SANCTUARY

By Lindsay McKenna

Blue Turtle Publishing

Praise for Lindsay McKenna

"A treasure of a book . . . highly recommended reading that everyone will enjoy and learn from."

—Chief Michael Jaco, US Navy SEAL, retired, on Breaking Point

"Readers will root for this complex heroine, scarred both inside and out, and hope she finds peace with her steadfast and loving hero. Rife with realistic conflict and spiced with danger, this is a worthy page-turner."

—BookPage.com on Taking Fire
March 2015 Top Pick in Romance

". . . is fast-paced romantic suspense that renders a beautiful love story, start to finish. McKenna's writing is flawless, and her story line fully absorbing. More, please."

—Annalisa Pesek, Library Journal on Taking Fire

"Ms. McKenna masterfully blends the two different paces to convey a beautiful saga about love, trust, patience and having faith in each other."

—Fresh Fiction on Never Surrender

"Genuine and moving, this romantic story set in the complex world of military ops grabs at the heart."

—RT Book Reviews on Risk Taker

"McKenna does a beautiful job of illustrating difficult topics through the development of well-formed, sympathetic characters."

—Publisher's Weekly (starred review) on Wolf Haven
One of the Best Books of 2014, Publisher's Weekly

"McKenna delivers a story that is raw and heartfelt. The relationship between Kell and Leah is both passionate and tender. Kell is the hero every woman wants, and McKenna employs skill and empathy to craft a physically and emotionally abused character in Leah. Using tension and steady pacing, McKenna is adept at expressing growing, tender love in the midst of high stakes danger."

—RT Book Reviews on Taking Fire

"Her military background lends authenticity to this outstanding tale, and readers will fall in love with the upstanding hero and his fierce determination to save the woman he loves."

—Publishers Weekly (starred review) on Never Surrender
One of the Best Books of 2014, Publisher's Weekly

"Readers will find this addition to the Shadow Warriors series full of intensity and action-packed romance. There is great chemistry between the characters and tremendous realism, making Breaking Point a great read."

—RT Book Reviews

"This sequel to Risk Taker is an action-packed, compelling story, and the sizzling chemistry between Ethan and Sarah makes this a good read."

—RT Book Reviews on Degree of Risk

"McKenna elicits tears, laughter, fist-pumping triumph, and most all, a desire for the next tale in this powerful series."

—Publishers Weekly (starred review) on Running Fire

"McKenna's military experience shines through in this moving tale... McKenna (High Country Rebel) skillfully takes readers on an emotional journey into modern warfare and two people's hearts."

—Publisher's Weekly on Down Range

"Lindsay McKenna has proven that she knows what she's doing when it comes to these military action/romance books."

—Terry Lynn, Amazon on Zone of Fire.

"At no time do you want to put your book down and come back to it later! Last Chance is a well written, fast paced, short (remember that) story that will please any military romance reader!"

—LBDDiaries, Amazon on Last Chance.

Available from Lindsay McKenna

Blue Turtle Publishing

DELOS

Last Chance, prologue novella to Nowhere to Hide
Nowhere to Hide, Book 1
Tangled Pursuit, Book 2
Forged in Fire, Book 3

2016
Broken Dreams, Book 4
Blind Sided, BN2
Secret Dream, B1B novella, epilogue to Nowhere to Hide
Hold On, Book 5
Hold Me, 5B1, sequel to Hold On
Unbound Pursuit, 2B1 novella, epilogue to Tangled Pursuit
Secrets, 2B2 novella, sequel to Unbound Pursuit, 2B1

2017
Snowflake's Gift, Book 6
Never Enough, 3B1, novella, sequel to Forged in Fire
Dream of Me, 4B1, novella, sequel to Broken Dreams
Trapped, Book 7
Taking a Chance 7B1, novella, sequel to Trapped
The Hidden Heart, 7B2, novella, sequel to Taking A Chance

2018
Boxcar Christmas, Book 8
Sanctuary, Book 9

Harlequin/HQN/Harlequin Romantic Suspense

SHADOW WARRIORS

Danger Close
Down Range
Risk Taker
Degree of Risk
Breaking Point
Never Surrender

Zone of Fire
Taking Fire
On Fire
Running Fire

THE WYOMING SERIES

Shadows From The Past
Deadly Identity
Deadly Silence
The Last Cowboy
The Wrangler
The Defender
The Loner
High Country Rebel
Wolf Haven
Night Hawk
Out Rider

WIND RIVER VALLEY SERIES, Kensington

2016
Wind River Wrangler
Wind River Rancher

2017
Wind River Cowboy
Christmas with my Cowboy
Wrangler's Challenge

Sanctuary

Copyright © 2018 by Nauman Living Trust
ISBN: 978-1-929977-61-1
Print Edition

Excerpt from *Dangerous*
Copyright © 2018 by Nauman Living Trust

All rights reserved. Except for use in any review, the reproduction or utilization of this work in whole or in part in any form by any electronic, mechanical or other means, now known or hereafter invented, including xerography, photocopying and recording, or in any information storage or retrieval system, is forbidden without the written permission of the publisher, Blue Turtle Publishing, PO Box 2513, Cottonwood, AZ 86326 USA

This is a work of fiction. Names, characters, places and incidents are either the product of the author's imagination or are used fictitiously, and any resemblance to actual persons, living or dead, business establishments, events or locales is entirely coincidental.

This edition published by arrangement with Blue Turtle Publishing

www.lindsaymckenna.com

Dedication

To my wonderful readers who inspire me to continue telling wonderful, heart-warming stories for them. You rock!

Dear Reader,

One of the joys of owning my own publishing company and creating the Delos Series, allows me to roam free as a writer to tell my stories for you. I can remember when my editor at a traditional publisher would tell me that I should never set a book in Africa, that it would result in "lowered sales."

I would like to think that if the hero and heroine and their challenges are powerful and riveting, it doesn't matter where a book is set. I love to write about areas that many of my readers would never travel to. For example, I've spent a lot of time in Peru, a very out-of-the-way country. And I've set many books from that area as a result.

And sometimes, I want to write about places that are on my bucket list, like Africa. This continent is over flowing with potential stories. And to prove that point, I set Sanctuary, Book 8 of the Delos Series, in Khartoum, Sudan, Africa. I spent a year in research on this country, its history, its people, traditions, religions and customs. I had so much material that I decided to write Book 9, *Dangerous*, at Port Sudan, on the Red Sea.

The history of Sudan, of the Nile splitting and becoming the White and Blue Nile, is romantic, but also saw the rise and fall of Egypt and other ancient historical countries as well. My readers know well that I love to share tidbits of truth about a people, a country, in hopes that you will not only be entertained by a great love story with a happy ending, but that you'll come away with actual knowledge of the people and land.

Be prepared for a wild ride created out of the wonderful woven history and landscape of the Sudan. If *Sanctuary* leaves you with warm fuzzies, please think about writing a review on it for me. Reviews are VERY important and helpful in bringing new readers to my series. If you would love to review but never have, just get a hold of me at docbones224@earthlink.net and I'll send you my little article on how to write a dynamite review! Thank you!

CHAPTER 1

August

NOLAN STEELE HAD a feeling his life was about to change and that made him damned uncomfortable. Being ex–Delta Force and thirty years old, doing mostly long-term undercover work in Africa, he'd learned a long time ago to listen to his gut. It had already saved his life more than once. He sat down in the mission planning room at Artemis in Alexandria, Virginia, the secret in-house security home for Delos Charities.

He looked around the large room at the two flat-screen TVs on two cream-colored walls, an oval tiger-maple table with ten comfortable black leather chairs surrounding it. He was the first to arrive for the 0900 meeting with Wyatt Lockwood, head of missions for the security company. A male assistant brought Nolan a cup of black coffee and assured him that everyone would be there shortly.

Nolan was eager to see Wyatt in person once again. He knew Wyatt from his Afghanistan days early in his career, and he knew Matt Culver, whose family owned the top-secret security company, even better. Matt, like Nolan, had been Delta Force, and there was always a tight bond between the brothers.

Culver's call to him from his home in Alexandria was intriguing. Nolan had had no idea this state-of-the-art security firm even existed because Matt had never talked about it. Obviously, it was off the radar, but since Nolan had top-secret clearance while in the Army, he was still surprised he didn't know about Artemis. The Delos Charities' security firm had gone dark in the secret world of shadow warriors. Nolan believed that was a wise choice nowadays since terrorists of every stripe were trying to locate such companies and destroy them.

Artemis was well hidden within a nineteenth-century, three-story farmhouse just outside Alexandria. It was surrounded by a working hydroponics farm from what he could tell as he drove in this morning. Anyone passing along on the rural country road would never suspect it was one of the most electronically advanced security companies in the world.

Matt Culver entered the room, a big, welcoming grin on his face and Nolan smiled in return. It was great to see his friend again.

"Hey, Nolan, good to see you." Matt came around the table.

Standing, Nolan shook his hand and they slapped one another on the back. "Same here, brother." He looked at the papers and files tucked beneath Matt's left arm. "This looks pretty serious. Do you have a situation here?"

"We do," Matt said. He sat down next to Nolan, handing him a mission brief. "Wyatt, Cav, and my sister Alexa are coming in shortly to assist in the briefing." He walked down to the end of the room and poured himself some coffee from a silver coffee station.

"This is quite a place," Nolan murmured, noticing the latest high-tech electronics.

"We're up to speed," Matt told him, sitting down beside him, sipping his coffee. "We're in the process of a massive expansion and assembling the right people for positions that need to be filled at Artemis. It's an ongoing process. My big sister, Tal, is CEO and runs the place." He grimaced. "I don't envy her. It's a tough job."

"What do you do, then?" Nolan asked. Matt was wearing a bright red T-shirt, jeans, and work boots. The last time Nolan had seen him, which was over two years ago, Matt had worn a beard, but now he was clean-shaven.

"I run the KNR—kidnapping and ransom—division of the Safe House Foundation. It's one of three branches that Delos created, and we maintain it around the world. My sister, Alexa, is the director of the Safe House branch. On certain types of mission planning, she's our go-to person and is up-to-speed on everything."

"Which means there must be a situation or I wouldn't be here, I assume?" Nolan asked, more curious than ever to learn why he'd been brought here.

Matt gave him a sly look, his gold-brown eyes glinting. "Right on, pardner. How are you doing, by the way? I heard you just got off an Ethiopian operation for the NSC, National Security Agency."

"Yeah," he said. Nolan couldn't say much because in their business, everything was classified.

"Successful?"

"It was, ultimately."

That told Matt a lot. He nodded, and then saw his sister Alexa, looking winded, dash into the room. He smiled. His type-A fraternal twin sister wore her red hair up in a bright pink plastic clip, making her look more like a Virginia farm gal than a top security executive. Right now, the East Coast was in the midst of the dog days of summer to everyone's continued discomfort.

"Am I late?" she asked, breathless, placing her electronic tablet on the table opposite the two men.

"Nope, you're right on time," Matt assured her, looking at the clock on the wall. "Meet Nolan Steele, Alexa. Nolan, this is my kid sister, Alexa."

Smiling warmly, Alexa reached across the table, shaking his hand after he stood up. "Oh, sit, Nolan. I love it when a man is a gentleman. But around here, it's a lost art," she chuckled.

Releasing her hand, Nolan nodded. "Nice to meet you, and yeah, I'm like your brother here—a throwback to the Neanderthal age." He liked her warmth and sincerity. Her hair made her look a little on the wild side, but hell, red-haired women were always only half-tamed, anyway. Nolan smiled to himself as he sat down.

"I'm here," Wyatt Lockwood greeted them in his deep Texas drawl, entering.

"Me too," Cav Jordan called, right on Wyatt's heels. He turned and pressed a button to close and lock the secure door.

Nolan watched Wyatt sit at the head of the planning table, with Cav on his left, Matt on his right, and Alexa across from him. Matt introduced Nolan to everyone in the room and handshakes were given.

Wyatt stood at the end of the table, half of it comprised of a surface computer built into it. He tapped the touchscreen, turning it on, both wall screens lighting up with photos and intel. "Did Alexa give you the mission brief electronically, Nolan?"

"Yes," he said, opening up his tablet.

"Okay," Wyatt said. "The people we have assembled here are directly connected with Mission 025. Your mission, Nolan." He tapped on a recording device. "And by the way, we record everything here."

Shrugging, Nolan said, "Fine by me," and then gave Matt a crooked grin. "I have nothing to hide."

That brought a collective round of laughter at the table, since they had all been in black ops and had secrets they'd take to their graves. Alexa wrinkled her nose and smiled, shaking her head.

"Yeah," Wyatt said. "You're about as transparent as granite. We all know that." He touched a key and gestured toward the wall screens. "Okay, I'm gonna roll with this mission. Keep your questions until I'm done. I want to give you an overview and then we'll get down to specifics later."

Nodding, Nolan appreciated the Texan's easygoing, yet organized, approach to presenting a mission briefing. "Go for it," he said, pulling a stylus from his pocket. The mission would automatically be transferred to his tablet so he could follow along.

"We just received a report from Kitra in Sudan. Kitra, which is Arabic for 'abundance,' is a Delos Safe House Foundation charity village. It sits about twenty miles southwest of Khartoum, in the desert of central Sudan."

Nolan studied the map of Sudan up on one of the screens; he was already very familiar with the area because he'd been part of an operation in Khartoum two years ago.

"Ayman Taban, our security chief at Kitra, sent us a report that got our immediate attention last week. One of his staff, who protects Kitra from being robbed by hungry, unemployed Sudanese, spotted Enver Uzan in the slums of Khartoum five days ago."

Nolan saw a color photo of Uzan appear on the screen. The al-Qaeda operator was dressed in typical Pakistani battle garb, the AK-47 butt resting against his hip. The word "black" immediately sprang to mind, from his obsidian eyes to his black beard and the long, greasy hair draping his narrow shoulders. His expression was angry, his eyes glaring.

"Uzan is an officer in the Pakistan Army, but in reality," Wyatt said, "he works as a captain for the Pakistani billionaire, Zakir Sharan. He's sent on a variety of missions to get Sharan's dirty work done."

Nolan flicked a look over at Matt. "You killed one of Sharan's sons, didn't you?"

Matt nodded. "Yeah, I took out Sidiq in Afghanistan. Tal killed his other son, Raastagar, a year earlier. Sharan's sworn a blood oath of vengeance against the Culver family and all the Delos charities around the world as a result. You know, of course, that that part of the world believes in 'an eye for an eye.' This past June, we asked each director of our charities to send weekly encrypted email reports to us on the political situation in their area, particularly on anything that might threaten them in the region where they are located."

Alexa leaned forward. "Nolan, we've also sent info on Sharan and the mercenaries he employs to do his dirty work to all eighteen-hundred charities. He's specifically targeting Americans working for them, although he's sworn to kill anyone who gets in his way. Uzan is an explosives expert. He's blown up buildings, set fires, and created maximum destruction against his targets."

Wyatt put another photo up on the screen, this one of Kitra, the village that sat out on the red clay desert of Sudan. "We believe he's in Khartoum to case Kitra and identify any Americans working there. And he's looking to either kidnap or murder them. We have no actionable intel yet because Uzan was spotted only once. Ayman is sending out three of his most trusted men into the slums, undercover, to see what intel they can pick up on why this al-Qaeda operative is in Khartoum."

Cav broke in. "All of us believe Uzan is there to make a statement by attacking Kitra, one of our showcase charities. We're trying to verify it, but until then, we need you to become a bodyguard for the American business administrator who helps run that charity."

"Her name," Wyatt said, "is Teren Lambert." He posted her photo on the other screen. "She's twenty-nine years old, an information technology and business specialist, and she's lived at Kitra since she was twenty-two years old. She's single, has built an Internet store for the abuse survivors who were taken into Kitra, and taught them how to sew and sell clothing. Teren speaks Arabic and helps Farida, the director of this branch, with all the daily details of keeping a huge conglomerate like this on its feet and thriving. She's from Somerset, Kentucky, smart as hell, and a computer genius. I talked with her via Skype two days ago. She's now aware that we're going to be sending over a security contractor to protect her."

Alexa said, "And we chose you for this mission, Nolan, because your prior Delta Force experience was in Sudan and Ethiopia. You speak fluent Arabic, French, and some local dialects. You know Sudan like the back of your hand. We need to put someone in there who has that kind of background, and you fit perfectly."

Nolan nodded, his gaze riveted on the photo of Teren Lambert. Someone had taken the photo in what looked like a barn; she was dressed in a sleeveless tan T-shirt and dark green trousers. This was no glamour shot—she looked sweaty, her brown hair piled messily on top of her head, long strands of it sticking to her high cheekbones. He saw sheep in the background. She had on a leather cuff around each of her wrists, a rope in her hands, and her attention was drawn downward. More than likely, Nolan thought, they were shearing one of the sheep.

It was her profile that made his heart beat a little faster. She looked lean and tall, clearly athletic, judging by the sleek muscled firmness of her arms.

It was the way her full mouth was tightened, those winged brows of hers drawn downward, that look in her stormy-gray eyes, that told Nolan this woman took no prisoners. It was the energy she radiated that said, "I'm not taking anybody's crap," that made his mouth faintly curve upward. This was a woman warrior, no question. Her eyes were large and filled with keen intelligence.

His lower body stirred as his gaze settled on that full mouth of hers. Damn, she was sensual and hot-looking, despite where she was and what she was doing. Suddenly, Nolan felt like the heavens had opened up and he'd been given a gift.

The pleasure thrumming through him as he absorbed Teren's photo surprised the hell out of him. Since he'd lost Linda four years earlier, he'd been frozen emotionally, dead inside. But right now, he felt a river of ice beginning to thaw and slowly snake through him, winding upward and encircling his heart, awakening his feelings once more. His reaction to Teren was deep and intense.

Nolan had seen his fair share of good-looking females in his life, but he'd never had this kind of reaction to any of them—and this was just from a photo!

So what was it about Teren? Was it that aura surrounding her that the photograph couldn't capture, but that he could feel with his now highly developed intuition? As focused as she was, her mouth gave away her woman's sensuality in a heartbeat. Teren was earthy. Like the word "terra," which meant "earth." That was a mouth that could send him to heaven in a helluva hurry, and Nolan allowed the pleasure of drinking that truth into himself.

Maybe he wasn't dead after all. Nolan had given up the thought of feeling anything remotely like this again. Like all operators, he knew how to stuff down the darkness until it never reemerged. At the time of his wife's death, he couldn't allow it out of that kill box inside him, or he'd have felt an overwhelming avalanche of grief. It had been devastating to lose both Linda and the baby she'd carried. And four years ago, Nolan couldn't deal with it.

Now, Teren's photo was popping the rivets off his sealed heart, triggering hope, fanning his sexual hunger and fascination for her as a woman. He'd always favored earthy women. How could one photo affect him this much? He'd never experienced that before.

Now he scowled, fighting down these new feelings so he wouldn't become distracted.

Then Wyatt flashed another photo of her up on the screen and Nolan groaned inwardly, even more hooked on the woman than before. This photo was a three-quarters view of her face and slender, strong body. This time, she was standing at a dusty table with shearing equipment, white fluffs of sheep hair here and there across its expanse. It was her wide-spaced eyes, a color that he'd seen on the mourning doves near his Virginia farmhouse. Teren had warm slate-gray eyes with black pupils and a black ring around the outer iris, giving her a penetrating look.

Nolan liked intense people. Operators were that way themselves. He tilted his head toward Wyatt, meeting his gaze. "Does she have a military background?"

"No," Wyatt drawled, grinning a little, "but she looks the part, doesn't she? When I first saw these photos, I thought for sure she was ex-military. But she's not. Teren is a civilian, with a two-year community college degree in computer repair and programming. I've seen some geeks who have the same look. She writes software programs for Kitra's business admin needs, plus for their online store, so Teren is a highly focused, disciplined person."

"Intense," Nolan murmured in agreement.

"You could say that," Wyatt said. "She's a woman on a mission. She's a type A whose word is her bond, and she gets things done. And she's a real ass-kicker if she needs to be."

"You'd have to be," Alexa added, "because Teren is the business hub and heart of Kitra. We need someone exactly like her there to keep all the balls our charity is juggling presently up in the air."

"Yes," Matt told Nolan. "Kitra is more than just a safe house for women. While they take in women and children who have been abused, they have also created since its founding in 1959, a thriving community. It has its own vegetable gardens, a fruit tree orchard, two wells, an electric substation, and a school for the children of these women survivors. Sewing with a treadle machine was introduced by an earlier director, and over time, Kitra established a school to teach women from surrounding villages how to sew as well. Their goods are sold online around the world. Plus, there is a thousand-acre sorghum field that is tended and the sorghum sold annually, which helps continue expansion of all that Kitra undertakes to get these women back on their feet."

"Kind of reminds me of an Israeli kibbutz, making a Garden of Eden out of a desert," Nolan said. The photo earlier had shown goats and cattle in pens with a nearby barn. There wasn't a Sudanese village that didn't have camels and these other animals as part of their livelihood. Sheep's wool was used to weave into clothing, goats for milk and meat, and camels for transport—these were the fabric of Sudanese village life.

"Kitra is in a class of its own within Delos," Alexa added. "Most of our charities are not this huge, but some do grow in this direction, depending upon the country they're in." She motioned to his tablet. "In there is the history of Kitra. You'll see how each director has added to it, expanded it, and how it has become a poster child for all our charities. Kitra shows what can be done with local help and great administrators running things. That's why our Delos people are so important to us, and why we need to do everything we can to protect them from terrorism in the world we live in."

"I would imagine," Nolan said, "that because it's so affluent and has plenty of food, water sources, and animals, you have a lot of people wanting to come in and steal from it."

Wyatt grunted. "Yes, which is why Farida, the latest director, hired Captain Ayman Taban when he retired from the Sudanese Armed Forces. She gave him a yearly budget and he hired men he trusted. There's twenty-four-hour security surrounding this village, and if Ayman's people weren't in place, the poor would rob Kitra blind in a day."

"Make that a few hours," Nolan replied, knowing too well the squalor and starvation of the people in certain areas of Sudan.

"Either way," Alexa said, "Ayman has been there for us, and he and his men make a major difference. There are way too many people who would steal food, animals, or equipment from within Kitra and get money for it in Khartoum. It's an ongoing issue."

Wyatt said to Nolan, "Ayman was a graduate of the Military College at Wadi Sayyidna, near Omdurman. It's a well-respected military facility, and I've talked to Ayman a number of times about setting up this mission briefing. He knows the lay of the land, the issues, the challenges, and how to keep Kitra safe."

"And he was the one who also had his man spot Uzan?" Nolan said.

"Precisely. Ayman is a real hawk—he doesn't miss anything. We all feel you'll get along well with him."

"He knows I'm coming?"

"Yes. But to avoid tipping off Uzan or any of his paid spies about who might be in the area, we've asked Teren to pick you up at the Khartoum airport. You'll be undercover as her employee, a second IT person coming into Kitra to help her. That way, it looks normal and won't raise suspicions."

"Good plan," Nolan agreed. He privately liked the idea of being close to Teren. Why? He hadn't been interested in women except for spending one night in bed with them and then walking out of their lives. Nolan never led a woman on—he was up-front about the fact that he wanted sex for the night and that was it. In the morning, he left. It was all he could handle right now, because inside, he was dead.

Sure, he could give a woman sexual gratification and pleasure, but he'd been unable to share the feelings he knew women wanted and deserved. He felt like a bank emptied of all its emotional currency. But when he looked at Teren's photo, he felt as if he were looking at a treasure chest he wanted to open, touch, and explore. It was a crazy situation; one he'd never encountered before.

"Questions?" Wyatt asked him expectantly.

Nolan looked at his notes. "Weapons?"

"Our people have cleared it with the Sudanese government. We already have a license in hand to give you so you can carry a concealed weapon at all times."

"Does their police department know about this situation?"

"No," Wyatt said. "There's too much graft and corruption. Cav here has someone inside the government who's a trusted individual. She's the one who approved your concealed-carry license. She won't talk. All this stays at a very high level of their government; it doesn't trickle down to their police department."

"Good," Nolan grunted, "because that place reeks of bribery and other crimes, and there are a lot of gangs in the area."

"That's a given," Cav confirmed. He was their expert on Asia and Africa. He took a folder and pushed it down to Nolan. "Here's everything you need for weapons use, confirmation that you're a Delos employee with proper credentials, and any other government-granted documents. There's an electronic copy that's been sent to your tablet, as well. You're not going to get hauled into a police station."

"Good to know," he said, taking the folder. Turning his attention to Wyatt, he asked, "What if we get into a firefight with Uzan?"

"Ayman is already in touch with the Sudanese Army, up high with a general. He's aware of the potential for conflict. And if Kitra gets hit broadside with an attack by Uzan and his mercenaries, the general will be sending in, by helo transport, a quick reaction force—a QRF—to protect Kitra and its people. They already have a detailed plan in place. That's also in the intel that Cav sent to your tablet. Always go through Ayman for anything you need. Don't go to the general directly."

"Got it. Is Ms. Lambert carrying?"

Wyatt shook his head. "No, she's a civilian." Then he added, "But Ayman keeps weapons in the armory within Kitra. He's trained her and she's a good, solid shot. She has a license to carry but doesn't. Ayman was a highly respected officer in the Army and he has a powerful network of friends whom he can trust, so Kitra is well off with him there."

"And Uzan? If I capture or wound him?"

"Ayman will step in and take over. Uzan is a wanted man in Sudan for many reasons, and the government doesn't want al-Qaeda operatives in their country. They've got their hands full with Darfur. They don't want men like him coming in and stirring up trouble."

"And I'm to keep Ms. Lambert safe because she's probably the object of Uzan's focus?"

"Affirmative," Wyatt said. "Ayman agrees with our analysis. We figure he'll try to kidnap her, demand ransom, and later, probably behead her, record the execution on video, and then put it across the Internet."

"And you want me to case Kitra for potential attacks? Work with Ayman if I spot deficiencies or weak points within the village?"

"Yes. He knows you're coming and he knows your skills. He's looking forward to working with you. You're one more gun in the fight as far as he's concerned."

"Sounds good," Nolan said, closing up the tablet. "I'm ready to kit up and take off." And he was damn sure no one guessed how much he was looking forward to meeting Teren Lambert at the Khartoum airport.

CHAPTER 2

TEREN WAITED PATIENTLY outside the customs area at the Khartoum airport. She had her cell phone in hand, scrolling through messages from her two office assistants. Her mouth tugged at the corners as she looked up at the double doors, expecting Nolan Steele to come through them at any moment.

His color photo flashed on her screen. He had an oval face and large, hawkish marine-blue eyes that reminded her of the ocean's depths. His mouth was something else—sensual, yet firm. He was almost painfully good-looking—far too handsome for his own good! He probably had an ego the size of Jupiter. She hoped not, because the moment the email from Wyatt Lockwood had appeared on her laptop, her whole body reacted to the stranger's photograph. Those eyes…so full of secrets and, Teren sensed, pain. It didn't appear on his unlined thirty-year-old face, but it was there.

She was just a year younger than him. She thought back to when she'd been an idealistic eighteen-year-old, filled with hope and the belief that the world was essentially a good place. She found out differently later that year and after her own traumatic experience, Teren had quickly revised her views about men. From that time on, they had been creatures she couldn't understand or relate to. She'd become gun-shy around them, and now, over a decade later, she still felt that way.

But as she studied Nolan's face, Teren felt her heart slowly begin to open, like petals on a lotus. Not wanting to feel like this, fighting it, she clicked her phone's screen off but left the phone on, because he had her phone number in case they missed each other here at the busy, crowded airport.

A potpourri of spicy scents filled the air. Men wore either light-colored silk business suits or the traditional *jalabiya*, a loose-fitting garment, collarless, ankle-length, and long-sleeved. Some wore caps, others turbans. Because it was August, a season of dry, blistering heat, the *jalabiyas* were either white, cream, or tan, made of cotton-linen or silk, to deflect the burning rays of the sun outside this air-conditioned facility.

She nervously smoothed her *tob*, a head-to-toe gown of white cotton topped by a white silk *hijab*, the traditional scarf Muslim women wore over their heads when in public. She wasn't Muslim, but Teren tried to fit in, not stand out. Knowing how dangerous it was to be a white, American woman in this third-world country, she didn't want to draw attention to herself any more than necessary.

Normally, she wouldn't have been here waiting for someone at the airport. She liked the red clay walls that surrounded Kitra, the sense of safety that was always there because Captain Ayman Taban ran his security force like the military man he'd been for twenty years.

So, where was this Steele guy, and was that even his real name or a cover one? After talking with Wyatt by sat phone, she knew he was going to be her personal bodyguard, and that he was ex-military, but Wyatt hadn't said anything more than that. Tapping her slippered foot, Teren began to feel restless. She didn't like being out in such a huge, bustling area with so many men and so few women. She knew she'd stand out because of her lighter skin.

In Khartoum, she dressed conservatively, the *niqab*, over her brow and nose, only a slit for her eyes, trying to hide her skin color. Here at the airport, her face was fully visible, the scarf draped around her head, neck, and shoulders. Steele had to be able to identify her once he came through the doors of customs. Sudan wasn't a safe place in many areas and it was especially dangerous to a woman who stood alone without a male escort in tow. Too many terrorists were lurking around, and it always made her tense. Her nervousness this afternoon was heightened because she felt inexplicably drawn to Nolan Steele.

Teren wasn't prepared when she spotted him at the exit doors of customs, along with several other Sudanese businessmen dressed in their robes. He was moderately built, wearing a tan T-shirt beneath a loose-fitting khaki jacket and trousers. Their eyes briefly locked upon one another, and Teren's heart began to accelerate. He was here! Why did it feel like a homecoming instead of a first meeting? Her lips moved and then tightened, and instead, she lifted her hand.

He gave her a bare nod, his eyes narrowing, and every nerve in her body reacted to that swift, intense perusal he gave her.

And then, just as quickly, he lifted his chin, his gaze sweeping around the noisy, busy airport. She had the distinct impression he was actually a lordly leopard in disguise, calmly surveying his kingdom, not a stranger coming to a strange country. He walked like a hunter, light on his feet, avoiding any living animal in the immediate vicinity.

She watched in amazement as he threaded his way through the crowd. He moved like water flowing around rocks, disturbing nothing, gaining no one's attention. Teren's respect for him as a security contractor rocketed.

His shoulders were broad, squared with pride, his hand on a single bag that appeared to hold a laptop. His right hand was free. And as his gaze swept to her once again and briefly halted, Teren felt in that one, scorching moment, he had memorized her from head to toe.

It wasn't sexual. It wasn't lust. It was something indefinable, but just the power of it stirred up the heat simmering in her lower body. Once he was clear of the bustling crowd, his gaze locked on hers once more, and Teren felt as if she were being surrounded by such intense protectiveness, it stole her breath away.

Protection! It had been so long since she'd felt safe. *So long*...and he seemed to be invisibly embracing her, the sense of safety he radiated even stronger the closer he drew to her.

For once in her life, Teren found herself speechless. Their gazes clung to one another, and something passed between them that made her throat tighten. She fought back old, wounded emotions as she absorbed the look in his eyes, feeling his quiet authority and power. Now she lifted her chin and realized that, on some level, she didn't want him to step away from her. It was the craziest, most out-of-this-world sensation she'd ever felt!

Almost dizzied by his palpable masculinity as he drew to a halt about four feet away from her, she stared up at Steele—gawked was more like it. Teren suddenly felt like an innocent eighteen-year-old who held all the hopes of the world in her heart.

Steele was a stranger. Ex-military. Black ops. So different from the world she lived in that what he was bringing with him was alien to her culture. Then his eyes warmed as he smiled down on her, and she felt heat sheeting through her, arousing her dormant body, ripping away all her fear, the sense of danger that always hovered around her. She felt a fire sparking to full life deep within her body, as if on some unknown plane of existence, she was meeting him after a long absence.

"Ms. Lambert?"

His voice was low and quiet. The vibration, though subtle, tingled through every cell within her. Teren barely nodded. "Yes." The word came out smoky and soft, so unlike her. Nolan Steele brought out her female quality with just his mere presence.

Looking deeper into his eyes, Teren didn't see arousal or lust. What she saw, however, was even more powerful: gentle understanding and yes, compassion burned in his eyes, aimed directly at her. How could that be?

She felt tongue-tied, scrambling inwardly to snap out of that magical cocoon he'd just woven around her. The feeling left Teren unsure of herself—normally, she exuded a quiet confidence wherever she went. Whatever magic he possessed made her feel excruciatingly female, and she gratefully absorbed it.

Steele gave her a wry smile, his eyes crinkling, the lines in the corners deepening. "Are you all right? You look a little dazed."

Teren felt heat burnishing her cheeks. She *never* blushed, but she was now. She managed an apologetic, "I'm sorry…long day." Well, that wasn't a lie, just not the whole truth. "The heat, too." She lifted her hand gracefully toward the automatic doors.

"Understandable," he agreed with a nod. Holding out his hand, he said, "Nolan Steele. It's nice to meet you, Ms. Lambert."

His large hand engulfed her thin, narrow one, and the touch of his callused palm sliding against hers sent wild electric sensations up her lower arm. His fingers were long, strong, yet gentle, as he lightly squeezed her hand in return. Teren felt his latent strength, reminding her once more of that proud leopard who, while in repose, looked tame and nonthreatening—but he wasn't. Skin against skin she sensed much more and couldn't hold off images that had nothing to do with a simple "hello."

Unsteadily, Teren pulled her hand free, her skin vibrating with his energy. "Do you have luggage?" she asked, trying to restore the impression of competence she'd brought with her.

"Yes." He broke contact with her flawless gray eyes, which brought to mind the color of the sky just before dawn. "I've been here before, and baggage is that way." He pointed in the direction of the highly polished hall that led to the right.

She blinked, her mind slowly returning online. "You have? I mean, you've been in Sudan before?" The way his lips parted in a grin, part boyish, part secretive, told her that Nolan wasn't wearing his game face. He was being genuine.

Wyatt had warned her that she probably wouldn't be able to read him or know what he was thinking or feeling. But that wasn't true, at least not here and now. It was as if they were both standing before each other, exposing themselves boldly and fearlessly. She could almost feel his essence, and it swept her away in a glorious cloud of heat, light, and promise.

"Yes, ma'am. In fact, I've been here too many times," he assured her. Nolan knew better than to cup her elbow and guide her down the massive, gleaming hallway leading to the escalator down to baggage. This was a conservative country, and a strange man could not touch a woman. Only family could touch family, and even then, it mattered which person in the family it was. Earlier, when they shook hands, any passerby would automatically think they were related and from the same family. They would think nothing of the greeting. Nolan gestured and said, "This way."

Tucking her phone into the white straw purse hanging over her right shoulder, Teren nodded. Again, women here never led the way; rather, they followed the men. She was curious about Nolan having been in Sudan before. He walked like he owned the place, but it wasn't arrogance. It was utter male confidence of the finest kind. She'd seen that same type of confidence in Captain Taban, the man who had won her deepest respect. It was quiet authority that no one dared breach or challenge. And yet, when Nolan barely turned his head, she saw his profile, felt his protectiveness envelop her even though she was a few feet behind and to the left of him.

Farida, Kitra's director, had been urging her to leave and go stateside, back to her family home in Somerset, Kentucky, but to do that, Teren would have to revisit her past. She'd grown up in the small town, mostly full of devout Christians, and their set of morals and values were strong and unwavering.

She'd honestly tried to live up to that impossibly high bar of expectations but had failed. Not only had she paid for it personally, she'd also lost the baby she'd been carrying. Teren had been profoundly shamed by her family, who had lived in that area for over a century. The generations before her had been hardworking farmers, plowing the land, raising cattle, and keeping their large families fed. To go home was to resurrect a past between her and her parents and the townspeople who lived there. None of them ever forgot—or forgave her for—the sin she'd committed.

Teren had tried to go home once, but after a few days, she felt the shame, the guilt, the horrible grief of loss, and she'd had to leave. And all the friends she'd grown up with were now married and had housefuls of children.

And here she was: single and alone—and lonely. But not lonely in all ways, because Kitra soothed her wounded heart and scarred soul. Her family loved her. They had tried their very best to move beyond their intractable beliefs to forgive her. Some days, Teren believed they had done it. Other days, it was painfully clear that the people in the community had not forgiven her for her actions. She was the town's "bad girl" and her reputation was forever ruined. It was a sin that kept on giving, and kept resurrecting itself every time she was home. It was just too much for her to deal with.

As she passively followed Nolan, her mind lingered painfully on the past. Could it be that this crazy feeling had taken over because she hadn't been home for the last three years? Talk about confusing! Teren had her life all sorted out, organized, every hour accounted for. She was needed, respected, and loved at Kitra. In fact, the village would plunge into chaos if she weren't there with the magic of her computer skills, her knowledge of electronics, and the world at large, far outside the country of Sudan. Here, she had a sense of purpose and knew she made a positive difference, and that meant everything to her. She worked closely with women who had been badly abused, raped, or kidnapped and forced into sex slavery or marriage. Teren felt lucky in comparison to them. All she'd received was abuse and the loss of her baby. These Sudanese women, with fear embedded beyond their eyes, had fled to Kitra to heal, to be protected from abusive husbands and families, to learn a trade and then be able to confidently start their lives all over again.

Their children would not starve. The women would not be beaten again, or end up with a nose or ear cut off, or have acid thrown into their faces because they were "bad wives" to their husbands, or worse, stoned to death.

The village of Kitra was Teren's life preserver, just as it was for the Safe House Foundation, whose entire reason for being here was to act as a protective haven for such women, no matter what tribe, skin color, or nationality they were. If they came to the gates of Kitra, small children or babies in arms, Farida's team took the young mothers in. Then they were fed and received medical care, as did their children. Each woman was given a hut of her own, clean and with rugs on the hard-packed clay floor, and mats, mosquito netting, and sleeping bags for all. She was then taken to Samar, the female psychologist, who was thirty-five years old, but seemed like she was a thousand years old to Teren. Samar had even helped her sort out much of her own guilt and shame.

Her mind moved forward as they left the escalator, and she saw Nolan read the overhead sign written in Sudanese Arabic, telling him which carousel would be dumping out his luggage.

Teren again noted how few women were here at the airport. She disliked certain Sudanese traditions and longed for the freedom not to wear a *tob* or other concealing garments. Instead, she longed to throw her leg over a horse and wear her beloved jeans and sleeveless tees. She could do that at Kitra, but not outside the walls of the village, where she again adopted the bearing of a meek, subservient woman. It was the only part of working in Sudan that she rebelled against. On most days Teren could handle it, but on other days, not so much.

At least she had the freedom of American clothes and she could move freely about the huge, enclosed, thriving village. It felt wonderful. Right now she longed to be back within the embracing walls of Kitra, wanted to tear this *tob* off her body, and toss it aside. But to do something that stupid would land her in Sharia court, and more than likely she would be publicly whipped or stoned to death for her insult to Islam.

There was just something about Nolan Steele that made her feel rebellious and want to throw off the trappings of her soiled past so she could feel free once more.

Nolan turned and eased the handle of his laptop bag into her hand. "Hold this for me for a moment? I see my luggage."

Her fingers curved, closing around the canvas and leather handle. "Sure."

He smiled at her then, that same deep warmth gleaming in the depths of his eyes, nurturing the spark of hope he seemed to bring her. Hope for what, Teren wasn't sure, but there it was. Nolan walked toward the baggage carousel where she saw two green canvas bags. Vaguely, she remembered Ayman's having had one too. They were called duffel bags by the U.S. military, if she remembered correctly. She watched as Nolan easily pulled them off the carousel, one in each hand.

"You okay carrying my laptop if I carry these?" he asked, halting in front of her.

She smiled faintly. "If I can wrestle a hundred-pound sheep to the floor of the shearing shed, I think I can handle a ten-pound laptop. Let's go out those doors to your right. The parking lot is just across the roadway, and my *hafla* is nearby."

"Sounds good. I'll lead the way."

Teren realized Nolan knew what a *hafla* was: a minibus that had a flatbed component, the most prevalent vehicle in and around Khartoum. She hadn't been looking forward to teaching her security contractor about Sudanese customs after he arrived, and it was a pleasant surprise to know that he knew Sudan and its conventions.

Often, she had to drive into Khartoum to pick up items that required a flatbed truck. Kitra had no fancy cars, and her *hafla* had no air-conditioning in this ninety-five-degree Fahrenheit heat.

Teren breathed another sigh of relief as Nolan moved out of the cool air-conditioned terminal and into the dry, scorching sun overhead. She wondered what else he knew. How often had he been in Sudan? And why? Teren had lots of questions for him.

The corners of her mouth curved as she held the lightweight, floaty *hijab* to her head. It would be a sin in this country to have it slide off, revealing her hair.

The wind was hot and dry, tearing at her fingers where she firmly held the scarf in place as they hurriedly crossed the busy highway between the terminal and the parking lot. The sky was a pale blue, the sunlight at this time of year harsh and stunning to outsiders who weren't prepared for it. Teren referred to it as "the burning" of the land, animals, and people. There was nothing comfortable about ninety- to one-hundred-degree heat in August. Even at night, it rarely got below seventy degrees.

Thank goodness Kitra had its own electric substation fueled with oil. It provided air-conditioning to the main administration building and the duplexes where she and others lived. This was truly a gift, because very few Sudanese, even within bustling Khartoum, had air-conditioning available. Only rich, huge skyscrapers and five-star hotels had such a desirable amenity.

Teren wanted to get back into that cooling air once again. Her admin office in the main building at Kitra was cool because the delicate computers, servers, and routers needed that kind of mild-temperature environment in order to operate.

She felt sorry for the Sudanese, who lived in huts and endured this awful summer heat. Everyone, by the time October came, was desperate for the cooler temperatures of the coming winter.

"Third row, white *hafla,* two cars down," she called to Nolan. Teren was grateful he didn't use his full stride—and he could have—leaving her to scramble to keep up. Instead, he monitored his pace for her sake, which she appreciated. She was eager to discover more about this tall, dignified operator whose very presence made her feel safe for the first time in years.

CHAPTER 3

MEANWHILE, TEREN HAD no idea that Nolan was confronting his own feelings about this unexpectedly shy woman who had met him at the airport. He just couldn't shake the intense, burning connection he felt with her. She looked like a white lotus that stood out in the Khartoum airport, littered with males in *jalabiyas* or business suits. He'd sensed where she'd be standing before he'd even laid eyes on her. And there she was, leaning against the wall, out of the way, hiding as it were from the overwhelming number of men here at the huge airport.

The simple, white cotton *tob* she wore was shapeless, purposely designed to hide her figure from men's prying eyes. Nolan didn't agree with the practice, he never had, but he knew they also wore the long, shapeless gowns—both men and women—to be comfortable in the suffocating heat of the region. This part of the world was ruled by Sharia law, which subjugated women and made them chattel, controlled by their husbands and male relatives. They had no separate identities and were not allowed to be independent in any way. Nor could they explore the myriad aspects of being a woman. Instead, they were relegated to being broodmares, to bring in a new generation of boys who would be brought up learning not to allow women their place at the table. They suppressed and controlled them, more or less, depending upon the country and its laws. However, not all Muslim countries embraced Sharia law.

Teren's head was wrapped in a white *hijab* of soft, fine silk that hid most of her sable hair. The edges of the *hijab* were hand-embroidered with gold thread, which highlighted the gold within her hair when she moved her head slightly, the window's light behind her glinting through a few escaped strands.

Teren Lambert wore no makeup, but she had no need for it. She was truly a natural beauty. Nolan's heart lurched as he connected with her soft dove-gray eyes once more. The photo of her at the mission briefing back in Virginia was a shadow compared to seeing her in person. She had a narrow face, high cheekbones, and a broad, unlined brow. Her large, intelligent eyes were the centerpiece of a stunning, exotic face.

Nolan made the mistake of allowing his gaze to drop past her straight nose to her lips, and he wasn't disappointed. This woman had a lover's mouth; that was all there was to it. A mouth made to worship, to part, to taste, to join, and feel her returning lushness and fire as a woman. There was no mistaking her earthy sensuality. So often in the past, Nolan had intuitive hits that had saved his life seconds before he could have been snuffed out of existence. This time, he used that internal radar of his on Teren.

She stood casual and relaxed, her hand on a white straw purse across her right shoulder. She reminded Nolan of a lean, languid cheetah roaming the red deserts of Sudan. But there was nothing weak or fragile about her. He could feel her inner strength and somehow knew that life had thrown a lot at her. Instead of being crushed by it, she'd survived it, and now she was thriving.

Nolan was always drawn to women who were warriors. Now, seeing Teren hidden in her *tob*, he wondered, as he slowly threaded in and out and around the men leaving customs, if others saw Teren as a warrior, too. Nolan doubted it. His peripheral sensing ability was off the charts and had been honed by years of life-and-death dances here in Sudan and Ethiopia as an undercover operator. But he sensed *all* of her—the understated elegance, the way her slender hand with those long, long graceful fingers hung relaxed at her side. She reminded him that women were like flowers: bright, beautiful, to be looked at, appreciated, each with her own intrinsic beauty.

Nolan shifted his appreciation to Teren's wide, flawless eyes framed by long, sable lashes. Her eyes reminded him of soft, gray diamonds, dawn light moving through them. Eyes that saw a lot, he guessed, because earlier she was far more alert than she appeared, as she relaxed against the wall.

And she was hiding. Nolan could feel it. Perhaps that *tob* gave her a feeling of safety. Nolan could understand how Sudanese women, brainwashed since birth to hide their bodies from lustful male eyes, would feel naked without the protection of the long garment that hid them from neck to ankle. Was that why she was hiding? Teren had been in this country for seven years and maybe she'd had some bad experiences. If so, the *tob* would be a useful shield to hide behind. Nolan wanted to protect her after sensing how raw and threatened she felt.

No man in the airport made any moves toward her, although a number of them took second and third looks at her as they passed her by. She kept her eyes downcast, as a good Sudanese woman would do in such a situation. But every once in a while, to Nolan's satisfaction, her gaze would automatically sweep the area around her. That was good. It showed the type of vigilance that she'd continue to need with Uzan prowling around like the hyena he was, somewhere in the area. Until he and Captain Taban could find the bastard and break up any strategy he had against Kitra and Teren, she was at risk.

As a Delta Force soldier, he'd often come to the aid of defenseless women, children, and even animals on occasion. He sensed hurt and pain in this woman: she felt like a minefield to him, and he was reluctant to take a wrong step with her. He felt she'd close up and never allow him entrance into her personal life. And Nolan wanted to manage to slide past her shields and know Teren on a deeply personal basis, right or wrong.

She was bringing out every masculine reaction he had within him, and like the cheetah he imagined her to be, had Teren run from something? Because the main survival skill of that graceful African animal was to outrun the enemy that wanted to bring it down.

Who had brought Teren down? His mind clicked over her file, but he could find nothing in it to indicate what he sensed around her now. That bothered Nolan deeply, because in the briefing room he had made an unexpectedly powerful connection with her. Now that connection was strengthening at surprising speed. He was more than glad to be her bodyguard while he was here in Sudan. She needed one, because he knew that Uzan would target her. But was someone else targeting her too?

Teren wasn't the helpless type, and Nolan knew she was not a fragile person, but something devastating had happened to her. And because of it, she was glad to be hiding in the *tob*—at least for now. Nolan knew that Kitra was a walled village, as many villages were in Sudan. The enclosure kept out lions, hyenas, and other predators at night, while also protecting the village's cattle, camels, goats, and sheep.

Did the walls of Kitra give Teren that additional sense of safety she needed? What Nolan couldn't put together was why someone in her late twenties, as young, beautiful, and vibrant as she, would hide here in central Sudan at a charity. She had the skills to hold a high-paying job as an IT person anywhere in the world. Why was she here in the middle of this godforsaken, struggling, third-world country? What drew her to Kitra and why did she stay?

The questions he had for her were many, and all were personal in nature, which wasn't supposed to be any of his business. He was to maintain an arm's length emotionally from her in order to do his job of guarding her, nothing less.

As Nolan approached her, he saw her cheeks grow even more pink, her full lips parting as she lifted her chin, calmly meeting his gaze. This close to her, Nolan instinctively inhaled deeply, drawing in her female scent. It stirred his lower body to vibrant life. He was glad to be wearing the heavy, sturdy bush trousers he always wore when in Africa. The zipper would keep his erection well hidden from the world, not to mention the short-sleeved bush jacket he wore over his tan T-shirt, which fell below his crotch.

Nolan hadn't known what to expect from meeting Teren, but what was happening between them on a nonverbal level was emotionally charged and exhilarating to him. She was such a sensual creature; he knew it as soon as he'd shaken her hand. He felt it, saw it in her wide, trusting eyes, in the perfect shape of her mouth, in the way she moved away from the wall to stand confidently before him. Nolan did not sense Teren was wary of him. And that was good.

He'd been hired to put himself between her and any dangerous situation that threatened her life, and that meant being willing to take a bullet for her.

Now, as he spoke her name, he saw her eyes change, widen for a moment, looking even more intriguing. Nolan could drown in the quiet pools of her eyes, be lost forever in her.

"This way," she called to him, gesturing ahead.

"I see it," he called over his shoulder. Teren was making him feel again on levels Nolan had never hoped to regain. It was her. That sense of being a woman tied strongly to the land, her hands in the warm, fertile soil of this planet. Those things appealed strongly to Nolan. Maybe it was his ancient Irish background, his mother teaching him a love of the land, the emotional and familial ties to it, that Earth was a living being, just like them.

Nolan moved his gaze slowly, absorbing and memorizing everything around him, whether cars or people. The sound of jets taking off shook the hot afternoon air, the obnoxious odor of jet fuel always present.

Spotting the *hafla*, the fender dented and rusted, Nolan felt right at home. Most cars in Africa had had the shit beaten out of them: the drivers were terrible, and only tough vehicles survived, just like the people who survived on this dark continent.

Halting at the vehicle, he moved aside as Teren came closer, their bodies nearly touching as she slipped the key into the lock, opening the passenger-side door for him.

He dropped his duffel bags on the flatbed. As Teren stepped back, he took the laptop she offered him, placing it gently on the plastic seat between them. There was a light film of desert grit across the plastic.

"There are some ropes down on the floor," she told him. "You can use them to tie your duffel bags to the frame of the *hafla*."

Grunting, he spotted and grabbed them, then turned, meeting her gaze. "You've thought of everything."

She moved aside, holding the passenger door open because the breeze was strong. "Out here, if you don't, you're screwed."

He chuckled, appreciating her dry humor. Quickly looping the ropes through the canvas handles and then tying them to the white, badly chipped metal frame, he said, "Yeah, out here you need a safety net, and if you don't have it, you're in dire straits for sure." Nolan saw her mouth curve faintly, her eyes glinting with silent laughter. *That mouth.* He was already in such deep trouble with Teren. "You want me to drive?" he offered, standing with his hand on the cab of the vehicle.

"No." And then she added with sarcasm, "At least with the Sharia law here in Sudan, women are still allowed to drive, unlike in Saudi Arabia. Hop in. There's no air-conditioning, so you'll need to keep the window rolled down or die of heat prostration."

Nolan chuckled and allowed her to pass him. She moved with such confident grace. There was nothing passive or scared about Teren Lambert. She hid herself well; the way she carried herself now that she was outside that airport was a surprising but welcome change. Nolan needed this woman to be strong, brave, and confident, because Uzan was a murdering thug who would kill her if she didn't know how to think through a crisis. And that was an area that Nolan needed to test, to see how Teren felt about it. Judging by her carriage, her shoulders thrown back, chin lifted at a saucy angle, he had a competent warrioress on his hands. That was good. It could mean the difference between living and dying—for both of them.

He opened the driver's-side door for Teren and she gave him a grateful look, awkwardly slipping inside and closing the door. As she rolled down the window, she pulled off the hijab, dropping it on the seat between them. Nolan felt pleasure in seeing her long hair as she removed the tortoiseshell comb, the long sable strands escaping, framing her oval face and strong chin. The sunlight glanced off it, catching the amber among her shoulder-length tresses.

"I'm going to change my looks," she warned him with a grin. Reaching over to the glove box, she drew out a black baseball cap, a set of dark wraparound sunglasses, and a thick rubber band.

"Okay by me," Nolan murmured, curious.

Teren quickly gathered up her hair and fashioned it into a ponytail, pushing it over her shoulder and placing it between her shoulder blades. Settling the dark glasses on her face, she pulled the baseball cap on, keeping the bill low. "When I go into Khartoum, or anywhere outside Kitra's gates, I become a chameleon of sorts," she explained, shoving the key into the *hafla* and starting the engine. "Most people can't tell if I'm a man or a woman when I drive the streets of Khartoum or the dirt roads to and from a village. There's very little chance of me being turned in to the police for being a woman, because in seven years, I've never been caught pretending to be a man behind the wheel."

His mouth twitched with amusement, and he said, "I like your strategy."

She drove out into the roadway, pressing down on the accelerator to keep up with the crazy taxi drivers who zoomed in and around other cars waiting to pick up passengers at the terminal. "It serves me. Being a woman here in Sudan has its own challenges. This is one of 'em." And then she glanced over at him, seeing that he was putting on his own pair of sunglasses and settling a dark green baseball cap on his head. Almost laughing, she said, "Gee, we could be twins, Steele."

He laughed and sat back, elbow resting on the doorframe, the hot air circulating through the cab. "I like your style, Lambert." He saw her lips twitch, but she said nothing, paying attention to the darting kamikaze-like taxis and speeding, shiny black Mercedes trying to escape the confines of the airport.

Nolan felt her laughter, and it seemed Teren was shedding some of her serious demeanor now that they'd left the airport. He understood the stresses of her being a white, American woman, the wrong color of skin and gender for this part of the world.

As a man, he could get away with being Caucasian because there were plenty of American businessmen in Sudan, especially the oil company executives who had a great interest in the production of Sudanese oil in the south of the country. Half of Sudan was red clay and grasslands. The lower third was hot, steamy jungle where oil had been discovered. A pipeline now crossed Sudan, passing close to Khartoum on its way to Port Sudan, where oil tankers from around the world sat waiting in line to have their vast bellies filled with the thick, black crude.

But a white, American woman here in Sudan? He understood Teren's safety measures: hiding her hair, making herself look mannish to avoid any kind of unwanted interest by others. And he knew that Sudan had plenty of militants, like members of ISIS, prowling the perimeter of the country as they tried to get a foothold in the slums of Khartoum. He also knew al-Qaeda was chipping out a foothold in the capital's economically deprived areas as well.

Fortunately, the Sudanese government didn't want either terrorist faction on their turf, so they were quietly using their police force and undercover military people to root out the murderous bastards.

Nolan kept quiet watch as Teren turned the *hafla* onto the major highway leading out of Khartoum. He knew from studying the maps prior to landing that Kitra was located on a small highway off a larger one. The fact that it was paved told him of Kitra's importance to the country. Most roads were dust, full of potholes, and were driven at a very slow pace to prevent axles from being broken.

"If you're thirsty," Teren said, jabbing a finger toward the glove box, "I put some bottles of water in there for us."

Touched by her thoughtfulness, Nolan opened it and took out a bottle. The water was warm, but he didn't care. "You want some?"

"Please."

Nolan opened the bottle, handing it to her. The *hafla* was a standard shift, something most Americans didn't know how to drive anymore. She needed two hands to drive and shift gears. Once the *hafla* was in drive, Nolan took pleasure in watching her lift the bottle to her lips, tipping her head up, exposing the slenderness of her throat, and drinking deeply.

"Thanks," she said, handing the nearly emptied bottle back to him.

Their fingers touched and Nolan felt a tingle from their momentary contact. "I'll finish it off, okay?" he offered.

"Sure, I don't have any viruses or bacteria. I'm clean."

"I'm not worried." He grinned.

She flashed a look at him, then smiled. "I'm glad you have a good sense of humor, Steele."

"Call me Nolan if you want, but I'll answer to anything." Because he wanted that familiarity, that closeness with Teren, he had to cultivate her trust.

"Okay, fair enough. Call me Teren. I don't stand on much ceremony unless I'm forced to."

"A woman after my own heart." His skin riffled when she gave a full laugh. It was as if she were touching him with just the sound of her smoky voice. The sensuality surrounding her was palpable in the cab.

Nolan recognized that Teren was not a flirt—that was part of the draw to the "earth goddess" kind of woman he favored. The soil was fertile, alive, creative, and alluring, and so was Teren.

CHAPTER 4

NOLAN WATCHED AS the flat grasslands stretched out before them on their way out of the capital. Sparse green brush and tufts of grass sprouted here and there. Khartoum was a sprawling city of six million, sitting at the confluence of the White Nile and the Blue Nile, which wound lazily through the center of it.

The capital city was nestled between the two rivers, and next to it were its sister cities: Omdurman and Bahri, or Khartoum North. He knew the areas well. There was a pall of pollution hanging over the city midafternoon, as usual, and in the distance, to the west, he saw thunderstorms building, which were welcome this time of year. It was about the only thing that would bring down the daily, blistering, hundred-degree temperature.

He smiled as he watched Teren concentrate on her driving. She wasn't a chatty female, but for him, that was a big plus. He would need her to be focused when he taught her what she needed to know while she was under his guardianship. And he wasn't about to break her focus by talking to her right now. Besides, the wind whipping in through the cab was noisy enough to dissuade talking. The diesel-spewing trucks whizzed past, blue clouds of smoke belching from their tailpipes as Teren navigated their vehicle swiftly past.

It took nearly forty minutes before she broke free of city traffic and was speeding along an asphalt highway. Another thirty minutes passed before Teren slowed the vehicle and made a left turn down a narrow ribbon of a black asphalt road. It was marked by a centerline, barely visible because the brutal sunlight bleached out all color. Up ahead, on a slight rise, Nolan saw what looked like a village in the far distance, the horizontal heat waves dancing, making it appear and disappear beneath their undulations across the burning land.

Teren didn't slow down. In fact, she sped up, driving more like an Indy driver in a race at the track. She was attuned to the sound of the engine, how the tires sang on the heated pavement, the movement of the *hafla* as they sped around the long, flattened-out curves of the road.

Nolan watched Kitra appear out of the mirage, slowly congeal and become real. There was a slight knoll, maybe fifty feet above sea level, where the enclosed village sat. The red clay walls were seven feet high, discouraging predators from leaping up and over them to get inside to the corrals where goats, cattle, and sheep were held. There was a huge entrance, black wrought-iron posts ten feet tall with a horizontal bar that had "Delos-Kitra" spelled out in Arabic across it. He was pleased to see that the two heavy gates were made of the same metal, and there was a guardhouse beside it. Two men were there, both dressed in the familiar Sudanese Army uniforms and armed with M16 rifles. *Captain Taban clearly knew his business*, Nolan thought with relief. Wyatt had assured him that the officer was the real deal. So often in these third-world countries, the military leaders were fat, spoiled, rich politicians or family members who had no military training. Taban wasn't one of that kind from what he could see so far.

Teren waved her arm out the window toward the guards as she approached. They both came out of the guardhouse, rifles on their shoulders. She halted, speaking quickly in Arabic, greeting each of them warmly by name.

Nolan saw their attention was focused on him however, as it should have been. One guard, six feet tall, muscular, and all business, asked Nolan in perfect British English for his passport, which he handed over. The other guard had a visitors' chart in hand and flipped through it, locating his name. Nolan then had to sign in. The first guard gave him a temporary pass to be carried at all times until a permanent one could be made. This was all good in Nolan's world. That meant someone couldn't just waltz into Kitra without proper identification. Uzan's photo had been sent to Captain Taban, and Nolan was going to assume for the moment that these two alert guards had memorized the bastard's face. He'd make sure later when he had an official meeting with the chief security officer for Kitra.

Tucking the plastic visitor's card into his jacket pocket, Nolan nodded his thanks. The guards stepped away and one pressed a button, and the large, black iron gates slowly swung open. Teren was tapping her fingers against the wheel, as if anxious to get on with things. She had taken off her sunglasses, hanging them on the throat of her *tob*. Off came the hat, too. She turned to him.

"First things first: I'm going to take you to your duplex so you can get cleaned up and unpacked, and you probably want to rest. I'm sure you have jet lag."

"Sounds good and yes, jet lag is guaranteed."

She looked at her watch, pulling up the sleeve on her slender left wrist. "It's three p.m. Farida, the director, has invited us over to her family's duplex for dinner at seven p.m. Ayman and his wife, Hadii, are also invited. Do you think you're up for that? Or would you rather crash and burn?"

"No, I very much want to meet them." Nolan liked the idea that Teren was going with him.

"Great." She shifted the *hafla* into gear and it leaped forward into the huge, rectangular enclosure of the village. "I'm taking you to our duplex." She frowned and drove very slowly once inside the gates. "I hope you're okay sharing the duplex with me. Captain Taban felt it important that you be near me since you're my big guard dog." Her lips curved teasingly as she sent him an amused look.

"Yes, I'm your guard dog, and yes, I do want to be close to you." *Much closer than you might imagine.* But he kept those words to himself.

She shook her head. "I think this situation is overblown, if you want the truth. But Captain Taban feels Uzan is a serious threat to Kitra and to me, so I'm playing along with what he wants. He's a good man and has always held Kitra's heart close to his own. And he's kept us safe for the five years he's been employed by us."

"Wyatt knows him personally," Nolan told her. "He feels Kitra is in good hands with Taban."

"That's music to my ears." Teren lifted her hand and gestured around the area as she slowed the truck. "You can get a bird's-eye view of Kitra from here. Up on that slight knoll is the U-shaped administration building. The medical clinic, the psychologist's office, our kitchen and dining room, my office, and the sewing area and sewing training center are all located within it. So is security, which is near to my office. The staff lives in the duplexes on the east and west sides of the U-shaped building. North of the main building are a hundred and fifty small huts. Those house the women survivors and their children, who have asked Delos for safety. Right now, we have about one hundred women here, mostly with children. Once she learns to sew and has a trade to bring in money to feed her family, she'll leave Kitra. Most go back to their families' home villages, where they set up their trade and enjoy a happily-ever-after of sorts."

"Sounds like Delos makes a serious effort to help these women," he said, spotting some of the huts, which consisted of wood, corrugated aluminum siding, and thatched roofs. They were far better constructed than what was available to most of the poor surviving in Sudan, and Nolan knew it. Most tribes moved their herds with the seasons across Sudan, living in huts made from local grass, with thatched roofs, and anything else from nature that they could scavenge in the area to create it.

Teren wiped her damp brow with the back of her hand. "Delos has always put people first, Nolan. We do everything in our power to support these survivors emotionally, mentally, and physically. The biggest worry for an abused woman is her small children. When she sees that they are cared for medically, that they have full bellies every day, that they get to go play on that huge playground over there and are babysat by women caregivers when needed, the woman survivor begins to thrive. She can focus on learning her new trade that she'll make money from."

Nolan stared at the playground, which was enclosed by a two-foot-high blue plastic wall. There was sand inside it, gold and sparkling. He saw about thirty children of various ages playing on merry-go-rounds, five swing sets, six teeter-totters, ten slides, and five sets of monkey bars. Even from a distance, he could hear their infectious laughter, making him smile.

Glancing over at Teren, he saw a kind of wistfulness come to her expression as she watched the children. She'd make a good mother, he guessed by the nurturing look on her face.

"This is impressive."

Teren smiled a little and said, "It's life-giving. Kitra means 'abundance' in Arabic, and this place gives back to those poor women who've been beaten down, scarred, harmed, and abused. They absolutely blossom here at Kitra." She urged the *hafla* slowly forward. "There's a beautiful fountain in front of the admin building, with lots of shade trees surrounding it. Everyone loves to come out here in the midafternoon and cool down. The kids play in the fountain, splash around, and there's a lot of laughter from everyone."

"Do you get splashed with water?" Nolan asked, watching the amusement in her eyes.

"Oh, as you get to know me, you'll see I'm usually the first person who takes off her sandals, strips down to her sleeveless tee and cargo pants, and leaps into the fountain, chasing the kids around in it. I do manage to get wet, of course, and I also get a lot of the adults who are sitting nearby wet."

His mouth pursed. "Anyone ever accuse you of being an instigator, Ms. Lambert?"

Her hands opened on the wheel. "A few times, Mr. Steele. A few times. I'm not someone who can sit in an office all day. I have to get up, stretch, move, get my hands onto something other than a computer keyboard. Usually, you'll find me out at the barn working with the men who care for the animals, or playing with the kids in the fountain, or at the playground. If I get lucky, I throw a leg over one of our horses and ride outside the village at dusk when it's cooler. I love to gallop along the grasslands, just being one with the land, the wind, and the sky."

"I'll join you on those rides."

She raised a brow and then chuckled. "Because you have to? Ayman told me a bodyguard goes just about everywhere with the person they're protecting."

"That's true; I'd join you because of that, but also because I want to." Nolan saw her eyes widen momentarily, and then warmth and some other undefined emotion shone in them.

"You have to tell me all about yourself. You must be a country boy if you want to ride with me."

"We'll cover that later," Nolan promised, interested in the many wooden corrals and huge three-story barns coming up on their right. In one pen were about a hundred sheep, in another the same number of colorful spotted goats. In the last one were at least fifty long-horned cattle. These were large corrals covering at least ten acres each.

There were a lot of trees around the outside of the corrals to give the animals shade, and inside each corral were filled rectangular concrete water troughs. He could see that there were also men inside them, delivering dried grass and feeding the herds. The animals' coats gleamed with good health. Usually, Nolan saw half-starved animals in Sudanese villages. Thanks to the grasslands, the animals owned by village tribes never reached the level of health and vitality that Kitra's herds did. He saw acres of water sprinklers giving that grass vibrant life. The grass, once it reached its mature height, would be cut and dried with a scythe by hand. It would then be hauled into a barn to dry, then fed to the animals over winter, ensuring their continued health. Outside of Kitra, those animals would quickly lose weight and become skin and bone by the time next spring arrived when grass would once again, become plentiful.

The duplexes were one story and large, the stucco painted white to deflect heat. They, too, had corrugated aluminum roofs. To Nolan's surprise, he saw air-conditioning units with each one. That was a game changer for him. He'd spent a lot of time in African desert countries and rarely encountered air-conditioning. To his left, far beyond the barn, he saw a small substation, the reason why there was enough electricity for the houses of those who maintained Kitra.

"This is actually a small city."

"Yes, it is." Teren pulled the *hafla* into a concrete driveway at the first duplex, parked, and shut off the engine. "Welcome home, Nolan." She smiled a little. "This is my duplex." She pointed out the window toward it. "You've been given the one next door to me. We knew you were coming, so a number of women went to work to really clean it, dust it, and make sure you'd have everything you need."

"That's a lot of work," he said, climbing out. "Thank you." He walked to the flatbed and released his two pieces of luggage, carrying the first of them to the door of his temporary digs.

Teren produced a set of keys from her purse and opened up the bright red painted door to his side of the duplex. Dropping the keys into his hand, she said, "Come in. Let me show you around." And then added wickedly, "Besides, it's much cooler in here."

Nolan followed her into the cool, welcoming unit and shut the door behind him. There was a black-and-white zebra hide across the gleaming white tile floor in the living room. A black leather couch and two other matching chairs made it look inviting. The coffee table was made of local wood, lovingly crafted, with a thick, clear glass top. Teren moved like a whisper, pointing out the small but well-stocked kitchen, his bedroom with a queen-size bed, and a tiled bathroom with a large, enclosed shower.

Nolan placed his first duffel bag on the bed and explored further, finding a small room off the bathroom for his office. A desk and a computer were already set up for his use, a landline phone nearby. Nolan particularly liked the handcrafted stained-glass light overhead.

Teren turned and walked through the living room and kitchen to a door at the other end. "This is the door between our homes. Generally, we keep them locked."

Nolan walked over to her, but not near enough to make her feel uncomfortable. He was beginning to see slight smudges beneath her eyes and realized she had likely been putting in long days before his arrival.

"Would it bother you if I asked you to keep it open?" he asked. "I promise I won't be waltzing into your place uninvited unless there's a serious threat."

She brought her arms against her breasts, her mouth tightening. "You mean, if I'm being attacked by Uzan and you hear it and come through it with guns blazing?"

Knowing she said this half in jest and half seriously, Nolan placed his hand on the doorknob. "It's a safety measure for you," he said quietly.

He had the feeling she was uncomfortable with his request. Did she not trust him? "Look, if you're in a relationship or have a special guy over, I promise I won't be bothering you. I know an attack when I hear one."

"Oh," she muttered. "No, I'm single and I don't have anyone in my life, Nolan, so no worries there."

"Then what *does* worry you?" Again, he saw her brow crease and she looked down for a moment, as if deciding whether or not to divulge her secret to him.

"I…umm…just like the sense of safety a locked door gives me." And in a rush, she added, "But I know you have a job to do. Wyatt gave me a short course on being a PSD, a personal security detail, and how I had to behave, and how you would protect me. I guess I'm still getting used to it." She looked up, searching his eyes.

Nolan had to physically stop himself from reaching out to touch her reassuringly. He saw her confusion and worry and eased his hand from the jamb, allowing it to fall at his side. "Can you see me as an extra, added layer of protection to keep you even safer than you were before, Teren?" It was the first time he'd spoken her first name out loud. Damn! It felt like sweet honey rolling off his lips. Her eyes lost some anxiety.

"That helps...yes."

"I don't know the lay of the land around here yet," Nolan confided. "Until I do, I'd appreciate it if you'd keep that inner door unlocked. You don't have to keep it open. After I have several meetings with Captain Taban, I'll have a clearer understanding of the situation. If he feels the risk to you is low, then I'll tell you to go ahead and lock your door. Okay?"

Instantly, Nolan saw relief come to Teren's eyes. Was he that much of an ogre to her that she didn't trust him? Nolan's gut rejected that thought as soon as it formed in his mind. Teren had given no indication that she distrusted him. Instead, he sensed she was embarrassed or ashamed of something. With time, Nolan hoped the immediate level of trust they had already established with one another would allow her to reveal whatever the secret was. He could only be as effective as she was honest with him.

"Okay, that sounds good," she said, her voice low and emotional.

Nolan looked at his watch. "I'm going to crash for a while after I get my other duffel. Then, I'm going to get a shower. Could you knock at my front door near dinnertime? I'm assuming we'll walk to Farida's duplex?"

"Yes, we're expected at seven p.m." She opened the door and stepped through it. "For now, though, I'll leave this unlocked for you, Nolan."

He gave her a faint smile. "We'll take this a day at a time."

"Yes...that's all we can do. One day at a time."

Nolan watched the door quietly close between them. He settled his hands against his hips, scowling as he turned and surveyed the cool, quiet duplex. Rubbing the back of his neck, feeling the fine grit from the open-air ride to Kitra, Nolan was bothered by Teren's most recent reactions.

He knew a lot of people didn't want to have a stranger in their midst, privy to their private life. And he shouldn't have been celebrating that Teren had no man in her life, either, but hell, he was. A lot of women didn't want open windows or doors where they lived. They were all afraid of an intruder slipping in and raping or killing them. And it was a very real fear around the world, not just in the U.S. That was probably why Teren had reacted as she did.

More than anything, Nolan needed to forge an unbreakable bond with Teren, because if problems arose, she'd have to know what to do and then follow his short, sharp commands if all hell broke loose.

He was glad that she wasn't a flighty, disorganized woman in any sense of the word. Teren was grounded, stable, commonsense, and practical. He could see it in everything she did and how she moved. Those were all great attributes for a PSD to have, because in the long run, it made it easier for him to protect her.

Letting it all go, feeling the exhaustion creeping up on him, Nolan went out and retrieved his other bag. After locking the door, he walked into the spacious bathroom. He was eager to dive into a long, cool shower to wipe away the jet lag and the Sudanese red grit clinging to his damp flesh. After that, a few hours of sleep would help him stay awake for the dinner tonight.

Best of all, Teren would be there with him. Nolan needed to see her interact with others, to get to know her as quickly as possible, so he could anticipate what she'd do in a crisis. Never mind his mounting personal interest in her now that he'd found out she was single.

CHAPTER 5

Nolan knocked lightly at Teren's door. Night had fallen, the stars glimmering in the black vaulted skies above Kitra. He heard the yips of a pack of hyenas out beyond the walled village. That was one animal he'd hated on sight. Their bone-crushing jaws could destroy a person's arm or leg in seconds. Plus, hyenas were aggressive predators, roaming the Sudanese desert in packs. With the corrals of sheep, goats, and cattle within Kitra's walls, Nolan was sure the scent of those animals made the pack he'd just heard want to get inside Kitra and perform their murderous slaughter. A seven-foot wall would deter them from any such attempts.

The door opened, and Nolan had to put on his game face. Teren was dressed in a filmy, white silk long-sleeved blouse. The bell-shaped sleeves made her look romantic and wispy. She wore a pale pink, ballet-length skirt with a set of sturdy but feminine-looking leather sandals on her feet. He smiled when he saw that she had pink polish on her toenails. Out here in this dry, gritty land, the ability to indulge in the luxuries of femininity was a rare occurrence.

He liked seeing her recently washed hair twisted up on her head, a beautiful tortoiseshell clip holding it all in place. Her filigreed gold earrings appeared to be from Turkey and hung halfway to her shoulders, increasing her exotic look. Teren wore pink lipstick too, which showcased the shape of her sensual mouth. There was a shine to her sable hair, highlighting gold strands and darker, wine-colored ones. The multicolored effect increased beneath the porch light from where he stood.

"I woke up on my own. I thought I'd come over and get you," he said.

"Thanks, I was just coming over to knock on your door. Good timing, Nolan." She stepped out, closing the door. There were well-placed lights all around the village, making it easy to walk around at night. Looking him up and down, she added, "You look cleaned up and rested."

Nolan noticed she didn't lock the door but said nothing. Training could start tomorrow. "I brought my African clothing with me," he said, and gestured to the ivory safari pants and jacket he wore. "My only concession to being an American is my red T-shirt." He grinned.

"We sort of look color-coordinated, even without consulting one another," Teren said, gesturing for him to walk with her. "Pink and red are brother and sister to one another on the color wheel."

Nolan pushed his hands into his pockets, cutting his stride as she took him down a redbrick walk that cut across the courtyard of the admin building, past the water fountain. There was no way he could think of Teren as his sister. But he nodded and said, "I hope I'm dressed appropriately for a Sudanese meal?"

"Oh, no worries," Teren assured him. "You've been in Sudan before and you know their customs, but here, within Kitra's walls, it's relaxed. It's more of an independent tribal village than hostage to those strict Sharia-law demands you'll find in big cities here. Usually, men eat together and women eat in another room with one another. Here, Farida and her husband, Ameer, have a huge, round wooden table where we'll all sit together. Farida received her doctorate in business administration from Stanford University in California. When she can, she prefers the American style of sitting down to dinner rather than the Sudanese one."

"Well, that's good to know." He cast her a slight, teasing smile. "A little bit of America in the heart of Sudan. Who knew?" Nolan picked up a faint fragrance on Teren's skin as she walked close enough for him to detect it. It was spicy with a hint of cinnamon. Her hair gleamed beneath the lights, and he wondered if she'd put cinnamon oil in it. Out in this dry desert grassland, many women liked to put oil in their hair. She smelled good. *Too good.* Like the world's tastiest dessert.

Nolan forced himself to keep gazing around, looking for any potential threat to Teren. He didn't have a weapon on him yet—he'd receive one from Captain Taban at some point—but Nolan had the abilities and skills to protect Teren even without one.

"Farida's been here at Kitra as long as I have," she said. "We sort of grew up here together. She's very Americanized, and I'm sure you'll feel right at home." She smiled fondly. "Farida's a real rebel."

"A bit like you?" he said, lifting an eyebrow. He saw her give him a wicked look.

"Touché. But I can reluctantly play the part of a subdued, well-trained female when I have to, believe me. Tomorrow you'll see me in cargo pants, a tee, and sandals. I'll probably remind you of a California surfer girl. I don't put on Sudanese dress unless I'm forced to."

"Like at the airport when you picked me up?" He saw her lips quirk.

"Yes, at times like that."

"Thank you for your sacrifice."

She grinned. "I'm glad you have a deadly sense of humor like me."

"Oh?" Nolan inhaled the dry night air. The cattle lowed every now and then as the pack of hyenas moved closer, yipping sharply as they approached. It was the time of the new moon, and dusk was spreading across Sudan, the area slowly darkening.

"I didn't know what to expect," Teren admitted, risking a look over at his deeply shadowed face. There was such quiet, lethal power around Nolan. She wondered if his last name, Steele, had prepared him for this kind of dangerous work. Teren thought of Damascus steel, a famously strong metal that had once been used to forge blades, and then made the connection to her bodyguard. "I mean," she said, stumbling over her words, opening her hands, "I'm just a girl from rural Kentucky. I know nothing of black ops or bodyguards."

"That's all right. I'll teach you. Just don't lose that soft Kentucky drawl," Nolan said, meeting her dark eyes. "It's part of what makes you beautiful."

His compliment was real, and Teren knew it. Even though Nolan appeared to be able to tease her, and did indeed have a good sense of humor, there was still a core of him that was deadly serious. She could sense it around him.

"Thank you," she whispered, feeling a surge of heat throughout her body. Thank goodness it was the gray of dusk and he couldn't see her blushing! "A lot of Sudanese ask me why I speak so funny," she said, smiling fondly. "I guess they think my Southern drawl sounds really weird."

"Doesn't to me," he offered. "It's soft, like you." And then Nolan wondered what the hell he'd just let fly out of his mouth. He had no business being personal with Teren, but damn, he couldn't help himself. Everything about her was personal to him. Her profile as they'd stopped to watch the kids play on the playground was burned into his mind. Their shrieks of delight had turned her expression maternal; Nolan had actually felt an ache in his heart. Teren was a toucher and hugger, he was sure, and the children here probably adored her, but he'd soon find out.

"Oh," she said wryly, as they passed near the bubbling water fountain and she waved to the children playing there. "There's nothing soft about me."

"The photo they showed me at the briefing at Artemis was one snapped of you in the shearing shed. I've sheared sheep, and it's not an easy job to heft a wriggling, panicked hundred-pound sheep on its back and butt and then shear the wool off it. Takes a lot of brute strength."

She gave him a measuring look. "You don't miss much, do you?"

"My job is to notice."

Opening her slender hands, she said, "No one realizes how strong I really am. I work out at our gym. And I run five miles every other day at dawn."

"Why do you work out so much?" Nolan saw her winged brows drift downward as she thought about a possible answer to him. Again, he could feel her retreating from him, just as she had when they discussed keeping the door unlocked and open between their apartments. There was a secret she carried, and when she compressed her lips, Nolan knew she wasn't going to be fully honest with him.

"I love hard, physical work." She tapped her temple. "I do so much heavy mental work as a computer tech that I have to balance it with an equal amount of physical exercise." That wasn't a lie, but it wasn't the full truth. For whatever reason, Teren felt guilty about not being fully forthcoming with Nolan. He was a man who invited her trust. Nolan seemed to be sincere, and she felt he genuinely wanted her to get to know him.

Wyatt had warned her that Nolan would dig into her on all levels, because if an attack ever came, he had to know how she'd react and how he could best protect her in such a situation. She'd asked Wyatt to take out part of her past in her file, because she wanted no one to know about it. His mission team had done a thorough vetting and background search on her, including police reports and court information. She just couldn't go there with a stranger. Wyatt agreed to remove it from the file he'd give Nolan, but he warned her that Nolan should be made aware of it once they had built adequate trust between one another. Teren pleaded with the head of Mission Planning to remove it and say nothing to anyone. He'd been as good as his word: he would remove the upsetting information from the file, and Nolan would be left in the dark, but that hadn't sat well with Wyatt.

"How often do you go horseback riding?" Nolan asked, his gaze furtive as he probed the shadows around the fountain. Within the U-shape of the building was a huge, long rectangular courtyard. He saw at least twenty wooden picnic tables, barbecue grills nearby, and more trees to create cooling shade throughout the area.

"At least twice a week if I can. Maybe tomorrow I can take you over to the barn and show you our horses. We have six of them. Ayman and I go riding sometimes. He's a true horseman, born in the saddle almost."

"I'll probably be with Ayman most of the morning," Nolan told her as they rounded the end of the fountain. He saw the line of duplexes on the western side of the admin building.

"I'm sure. There are a lot of layers of security to this place. Wyatt said you'd be casing the joint." She smiled faintly.

"I need to commit this whole place to memory."

"Really? That seems impossible!"

"A security contractor has a different type of brain than most people," he assured her. "We're asked to memorize manuals a hundred pages long on some ops, so memorizing the layout of a place like this is easy in comparison. Memorization of the surroundings is imperative. That way, I can tell what is out of place and a potential threat to my detail."

"Wow," she murmured, staring over at his shadowed profile. "Really? A hundred-page manual?"

"Yep," Nolan assured her, meeting her wide eyes. She was clearly impressed. Teren was going to be easy to talk with, to delve into, precisely because she had that catlike curiosity. Still, he reminded himself of the land mines around her, too. There was nothing in her file to indicate anything bad had happened to her, but damn it, her reactions told him differently. What was she hiding? Had she hidden it from Wyatt and the Mission Planning team at Artemis, too?

"You're an enigma," she said with a partial laugh, gesturing for him to turn down a narrower walkway that ran in front of the many duplexes.

"And you aren't?"

She chortled and held up her hands. "Guilty on all accounts."

"And Wyatt did warn you that you and I are going to have some serious sessions with one another?"

"Yes," she said, barely holding back a smile. "He warned me you'd dig to China and back with me. All in the name of figuring out what I'd do in a crisis."

"Right," Nolan agreed. Teren stopped in front of a duplex with a brightly painted blue door.

"This is Farida and Ameer's home. I know everyone is excited to meet you and get to know you." She laid her hand on the sleeve of his ivory safari jacket, feeling the hard muscles tense beneath her fingertips. "You're going to be the star tonight, Nolan."

TEREN ENJOYED THE cold hibiscus tea in a large glass, a sprig of fresh mint in it. Watching Ayman and Nolan together was like watching two old friends who hadn't seen each other in a long time. And Nolan's ability to greet the men in the customary Sudanese fashion went a long way with everyone. Men remained with men in another room while the women gathered in a nearby one.

Farida came over to her and whispered in her ear, "He is *very* good-looking, Teren!"

Teren nearly choked on her tea and turned, meeting Farida's gold-brown eyes, which were dancing with merriment. When she could, the director preferred to wear pantsuits instead of a *tob*. Tonight, she wore a pale yellow linen pantsuit. She wouldn't be able to get away with wearing it outside Kitra's wall, but Farida had, long ago, been seduced by American clothing. "I didn't know what to expect," she admitted.

Farida sat down at the huge table that they had just laid out with salads, meat, and rice dishes. She held her hibiscus tea between her small hands. She was barely five feet two inches tall, but in Teren's eyes, the woman was a dynamo of nonstop motion and passion for Kitra.

"Ayman had shown me a black-and-white photo of Nolan, but it sure didn't do him justice," she said, giving Teren a sly look that spoke volumes.

"Oh, no," Teren said, holding up her hand. "There's no way I'm getting into a relationship with him. My last one was a certifiable disaster, Farida."

"Yes, but he was a Frenchman, Teren. They're known to be so fussy." She shrugged her shoulders dramatically. "This man, Nolan Steele? He's very solid. Steady. And he listens closely to what we say and doesn't interrupt."

"Unlike Henri," Teren glumly agreed. Two years ago she'd met the French importer-exporter in Khartoum by accident. She'd been so lonely for so long. When Teren looked back on that debacle, she knew she'd made a poor decision regarding the forty-year-old Frenchman, who had passionately courted her. And she had fallen for him. The sex was great, but Henri's fussiness, as Farida called it, drove her crazy. She didn't want a man who was a drama king, who nagged and pouted when he didn't get his way. And it had brought too much of her dark past back to her. Teren had broken it off, much to Henri's very vocal objections.

Hadii, Ayman's wife, brought in *mouloukhiya* stew, thick with chicken and vegetables. She set it down and then joined them. After she poured herself more tea, she took some *kissra* bread and dipped it into the yogurt and tahini sauce. "Teren, I think you have been blessed."

"Oh?" Teren met Hadii's serious demeanor. She was the mother of two strapping sons who were now guards here at Kitra with their father, Ayman. Hadii was forty years old, and her dry sense of humor always made Teren laugh, even when she was having a frustrating day with her cranky computers.

"Well," she said, draping her manicured red nails over Teren's lower arm, "I think we women can agree that your new shadow is quite delicious-looking. Not that we should be talking about a strange man who is not one of our relatives, but really, he is to be savored."

Farida leaned over and said in a dramatic whisper, "In America they'd call him a hunk, Hadii." Then she added drolly, "Or maybe a stud?" and slanted a meaningful look in the direction of Teren, who sat between them.

Teren colored fiercely as a knowing look danced in Farida and Hadii's brown eyes. "Oh, come on, ladies. I wouldn't know!"

Hadii raised a thin black brow, giving Nolan a critical, assessing glance. All three men were in the living room, including Farida's husband, Ameer, discussing something in low voices. Probably politics or soccer. "Well, if I'm any judge of a stallion, my dear Teren, he is certainly all of that."

Pressing her hand against her mouth, Teren muffled her laughter. Farida and Hadii were like two doting older sisters who made it their objective to constantly try to marry her to a handsome young man. "You two are embarrassing me!" she whispered, giving each of them a baleful look.

"Pooh," Farida said, lifting her fine, thin nose into the air. "You forget how beautiful you are, Teren. You are getting past the age to marry. You don't want to be one of those old maids from America, now, do you?"

She shook her head, giving her dear friends a warm look. "I just haven't met the right man, is all. I keep telling you two plotting and planning strategists that."

"Well," Hadii said in her own defense, "I had Ayman bring Captain Joseph Adler from the French Foreign Legion out here to introduce to you. He was a well-built man in every respect. Very nice, too."

Groaning, Teren remembered meeting that German officer with the scar on his jaw. "I didn't like him, Hadii. He was hard, and he'd lost his ability to trust someone emotionally. I don't want a man who's locked up. I want someone…well…like Ayman or Ameer. Your husbands are wonderful men, they're great fathers to your children, and they love you fiercely. That's the kind of man I'm wanting."

"Tut-tut, child," Hadii murmured knowingly, smiling. "If I'm any judge of character—and I believe I am, because look who I married—this young American stud, Nolan Steele, seems to fit all your requirements."

Teren rolled her eyes, knowing that when Hadii and Farida picked on her, she had already lost the battle *and* the war.

Farida jumped in, her voice keyed with excitement as she whispered to them, "I see the way he looks at you, Teren, when you aren't aware. I have eyes in my head."

"So do I," Hadii intoned, giving her a knowing nod.

"Well," Teren said, "the food's going to get cold if we don't serve it soon. Shall we, ladies?"

Both women groaned and agreed, pushing away from the table and standing up.

"I'm seating Nolan next to you," Farida said, not taking no for an answer as she stabbed her finger at the two chairs to her left.

"Let me help serve first," Teren insisted. Farida was such a matchmaker, and Hadii was her right arm! As Hadii walked past Teren, she rubbed her hands together, glee in her sparkling eyes, a wicked look in her expression.

Teren knew she was in trouble now. These two had both just agreed that Nolan was the perfect mate for her. And they'd do everything in their considerable power to ensure she was going to be with him far more than she'd thought she would be.

As she followed them to the kitchen, the air pungent with fragrant spices such as cinnamon, cardamom, and mint, she smiled to herself. For sure, Nolan was a man's man. As the women brought out the rest of the spicy food, at least fifteen white serving dishes bearing different fare, Farida called the three men to come join them. And like the traffic cop she was, she directed each man to a particular chair at the round table.

Teren loved the colors of the dishes, from the red tomato salad mixed with diced green onion and green chili peppers, slathered with a peanut butter sauce, to the mouthwatering *mouloukhiya* stew, to the Sudanese rice mixed with butter, coriander powder, and turmeric, which gave the grains a yellow color. The table looked like a palette filled with paint pots, each dish fragrant and begging to be sampled. She passed a huge platter of *kissra* bread made from rye and wheat flour. The round, baked bread, which reminded her of the flatbread found in the U.S., was a staple here in Sudan.

When Nolan came and stood behind her chair, Teren felt heat rush to her face again. No man had ever made her blush like he did. Farida and Hadii gave her great big smiles that translated to "I told you so," because Nolan was acting like a gentleman. As Teren wrinkled her nose in response, both her friends tittered between themselves and sat down around the table with their husbands. Teren hoped they weren't going to be suggestive or sly in their remarks as dinner progressed. That was all she needed! Here were two happily married women wanting to match her with the man they thought was perfect for her. What a night this was going to be!

CHAPTER 6

"ARE YOU AS full as I am?" Nolan asked Teren as they slowly made their way back from Ameer and Farida's home. It was eleven p.m. and he noticed her hand resting on her stomach as they walked.

"I feel like a proverbial Thanksgiving turkey," she groaned. "Farida and Hadii make fabulous Sudanese food, and I always love getting an invite to come over and eat with their families. But afterward, I'm stuffed for a week."

"Do you cook for yourself?"

"Yes, all the time. I love this country's food, but I adore barbecue."

"I saw the barbecue grills in the courtyard. Was it your influence to put them in?" he asked, suspecting he knew the answer.

"Yep," she chuckled. "When Farida was hired after our last director retired, she'd just returned from the States. After being in California for six years, she'd fallenin love with love the cuisine there, but she also got hooked on good Southern-style barbecue."

"And you, being from Kentucky, Southern by upbringing, just pushed that cart down the hill with her, right?" He saw faint laugh lines crinkle around her eyes.

"Oh, at a gallop, believe me. Now, the Sudanese, as you probably know, do have a form of barbecue, but our sauces are a whole lot better—at least, that's my personal opinion. As a celebration gift to Kitra when she became director, Farida ordered six sturdy metal barbecues that we set in concrete in the courtyard. They're permanent and very well made."

"So are you the sauce maker?"

"Guilty as charged."

"What kind of sauce? Mild?"

"Well," Teren said, "the Sudanese were raised on red-hot peppers and hot, spicy foods."

"Yes, I've burned the first layer of skin inside my mouth eating some of it at times," Nolan admitted wryly.

"I like hot and spicy, but not the type that numbs your tongue and mouth so you can't taste it."

"Again, you're a woman after my own heart. So?" He raised his brows. "When's the next barbecue around here?"

"Well, Farida and I were talking about that before you arrived. This Saturday we're celebrating twenty women and their children returning to the villages where their parents live to start their lives over. Farida thought it would be nice to hold a barbecue for them, and then they'll be trucked back to their villages by our drivers afterward."

"Sounds good. Are you making the sauce?"

"Yep, but Farida's is just as good. She makes a green sauce that will burn your mouth off, but a lot of the Sudanese women and children love it. They call my sauce *da'iff*—weak."

Her Sudanese Arabic was soft and melodic, rolling off her tongue. "I'll definitely have to try your sauce," Nolan promised, pressing his hand to his heart. He was rewarded with a wide smile, Teren's teeth white and even against her full lips. "I heard you speaking Arabic half the night and the other half in English, Teren," he continued, reflecting on the evening they'd just spent. "Your Arabic is excellent."

"It's so easy to slip between them, I don't even realize when it's happening," she admitted. "Farida said I had an ear for languages. If you ever walk in on us in her office, you'll hear us swinging back and forth between both languages. She loves American slang and uses it anytime she can."

"It feels like you've got a really tight, cohesive team here," Nolan noted as he continued looking around. Although there were three surveillance jeeps that slowly drove outside of the walled village at night, Nolan needed to remain alert. An enemy operator could time those jeep movements, waiting till the vehicle had driven around a corner of the village. Then, before another jeep's lights could reveal his presence, the enemy could struggle to climb over that seven-foot wall and disappear.

Earlier tonight, after dinner, Ayman had taken Nolan to another room, where he'd handed him a Glock 18. The officer had given him enough magazines filled with bullets to do a very thorough job if needed. Tomorrow, he'd get other weapons from the armory. Nolan didn't want to upset Teren by letting her see the pistol he'd pushed down into the back of his belt, hidden by his loose safari jacket.

He had to admit that he felt relieved to finally be carrying a weapon since a hit on Teren or on the enclosure could happen at any time. His team needed to find Uzan again, and Ayman had indicated that his three undercover soldiers were following his trail through the slums of Khartoum. He believed that soon they'd spot the bastard.

"Everyone who works here, Nolan, is fully committed to Delos and its objectives. It's our passion," Teren said, seeing his serious expression. Had she sensed his concern?

"Why did you choose to come here, Teren?" Nolan asked, changing the subject. He'd been curious about this since he'd met her. She looked down and became thoughtful, clearly wanting to give him a fair answer.

"I've always loved Africa. I don't know why—maybe I lived here in a past life. This continent holds a special place in my heart. I hate to see children and women suffer, and I know it's really bad over here for some of them. I guess I just wanted to make a positive difference in their difficult lives."

"In the file that Wyatt gave me, he said you'd worked at the UN camps in Darfur for a year."

"Ugh, that was hell on earth. I handled it, but I didn't have the internal fortitude to do it for more than a year. It burned me out emotionally."

"Seeing victims die every day isn't something most people can take, Teren," he said gently, seeing a quick flush of shame on her face. Then it was gone. But at that moment, he realized that she did not see herself clearly. Rather, she rated herself by what others did for those poor Darfur survivors.

This raised Nolan's concerns. For her height, she was a good fifteen pounds underweight, and he noticed she hadn't eaten a lot tonight. Hadii was always verbally poking at her to eat more, and so was Farida. They were like two mother hens clucking over their little chick, Teren. He was pretty sure that she was more like their adopted daughter, and maybe that was a good thing. It was obvious that those three women clearly loved one another.

"I guess," she said, halting on the walk near the burbling water fountain. "When you put it that way, it's something to be proud of. I shouldn't call myself a wimp because I couldn't take it in Darfur longer than others did."

Then Nolan did the unthinkable. There was a long, loose strand of Teren's hair at her temple, the breeze moving it against her high cheekbone. He lifted his finger, grazing her warm, firm skin and easing it behind her ear. "You can never compare yourself to others." He saw her eyes widen, her lips part, surprise in her expression. And then, Nolan saw her barely sway toward him. It wasn't obvious, but he recognized that Teren liked his touch—and wanted more.

She stopped herself from stepping forward, and he gave her an apologetic look. "I shouldn't have done that. Sorry." *Sorry I can't do it again*, he thought. He wondered what she was thinking as she bent her head, as if to hide her reaction to his unexpected touch.

"I understand," she whispered, turning, beginning her slow walk toward their duplexes, which were shadowed by the night. There was a small light above each door to chase away the darkness and make it easy to see where they were going.

Teren tried to push her regret away. Nolan's gesture had been so natural between them, as if it were a familiar sign of affection. A small ache grew in her heart, her cheek still tingled where he'd barely brushed her with his index finger. Teren realized Nolan was just as drawn to her as she was to him.

She made such poor choices when it came to men, always leaping before she looked, too impatient, thinking she knew the man well enough when she really didn't. And then, later, she'd regret her decision to get closer to him.

She wrestled with her curiosity about Nolan Steele, because he was *not* like any other man she'd run into during her lifetime. He was very different, a lone leopard. When a young male leopard is chased out of the territory where he was born, he moves off to find his own territory. He'd roam the red plains of Sudan in search of another family to make his own.

Now, with Nolan, even though she was powerfully attracted to him, she'd not flirted, not let on how she felt toward him, thinking it was one-sided. Well, judging by the burning, aroused look in his narrowed eyes, it was mutual. And the only thing Teren could celebrate was that she had not made the first move for once. Maybe things would turn out better this time.

She felt Nolan fall into step with her, felt the warmth of his male body close—but not too close to her. Teren felt that all-encompassing sense of safety he surrounded her with once again. She wanted to discuss that with him. She'd never felt anything like this before—only with Nolan.

"What does your schedule look like tomorrow?" Nolan wanted to get them back on a professional footing. He was afraid she'd been shaken by his spontaneous act of intimacy with her.

"I get up at five a.m., and then I go for my five-mile jog."

"Where do you run?"

"Outside the gate on the grassy plain. Usually I jog close to the highway because the soil is more hard-packed than on the nearby grasslands. It's five miles one way from Kitra to the turnoff from the highway to Khartoum. I go two and a half miles toward it and then turn around and come back. Then I shower and eat breakfast, and I'm in my office by eight a.m."

"Do you get up a lot from your office and go various places?"

"Yes, I can't stand sitting for too long. I leave my office between five to six p.m. and come home, fix a meal, and crash. I'm usually in bed by ten p.m. That's my day in a nutshell."

"Okay, sounds good. At 0900—I mean, nine a.m., I'll be over at the security office, where Ayman is going to introduce me to the security system around here. It's probably going to take at least until noon."

He glanced down at her, admiring her profile, which was so beautiful, although right now her lips were compressed and her brow furrowed. Nolan thought he'd really done it this time by spontaneously touching her. She hadn't been expecting such intimacy. He recognized that his feelings for her were growing quickly, whether he wanted them to or not. She must have sensed it, because she was giving off the vibe of a scared rabbit facing off with a predator. Him.

He walked her to her door and aiming again at a professional tone, instructed, "Listen, you need to start locking your home when you leave it."

Turning to look up at him, she said, "You're kidding me, right? We always leave our doors unlocked. I know you said there was a threat, but look at that seven-foot wall." She gestured toward it.

"Wish I was," Nolan said, using his most patient tone. "Tomorrow morning, how about if I join you for that jog. Then, after I finish with Ayman, I'd like to sit down with you in your office so we can discuss the ins and outs of working together. Being protected can get on the subject's nerves pretty quickly, Teren. I'll try to head off that possibility by telling you what to expect beforehand and what we can expect from each other. How's your calendar look for tomorrow afternoon?"

"It's free after two p.m. Will that work?" Nolan was so close she could breathe in his scent—strong and masculine. It was part desert, part sweat, and part something else so powerful that she felt her body respond with a sexual longing that rocked her.

"We need to keep you safe, Teren, so once you're inside your home, lock that front door. Tomorrow, I'll check out any weaknesses and we'll remedy them."

"I just hate the idea of having to do it, is all. I realize this isn't your fault. You're trying to help me, but it angers me that one man can change another person's life so suddenly and dramatically."

"One good thing about all this is it's not going on forever, Teren. If you can work with me, this situation may be over sooner than later. What you don't want is Uzan or one of his henchmen lying in wait for you inside your house." He gestured toward the interior.

Teren felt herself tensing; she hadn't even taken something like that into consideration. Could he be right about the need for extra security measures?

"Right now, I'll go in ahead of you. I want you to remain out here, beside the door, but not standing in front of it. I need to clear every room before you go in."

She moved to the other side of the door and waited. "Can you teach me what I need to know?"

"Tomorrow when we meet and talk in your office." Nolan silently praised her teamwork attitude. He knew Teren had her own rhythm and fixed schedule. Every human being did. Now he was coming in and destroying it, then replacing it with a PSD routine instead. He opened the door slightly. It was dark inside and he reached behind him, taking the Glock out of his belt, unsafing it. There was already a bullet in the chamber. Pushing the door wide open, he reached inside and flipped on the overhead light switch. He heard Teren's soft gasp as he revealed the weapon from beneath his jacket.

"It's smart to always keep a light or two on in your home when you leave it."

Teren watched in silence. He was putting himself in harm's way for her. Nolan was all business, his focus suddenly like a laser, his eyes narrowed. In some ways, he made her think of a leopard, stalking a potential kill. He moved soundlessly. Her cheek tingled, reminding her of that molten, beautiful, and unexpected moment with him earlier. How close she'd come to stepping forward, leaning upward, and kissing that chiseled mouth of his.

Maybe Farida and Hadii had been right. Nolan was eye candy. For once could she not leap before she looked? Just appreciate him as a man? Give herself time around him so she really knew him? Confusion swept through her as she patiently waited. Finally, Nolan reemerged, sliding the Glock behind him into his belt. He gave her an apologetic look.

"It's clear. Come on in."

A faint smile lurked on her lips. "I've been living here for seven years, and the only thing I've ever run into was a scorpion in the middle of the living room one night." She saw him tuck a smile away, his eyes gleaming with amusement.

"I understand."

Sweeping into her home, Teren heard the door close. Turning, she said, "I'll take all of this seriously, Nolan. I know you mean well, and so does Wyatt. It may look like I'm not grateful, but I am."

"It's tough to get used to a new routine." Standing by the door, he said, "After you're inside, you should check your windows to ensure they also remain locked. Check them every day. Does anyone else ever come in here? Like a cleaning woman?"

"No, I do my own cleaning. I'm the only one ever here, unless of course, I have friends over for dinner." She walked to the kitchen, grabbed a glass from the cabinet, opened her fridge, and pulled out a pitcher of cold water. "Do you want some?"

Nolan shook his head. "No, I'll let you have your space." He gestured to the inner door. "Mind if I go this way?" The expression on her face was one of concern. He understood why. It wasn't easy to give up one's privacy to a stranger, no matter what the reason or how important it was. "I'll see you at five tomorrow morning, Teren. Good night."

"Good night, Nolan. Thank you…" She watched him walk to the door and disappear. He quietly closed it behind him. After gulping down the cold water, she set the glass in the white tile sink, feeling vaguely disturbed. Why? Walking over to the door, Teren wanted to lock it.

Nolan was taking her control away from her. Normally, she was the one who was in charge—here at Kitra, she was the number three person. She turned, leaving the door unlocked, and went to the kitchen. Leaning against the counter, she rubbed her face with her hands, making a muffled sound of frustration.

What was this really all about? Nolan was only doing his job. He cared enough for her life to educate her.

She knew exactly why she was reacting like this. It had happened years ago, when she was eighteen. She had been so naïve and trusting, and smiling, handsome Tony had taken advantage of it. After inviting her to a motel room, he had drugged and raped her, then left. She'd awakened alone and naked hours later.

With a growl, Teren pushed off her sandals, her feet against the coolness of the pale orange tiles. The sensation felt steadying to her roiling emotions as the past was brought into the present once more. Why couldn't she just get over the fact that she'd been drugged and raped? Of course, that wasn't the worst part. That came when she'd found out she was pregnant. She had been too ashamed and frightened to tell anyone, especially her family, about it. Humiliation, that sense of being a failure to her family, struck her strongly as it always did. Her innocence had been destroyed at eighteen. And her family, who cherished strong morals, had disconnected from her as a result of her traumatic experience. Consequently, Teren learned to live on her own without their support because they were embarrassed by her behavior.

Her life had changed forever when she'd left home after high school and gone to a neighboring town that had a community college. She found it wonderful to live in the scintillating, exciting, and unknown world instead of at her family's large dairy farm. She was the only girl, the baby of the family. She had three stout, hardworking brothers who coddled her, protected her, and chased away any boy who might be interested in her during her high school years. Her family had filled her head with the fear of getting pregnant. Of having sex before marriage. Of being called a slut like so many other girls at her high school. They all vowed she'd be a virgin when she graduated, and she had been.

Her social skills were less well-honed as a result of their over-protectiveness. At a school dance, her tall, brawny brothers would glare down at any boy who asked her to dance. If the boy moved his hand from the small of her back, one of her brothers would come over, forcibly separate them, and tell the boy to get lost. It was so embarrassing to Teren. And then there were the constant, daily fights with her stern mother over the kind of clothes Teren wanted to wear. Her mother accused her of looking like a biblical harlot if she deemed a dress too tight or too short. Teren remembered those years of high school and indeed felt as if she'd had three bodyguards, plus her mother checking her out thoroughly before she went to catch the school bus. Her three brothers had been protective and watched out for her since the first grade until the day of her high school graduation.

Frowning, Teren sat down in the living room, placing her feet on her carved wooden trunk with leather straps for hinges. It was her idea of a coffee table. Inside the chest were all the personal belongings she rarely shared with anyone. Her mind bounced from her past to what Nolan had just done tonight. It made her feel as if she had a big brother lording over her once more, telling her what to do, controlling her every movement. Only Nolan wasn't looking at her clothes, perceiving she was a slut like her family, her friends, and the people in her town thought she was. No, when he'd first come to the door to pick her up at seven p.m., she'd seen pleasure come to his eyes as his gaze moved slowly from her head down to her sandaled feet and back. She'd felt his approval of what she wore, saw that slight, boyish smile curving one corner of his well-shaped mouth. If anything, he made her feel beautiful.

But she was a harlot of the worst kind in the eyes of her family and community. Tipping her head back against the butter-colored leather couch, sinking against it in surrender as her past unwound within her like an ugly story with a bad ending, Teren closed her eyes. She wouldn't cry. God knew, she'd cried buckets of tears over the years because of her drugging and rape by Tony. After her best girlfriend, Erin, listened to Teren list what she thought were digestive symptoms three months after the rape, it changed Teren's life forever. Teren had been nauseous all the time, vomiting, her stomach roiling off and on for no reason. Erin became very somber and suggested she pick up a pregnancy test at the drugstore. She said that from the symptoms Teren was describing, she might be pregnant.

Teren didn't want to believe Erin, but the test had verified her suspicions. Finally, she told Tony the test results, and the earth fell out from beneath her feet, her life never to be the same again after that horrifying night. He'd beaten her unconscious, and she'd miscarried and woken up in the hospital with her parents, who had shame in their eyes, at her side. Later, after recovering sufficiently, she went on to complete her two-year computer science degree. Coming to Africa had been good for her. Teren had time to grieve, mature, and deal with the tragic choices she'd made when she was so young.

Now, opening her eyes, Teren stared up at the handmade metal and glass light above her. She wanted to focus on something positive. The light had been made by women here who wanted to learn the art of working with metal and stained glass in order to create beautiful lamps. These lamps usually carried oil in them and were designed to be used by villagers. This one worked on electricity, but it was still beautiful, and Teren appreciated the rainbow colors of the hand-cut glass throughout it.

Slowly rising, she rubbed her brow, a headache coming on. It always did when she refused to cry. If she cried, she could avoid the headaches. Maybe a warm shower would help to wash the old memories away. At least she hoped so. She felt her throat closing, the tears right there, aching to be shed for so much of herself that she'd lost that awful, life-changing night.

Undressing in her bedroom, she carefully laid her clothes out on the white chenille bedspread and moved to the bathroom, naked. She turned on the faucets, grateful that each duplex apartment had a hot water heater, so she could enjoy such a luxury in this struggling African country. Most people in Sudan didn't even have a shower, and one with hot water was unheard of.

She unclipped her hair, allowing it to fall around her shoulders, placing her favorite comb on the counter. Picking up a washcloth and cinnamon-scented soap, she stepped into the steamy enclosure. Just the soft, warm spray splashing across her head, the water soaking swiftly into her hair and darkening it, running in trickling rivulets across her upturned face, made the past begin to slowly dissolve. Water always helped Teren.

With her eyes closed, she saw Nolan's dark, shadowed face once more as they walked across the village and back to their duplex. He had a kind face, not a judgmental one like her father's. And Nolan had extended his patience to her tonight, even though she'd been somewhat reluctant about allowing him to protect her.

Nolan had inadvertently struck a deep wound that had never healed. Her three brothers, to this day, barely spoke to her because of what had happened. When the police found her in the motel, unconscious with a concussion, nose broken, cheek fractured, several teeth on one side of her jaw loosened, her family came to her aid. But they never understood why she'd gone to that motel room, although she'd tried to explain it. She'd been too emotional, too charged with grief and guilt, to share why she'd done it.

Teren would always be grateful that her family had not abandoned her in her hour of need. She'd lain in a coma for three weeks, miscarrying but not knowing about it until later. After she opened her eyes, disoriented, not knowing where she was or how she'd gotten there, she saw that her family had stood watch and prayed for her. Their church pastor and the parishioners had prayed for her as well. And there was always someone, either family or friends, who remained faithfully at her bedside in that hospital, twenty-four hours a day. Teren believed to this day it was the power of their prayers that had pulled her through.

Lifting her face to the water once more, she allowed those gutting memories to wash away, at least for now. Teren could only remember so much. It became too painful to remember it all at once. Her reaction to Nolan's trying to control her had brought back her parents' and her brothers' attempts to control her. It wasn't the same, but that's how she'd started to take it until she caught herself and separated her past from her present.

As she soaped up her shoulders and arms, washing away the perspiration and fine grit that was always carried on the desert breeze, she felt guilty over not being a more willing PSD. But he didn't know her past and she hadn't been aware of why she was balking until just now.

Teren was sure this wasn't the first PSD he'd ever been on. She knew very little about Nolan and his life as an undercover military operative and longed to sit down and really talk to him. How badly she wanted him to open up to her.

Of course, Nolan didn't know about her ugly past, and his impression of her would surely change if he ever found out. Her lips tightened as she washed her breasts, torso, and belly. Grateful that Wyatt had left her sordid past out of her file, Teren knew she needed to apologize to Nolan. He was doing his job, and Delos was paying him a lot of money to guard her and keep her safe.

Tomorrow morning when they went for a jog, she would tell him she was sorry and would try to be a better student, a better partner in this PSD dance that had landed at her doorstep. And most of all, Teren had to push aside the memory of that caring touch across her cheek, the way the heat had tunneled downward, her breasts firming up, her nipples puckering beneath her blouse. All the man had to do was lightly touch her, give her that smoldering look of wanting her, and she was already melting and wanting him, too. What was she going to do?

CHAPTER 7

TEREN HAD JUST stepped outside her duplex at five a.m., the western horizon a pale pinkish color, when Nolan joined her. She tried to hide her appreciation of his long, muscular legs encased in a pair of loose-fitting, dark green shorts. His tan muscle shirt showcased the power of his upper chest and broad shoulders. He was not wearing a pistol from what she could see.

Casually, she nodded in his direction, then quickly fashioned her hair into a long ponytail with a rubber band. Noting his beat-up gray sneakers, Teren smiled. "You must jog regularly," she said, pointing to his worn Nikes. She had thrown on a sports bra, a sleeveless lavender muscle shirt, and dark purple shorts that came halfway down her thighs.

"Yeah, I do."

She did a few stretching exercises on the porch, warming up. "How many miles a day?"

"Three to five, depending upon what's going on."

"I thought so," she said. Today, Nolan reminded Teren even more of a young, powerful leopard. There was no fat on this man's body. Every muscle was honed, but not overdone. She doubted he was a weight lifter and figured he followed a regular daily routine, such as jogging, to keep him in shape.

Nolan had already observed that Teren was dressed like an American jogger, since here, in the middle of nowhere, there were no conservative males to report on her. Here, she could wear typical American sports clothing and get away with it. He found her athletic build a real turn-on.

Teren was in excellent shape, thanks to her regular workouts, and Nolan was glad she was, because her personal safety partly depended on it. Much as he hated to think about it, he was here because she might need all her strength in the coming days, and his job was both to protect her and to teach her how to protect herself.

"Did you sleep well?" he asked while doing his warm-ups, stretching his legs like a fencer preparing for a match.

"Yes, but not for long periods…it was off and on."

"Why? Did I give you nightmares last night about all the bad things that could happen if you didn't lock your windows and door?"

She met his gaze and saw he was only half joshing her. She instinctively sensed that warm blanket of security he emanated, wrapping itself around her. There was no question that it was coming directly from Nolan to her. She was amazed at how good she felt as it embraced her.

The teasing in his low voice and the glint in his dark blue eyes made her smile. "I guess I have an overactive imagination, and sometimes it keeps me up at night."

"Sorry to hear that," he grunted, then stood up, ready to run. "I realize it's hard for a civilian to suddenly be thrown into an op where her life could be at stake."

"Well, speaking of that, I owe you an apology for last night," Teren said, walking with him toward the closed iron gates to Kitra. He slowed down a bit so she could keep up, and they walked beside each other, comfortable in one another's company.

"No, you don't owe me anything. Getting you up to speed is all part of my job. Sometimes people don't take to it right away."

She glanced out of the corner of her eye, luxuriating in the warmth beginning to flow through her, making her feel strong and free. "Look, Nolan, normally I'm not like that. I behaved very immaturely last night." She broke into a slow jog and he joined her.

Nolan nodded. He appreciated her gracefulness as she moved beside him. "Forget it," he said. "It's a new day." He was studying how different Teren was from other women who ran. She jogged like an athlete. That was why her body was so taut, sculpted, and beautiful. She had the nicest set of legs he'd ever seen on a woman, and his hands itched to slide up from her slender ankles, feeling her body react as he learned what aroused her when he touched her.

Catching himself once again, he tucked away those yearnings. Teren was his detail, not his lover, despite what he'd fantasized about last night in a series of torrid dreams.

"Are you always this patient with other people?" Teren asked. They slowed down as they approached the guard hut and gate. Two soldiers stepped out, saw who they were, and pressed a button. The black wrought-iron gates swung open, and Teren greeted the men by name, smiled, and waved. They came to attention, smartly saluting the pair as they headed out the gate.

Nolan liked the professionalism of Ayman's soldiers. Although Teren was friendly with them, they maintained a discreet distance, which was good. As soon as they cleared about a hundred feet, she chose the harder, packed red clay berm instead of the paved road. Nolan silently approved, knowing that the shock of hard pavement could tear at a runner's joints, while jogging on dirt softened the constant blows, much like a cushion. There was enough room on the berm for both of them, and he automatically looked around, forcing himself to stop watching Teren move. She was so damned sensual, whether she walked or jogged. There was a boneless movement to her he'd rarely seen in anyone except those who had the right jogging DNA. Now he was sure she was part cheetah—her grace was definitely catlike.

As he heard her easy breathing, he looked forward to the first mile, which would warm them up. Then the fluidity of motion would take over and lead to the runner's high they both awaited. For Nolan, it was like a moving meditation, and he always looked forward to finding that sweet spot where his body and mind worked effortlessly together. He called it "the song of the body," a time when he could luxuriate in the strength and power of his muscles.

But he wasn't going to be lulled into pleasure now or in the future as long as Teren was his PSD. It was his job to look around, to memorize the flat, red landscape scattered with brush and clumps of green grass.

He saw a rabbit skitter from one bush to another, and looking up, he saw birds flying overhead, leaving their night roosts in search of food for the day. Not a breeze stirred. The sky was losing its darkness above them, chased away by the sun approaching the horizon, which it would rise above in another fifteen minutes. Right now, the grasslands looked peaceful, even beautiful. When that August sun rose, though, it would quickly turn the land into an oven, brutally baking everything in sight. Most of the grass spreading out in every direction was yellowed and dried-out, but some brave clumps were still green here and there.

Scanning the curved black ribbon of road ahead, north of them he could almost make out the main highway in the distance. He was lucky he could see in all directions, thanks to the flat land, so it would be easy to spot any predator—on four legs or two—approaching from a long way off. Nolan felt fairly certain that Teren could safely jog out here, but he'd teach her some things to look for to alert her to possibilities, just in case.

He had noted the faint shadows beneath her eyes this morning. Although Teren had wanted to allay his concerns over her not getting enough sleep, Nolan sensed that either something had kept her from going to sleep or a dream had woken her up—and his gruffness and painting a threatening picture for her of someone hiding and waiting to jump her in her duplex had caused it.

Nolan knew that she needed to be aware of this disturbing possibility—and she was. Still, he didn't like upsetting her, because she was a sensitive creature, and he wasn't surprised that she had a wild imagination. He'd have to toughen her up regardless. Her life might depend upon what he taught her.

Their footfalls were cadenced and firm. Nolan enjoyed their closeness, their elbows sometimes brushing against one another. The berm was about four feet wide, which didn't allow him to swing out farther to give her the room she probably wanted. He was pleased that Teren didn't appear to mind those moments of contact. She hadn't pulled away, and she hadn't opted to jog on the highway or asked him to give her more room. Nolan knew he was a thief enjoying those accidental connections with her perspiring flesh. Sweat was trickling down his temples as she increased the pace after that first mile.

Smiling to himself, Nolan silently applauded her for pushing herself at this point. Her body was fully warmed up and fluid now. This was where the stride increase had to happen if one was serious about jogging—and Teren was very serious. She was all legs, and he watched as she let herself take off, her stride increasing. It allowed him to reach his full stride, which was surprising. Although she was just five feet seven, her legs were long, and she was using her genetic gifts to her advantage, really covering the distance now with practiced ease. She glanced at the watch on her wrist.

"What are you shooting for?" Nolan asked.

"Seven-minute miles."

He grinned. "You're a ballsy woman, Ms. Lambert."

She laughed. "Oh, I think you can keep up with me, no problem at all, Mr. Steele."

He felt good, enjoying their banter and the way her lips curved. Her ponytail swung in cadence between her shoulder blades, like a metronome moving back and forth, establishing a rhythm. She was now running strongly and blushed when Nolan sang out, "Hey, can I compliment you and say you run like a man?"

She laughed. "Thanks. Compliment accepted!"

"You're welcome." They were rapidly approaching the two-mile mark. "You've been at this a while."

"Ever since I was nineteen."

"Well, you're good."

She gave him a wicked look. "Are you up for a longer run, Steele? Say, nine miles instead of five? I can do it. Can you?"

Spunky and showing off a bit, he thought. *That's a good sign.* "Sure, nine's good. You're on."

"I guess having a good running partner is inspiring me," she laughed, giving him a merry look.

"It doesn't hurt to go longer or shorter distances every week," he said. "That way, your body doesn't get bored and turn lazy on you."

"Well," she said between spaced breaths, "since you're in my life until this thing with Uzan is settled, I might as well take advantage of you."

Oh, no question, Nolan thought. He wanted her to take advantage of him.

He was dying to sit and talk to her in depth. He was infinitely curious about what she thought and felt, what was important to her, and what bothered her. He didn't want to admit that no other PSD he'd been charged with guarding had opened him up as Teren had. It was her. It wasn't that she'd done anything except breathe and be her beautiful Kentucky self.

Teren was like a Chinese box puzzle, one Nolan wanted to intimately explore in every possible way. If he told her that now, of course, it would be too soon; Nolan knew she'd run the other way. He'd gotten a taste of that last night when he'd been spontaneous and touched her cheek, curving that lone strand of hair behind her delicate ear. And he yearned to do much more to please her. He imagined watching her turn and twist, caught up in the ecstasy of a man giving her the heat of intimacy—his intimacy.

No one had inspired such need in him, not even Linda. Nolan didn't know what the hell was going on with him or why this was happening now. It had all started in the Artemis briefing room, when the first picture of Teren had been flashed up on that screen. He'd felt as if someone had opened up his heart, tearing away the old walls of grief and loss surrounding it. Those layers of sorrow had dissolved in that moment when he'd stared at her profile, her eyes haunting him, her mouth urging him to ravish it.

But it was so much more than a physical sensation that had suddenly exploded within him. Nolan couldn't explain it; he could only feel it. He felt like one of those ancient African baobab trees from Botswana that had such deep roots and were thousands of years old. Teren affected him that deeply. He was so attuned to her moods, her needs, and he sensed, beneath these, her yearnings.

He'd lain awake for a long time, naked, on top of the bedspread, hands behind his head, staring up at the dark ceiling. He was always in control of himself, especially with his emotions. It was vital so he could function successfully as an operator.

He was concerned that last night he'd let his control slip when he touched her cheek, and that since then, he'd been thinking nonstop about Teren in a distinctly unprofessional way.

Damn! He'd had plenty of PSD assignments in his life as a Delta Force operator, but never had his emotions ever gotten out of that internal box where he kept them. But when Teren had stopped, facing him, and the starlight had graced her shadowy, exotic face, something had opened up inside him. Something good, healthy, and whole.

For whatever reason, Teren hadn't stopped him from being intimate in that one gesture last night, but that was beside the point. This was all his doing, and it wouldn't benefit either of them. He'd seen the surprise enter her eyes when he'd connected with her, followed by arousal and need. Sure, he knew when a woman wanted him, and it was staring at him in her stormy gray eyes after his brief contact. And when he quickly pulled his hand away, he'd seen regret replace arousal—could it be regret that he'd stopped? Women didn't like to be led on, and she was probably no exception.

Hell, he had to admit it. Teren was attracted to him, so it wasn't one-sided, which was both good news and bad news. It was right in front of them, in the darkness that had surrounded them on that walk, the warm breeze wafting like invisible lovers' hands tugging at them to move closer to each other, not step away.

But they had wisely separated because Nolan was embarrassed by his spontaneous act. Maybe that was why Teren had become cool with him at her duplex. Maybe it wasn't that he'd scared her, it was that she'd yearned to taste him, kiss him, and more. He could wish.

On the last mile toward Kitra, the ninth one, Teren held up her sweaty hand as the first rays of sunlight shot across the quiet grassland. "Can we slow and cool down?" she asked. "You okay with that?"

"Sure, seven of those nine miles you were wide open and pushing." He gave her an appreciative look. "You were doing seven-minute miles. Pretty impressive."

"Yeah," she huffed, shifting into a walk. "It felt good to really challenge myself this morning." And then her eyes gleamed with amusement. "I guess you inspire me, Steele."

Taking a mock bow in her direction, he said, "I think we work well together. You're no cream puff, like I originally thought you might be." He shot her a boyish grin, and she knew he wasn't serious.

Lifting her chin, Teren wiped the sweat off her brow and temples with her fingers. "Get over it, Steele! What if I called you something derogatory like that? How would you feel?"

"Oh," he said slyly, "but a woman being a cream puff is hardly an insult, Ms. Lambert. Just the other way around. She's sweet to taste, to savor, to be placed in the category of a very special dessert."

Nolan hoped she recognized the double meaning as her eyes narrowed a bit. Food for thought? Maybe curiosity? That was good. He wanted to engage her on that level, let her know that he thought she was one helluva delicious treat and that he appreciated her. Still, he realized there were sexual overtones to his word choice, and he saw a more thoughtful look enter her eyes.

"Well, I'm no one's cream puff," she replied, still trying to analyze his statement.

"Women are beautiful by nature," Nolan said, keeping his voice light as they walked. "I always think of them as one's dessert in life."

"Not meat and potatoes? As *dessert?*" How he enjoyed her rejoinders. She was certainly easy to tease! "Not even. I suppose if I said you reminded me of a steak, you'd take that as a compliment?"

"Sure, as long as it was medium rare, I would."

It was her turn to laugh, and she did, heartily, to Nolan's delight. Her hair was mussed, with long strands around her face, some of them sticking to her perspiring skin, and he couldn't suppress flashes of her lying on his bed, her hair spread out on the pillow as he licked the place behind her earlobe where an erotic reaction was guaranteed. He wanted to taste her long, smooth throat, move his tongue across her exposed nape, and watch as her breasts and nipples tightened to his exploring touch.

His erection thickened. *Get a grip*, he warned himself.

But it was too late. Teren was well aware of his erection and pretended not to notice. "I'm glad you have a good sense of humor," she said, meeting his eyes. Instead of feeling insulted, she felt excited. Heat swept through her lower body with a promise of something so pleasurable she felt her thighs tighten.

Now it was *her* turn to scold her body. She'd never had a good lover, according to Farida and Hadii, who had managed to get her to admit to her very limited knowledge of true ardor. They'd both given her sad-eyed looks, telling her a real man knew to please a woman first, not last. A real man knew how to make his woman growl like a satisfied cat after being taken by her male lion lover. Of course, Teren pretended to understand, but she didn't really. The two women talked excitedly about orgasms, how wonderful they were, how having one threw them into a frenzy of wild pleasure.

Teren would nod, as if in agreement. Though she suspected they knew she had never encountered such pleasures, she didn't have the guts to admit it. And after all the trials she'd gone through with her family, she didn't want anyone else telling her how inexperienced she was.

Not that Farida or Hadii would ever say such hurtful words to her. Instead, they clucked like wise hens who had raised many broods of chicks. For them, Teren was just one more chick to love and educate. They never made her feel insulted, only cared for and nurtured. In fact, Teren had often admitted to herself that she wished either of these wonderful Sudanese women had been her mother, instead of the stern, unforgiving one she'd been given.

Nolan wiped the sweat off his brow. Smiling, he said, "I like hearing you laugh, Teren. I wish you could see what I do when you let go."

Giving him a confused look, she didn't know what to say to his husky declaration. Was that burning look a yearning for her? She had no doubt that this man wanted her, and for once, Teren wasn't afraid or disgusted by it.

Maybe Farida and Hadii were correct—maybe Nolan was the right man for her. She relied on their insight into men, having no trust in herself because she'd been such a failure at finding the right men to love. Brushing away the trickles of sweat from her face and arms as they walked in the warming air, Teren saw it was almost seven a.m., and already the heat of the day was reaching furnace levels. What little cool air had breezed past them during the run was gone.

The two soldiers at the guardhouse came to attention as Teren and Nolan passed through the open gates. Teren saw the community awakening. Women in colorful clothing were standing in line to pick up trays and get breakfast in the huge dining room of the admin building. She smiled softly, watching the smaller children running around their mothers or playing happily with other children in line.

These children had known only the pain and abuse of their fathers' closed fists or open hands—now they laughed and played happily.

It was a scene that always made Teren's heart swell with joy; this moment made the whole day worthwhile. She knew every mother and child by name. The tragic stories of rape, abuse, and kidnapping for use by sex traffickers were a common thread among these women. Each had come to Kitra for safety, help, and healing. Some of their children had been sold by their fathers to male predators for sex; the money from these sales put food on the table for the family.

It was a tragic way of life in Africa. Teren had witnessed the positive changes after a family had lived at Kitra for a year. The transformation was almost miraculous. She'd seen lives turned around as wounds were tended and mothers and their children began to heal, as the mother gained self-confidence instead of being browbeaten and abused. Over time, she learned the trade of sewing on a treadle machine. Sales were assured, as everything she created was sold in Kitra's global Internet store.

The women now had monthly incomes and their families would not starve. It was an altogether powerful testament to a charity doing things the right way for those in need.

Teren often wondered if, had she been given similar help after her sexual abuse, she might have turned out differently—better than she found herself today.

"Those kids look like they're enjoying themselves," Nolan murmured, bringing her back to the present. "Are they like this all the time?"

"They are," she answered softly, slowing down, then coming to a halt. She told Nolan about the women and their children and their difficult journeys to get to Kitra. She saw instantly how moved he was by her stories, and she realized he could replace that professional game face with a glimpse of his deepest feelings. Wyatt had warned her that an operator would always maintain a stoic and unreadable demeanor. But she could see Nolan wasn't like that. She could read him easily because for some reason, he was willing to allow her entrance into his private self—the man, not the operator.

After she finished telling him about the women's transformations, she said quietly, "Every day, Nolan, I receive the gift of seeing these women heal just a little more. Their children are healing. When a child first comes here, he or she is so frightened, just a silent shadow afraid to speak, wincing when someone lifts a hand, thinking they're going to get cuffed or a fist in the face." She saw the anger leap to his eyes, saw the tightening of his mouth.

Reaching out, she touched his arm, which was damp with sweat, gleaming in the sunlight. "Farida, Samar, Nafeesa, and Charuni, who all work here, use every chance they get to hug, kiss, and hold these wounded children. They embrace the mothers too. And everyone here responds to the love."

She wanted to keep contact with him but pulled away as she saw arousal in his eyes. His look sent heat streaking down to her lower body, making it throb and ache with an unfamiliar sensation.

"Love is always the greatest healer," he replied, watching the group and trying to get his equilibrium back after the silent message of her touch. "I've met the people who created Delos, and I can tell you that they're the same way."

Her gaze lingered on his. "And do they hire men such as yourself who have heart, who are able to reach out and do the same as we do here at the charity?"

"What do you mean?" he asked, unsure where this was going.

"Wyatt warned me about you. He said you were an ex-military operator and that you would wear your game face when you were around me." She gave a negligent shrug. "He said I'd never really know what you were honestly thinking or feeling." She gestured toward the highway. "Yet, this morning on our run, you didn't wear a game face. You laughed, smiled, talked, ran. I could sense things around you…"

He put his hands on his hips, because if he didn't, he was going to take a step forward, frame Teren's gleaming face, and kiss her senseless. She wanted to kiss him. He saw it in her eyes, felt the desire around her. Nolan wouldn't tell her how keen his sixth sense was because he knew it would embarrass Teren.

She was fragile in a different way, he realized. She didn't seem confident about her feelings toward him. At her age, most women had a very solid understanding of themselves in that regard, but she didn't. And he couldn't be like a rogue elephant in her life, stomping through it, tearing it up as a result.

Choosing his words carefully was important. "Well," he rasped, giving her a warm look, "I find that around you, Teren, that mask I'm supposed to wear melts away. I'm not blaming you. It's just you. You invite me to be who I really am, not what I'm supposed to be for you. And yes, I can put that game face on in a heartbeat. But you know what? Around you, I don't want to."

He saw instant relief come to her eyes. "That's good," she whispered unsteadily, touching her brow, pushing strands of hair away from her eyes. "Because I like being around the real you, Nolan. I hate people who put on an act to hide who they really are."

"Good. Does that mean you accept my presence here, even though you're my PSD?"

Her blinding smile went straight to his heart, accepting him fully and arousing a fierce yearning to make her his, to please her in every way possible both in his bed and out.

"Yes…yes, I like seeing how you're really feeling, Nolan. Don't ever apologize for being who you really are around me. I love it…"

CHAPTER 8

THE ODOR OF raw sewage stung Enver Uzan's nostrils as he walked near the White Nile riverbank. His eyes watered and he wiped them, muffling a curse. Khartoum's slums were endless. It was a city of six million and probably half of it was comprised of starving Sudanese from the south, who had come here hoping to find help, jobs, and food for their families. But no such luck would be with them. The refugees set up their sagging canvas tents for miles on yellow dirt on this side of the slow-moving Blue and White Nile Rivers, which both flowed through the city southward.

Although the river water was filled with sewage, the wives took their five-gallon plastic jugs daily to the riverbank and filled them up. They would boil the water to use for cooking, drinking, and bathing.

Uzan loathed the smell of sweat combined with dirt on the tent-lined avenue, and he turned away from the thin, dirty children, their bodies shrunken so that their heads appeared twice their normal size. They stared up at him with glazed eyes as he passed. And why would they pay attention to this man who wasn't wearing new clothing that would've instantly flagged the attention of one of the city's roving gangs? They would want to kill him and tear the clothes off his body for starters, then rob him and slit his throat.

Uzan wiped a hand across his trimmed black beard to dislodge the sweat. He was searching for a particular faded green tent with a gold lion painted on the side of it. He hated Khartoum, preferring to be back in Pakistan, but his lord, Zakir Sharan, had sent him on this sordid mission. Although he would never turn down an assignment, this one made him nauseous. He felt as if he were walking through the bowels of hell. The people were pitiful to look at and the children quickly scurried out of his way like wild animals, sensing he was someone important, perhaps dangerous.

Finally, he stopped and asked a man leading a donkey—which was wobbling along with a heavy load of mud bricks—where he could find the caliph of Aziim Nimir, Great Leopard. The man quickly told him, his eyes hooded with fear as he jerked on the rope, the donkey braying in protest as the man and his beast lumbered off, wanting to get as far away from the stranger as they could.

Uzan made a turn, walking down another long row of faded tan, white, and green tents. And just as the man had directed, there was Bachir's "palace," as he'd grandly referred to it on a satellite phone days earlier. Hell, decided Uzan, it looked like all the other ragged, thin, torn tents, with one exception: there were two *haflas* with food supplies piled high on the truck beds, zealously guarded by a motley crew of aggressive youths high on drugs. They strutted around the perimeter of the trucks like young lions, carrying AK-47s, looking fierce and threatening. The crowd surrounding them was hungry and saw there were sacks of sorghum, wheat, and rice on those beds. While they desperately wanted to get to them, the warning glares of the soldiers with their AKs stopped them. The crowd knew that if anyone tried to grab a sack, he would be shot.

Making sure he kept his Glock 18 well hidden among the folds of the robe he wore, Uzan aimed for a young man with a missing eye standing at the half-open tent entrance. He, too, was armed and probably no more than eighteen. The boy glared at him and Uzan knew he was dangerous. Starvation could make a man crazy.

These men were not like his al-Qaeda brethren, who came from villages in Pakistan and Afghanistan. They were well enough fed, their brains worked adequately, and they weren't on drugs like this sorry excuse for an army.

This was the first time he had visited Sudan, and he wasn't at all impressed with the quality of the soldiers here. They all had shrunken stomachs and huge, protruding eyes. He estimated these men hadn't eaten in days, but as he neared the tent, he smelled roasting goat meat being cooked inside, among other pleasant food odors.

"I'm Uzan," he told the boy. "Caliph Bachir is expecting me."

Instantly the boy's eyes widened, and he looked the visitor up and down. Uzan was five feet eight and nearly twice the weight of this pathetic soldier.

"Enver Uzan?"

Surprised, Enver nodded. The boy had a memory, at least. "Yes." He pulled a scroll from within the folds of his robe and handed it to the young soldier. "Give this to your caliph. It's from Lord Sharan."

The young man disappeared, gripping the scroll. Uzan was uncomfortable here in this deadly slum, feeling out of his element. He knew how to operate in Afghanistan and Pakistan, but not this sordid African country. Lord Sharan's passion for destroying Delos Charities was uppermost in his mind. Uzan was one of twenty top officers who served his master, and they had all received orders and were being sent out to places around the world. Each had, as his priority, a specific Delos charity.

Uzan had taken part in the planning of this imminent massive global attack. Because the Culver family—who owned the far-flung charities—had killed Sharan's only two sons in Afghanistan, his lord was seeking an eye for an eye—nothing would stop him.

Uzan considered himself fortunate not to have been sent to the hot, moist jungles of southern Africa or South America, as others had been. At least he was in a dry, hot climate—he'd been born in Pakistan and was used to it.

The soldier reappeared. "Come," he ordered in Arabic.

Uzan slipped through the folds, suddenly surrounded by the pleasant, spicy odors of food being served. His stomach betrayed him by rumbling and he realized he was very hungry.

He saw a man on a wooden throne, dressed in a white *jalabiya*, a white cap on his short black hair. This had to be Caliph Bachir, a murderer, a sociopath, and the leader of Aziim Namir, which had a fragile alliance with an al-Qaeda affiliate in Pakistan. Well, he'd find out shortly if he could work with the crazy Sudanese warlord.

The Delos Safe House Foundation in Kitra was his target. Would this madman help him or not? Uzan carried enough Sudanese pounds in a heavy knapsack on his back to gather a mercenary army. But looking at these starved soldiers, he now wished fervently for a good group of Taliban or al-Qaeda–trained operators instead.

Unfortunately, his orders were to work with Caliph Bachir. He was cursed.

NOLAN WAS TRYING to quell his need to see Teren. He'd just left Ayman's busy security office and was heading toward her office in another part of the administrative complex. Inside his black calfskin briefcase were documents for Teren. The other papers he was carrying had been given to Ayman.

As he moved down the sparkling white tile halls, he met women of all ages, some in colorful Sudanese *tobs*, others in more contemporary clothing, moving between offices. There was a quiet sense of urgency coupled with compassion among the employees of this charity.

Smiles were frequent, kindness everywhere. Was he lost? Did he need help finding Teren's office?

The windows were plentiful in each office, allowing lots of light into each massive room. He spotted Teren's name in Arabic beside her open door. Nolan had not seen her since early this morning—funny, he thought, how she'd taken up residence within his heart.

He quietly stepped into the outer room. Beyond it was another open door, and he was sure that was Teren's busy office.

"May I help you?" a young woman asked from behind the desk.

"Yes. I'm here to see Ms. Lambert. Will you tell her that Nolan Steele is here?" He looked at his watch. It was nearly two p.m.

"Of course, sir," she said quietly, pressing a button on her speaker box. She spoke in Sudanese, but Nolan followed the short conversation. Teren's soft Southern drawl came over the speaker.

"Tell him to come on in. Thank you."

"Please, go in, sir," the woman said, smiling. She stood, gesturing gracefully toward the door.

Nodding, he thanked her in Arabic. Her brown eyes widened and she smiled broadly because he knew her country's language. Nolan was sure that she hadn't expected a white man to know her language at all.

Sauntering in, he saw Teren, with three large screens sitting on her massive wooden desk. She had three keyboards as well. On one corner of the desk was a pile of files. On another corner was a half-empty glass of pink hibiscus tea. She was wearing a bright orange cap-sleeved tee, jeans, and sandals, the same outfit he had seen her leave her apartment in after a shower and breakfast.

There was something touching about her sable hair, now twisted upward and tamed into the barest semblance of order with a tortoiseshell comb. Teren looked up, beaming at him.

"Hey, come in and make yourself at home. I'll be with you in just a minute," she said, and turned in her chair, her full focus on one of the computer screens.

Nolan brought over a four-legged stool and set it down near her desk, between the stacks of files. He watched her long fingers fly across that keyboard. She had amazing speed. Looking up, he realized that she was writing code for a piece of software.

He could hear phones ringing up and down the hall. There was a red landline phone sitting on Teren's desk, and Nolan idly thought that Teren was probably the go-to person for any and all emergencies that occurred around here of a computer or server nature.

"There," she finally murmured in a pleased drawl. "All done for now." She turned in her black leather chair. "Are you thirsty? Would you like some chilled hibiscus tea?"

"No thanks, but a bottle of water sounds good, if you can lay your hands on one."

She nodded, getting up and rubbing her hands together. "That's an easy fix." Walking around her desk, she went to one corner, where she had a small refrigerator. "You're living large, Steele," she teased, taking out a bottle and closing the fridge. Handing him the chilled bottle, she added with a slight grin, "Cold water here in Sudan. Now, that's a real luxury."

He twisted off the cap. All bottled water in any African country was "gassy," or carbonated. Still water was likely to have been taken out of a bad well—or worse, the dirty Nile—and sold as clean, safe drinking water. "Thanks, and you're right, it's a rare luxury." He followed her movements with his gaze while chugging down half the contents. Few Sudanese had a fridge or the electricity to run it, and even if both were available, most of Sudan couldn't afford either one. Even fewer had good drinking water. Nolan knew how fortunate he really was.

"The fridge your idea?" he asked, capping the bottle and setting it on the edge of her desk.

Teren shut the door to her office and turned around. "No, actually. Nafeesa, our chef, found an Alibaba website deal online about two years ago. If we bought ten small fridges, we'd get them for a steal. So, Farida looked at our budget's bottom line and declared it done. Before that, we were all spending a lot of time walking to and from the dining room way on the other side of the building to get a drink of water and ice cubes. Buying the fridges was cheaper than redoing the piping to put in water dispensers all around this old building."

"You make do with what you have," Nolan agreed, watching the gentle sway of her hips. Watching Teren was like watching a ballerina. She was nothing but grace. She sat down, sipping her hibiscus tea.

"Okay, so you're going to teach me more about being a PSD, right?"

"Yes." Her eyes were alight and he could feel the happiness around her. Teren's morning must have gone well for her, and he was glad. "Do you want notepaper and a pen?"

"No, if I need anything, I'll just type it in on this screen," she said, gesturing to the black keyboard in front of her. "And don't worry. Everything we deal with here is encrypted. Part of Artemis's new orders was encryption of all documents and emails, so the charities could talk with the security firm without worry of being hacked."

"Yeah, sadly, the world has come to that." Nolan opened his briefcase, setting several files on the desk in front of him. "I'm going to lead you through a lot of intel, Teren. If at any point you want further explanation, just shoot."

"Okay," she sighed, sitting back in her chair, rocking it slowly back and forth, frowning. "I wish things hadn't escalated to the point where we have to do this, Nolan."

"Me too," he admitted, sympathy in his low voice. Nolan was even more protective of Teren now that he had feelings for her. It was clear to him that something good, possibly even beautiful, had taken root between them. Putting those thoughts away for now, he opened the first file, turning it around and pushing it in her direction.

"The story behind the story," he told her. Nolan told her how two of the

Culver children, Tal and Matt, had killed Zakir Sharan's only two sons in Afghanistan. And Agnon Rasari, son to Valdrin Rasari, a Malgarian billionaire who was one of the world's biggest sex traffickers, died with Raastagar. Zakir Sharan and Valdrin Rasari joined forces because their sons were murdered by the Culvers. Before that, Sharan had a huge sex-trafficking trade in children stolen from Afghanistan and Pakistan. He linked up with Rasari, who was the kingpin of the global trade. The fact that their two sons were murdered together made them bond on another, more lethal level and vow to destroy Delos wherever and whenever they could.

Nolan showed her a picture of the Pakistani and Malgarian billionaires. She picked them up, studying them, frowning more.

"Could the killings have been prevented?" Teren asked, looking over at him. "I mean, the murder of these three sons?"

With a shake of his head, Nolan said, "Sidiq and Raastagar Sharan were in Afghanistan to increase the opium trade to sell around the world. And they also kidnapped young girls and boys, hauling them across the border into Pakistan to be sold as sex slaves in a global marketplace that operates out of that country. Sharan makes money in various ways, legal and illegal. Both his sons were in illegal trade. They were affiliated with al-Qaeda. In fact, Sharan is one of the major backers of that organization, pouring millions into it every year."

"That's horrible," she said. As if the photo were germ-ridden, she dropped it on her desk and pushed her fingers against her jeans, wiping them off.

"Valdrin Rasari is even worse. He's one of the biggest sex traffickers in the world. His son, Agnon, was learning the trade from Sidiq and Raastagar when they got tagged. That's three vermin that will no longer infect our planet," Nolan muttered. "Don't feel sorry for any of them, Teren. They take part in creating the suffering that's going on around the world."

He pushed another photo to her.

"This photo is one you want to memorize and know like the back of your hand. This is Enver Uzan, thirty years old, a captain with al-Qaeda, and one of Sharan's top men, who carries out his orders, whatever they may be. The CIA picked up cell phone traffic from Sharan's office. They only have pieces of the intel, but Kitra was mentioned as an attack site and as one of the jewels in the crown of Delos. So it's a worthwhile target to hit."

A cold chill ran down Teren's spine as she stared at the dark-eyed, black-bearded man named Uzan. He wore a brown Afghan rolled cap and a black vest over a white long-sleeved cotton shirt. And across his chest were bandoliers of bullets. His mouth was thin, like his face, his eyes cold and lifeless. Automatically, she pulled back, releasing the photo as if her fingers had been burned. She could feel the hatred emanating from the man—hatred of everyone who was not like him.

"His eyes are dead," Teren said, her voice cracking. She glanced over at Nolan. "Is he after me? Or does he want to destroy Kitra to make a statement for his boss, Sharan?"

Nolan heard the low quaver in her voice, saw the fear in her eyes as she clung to his gaze. She was a civilian and believed in doing good in the world. Uzan believed in destroying any world that wasn't just like his, and he had no qualms about doing it.

Feeling her shock, her disbelief that she could be a target, he said quietly, "Teren, these people are terrorists. They're fanatics with only one goal, and that's to rid the world of anyone or anything who doesn't believe exactly as they do."

She wrapped her arms around herself, moving her palms slowly up and down her arms, staring at Uzan's piercing eyes in the photo. Biting down on her lower lip, she asked hoarsely, "Do you know? Does Artemis know?"

"Know what?"

"If Uzan and Sharan are going after Kitra? Or after me?"

Straightening, Nolan told her what he knew. "The CIA listeners picked up bits and pieces, Teren. They heard Kitra mentioned. Your name was mentioned."

She frowned. "What does that mean?"

Shrugging, Nolan rasped, "No intel is perfect, Teren. Artemis has some of the most advanced satellite, photographic, and listening equipment in the world. The best security people in the world are working for them. They've got the CIA and NSA tapes from these conversations. Their intel people think that Uzan's plan is twofold. In order to satisfy Sharan, who seems fixated on Kitra as a world model of the Delos organization, he wants to destroy it." Shaking his head, Nolan muttered, "This place is so damned big and sprawling it would take a nuclear bomb to wipe it off the map. That's not going to happen. Sharan, so far, does not have a dirty bomb or any nuclear weapon in his possession. So, to destroy Kitra, he'd have to have a sizable army of men with him. And with the Sudanese Army already trying to eradicate these terrorist groups from their country, Uzan isn't going to be able to mount that kind of overwhelming attack against Kitra."

She moved her finger across the shining reddish wood of her desk. "So? Plan B is what? Kidnap me? Make an example out of me to the Western world? Behead me on a video and put it on the Internet?" Her eyes narrowed and she saw a lot of unspoken emotion in Nolan's eyes. His mouth compressed.

"Artemis is thinking along those lines, yes." He hated saying it but was surprised to see strength and resolve come to her face. Maybe she was a lot stronger emotionally than he'd first thought. Although she wasn't military, she had already realized Sharan's strategy. His respect for her grew even more. This smart, practical woman had swiftly sized up the situation.

"Do you agree with Artemis, Nolan?"

He heard the concern underlying her cool, authoritative tone. He didn't want to nod, but did, looking into her darkening eyes. "I do. You're the route of least resistance that will allow Uzan to partially succeed at this task. It's easier to pick you off, a lone female in this very male-dominated society, than to try to attack and destroy Kitra itself. You are the American face of Kitra. That would be enough to make their point newsworthy, globally."

She wove more patterns with her fingertip onto the top of her polished desk. "This doesn't seem real," she confessed, looking up at him.

"I know. It's not part of your worldview," he said apologetically, seeing her fear mixed with confusion. "You're an innocent in all of this, Teren. You've done nothing wrong. You live in your heart; you live your passion to support others who struggle and need help. You're a saint in comparison to these sick bastards who are plotting against you."

Hearing the deep anger in his low voice, she closed her eyes, trying to think, to put this all into perspective. Opening her eyes, she asked, "If I leave Kitra, will the attack stop?"

Snorting, Nolan said, "I don't know, Teren. No one knows. Artemis intel has played out all possible scenarios. Wyatt has looked at it every which way. He feels, ultimately, that wherever you are, you will be the easiest target of opportunity." And then his voice faltered. "I'm sorry…" He stared at her, seeing real fear in her eyes for the first time as this new reality started to sink in.

Teren sat up, rubbing her damp palms against her jeans. "If I left, would Uzan follow me? Could we lure him into a trap, Nolan? I'm not taking this sitting down. I'll be damned if I'll be a sacrificial lamb for this bastard!"

She suddenly stood up, needing to move, to run, but there was nowhere to run. She wouldn't leave Kitra, and all her friends, open to an attack from this insane terrorist. Pushing her fingers through the loose strands near her temple, she paced the length of her office, scowling.

"I don't know," he said, straightening, watching her pace like a caged cheetah.

"Then why don't you call Wyatt and ask? What if we could turn the tables on him, Nolan? What if we could trap Uzan instead?"

"We discussed that possibility during the mission briefing," he told her gently. "They left it up to me to determine, based upon ground conditions at the time."

"If I could lead Uzan away from Kitra, it would keep this place safe. That's all I really care about, Nolan."

He stood and stepped across the office, gripping her shoulders, bringing her to a halt. "We're not there yet." He kept his fingers still on her shoulders, wanting to shelter her, because he heard the terror banked in her husky voice. She was more concerned for the people of Kitra than herself. "Take a deep breath, okay? There is no overt threat that has arisen yet."

"But," she whispered, anguish in her tone, "I worry for the people here. I don't worry about myself. I'm a survivor, Nolan. They shouldn't become targets…and I care so deeply for all of them." She choked, giving him a pleading look.

"I care about your life too, Teren," he said, locking on to her startled gaze. Her flesh was so firm and strong beneath her tee that Nolan could feel the heat of her skin. He wanted desperately to protect this brave woman, who had no idea what she was suggesting.

"Look," he rasped, his fingers holding her upper arm gently. "I know we haven't had time to talk much personally, but I'm too damn familiar with the slums of Khartoum. I was undercover in that hellhole for a year. Those who live in those deplorable, ungodly conditions are slowly starving to death. They're turned into mindless soldiers, addicted to drugs, and they worship their local warlord. And they'll do anything he orders without giving it a second thought. Ayman has already sent three of his best men undercover to seek out Uzan. It's dangerous to all of them, with no guarantee of success."

Teren relaxed beneath his large hands, heard the emotion vibrating in his voice, saw the concern in his eyes for her. "I don't want to put anyone at risk. I don't." Hot tears gathered in her eyes. "You know how much I love these people, and they love me."

"I know that," he said, seeing her eyes glisten with tears. Nolan could handle anything but a woman's tears. It just tore him apart, and he had no way to fix it or them. The helplessness tunneled through him as he saw Teren fighting to stop from crying. He could feel her terror—she was trapped. And to her credit, she was trying to figure a way out of this, so she could protect Kitra and those she loved. Nolan ached for her. Damn, she was brave—and selfless.

Teren wasn't military trained, but she had the heart of a soldier, the heart of a Delta Force operator. She was willing to sacrifice herself to save others, and that was a part of their creed. Nolan didn't want to lose this woman. She stood there before him, warm and alive, and he inhaled her spicy scent as he gazed into her wide, searching eyes.

"I'll talk to Wyatt further about this. I'll let him know what you'd like to do, but there's no way to know what his decision will be, Teren," he told her heavily, forcing himself to release her. For a moment, she swayed toward him and then caught herself once more. Nolan wished Teren would allow herself to fall into his arms so he could hold her and give her a sense of safety. She now fully recognized that she was a target and he imagined she felt like the defenseless rabbit he'd seen out on the grasslands this morning. She was now facing down a hyena called Uzan, who had every intention of tearing her apart, one limb at a time. And all he could do was stand there and watch as the terrifying reality finally sank in.

CHAPTER 9

TEREN STOOD BEFORE Nolan, feeling real fear digging into her soul. She wished he still had his steadying, firm hand on her. Wrapping her arms around herself, she whispered, "This is a nightmare. Never in my wildest imagination did I think something like this could happen."

Nolan felt like hell, because he had been the bearer of the worst news possible—news that had just shattered her reality and changed the course of her life. "I'm sorry, Teren. I really am." Dragging in a deep breath, he took her elbow, gently nudging her toward her desk. "Come on. There's more that you need to know."

"I'm not sure I want to hear any more," she replied heavily, though the feeling of his palm beneath her elbow gave her a sense of protection—at least, for now.

"Forewarned is forearmed," he assured her. He saw how her shoulders sagged, heard the shock in her voice. Not many people were told, "Hey, you're the target of a terrorist." And it wasn't just any terrorist. Sharan was one of the biggest supporters of al-Qaeda.

Teren sat down and leaned back, arms folded against her chest, staring at Nolan as he pushed another paper across the desk in her direction. She stared down at it, not wanting to touch it, as if she would be further contaminated by what was happening around her. "What's this?"

"It's military-grade information," Nolan said. "I've spent all morning in Ayman's office, going over the more tactical part of the intel with him."

"What does he think about this?" This had to upset him as well, because he took great pride in keeping Kitra and all its inhabitants secure and safe.

Nolan snorted. "He doesn't like it. No one does. Tomorrow morning all the heads of the departments here at Kitra are going to be asked to gather in Farida's briefing room at nine a.m. Ayman and I will give all of you the briefing. I'm giving it to you today, ahead of time, because I don't want you caught off guard with others around to see your reactions. This is personal, between you and me."

"Thank you," Teren whispered, feeling a headache coming on.

"I'll keep you out of the line of fire as much as I can," he told her quietly as she struggled not to cry. If only he could gather Teren into his arms, hold her, give her a sense of safety—but he couldn't.

"I know you will."

He nodded, not feeling any better. "Knowledge is power in our world, Teren. That document before you outlines the mission objectives of Sharan's organization as far as we know at this time. Based on cell phone chatter, we know he's going to hit other Delos charities too, but we don't know which ones. The CIA continues to monitor all his conversations. What we know right now is that Kitra was mentioned and your name was brought up."

"How on earth did they get my name, Nolan? I rarely work outside of Kitra. I'm rarely in Khartoum. My life is here," she said, and jabbed her index finger down at her desk.

"Well, that's part of the puzzle," he admitted. "We honestly don't know. Ayman thinks that someone who worked here but who has left Kitra might have given up your name to someone in the al-Qaeda organization." He shrugged. "Ayman is asking Farida's office for a list of employees who left Kitra in the last seven years. He'll have it shortly, and we'll all go over it together."

Her mouth turned down and she muttered a curse. "Don't bother. I know who it was."

Cocking his head, he said, "You do?"

"God, this is a mess," Teren whispered, shaking her head.

"Tell me."

"Two years ago, there was a young man who applied to Kitra to be a janitor. Ayman did a background check on him, and he came back clean. His name was Nazir. He came out of the slums of Khartoum. He was a hard worker, earnest, responsible, and promised to do a good job at Kitra. Our head janitor, Abit, needed help, so Nazir was hired."

Nolan wrote down his name. "What happened, then?"

Grimacing, Teren whispered, "Nazir was always drawn to me. You know how friendly we are here, Nolan. I guess he took my friendliness for something more than it really was. He tried to come into my duplex one night." She saw Nolan's eyes narrow instantly as his sense of protectiveness wrapped around her. "He thought I liked him well enough to go to bed with him. Luckily, Ayman was walking nearby at the time. Nazir knocked, I looked through the peephole and saw him. I opened my door to see what he wanted. I knew who he was and I thought nothing of it. He said I was his woman and he was going to bed me. I panicked and I tried to shut the door and keep him out. Ayman was there in a flash, grabbing Nazir, and throwing him down on the porch. I was so scared. I-it brought back a lot of bad memories for me..."

He heard the suppressed anguish in her voice. Nolan wasn't going to remind her that keeping her door locked was a good idea, because in this case, Nazir had knocked and she'd opened it, thinking nothing of it because he was someone she knew. What Teren didn't know was the man's true intentions. He was a hyena in disguise. "That had to rattle you."

"Oh," she said, her voice choked. "More than you could ever know."

"Nazir was fired?"

"Ayman hauled him out of my doorway that was half closed, by the collar, with two of his soldiers assisting, and took him to a *hafla*. One of his men drove Nazir into Khartoum and dropped him off in the slums. He was fired on the spot." She gave a shrug. "We never saw him again."

"He sounds like the right person to investigate," Nolan agreed, seeing the pain in her eyes.

"He could have given someone in the slums the info to get even at me for rejecting him."

"Entirely possible. The slums of Khartoum are nothing but gangs of men. They might own a half an acre of that sorry place, but it's theirs, and they fight to maintain or expand it. Ayman is going to have to pull Nazir's employment records. We might get a lead from that."

"But Ayman has strong ties within the Sudanese Army, right up to the top generals who run it today," Teren said.

"I'm sure he'll do everything in his power to uncover more about Nazir as a person of interest. Until he does, we have to wait for intel."

Mouth tightening, Teren said, "Nazir could have spilled my name or worse, sold it to one of those gangs for money."

"Yeah. Bad news travels fast in the slums," Nolan glumly agreed. "At least it's a strong lead, Teren. If we can pin Nazir down, find out if he joined a gang and if that gang has an al-Qaeda affiliation, that intel can help us a lot. It will allow us to understand who and what we're up against."

Her headache continued to mount. She rubbed her temple. "What do I do then while we wait?"

"Stay within Kitra's walls. Don't leave them without me at your side. Or, if you have to go somewhere by vehicle and I'm not around for whatever reason, have one of Ayman's soldiers go with you. At no time are you to be left alone, Teren. Not until we can get this fixed."

"Is it fixable, Nolan? Really?"

He heard the derision in her voice and understood her sense of helplessness. "Ayman is on this. He's already got three of his best men undercover in the slums, searching for Uzan."

"When did he send them in?" Teren sat up, hands resting on her thighs, digging into Nolan's darkened gaze.

"Wyatt called Ayman three weeks ago after Artemis figured out what possible strategies Sharan might employ against Kitra. They talked by satellite phone and it was encrypted, so no one could break in and listen to what they were talking about, Teren. Ayman had three of his soldiers volunteer for the mission to find Uzan, and right now, they're actively hunting for him. They're searching a huge area along the banks of the White Nile, looking for a needle in a haystack. They've got his face memorized from a photo Ayman had. They're posing as Sudanese looking for work, moving among the gangs, trying to locate him."

"That's so dangerous."

He held up his hand, hearing the anxiety in her tone. "They're soldiers, Teren. Ayman trained them. They're loyal to him, to you, and to Kitra. They want Uzan as bad as we do, believe me. They are outraged that anyone would try to destroy Kitra or harm you."

"Oh, no…" she whispered, pressing her hands to her eyes. "I saw them leave Kitra that morning in a truck. I didn't realize what they were doing. I just thought…" She allowed her hands to fall to her lap, staring at Nolan. "I thought they were leaving on some special assignment that Ayman had given them."

"Well, you were right, Teren. You just didn't know what it involved." Nolan stood up and halted in front of her chair. "Look, these are good men. They were born in Khartoum, they know the lay of the land, and they were undercover operators working for the government for at least ten years before they came to work here at Kitra. They've been in those slums before, and they know what they're doing. Don't worry so much about them, okay?" He put his hand on her slumped shoulder, seeing the suffering mount in her eyes. This was Teren's family, and it was devastating to her. His fingers moved gently across her shoulder, and he felt the warmth of her flesh beneath the thin tee she wore.

"Now that you've pinpointed Nazir," he said, crouching down in front of her, his hands on the arms of her chair, holding her shaken gaze, "Ayman's going to be able to get ahold of his soldiers and redirect their efforts in the slum. I need to go back to his office and give him this intel, Teren. Will you be all right here?"

She felt a rolling quiver go through her gut. Whenever she got severely upset, she would throw up. And she felt close to that right now. "I'll be okay," she lied. "I need to go to the restroom."

Nolan nodded and stood. "As soon as I get done speaking with Ayman, I'll come back here and let you know what he found out, okay?" He saw how pale she'd become. He curved his fingers around her lower arm and squeezed her reassuringly, then released her. She hurried out of the office ahead of him and disappeared down another hall where the women's restroom was located.

Cursing softly, Nolan placed all the information into his calfskin briefcase, snapping it shut. It was time to see Ayman.

MISERABLY, TEREN WIPED her mouth with a paper towel as she hunkered over the toilet bowl. She slugged a mouthful of water and then spat it out into the toilet. Then she heaved again and again until her stomach ached. She wished she weren't so affected by shock. Her mother had been very disapproving of her "sensitive" stomach. Even as a child on the farm, when she'd see her father chop off the head of a chicken, she'd throw up on the spot, horrified by the blood and the sight of the headless chicken as it raced in circles around his feet. She'd heaved three times that day, and her mother shamed her, and her brothers taunted her for being a sissy.

Teren washed her mouth out again, pushing herself off her shaky knees and slowly emerging from the stall. Luckily, no one else was in the restroom, and for that, Teren was grateful. She didn't want to look at herself in the mirror as she cupped water from the faucet, rinsing out her mouth one more time. Her flesh was pale and damp, her eyes like wounded holes staring back at her. Grimacing, she avoided looking at herself again and wiped her mouth dry with another paper towel. There was work to do. Things couldn't wait on her just because she was upset.

She longed for Nolan's nearness, but she realized he had a job to do. She had no business asking any more of him, because she saw that he wanted to shield her as much as he could. But when he'd wrapped his hand around her lower arm, squeezing it gently, she could feel him feeding her something special, something so necessary to her heart and soul that she welcomed this kind, unexpected gesture. How badly she wanted to crawl into Nolan's arms and be held.

Right now, she felt like she had when she was eighteen, when Tony had stalked her, and he was much stronger than she would ever be. When Nazir had come knocking at her door that night, she'd opened it, thinking he needed help with something. Never could she have imagined that he would come to have sex with her, which was what he told her he wanted.

She'd been drugged and raped once, and the shock of Nazir's blunt request to her, his foot wedged inside the door so she couldn't shut him out, had brought back all those sordid memories, the pain, her injuries, the loss—

Teren made a rough sound, turning away from the sink, her hands in fists, eyes tightly shut. She would not go there! She just couldn't! Tears ran down her cheeks, running off her chin. Angrily, she swiped at them, fighting them back, swallowing hard.

She stood staring numbly at the pale green wall in front of her, wondering what the hell kind of bad karma seemed to be following her around. First Tony. Then Nazir. And now? A rich billionaire in Pakistan wanted her dead. He wanted to make a statement to Delos, and he was going to use her to try and do it.

Rage mingled with her fear, driving away her numbness. Now anger trumped everything as it tunneled through her. Teren would be damned if she was going to be a "soft target," as Nolan had referred to her during the briefing in her office. She would not go down without a fight. But she also worried that Kitra might be attacked if she remained there.

Torn, she knew Ayman would do everything in his considerable military power to keep Kitra safe. She was relieved the man was here among them and that he loved Kitra like all of them did.

Her headache was subsiding now, and Teren figured it was from all the vomiting, which had relieved the pressure in her head. Next time, she decided, aspirin would be a better way to relieve her headache.

Pushing away from the white porcelain sink, she forced herself to go back to work. Maybe Ayman and Nolan could find out more about Nazir. She became focused on the new software she was writing for the online store. She wanted to get lost in it, because she didn't want to think about the threat swirling around her. An hour later, her phone rang. Picking it up, she heard Ayman at the other end.

"Teren, dear, could you come to my office now?"

Her stomach clenched. "Sure, I'll be right there, Uncle."

What now? Teren didn't have a good feeling about this, hurrying down the long hall toward Ayman's office. This wasn't going to be good news and she knew it. Lifting her hand to his assistant, she opened the inner door. Nolan was sitting in front of the large desk. Ayman looked stern, and when he put on that kind of mask, Teren knew he was hiding his emotions. Nolan was wearing his unreadable game face, and the iciness of the atmosphere made her skin crawl.

"Have a seat, my child," Ayman urged, gesturing to the second chair in front of his desk, next to where Nolan sat.

"Thank you, Uncle." She sat down, closing her cold, clammy hands in her lap.

"I wish we had better news," Ayman began heavily, giving her a concerned look. "Nazir came from the slums of Khartoum. On his application form"—Ayman slid it in her direction—"he says he is originally from western Sudan, the Darfur region."

Teren picked up the paper. Nazir barely knew how to write, the inky letters wobbly and nearly unreadable. Luckily for her, she read Arabic. Scanning it, she said, "He's put down a man named Bachir as a reference."

"Yes," Ayman said. "When I originally had my men do a background check on Nazir, they noted the name. Two years ago, we could not find such a man in Darfur because of the civil war. I think Nazir put the name down because he knew the man when he lived in Darfur. And in my notes about him, that's what I wrote down. With Darfur and western Sudan in continued crisis, there was no way we could track this Bachir down any further than we did."

"At that time," Teren said, feeling hollow inside. She cut a glance toward Nolan, who was watching her, his eyes alive with concern for her. It helped steady her. He wasn't touching her, but she could feel the warm blanket of his caring wrap around her.

"Yes," Ayman muttered. "I just got off the phone with a military contact high up in our government. Bachir is a known entity now." His mouth puckered and he added, "This is a man who ran a rebel gang in Darfur known as Aziim Nimir."

Instantly, Teren's brows raised. She read the Khartoum newspaper daily. It was all in Arabic and it helped her learn the language. There was always a lot about Darfur and the ongoing atrocities and murders there. "I've heard that name," she said.

"Yes, unfortunately," Ayman agreed, shaking his head. "Bachir was a murdering thug in Darfur. He had a hundred-man gang of child soldiers who learned the art of killing from him. Bachir moved up to Khartoum about a month after I'd tried to track him down as one of Nazir's referrals. He's carved out a chunk of real estate in the slums and now calls himself 'the caliph of Aziim Nimir.' Today, he's like a king who owns a tiny patch of the White Nile riverbank."

Nolan reached over and touched her arm in a calming motion. "Bachir is now a loose al-Qaeda affiliate operating in this country, Teren. We figure that's how Sharan got a hold of your name. We both think Nazir is one of Bachir's soldiers."

"And he may well have been a child soldier before he left the gang in western Sudan to come here," Ayman said thickly. "I think he left the gang, came east, and wanted a clean start to his life. He had some education and he was intelligent. So he came here to Kitra to apply for a job as a janitor."

Nolan's hand grew more firm around her arm. Teren felt as if her stomach had dropped out of her body. She stared numbly at Ayman, at a loss for words. Only Nolan's hand on her arm kept her in that chair. Right now, she wanted to run—though she didn't know to where—just as she had so long ago, after she'd graduated from college. The people in her life at the time were suffocating her, judging her, making her feel as if life was trickling out of her.

So she had run to Delos. There, the Culvers had breathed new, purposeful life into her. They'd taken her in with open arms, never judging her, only supporting her so she could become healthy.

She was pulled back to the present by Nolan's low voice. "Ayman has been in touch with his men on the ground in the slum," he said quietly. "They're going in to locate the area where Bachir is operating. Chances are they'll find Nazir there too. If they do, that explains how Sharan got hold of your name."

"I-I see," she choked out.

"It's very possible that Uzan or his employer, Sharan, found out you were the only white American woman here at Kitra," Ayman said gently to her. "And because Sharan wants to strike out at Delos, and it's an American-, Turkish-, and Greek-owned charity, he would be looking to hit American employees at Kitra. Men like Sharan hate Americans more than any other people. Turkey is a Muslim country, so I don't believe they will attack that part of the Delos family. Perhaps they will hit the Greek part of the family, but Americans top their list. You're the only American here," he said. "The rest are Sudanese."

"We are his enemy," Teren muttered, shaking her head, stunned by the revelations.

Nolan moved a little closer, placing his hand over her cold, damp fingers. "You got very lucky when Nazir pushed your door open to get to you, Teren. If Ayman hadn't been passing by…"

Swallowing convulsively, the specter of her life at eighteen rose before her eyes. "No…I get it. Those gangs in Darfur routinely rape women and children. He would have raped me…" The word came out huskily, laden with emotion. Teren had never told anyone here at Kitra what had happened to her. And it could have happened again.

Nazir was a strong young man, and he could have easily overpowered her. He could have raped and killed her. She gripped Nolan's hand, needing his physical support right now. His fingers tightened a little more around hers, as if sensing the depth of her terror. How close she'd come to being a rape victim once again. And Nazir was also a murderer. She remembered reading about that gang. They used machetes to cut off the arms and legs of their enemies, watching them bleed out and die. A chill coursed through her.

"So," she said, her voice cracking. "This is the gang that's after me? They work with Sharan and Uzan?"

"We think so," Ayman said. "But it's too early to say for sure. My men are closing in on Aziim Nimir in the slums right now. We've sent photos of Bachir and Nazir to their cell phones so they know who to look for."

"What happens then?" Teren asked, her voice sounding a million miles away from her. She kept her focus on Nolan's hand, which had swallowed her own. It was the only warm place on her whole body right now, and her insides felt like quivering Jell-O.

"If my men verify one or both of them," Ayman said briskly, "then I alert our government. As you know, there is a strong effort to keep any kind of terrorists out of Sudan. Bachir is a known affiliate of al-Qaeda. If they verify his presence, the Army will send in a big enough contingent to find and capture him. They will destroy his entire operation and round up his soldiers."

"That could become a bloodbath," Teren whispered. "He wouldn't go down without a fight and you know that."

"It's out of our hands," Ayman said philosophically, shrugging.

"If they do capture or kill him, what does that mean about the hit Sharan has taken out on me and on Kitra?"

"My men are looking for Uzan as well. He's a well-respected captain within the ranks of that terrorist organization. He would know if there were any al-Qaeda ties to any gang in those slums. And I'm sure he's either made contact with Bachir or will shortly."

"Teren, Ayman's men are going to play it low-key. They want to try to find all three players. Mostly, they want to net Uzan, if they can," Nolan added.

She looked into his hooded eyes, needing him desperately. "What do you mean 'low-key,' Nolan?"

"They will scout the perimeter of Aziim Nimir's territory once they locate it. They'll blend in, try to find some of Bachir's soldiers, buddy up to them, try to get intel out of them. They're good at what they do, Teren. They work in the shadows and aren't about to tip their hand."

"This may take weeks or longer," Ayman warned her. "No one goes into Sudan like John Wayne, with guns blazing."

"Oh, that fantasy," Teren growled. "He made war look romantic. And it's just the opposite."

"You won't get any argument out of us," Nolan assured her, giving her a slight smile.

His half smile chased away some of her dread. "What do I do in the meantime?"

"Just do what you always do," Ayman urged. "But under no circumstance do you go anywhere near Khartoum. Here at Kitra, you are the safest. Plus, you have this man protecting you." Ayman gestured toward Nolan.

"But there's a medical group coming from Belgium in two weeks to go to a village twenty-five miles south of us. I was to be a part of it as their interpreter, not to mention I must coordinate it too."

"We'll see as that time grows closer," Ayman counseled, waving his hand in a downward motion.

"But it's safe," Teren argued strongly. "It's out on the grasslands. You can see a person coming for miles. You could send some of your soldiers with me if you are worried, Uncle."

"All of that is possible, dear Teren. I just cannot give you any firm answer right now. This is a dangerous game we are playing with Bachir. We have to be careful. I don't want to lose you or any of our men to that hyena."

"No, I don't want you to, either," Teren said solemnly. "But this medical group has been in the mix for nine months. I was to lead the convoy to that village. I know the elders there well, and I'm a known entity to them. I'll be doing the translation—"

"Please," Ayman said gently. "I will look at this trip closer to the date, Teren. I will not risk your life. You must understand that."

Deflated, she nodded and collapsed against the chair, feeling suddenly drained. "Yes…okay…you're right, Uncle. I'm just…shaken, is all…"

"And you have every right to be," he murmured sympathetically. "Why don't you take the rest of the day off?"

"No, I can't. I don't want to. Working stabilizes me. I won't think about this if I'm focused on writing code. I'll leave at five p.m. like I always do." She stood up, releasing Nolan's hand, giving him a look of thanks. Her knees felt mushy. Straightening her spine, she tried to look stronger than she felt.

"I'll walk you back to your office," Nolan offered.

"Yes, I'd like that."

Ayman stood, his thick black brows scrunched. "Teren, dearest, you must allow Nolan to remain close to you at all times. He becomes your shadow until we can understand the strategy that Uzan and Sharan have created."

"Yes," she promised with a weak smile, "I'm more than happy to have Nolan with me now, after hearing all of this." And she was.

As she walked slowly down the hall, Nolan at her shoulder, she said in a low tone, "I'm reeling, Nolan."

He reached out, cupping her elbow. "I know you are. It's a helluva lot to absorb. Your life just got turned inside out, Teren. I'm sorry." He gave her a caring look and squeezed her elbow. "And I'm here for you. Just let me know how I can help, okay?"

Nolan knew that some people, when cornered like this, wanted to be left alone. They crawled into an inner hole within themselves to hide, wanting no one around, wanting as little contact as possible. It was their way of coping, and it might be her way, too.

He wasn't about to assume anything with Teren right now. She was pale, her eyes dark, and she seemed to him like an unraveling ball of emotional yarn. What he wanted to do to help Teren was probably not what she wanted or needed.

She sighed and gave him an abject look. "Remember how much fuss I put up about the inner door being locked between our apartments?"

"Yes."

Her lips compressed. "Would you mind if I not only kept it unlocked but opened it up a bit? I'm feeling really scared, Nolan. I just need to know you're nearby. I feel safe with you. I know that sounds crazy under the circumstances, but you give me a sense of protection." She touched her furrowed brow. "And right now, I need that. Really badly." The past was coming back to haunt her. She'd been brutally beaten by a man before and now this time, men wanted to kill her. It was simply too much for her to absorb right now and left her feeling raw and vulnerable.

CHAPTER 10

Nolan met Teren at her office later that afternoon. She looked pale and withdrawn and he sensed how upset she was about the situation. He wandered in, hands in his pockets.

"It's five in the afternoon," he greeted her. "I thought I'd walk you home." She lifted her head and looked up toward him, and he instantly saw relief in her eyes. Teren was the kind of person who couldn't hide her feelings if she wanted to. She was so readable. He took his hands out of his pockets and saw the stack of files had dwindled since the last time he'd been in here.

"Thanks," she murmured. "I'll be ready in just a moment."

She was struggling to act like nothing had happened. Nolan got that. It was a standard defense most people would employ against shocking news. For Teren to look at the true nature of the threat against her would probably be overwhelming.

Nolan would have done the same thing. He compartmentalized himself all the time. But it didn't seem as if Teren was very adroit about it because she was still clearly shaken.

Leaning his hip against her desk, he said, "I took the bull by the horns and tried my hand at making us dinner tonight."

Her heart swelled with so many wonderful feelings as he caught and held her gaze. "That's so sweet." She made a few last keystrokes and the computer powered down. "What are we having?"

"Something light," he murmured, assessing her. "I know most people don't eat much when they're upset." He saw damp spots on her tee. She'd been crying. Probably closed the door and bawled her eyes out. Why was Teren trying to handle something so overwhelming as this by herself? Nolan knew she had friends here at Kitra she could confide in and ask for help and support, so why hadn't she?

"I'm one of those people for sure," she said, rising. "I've been accused of having what is called a 'sensitive stomach.'" Double-checking all the equipment and making sure it was shut down, she picked up her white straw purse, slinging it over her shoulder. "Are you a decent cook, Nolan?"

He felt her trying to shift, to pretend everything was normal. He played along, having no desire to make her suffer any more than she already had. "I went over and saw Nafeesa. I asked her what would be a good meal for you, because you weren't feeling very well. She gave me some things to put together for you tonight."

"That's so sweet of Nafeesa. And you, too. Thank you." She grimaced as she came around the desk. "Now everyone will gossip about me not feeling good. They'll all worry."

He cupped her elbow and liked that she moved into him, their bodies almost touching. "No one can know what's really going on. We'll inform all the department heads tomorrow at nine," he assured her. "Otherwise, it remains top secret for now."

"There's no sense in scaring everyone to death around here, Nolan." Teren turned and shut her door, locking it with a key. "See? I do lock *some* doors." She forced a slight smile. A corner of his mouth lifted, and she melted beneath the caring look he gave her. "I'm trying," she growled defensively.

"You're doing fine, sweetheart."

The endearment nearly brought new tears to her eyes—tears of gratitude and hope. Once again, Nolan had made her feel warm inside, thawing that icy fear that had held her in its grip since her talk with him and Ayman earlier in the day. Now he guided her down the hall toward a door that would take them out into the courtyard. How did he know she loved to walk down that lush green grass beneath the shade of the trees? Sometimes, Teren wondered if the man read her mind. For someone she'd just met, he seemed very attuned to her needs without her saying anything.

Everyone was leaving work, walking back to their duplexes for the evening. The sky was a light, bright blue, the heat of the day, in the high nineties, unbroken. The breeze was hot against Teren's face. She remained close to Nolan because he gave her the care she so desperately sought right now. The gates were closed in the distance and she could see the mirages dancing across the flat grasslands outside of them. Her mind wouldn't remain still, leaping over so many conversations, those photos, and the past coming sharply back in focus, staring at her once more.

"Penny for your thoughts?" Nolan asked, looking down at her set features. He was coming to realize that when Teren was upset, her brow furrowed, and she'd sometimes chew on her lower lip. "Or," he added drily, "maybe a dollar or two?" That brought out a vague half smile from Teren. A hint of pink tinged her cheeks and he realized he'd reached her. It felt good to know he could influence her. A woman didn't blush unless she cared about the man she was with. His fingers lightly caressed her elbow, and he saw her frown begin to soften. She was extraordinarily sensitive; just the brush of his fingers, a light stroking motion reassured her. Knowing this warmed him more than she could have imagined.

"You'll need a thousand-dollar bill," she murmured, lifting her chin, meeting his eyes, and feeling the ice inside her begin to melt. Right now, Nolan didn't have on his game face, nor did he try to hide the pleasure she saw burning in his eyes for her. No question, there was something strong and good between them. Teren hesitated to give any more of herself to Nolan because her choice in men had been so awful. Farida told her not to worry about it, that she had to go through a lot of bad boys to attract a real man to her. A man like her husband, Ameer. In many respects, Teren saw how much the Sudanese man was like Nolan. And vice versa. It was as if they had been cast from the same mold. But maybe the military molded all men that way.

"Okay, I can afford ten dollars," he said, pulling his wallet out of his back pocket. He released her elbow as they wandered slowly down the shady courtyard. Pulling out a ten, he placed it in her hand. "There."

A chuckle escaped her. "No…take it back. I was just kidding, Nolan."

"Keep it. Give it to your favorite child on the playground. He or she will take it home to Mom and she'll think that Allah blessed her. A U.S. ten-dollar bill equates to fifty-five Sudanese pounds. In this country, for someone who's poor, that's half a year's pay."

Teren folded the bill and tucked it into her jeans pocket. "You're right. Thank you." She smiled up at him. And then something unexpected, something wonderful, happened.

"Come here," he rasped against her hair, sliding his arm around her shoulders, drawing her beneath his arm. "You look like you want to be held for a little while. Am I right?"

She slowed, savoring his arm sliding across her shoulders, hand on her upper arm, barely tugging her toward him; he didn't assume she wanted him. Teren realized it was a way of asking if she would accept his embrace or not. She did, and melted against him, their steps and stride the same. "How did you know?" she asked hoarsely, pressing her cheek briefly against his shoulder.

"You'd never make it as an undercover agent, Teren. Your every emotion is written across your face and in your eyes." Meeting her upturned gaze, Nolan was drawn to kiss her, but he didn't. They were out in public and this was enough of a personal gesture on his part toward her. He knew it would be seen by those nearby and he was sure it would fire the gossip at the dinner tables tonight with the staff. They all loved Teren. They wanted only the best for her. And so did Nolan. He was taking one hell of a risk by being this intimate with her so soon.

"I always got accused of being like that at home, too. My family could read me like an open book," she admitted sourly, surrendering to his strong, tall body, absorbing his protection, other feelings awakening in her, chasing away the rest of her shock and fear.

"Don't ever change," he told her, his voice suddenly thick with emotion. "I like you just the way you are, Teren."

"You're the only one, then. I mean"—she opened her hand—"my family thinks that I'm a wimp and weak. I'm the youngest of four kids, with three older brothers."

He snorted. "Well, there you go. You didn't stand a chance."

She grinned a little, the darkness that surrounded her beginning to lift. Nolan led her up to the round concrete fountain that spewed water six feet into the air. He halted in front of it and turned Teren so that she was facing him.

Teren laid her hands on his lower arms, studying Nolan's serious face beneath her sable lashes. He was strong where she was presently weak. She'd been stunned by the information he and Ayman had shared with her. Teren could feel him adjusting, shifting to read her, to fulfill her demands right now even though she hadn't asked anything from him. His large hands slid in a caressing gesture across her shoulders, making her skin leap and tingle wildly. That heated sensation raced down through her, and she savored the feelings of being a woman desired by this man. Instinctively, she wondered if Nolan would be a good lover, a man who shared, who didn't just take and then get up and walk away, leaving her aching and wanting. Teren's choices in men had always left her unfulfilled and feeling as if she had missed something in the connection.

"Right now," he told her in a low, gritty tone, "you need a little pampering and care, Teren. I want to be the man who gives it to you, but you need to let me know just how far it goes. Or if you want it at all. Tell me what you need because I don't want to overstep my bounds with you. You've been hit broadside with some serious news. This is not me, the operator, talking to his PSD. It's me, the man, talking to you as a woman I care about."

Nolan knew he was taking a huge risk with Teren. She was already overwhelmed and he was stepping in to push a personal boundary with her. It wasn't fair, but he couldn't read minds, either. And she wasn't one to be forthcoming unless he coaxed her into talking with him.

In many ways, Teren was just like him. Nolan knew why he acted the way he did. As an operator, it was necessary. But Teren wasn't one. So what the hell kind of family made her react this way? Most women opened up without being asked. Women were able to easily speak of what they thought and felt with a man—but not Teren.

Nolan hung on to his patience about Teren's unknown past. He'd gone through her file once again, looking for clues. Frustrated, he'd found nothing that could explain why she was so defensive about sharing herself in ways most women found easy. Searching her stormy eyes, he saw that she felt torn by his request. He'd gone far enough with intimacy with her already and had no desire to crowd her. But damn it, he could feel how much she was hurting, how much Kitra meant to her. This was her world. This was what she loved to do.

And now the life she'd known for years was getting ripped out from beneath her. It was changing by the minute and it wasn't giving Teren a breather to absorb it all. It was a lot for anyone to take in, much less someone as sensitive as she was. She was strong in many ways, but in other ways, Nolan saw deep wounding in her. He didn't want this woman hurt any more than necessary.

"It's funny, Nolan," she whispered, moving her hands up and down his forearms. "After everything I was told today, I went back to my office. I was wishing I could just crawl into your arms and be held." Her lips pursed and she looked away for a moment, trying to find the right words, because the concern burning in his eyes told her so much. She lifted her lashes, holding his narrowed gaze. "I'm not very good at choosing a man to be in my life. Farida and Hadii will confirm that I'm an abysmal failure. I'm torn about you. I want to run to you, but I'm afraid."

There, the truth was out. She saw his tight mouth relax a little, his caresses continuing along her shoulders, sending soothing sensations throughout her.

"I don't want to hurt you, Teren," he began, his voice low. "You're reeling right now. Anyone would be under these circumstances. I do care about you. I know I shouldn't, but I do. I was hired to protect you, and you were going to be just another PSD I was assigned to guard." His voice changed; his hands stilled on her shoulders. "But you're becoming much more than that to me. I didn't walk in here expecting to be personally interested in you, but I am." Fear ratcheted up inside him, but he pushed through it, because for the first time Teren was lowering those walls she hid behind so well; and he needed to come clean with her too.

"I never meant for this to happen, Teren, but it has. I realize we're in a dynamic situation, and protecting you will always be my first order of business. It hurts me to see you suffer. I find myself wanting to do something to help you, to give you a little island of peace in this storm cycle we're caught up in. I want to be there for you in whatever capacity you define. I won't make a pass at you. I won't place you in an uncomfortable situation with me. But because I can't read your mind, I need to hear it from you first."

Swallowing, she felt warmth flowing through her, lessening her fears. "I'm not very good at talking intimately to a man, I guess."

His mouth crooked. "Well, with three big brothers probably hovering around you, keeping you safe from the big, bad world of boys growing up, it's no wonder."

She smiled faintly and nodded. "They were *very* protective of me. Too much so. And yes, they really made my growing up years very different from what most girls might experience without three guard dogs lording over them."

Nolan saw her wry look, the soft corners of her mouth lifting a little. "Were you able to have a boyfriend? Go to dances?" he teased.

"When I'd go to a dance, which wasn't often, my brothers were right there, and they threatened any boy who showed the least amount of interest in me. They chased them off."

"You didn't really have breathing room to find out about boys then?"

She shook her head. "No. Farida and Hadii told me a long time ago that my socialization skills, as they referred to it, got stunted early." She gave Nolan an embarrassed look. "They said that because of my background, I wasn't able to know a good man from a bad one. And they're right, because my personal relationships from the time I was eighteen and left for college have been exactly like that, Nolan. I don't trust myself with men anymore. I consistently make bad choices. That's why I'm so hesitant with you."

Nolan kept his expression bland. Teren had been guarded by her three brothers and it had made it impossible for her to learn, grow, and make normal mistakes through relationships. "I see. There's no way for me to overcome that with you, Teren. All I can do is be honest with you, ask you a lot of questions, talk with you, and try to gain your trust."

"And this is coming at the very worst of times, Nolan." She lifted her hand, pushing strands away from her brow. "I wasn't looking for a possible relationship."

"Neither was I," he admitted wryly. "But I get it." He held her unsure stare. He could feel Teren wanting what he was offering her and at least now he knew why she was so hesitant. Her personal life had been an ongoing disaster, thanks to her helicopter brothers and parents smothering her attempts to grow up and mature, following her every move through high school, where kids just naturally grew, made mistakes, and learned from them. Teren hadn't been given that opportunity. Nolan suspected her parents were probably even more protective than her brothers. They hadn't gotten that way without parental molding, either.

"I'm drawn to you," she said quietly. "You do make me feel safe, Nolan. Oh, I know it's your job and you do it well, but this goes beyond that. From the moment I met you at the airport, I felt…well…this wonderful sensation. It made me feel so secure and safe." She frowned, searching his eyes. "And it came from you. I know it did. And you didn't even know me, but from the moment our eyes met, I felt this warm blanket of protection wrap around me.

There's no other way to describe it."

Nodding, he felt her confusion. "I don't think you realize just how beautiful you are, Teren. When I saw you standing in that airport in your white *tob*, you looked like a flower among hundreds of men rushing back and forth. You have no idea how fresh, how pretty and desirable, you were to me."

"Was that why I had that feeling then, Nolan? That warmth wrapping around me?"

"I guess so. I mean, I didn't consciously know it happened, Teren. But from the moment I laid eyes on you, I felt this incredible connection with you."

"Does it always happen to you?"

Shaking his head, he muttered, "No, it's never happened before. Not like this."

"I like it. It helps me feel better, Nolan. Honestly, I feel like someone just threw me over a cliff and I'm in free fall." Her voice broke. "I'm not very tough in some ways. In others, I am. I'm super-sensitive about everything. I don't take emotional blows very well. And you walking into my life right now feels like an oasis in a desert with a dust storm approaching. You make me feel safe, whether you know it or not."

"That's all good," Nolan rasped, forcing himself to keep his hands where they were. He felt his heart opening wide to Teren, felt the need to do so much more for her, but she had to define those boundaries for him. "Look, you have another decision to make here. A security contractor isn't supposed to get personal with the person he's guarding. And I have. You need to know you can ask for me to be replaced. I can call Wyatt and ask for another contractor to guard you. If I make you feel threatened or uncomfortable in any way—you will have to replace me."

"No! You do just the opposite for me, Nolan. I don't want another bodyguard—ever."

"Tell me what makes you feel comfortable around me, then. How can I help you, Teren? And be specific." Her eyes widened, the black pupils enlarging. Groaning inwardly as her lips parted, all Nolan wanted to do was pick her up in his arms, carry her to his duplex, and love her. But that was sexual, not necessarily the emotions Teren needed. He doubted she felt any sexual hunger, given what she'd been told a while ago. She was in shock—she wasn't in heat.

"I like the idea of having dinner with you," she began hesitantly. "And keeping the door open between our duplexes. I like you touching me like this. I'm starving for that connection from you, because when you touch me, it makes me feel better, more stable. My world has blown up on me, Nolan. I'm just a civilian. I'm not military or trained in that way. I'm committed to this place, heart and soul. I don't dream of anything else, because I'm fulfilling my dream every day here at Kitra. I love what I do and I know I make a difference."

"You are a very necessary part of why Kitra is so successful, Teren," he agreed. Nolan was relieved that she wasn't leaning into him, that their hips weren't fused with one another.

She was gun-shy and with good reason, now that he understood some of her past. Still, Nolan knew they felt a mutual intimacy, which was a good start. If he told Teren his dreams of them together, it would probably shock the hell out of her, and she'd already had her fair share of shocks today. He didn't need to add to them. Instead, Nolan would keep how he felt about Teren his secret. They had this mess with Uzan to get past first. Everything between them was tentative. Nothing was written in stone.

Teren was right: she was in free fall. All he could do was fall with her. Nolan couldn't stop Uzan from stalking her. All he could do was be there to protect her if the soldier made an attempt to take her life or kidnap her.

"We've met at a very awkward time, Nolan."

"Yeah, that's occurred to me more than once."

She smiled a little, moving her fingers up and down the sleeve of his light cotton safari jacket. "Farida and Hadii think you're a good man. That you're right for me."

He cocked his head, surprised. "What do you think? That's more important to me, Teren."

"I feel drawn to you but I keep resisting it because of my less-than-glorious past."

"Have you ever been drawn to a man like this before?"

Shaking her head, Teren said, "No. Not ever. It's new to be powerfully attracted to a man." And then she searched his eyes, which were a deeper blue, seeing the yearning for her in them. "You're different from the rest of them. And I know you were sent here to do a job. It really wasn't about us on a personal basis. This is all so crazy."

"Then," he offered, releasing her, urging her to walk beside him, "let's take this an hour, a day, at a time. Whatever is there, if it's real, Teren, it will naturally unfold between us. And right now, your life is on the line, so my first priority is keeping you safe, not courting you, as much as I'd like to."

She met his very male look, saw the truth in his eyes. "I can't see beyond what's happening right now," she admitted. "But it's lovely to have you here and I'm actually beginning to trust you."

Those were the words he needed to hear more than any other. Smiling, he walked at her side, their hands sometimes brushing against one another. "And that's the most important thing we can share between us right now, Teren. If you trust me, it can mean the difference between you living and dying. I don't mean to put it so dramatically, but it's the cold, hard truth. If I tell you to run a certain way or drop to the ground, you need to trust me and instantly do what I ask."

"I will," she whispered. They walked from beneath the shade, back into the late afternoon sunlight still stretching across the grasslands that surrounded Kitra. "I'd be too frightened not to."

"You will be. It's a natural reaction. But you need to move beyond that fear and listen to what I'm telling you to do. If you can do that"—Nolan gazed down into those incredible dove-gray eyes of hers, now filled with less anxiety—"then you'll live."

"I still feel like I'm in some weird other dimension, Nolan."

"I know you do."

"And sometimes I wonder if you're real."

He grinned a little. "Oh, I'm very real, all right."

"I'm glad Wyatt assigned you to protect me. I don't want you replaced. Promise me you'll stay?"

"I'll stay," he growled, giving her a heated look, wanting her to realize that she was a helluva lot more to him than just his PSD. Teren seemed at peace now, walking close to him. Nolan knew that as good as Ayman and his well-trained soldiers were, Kitra was not impregnable. The right terrorist with the right experience and training could easily come over the red wall that enclosed Kitra. He would become a stealthy hyena loose among unsuspecting prey.

The air was alive with the smell of spices and food cooking. He heard children shrieking with laughter now and then. All the families of Kitra were preparing dinner. Nolan knew from being in Sudan that food wasn't a guaranteed thing for any tribe or village. The women survivors who lived here with their children must have thought that Kitra was a dream come true. To have enough food to fill a belly daily in this country was not normal. And in western Sudan, where he'd operated most of the time, Nolan had seen starvation daily. It was gut-wrenching, but at least the Delos charities were doing something to ease this terrible situation. It was a drop in the bucket, he realized, because thousands died yearly from lack of food. This was a harsh third-world country that took no prisoners, and starving people were always desperate to survive. That was why he would always be fully alert, even within the walls of Kitra. Starvation made companions of people like Uzan who prowled among them with money to assure them that they wouldn't die.

And more than anything, Nolan wanted this woman to survive this plot and coming attack. He knew the odds weren't good and they were stacked against Teren. He knew it because he'd performed too many PSDs over the years as a Delta Force operator. There was no way he was going to tell Teren any of the possible outcomes. He'd just started gaining her trust. That was a huge step forward for them to be a good, working team. And maybe his ability to reach out personally, man to woman, had fused that bridge between them. Nolan wouldn't allow himself to dream of a future with Teren. He was too much of a pragmatist in this dark world he worked within. She just had to survive this. And so did he. Then a life with Teren would look a lot more possible than it did today.

CHAPTER 11

NOLAN UNLOCKED THE door to Teren's duplex and she dutifully stepped back, as he'd trained her to do. She knew the drill now: move off to one side and let him clear the duplex for her. Nolan did just that, pulling the Glock from beneath his jacket and silently moving inside.

Teren felt an immediate shift within Nolan: he was now a focused predator on the hunt. It was quite a change from his usual approach to her, as a soft-spoken, gentle protector. In fact, his ability to handle her moods was something she'd never experienced from a man before.

Since Teren had come to Kitra, Ayman, Ameer, and Abit had treated her like a beloved adopted daughter, and for the first time in her life, Teren had been lavished with love and kindness from men. The difference between her own father and her Sudanese friends had been life-changing and eye-opening for Teren. Whether they knew it or not, they had helped her to heal too. She was no longer fearful of men because of their love, respect, and kindness toward her.

But she'd had no American friend to discuss her discoveries with until now. Nolan encouraged her to share with him, because he cared. He listened with real interest to whatever she said, unlike her family, who tended to dismiss her observations, questions, and chatter.

"It's all clear in here," Nolan now told her. "Come on in."

Teren nodded and shut the door behind her, locking it and appreciating the cool air, thanks to her air conditioner. She saw that her kitchen table had been set earlier by Nolan and she smiled gratefully. "You've been busy."

Nolan kept the Glock in his hand as he moved toward his duplex. "A little. I'll be right back."

A new sense of peace descended on Teren as she went to her bedroom and changed into a pair of comfortable blue terry-cloth shorts and a sleeveless white cotton tank top. She removed her tortoiseshell comb, her hair tumbled down, and she brushed it until it had a soft, burnished look in her dresser mirror. Nolan had asked her to keep the curtains closed over the locked windows in every room, and she missed the light but understood his reasoning. Threading strong, clean strands between her fingers, she glanced at herself in the mirror. No longer was she as pale-looking as when she got today's difficult news and the shadows had dissolved from beneath her eyes. There was a hue of pink across her cheeks, and she knew it was because of Nolan's concern and caring toward her.

Sighing, Teren frowned, slipping on her sandals. It wouldn't last. Even if this crisis was settled, Nolan would have to leave her for another assignment somewhere else in the world. And then she'd be without him in her life. She tried not to consider that scenario. The question was: how could she withhold her feelings for him? Teren didn't think it was possible. Every day the longing for this man grew within her, taking root in her wounded, wary heart, healing her pain from the past. Nolan had given her hope—unlike the men she'd known before. He was one of a kind.

Pensive, Teren walked out into her kitchen and saw Nolan enter her home. Like her, he'd changed, wearing a pair of jeans and a muscle shirt that showed off his impressive upper body. She tried not to stare at him, but maybe she'd become a female cheetah in heat, just as her women friends had described would happen when she met the 'right' man.

Her body felt a power surge whenever he was close to her. Teren was amazed that one human being could sexually influence another so profoundly.

Nolan walked over to the stove, where he had placed a small pot with a lid on it. "I made us a small salad," he told her, pointing toward the refrigerator. "And I got lucky. Nafeesa was in the middle of making chicken broth for a Sudanese soup and I persuaded her to make you some chicken noodle soup. I figured that was pretty light and might sit well in your stomach." He took the lid off and the steam rose, spicy and fragrant.

"That sounds perfect, Nolan. Thank you. I'll have to thank Nafeesa tomorrow morning. I'm sure American chicken soup wasn't something she was used to making." She opened the refrigerator and saw two small salad bowls wrapped in plastic. She appreciated that Nolan had sealed the greens to keep them fresh. The man didn't miss a thing.

Nolan chuckled a little, stirring the soup with a wooden spoon. "I told her and she gathered all the ingredients and then made it for you."

"Did she taste the final product? How did she like it?"

"Yeah, she did. She'd never thought about putting egg noodles into a soup before and really liked the idea. I think she might make a huge pot of it for lunch someday soon for everyone to try."

"We're Americanizing them, Nolan," Teren said, smiling, as she took the plastic wrap off the salads and set them on the table.

"Why not? The world's global now. There's bound to be cross-pollination between cultures."

"You probably know that better than most," Teren said. She walked over and retrieved two soup bowls from the cupboard. There was something special about doing something as simple as preparing a meal with Nolan. Unexpected, but wonderful. She tucked her reaction away, knowing that if she survived this possible attack, Nolan would one day walk out of her life, never to be seen or heard from again. That was the realist side of herself. Her heart, on the other hand, wanted to believe that when he talked about having her in his life, he meant long-term. The two realities just didn't mix and she knew it. Still, her silly heart wanted to pursue the burgeoning relationship with Nolan.

"In a way," he said. He took the soup ladle as Teren held the first bowl in front of him to be filled.

"Can you tell me what you did in the Army?" Teren asked, curious to know about his background.

He slowly filled the bowl, not wanting to splash her with the hot, steaming soup. "I can give you some information, but everything I did was top secret, so I can't say much about most of it."

"Tell me what you can, okay?" She set the bright orange bowl on the counter, picking up the other one.

Nolan slid her a quick look. Teren was so close to him, her arm almost touching his from time to time. She invited intimacy.

"Why do you want to know?" he asked her lightly, filling the bowl.

"Because I want to know you." She smiled a little and took the bowl to the table, then came back for the second one.

"It's a good enough reason," he said, placing the lid on the pan and setting it off to one side. Nafeesa had given him several round *kissra* bread loaves, and he brought the plate of them over with him. Nolan held a chair out for Teren, and she gave him a glance.

"I could get used to this. You're spoiling me, Nolan."

"My parents taught me to always be a gentleman," he teased.

She sat down at his elbow. Nolan knew he would never tire of watching how Teren moved. There was such innate grace in her.

She broke off a crust of *kissra* and dipped it into her soup, giving him a curious look. "Okay, I'll ask you questions and since you're top secret, you can choose which you'll answer. Was your father in the Army?"

"He was, for four years. Worked in the intelligence section at the Pentagon. Then he got out and went to work for the CIA as a case officer. His cover was that he was a businessman who owned an import-export business. He did all his undercover work here in Africa." He sipped the chicken-laden soup, hungry. Teren ate more slowly and with delicacy.

Her eyes grew shadowed. "He was a spy, then?"

"Yes."

"Did you know this as a child?"

Shaking his head, Nolan said, "No. All I knew was that he was gone a lot. I never knew anything more until I was seventeen, when my father died in a shootout in Africa." He wasn't going to tell her it was here, in Khartoum, in the slums. Coming back here had brought up a lot of grief and loss for Nolan. Even his mother hadn't known where her husband had died. He'd found out through back channels when he was in Delta Force.

Teren reached out, sliding her hand across his arm. "I'm so sorry, Nolan. That's awful."

"Thanks. I didn't see him a whole lot as a child, Teren. I lived with my Irish mother in McLean, Virginia. He was usually gone nine months out of every year and we didn't know he worked for the Company until after he died. It was a helluva shock for both of us."

"I can't even begin to imagine," Teren said sadly, removing her hand. She'd seen his eyes darken when she'd reached out and made contact with him. Teren liked touching Nolan. It sent pleasure through her, fed her. "You were seventeen at the time. What did your mother do after she lost your father?"

"My mother, Aislin, was born in the Galway Bay area of Ireland and I have dual citizenship in America and Ireland. She needed to go home, because she missed her country and relatives so much. She waited until I graduated before putting the house on the market. There was nothing left for her in the U.S. I was going off to the Army. For her, it was an easy and right decision, and I supported her in moving back to her home country during my summer vacation. All our relatives from her side of the family live there."

"And what did you do?" she asked, savoring the rich, warm chicken broth.

He smiled a little. "I went with her. I wasn't entering the Army until the fall of that year. We flew into Killarney. I was already very familiar with her hometown. She'd never sold her family's house that was on the bay, so we had a home to go to."

"Is she a woman of the land or the sea?"

Nolan liked Teren's interest in his mother's background, even though she didn't know her. "She's a creature of the sea and a very famous landscape artist. She's painted beautiful seascapes of the Galway area. In fact," he said, "you remind me of my mother in some respects."

She smiled shyly. "I'm not a painter, Nolan. I can barely draw a circle."

He chuckled. "No, I mean emotionally. My mother is like the ocean. She has her moods and she's very sensitive, like you. She had always had respiratory issues and she didn't like living in McLean because of the pollution. She yearned for the clean salt air of Galway Bay. When she was upset about something, she loved to walk on the rocky beach and let the ocean soothe her. I used to go along with her and skip flat rocks into the water." Those were fond memories for Nolan.

"I'm afraid my kind of 'sensitive' isn't as good as hers is." It seemed that her stomach was accepting the food and she found herself much hungrier than she had expected.

"What do you mean?" Nolan saw a shadow cross her eyes. He'd hoped that if he opened up to Teren, she'd reciprocate. Normally, he never talked of anything personal with a PSD.

Giving an embarrassed shrug, Teren said, "I'm sensitive to violence or blood of any kind. And really, it's not very nice table talk."

He studied her for a moment. "Physically sensitive?" He saw her mouth turn down. "As in a sensitive stomach that you mentioned earlier?"

"Yes."

"My mother," he admitted ruefully, "is built the same way. In fact, her side of the family has that very same gene."

"Oh," she groaned, closing her eyes for a moment. "We really are more alike than I'd originally thought."

"Just because you don't paint doesn't mean you aren't an artist. I was looking at your store website for Kitra and there's a lot of detail and imaginative imagery in the web pages you've built, Teren. You're just a different kind of artist who doesn't use brushes, but instead uses pixels." He smiled kindly over at her. "I think you and my mother share a lot more in common than you know."

"Does she love children?"

"Very much. I was an only child, but there's an orphanage near her home, and she makes a point of going over every Wednesday to teach the children a class in drawing and art. They love her. She's very much a toucher, like you."

"That's amazing," Teren said, shaking her head. "Sounds as if you get along well with her."

"We're very close," Nolan said. "That's how I knew I'd get along with you. You're an easy keeper compared to some PSDs I've had to herd around." He smiled wickedly over at her.

Her lips moved into a curve as she continued to sip at the soup. "Well, once I understood what you wanted from me, I found it easy to get along with you, too."

"Good. We need to become a well-oiled machine so I can keep you safe."

She sobered, feeling her stomach clench a little. "For a moment," she whispered, "I forgot about all of that."

"Then let's keep talking. Tell me about your family and those three big, overbearing brothers of yours."

"Ugh, it doesn't have a happy ending, Nolan." Teren pushed the bowl gently aside, picking at the *kissra* bread, nibbling distractedly on it. At least she'd eaten ninety percent of the huge bowl of soup.

"I want to know," he coaxed her, holding her uncertain stare. And then he added, "Because I care about you, Teren. This isn't idle chitchat between us. I *want* to get to know you, the person. Not as the PSD."

His roughened tone, the emotion banked in his voice, pulled open that dark box Teren hid so deep within herself. "Well," she muttered, "it's not a pretty story."

"And yet," he murmured, "you've turned out to be one of the most beautiful and caring women I've ever met. And if it wasn't because of what your family instilled in you, Teren, then it was born inside of you. My mother always says that every person is like an oyster, but some special people are born with a pearl inside that oyster. You're one of those people in my book."

His gentle look convinced her she could open up a bit more with him. "That's a wonderful analogy. Your mom even thinks in images."

"So do you." He finished off his soup and pushed the bowl aside. "Tell me about yourself. Where did you grow up?"

"Well, it's probably all there in my file. I was born in Somerset, Kentucky. It's near Daniel Boone National Forest. My father, Alex, is a dairy farmer. My mother, Annie, is a world-class seamstress. We've had our farm in the family for a hundred fifty years. My mom had three boys first; I was the last to arrive. Everyone treated me like I was a brainless, helpless, stupid little girl who was always underfoot."

"I started to learn about dairy farming when I was eight years old. I wanted to help my father in the barns while the cows were being milked. But he said no, that it was a man's work, not a woman's work. I was disappointed, because I loved being outdoors and always have."

"I know you like to ride horses," Nolan said, pulling apart another piece of *kissra* bread. "What else did you do? I have this vision of you running barefoot, a young, wild little girl untamed by the world." He smiled a little.

Snorting, Teren said, "Hardly wild, although I wanted to be. My parents are very, very strict, very religious, and highly conservative."

"And you were the only girl in the family," Nolan murmured, beginning to see a broader picture of Teren. He could see hurt, frustration, and unhappiness in her eyes and voice as she spoke more personally about her family.

"Yes. My parents treated me as a problem because I was a girl. The boys could go out and help my father. They were big, brawny, and strong like him."

"And your mother? Do you have a close tie with her?"

Looking away, Teren said, "Not hardly." She laid the bread aside, her stomach tightening as she studied Nolan. His care drenched her, and she saw genuine empathy in his eyes. "She's an incredible seamstress. People know she's an artist with thread and fabric, and she gets paid well for what she does."

"Unfortunately," she continued, "only she can do it. She can't hire others to do what she does. So, she didn't need a whiny little girl always coming into her sewing room needing something from her. I also think she was tired of being a mother, if you want the truth. She raised three boys ahead of me. Plus, I know the sewing gave her a good feeling and a sense of confidence. She was earning good money and got a lot of well-deserved praise. It made her feel valued."

"And you felt like a mere addendum to your parents?"

Nolan had spoken the words gently, but it still hurt to hear them. Rubbing her forehead, she rasped, "Yes. Exactly."

"Did that give you a kind of freedom from them, though?"

"It did," Teren agreed, taking in a deep breath and releasing it. "I learned to take care of myself from a very early age, for the most part. I knew when Mom had that door to the sewing room closed, I wasn't to disturb her. I loved the Apple computer in my brother Ted's room and spent hours on it. And I learned a lot from him, because he wrote software and taught me how to do it."

"But then you went outdoors to ride your horse?"

She smiled fondly, resting her chin against her hands. "Yes. Domino, my black-and-white pinto gelding, and I would spend half a day running around on my father's thousand-acre farm. I had special places we'd go. A stream to sit and dream by. A small hill where I could lie with my back on the grass and watch the clouds shift into animals, birds, or other shapes. From the time it was warm enough in the spring until late fall when it got too cold, I'd go riding nearly every day. It got me out of the house. Mom was always in a better mood when I got back, just in time for dinner. If I was early, I'd go to my room and do my homework. If I finished that early, I'd go to Ted's room and be on the computer."

"Because that way you weren't underfoot?"

Wearily, she said, "Yes."

"I'm sorry, Teren." Nolan could see why she often felt underappreciated. In a way, Teren had been abandoned by both parents. It probably wasn't done on purpose, but it had happened, and she'd gotten the message loud and clear from an early age. It was hard to have four kids to clothe and feed, and Nolan was pretty sure the family wasn't wealthy by any measure. They worked hard every day, seven days a week, to keep the farm. They just didn't have the time to be doting parents to their children.

"So? Did you have friends you could hang out with and confide in?"

She cut him a glance. "I couldn't have a boyfriend. My brothers made sure of that. And my girlfriends were few, because my brothers were very judgmental about them. If my friends weren't religious, if they wore clothes that were too suggestive or sexy-looking…you know the routine. I wasn't allowed to have friendships with them."

"A few friends?"

"Two. They were a lifeline for me," Teren admitted.

"Did you do girl things together like sleepovers?"

"Are you kidding me? My parents didn't think the parents of my two friends were good enough for me. They didn't go to church; therefore, they were going to hell. And I sure wasn't going to invite them to a sleepover at my place. My parents were harshly judgmental."

He nodded and clasped his hands. "Sounds like the Sharia law practiced over here in Sudan came to Kentucky," Nolan said lightly, trying to lift her spirits. There were eighteen years of hurt lingering in her eyes and it was there for him to see. He ached for Teren. He could imagine her spindly legs, so long for the rest of her slender body, as she rode her horse, lonely, without many friends. Nolan was sure her horse became her best friend, and she probably talked to that gelding all the time. The horse was a lifesaver for a lonely little girl.

Managing a short laugh, Teren sat back, rubbing her hands down her shorts. "Yeah, it was the same kind of prison that women get put into over here in Sudan, no question. I had something similar, only it came in the form of my parents' strict belief system and my hardheaded brothers. They all called me 'Rebel.' And it wasn't said nicely. It wasn't a nickname—more like a curse. Not that any of them cursed…"

"I can imagine you as a rebel," he laughed. "I like you being independent, Teren. It suits you. I'm glad you stayed who you are, because look what you've accomplished over here for the seven years you've been at Kitra. Look at how many lives were improved. You should be proud of your accomplishments. Not many people could do what you've done for so many."

"Now you sound like Farida and Hadii," she said, smiling warmly over at him. "It's nice to be wanted, Nolan. To be respected, not considered an outcast or weirdly different." Right now, Teren wanted desperately to tell him what had happened to her. Instinctively, she knew Nolan wouldn't judge her as everyone else had. Swallowing, she thought she'd said enough for one day. "Besides," she added, "I wasn't always a good girl. I gave my parents a lot of grief too." It hurt to even think of admitting they called her a "bad girl."

Nolan shook his head. "Every teenager does that to their parents." He smiled.

She stood, gathering up the bowls and flatware. "No, I made a horrible mistake one time and it…well…it tore my whole family apart. And as a result, things just haven't been the same between us since." She turned away, seeing his eyes narrow instantly, as if he were sensing what she hadn't said. That scared her. Teren wasn't ready to go there. At least not yet.

Placing the bowls in the sink, she washed them out, feeling nervous, worried that with Nolan's ability to see beneath her surface, he might suspect what had happened to her. It was such an ugly, dark, seething secret that Teren wished she could get rid of it, but she knew it would never go away.

She felt Nolan come up behind her, his hands lightly cupping her shoulders. She nearly dropped the bowl and stood there, waiting.

"Whatever it is that you're carrying, Teren..." Nolan's voice was low and gruff.

"Yes?" Her voice was barely above a whisper, hands hovering paralyzed over the bowls in the sink. His fingers caressed her shoulders and upper arms, soothing her as a parent might soothe a fractious child.

"There isn't one of us that doesn't lug around that kind of baggage. Try to look at it in another way, okay? You did the best you could under the circumstances. None of us is all-knowing and you're carrying something pretty devastating deep inside you. I don't know what it is, Teren, but I can feel what it's doing to you. I wish I knew how to make it better for you. I know the situation we're in right now isn't helping, either."

She felt her heart burst with such passion for this man that she closed her eyes, her hands still resting over the wet bowls. Nolan's sincerity overcame all the resistance from her fractured soul. She breathed in the acceptance that vibrated from him and prayed that his words would help her heal from the worst decision she'd made in her life. Slowly opening her eyes, pain in her tone, she managed to choke out, "I want to believe you, Nolan. I really do."

"That's a start, sweetheart." He moved his hand across her hair, taming a few strands into place along her shoulder. "It's just a sense, but after talking with you, I get the feeling that you've never really found a home where you were honestly loved for who you were until you got here to Kitra. Is that true?"

Her throat constricted and she moved away, lifting a towel hanging on a hook off the cupboard near the sink. Nolan stepped back, giving her room. Turning, she saw his expression was one of deep regret for her.

"That's true," she admitted, her voice sounding broken, too many feelings surging through her. "After what happened, I ran away from my family, Nolan. I graduated from the community college and then left. Too many people were judging me, blaming me for what happened. I was too young, incredibly naive, and didn't know..." Teren sighed raggedly and set the towel on the counter, wrapping her arms around herself, something she always did when she needed comfort and holding.

"I'm sorry your family wasn't there to support you," he said heavily.

"They were, for part of it," Teren said, not wanting him to think her family were unfeeling monsters, because they weren't. "They did help me for a while, and I rebounded." She shrugged, resting her hips against the counter. "In the end I couldn't handle the town's ongoing judgment of me. They all knew what happened, so I had to leave to make a fresh start for myself."

"I know I don't know the story of what happened to you, Teren, but like I said, we all go through some really bad times. And you have to try to forgive yourself, tell yourself you did the best you could at that time, and let it go."

Nolan's mouth flattened and he drew in a deep breath. "I was married once. I swore I wouldn't marry while I was a Delta operator, because I'd be gone so much of the time on undercover assignments." He gave her a slight smile. "But meeting Linda made me forget everything I said I was going to do, and we got married. We settled in McLean, Virginia, where I was based. She got pregnant just before I left for another assignment to Sudan." His voice lowered as the scenario began to replay itself. "I was six months into the assignment when I got ordered back to the U.S. by my handler—there was a home emergency. They wouldn't tell me what it was, or who it concerned, and I was left in the dark."

"When I arrived at Andrews Air Force Base, my handler was there to meet me and drove me to the county morgue. My wife had been attacked by an intruder. She fought back and he murdered her." Moving his fingers through his short hair, he added roughly, "And the baby she was carrying died too. No one knew about the attack upon her until the next morning at nine a.m. when she didn't show up for work. By that time, my baby daughter was dead. If…if things had been different…if help had arrived shortly after she'd died, they might have saved my daughter. But it wasn't meant to happen."

Teren stared in horror over at Nolan. He stood before her, his shoulders sagging, and she didn't know what to say. Without thinking, she pushed away from the counter, taking those few steps to wrap her arms around him, crushing him against her, her head buried against the line of his hard, unyielding jaw. Anguish radiated from him—then slowly, his arms slid around her waist, holding her, clinging to her, his face buried in her hair.

Tears ran down her cheeks and she didn't try to stop them. All along, she'd felt something so brutal, so overwhelming, living secretly within Nolan. And now she knew what it was. His quiet admission was incredibly powerful and she was grateful that he trusted her. Trusted her compassion. Her heart.

Her eyes squeezed tightly shut, Teren felt the tension in his body as they held each other. It felt as if he were clinging to a life preserver and if he released her, he would drown.

CHAPTER 12

Nolan absorbed Teren's womanly strength and her deep compassion. The cinnamon scent of her hair, where he'd buried his face, lingered as he pulled away slightly to look down at her. He felt the slender curve of her body, her small, perfectly formed breasts against his chest. Heat pooled in his lower body as her belly sank against his thickening erection. A groan tore out of him as her arms curved and held him tightly against her. He could feel her breath, the rise and fall of her breasts, the moisture against the column of his neck. She was perfectly fitted against him in every possible way.

Just once…just once he wanted to let go of his steely control. His brain was screaming at him that she was his PSD, that he had no business inviting her into this kind of situation. Nolan knew that his story, the painful past of his life, had triggered Teren's unabashed, unselfish reaction. He knew deep within that she was sensitive to the plight of others who suffered. Why the hell had he told her about the worst night of his life? Why?

And yet, he hungrily sponged in the fluttering beat of her heart against his chest, felt life infusing him, instead of living in a land of limbo where there was no warmth, no intimacy, no—nothing. Teren inspired him to dream once more, whether she knew it or not. She fed his aching soul, one stained with so much grief, loss, and regret. And she did it without realizing it.

He nuzzled his face into her hair, feeling its cool silkiness against his flesh. Nolan heard a soft moan come from within Teren, her arms a little tighter around his shoulders, as she tried to press herself even more solidly against him. She felt so damn good to him and he couldn't help it; his lower body exploded with a raging hunger for her, wanting her now. His resolve was ebbing away from him, her instinctive seductiveness luring him, although Nolan knew she wasn't doing this to seduce him. She was trying to comfort him and find comfort for herself, too.

Teren was holding him with all her woman's strength and love right now because she was hurting for him, for the loss of his wife and baby. And her decency was what stopped Nolan from taking her. To cheat Teren like this, to use her desire to comfort him as a reason to take her sexually, was against his values. He wanted a woman to come to him with the intention of engaging in lovemaking with him. He was no damned wolf in sheep's clothing, and Nolan would never try anything with Teren because she had enough to handle right now.

He slid his hands down her back, a caress, a silent thank you for her support, then reluctantly released her, taking a step back when it was the last thing he wanted to do. He saw her lashes drift upward, arousal and compassion in her lustrous gray eyes. Pink tinged her cheeks, her lips were slightly parted, and she was breathless. Nolan could feel her wanting him, but damn it, she had to say those words, had to verbally move across that line that stood between them. He was not going to take advantage of the situation or of her. If he hadn't had that strong moral compass that always guided him, he would have been lost in the ugly world of secrecy. And maybe his mind, shaped by the military, made it easy for him to keep things in that black-and-white perspective.

Nolan saw confusion in her expression as he eased away from her. But he didn't want to stop holding her in his arms, his hands coming to rest on her waist, maintaining her lambent gaze, feeling such raw desire on her part toward him. Would she transcend her secret past? Could she speak the words, ask him to love her? That's what it would take, and Nolan sensed she was close to doing just that. But at what risk to herself? Teren had intimated something terrible had happened in her past. And until he knew what it was, he was reluctant to make love with her, as badly as he wanted to.

Tragic wounds changed a person forever. And someone blundering into another person's life required patience and time, because without knowing the dark secrets someone carried, it could backfire on both parties.

No, Nolan would rather continue to get to know her, understand what fueled her passionate life, and continue to slowly draw Teren to him for all the right reasons. Never mind this erection, which was now aching. He would rather suffer. The reward was the look in Teren's eyes, which spoke of utter trust toward him. That was the ultimate gift one human could give another, and Nolan recognized the gift for what it was.

"Hey," he rasped, moving his fingers along her waist. "Has anyone ever told you how beautiful your heart is?" He saw the corners of her lips pull up just little, heard her breathing become a little ragged. Her fingers tightened on his forearms, and Nolan felt as if she wouldn't be able to stand on her own just yet. He hadn't even kissed her, and that's exactly what he wanted to do.

"No…" She gazed up at him, her pupils large and black as she studied him in the heated, swirling silence around them.

He lifted his hand, taming her hair and pushing it away from her face. "Well, it is, sweetheart." And she did indeed have a sweet, innocent heart that she had just given him. That was the trust throbbing strongly between them. Nolan knew it was only a matter of time now before Teren came to realize that whatever issues stood between them, they would dissolve, because the bottom line was that they trusted one another.

"I'm so sorry for what happened to you, Nolan," she whispered unsteadily. "I-I can't even begin to imagine the pain you felt…the loss…"

"I was twenty-six at the time," he said, cupping her cheek, looking deep in her eyes, which now glistened with unshed tears. "I'm thirty now. Time has helped. It's about the only thing that has," he added, sadness in his tone. "I never thought in a million years that our home, which was in a good section of town, would ever be broken into. It just never occurred to me."

Shaking her head, Teren said, "It wouldn't to me, either, Nolan. My God, you must have been so devastated. I don't know how you survived."

Just holding Teren was helping him to come to terms with his grief-stricken past. He realized he'd been waiting for this kind of woman, this moment, for a long time. "I was numb for a couple of years. I couldn't even cry. And then, one day, the dam burst and I couldn't quit crying. I was out on an undercover op in Ethiopia when it happened. And fortunately, when it all came down and broke me, I was out in the desert, alone."

"How did it break you?"

"The pain, the grief that I'd sat on so long, came vomiting up through me, Teren. I can't explain it. It was like a fist violently shoving up inside of me, forcing me to let out all my screams, my anger, my grief. I was at a safe house, waiting for a PSD who would arrive a week later. I had those seven days to get it all out of my system, release the bulk of it, cry until I had no more tears left, but the sounds were still tearing out of me. I lost track of night and day. I couldn't eat. I forced myself to keep drinking a lot of water, because I knew I had to stay hydrated or I'd die."

CHAPTER 13

Suddenly, Nolan's radio, which was connected to Kitra's security network, blared to life.

"Nolan? This is Ayman. We have a situation. Will you please meet me at the main gate?"

Giving Teren a look of apology, he released her and pulled the radio out of his back pocket. Their intimacy for the evening was at an end.

"Copy that." He looked over at her. "Stay here. Lock the door after me. I'll get back to you as soon as I can."

"Okay," she said, frowning. Standing in the kitchen, she watched Nolan quickly move to his duplex. When he returned, he was wearing his safari jacket, and she knew he was carrying his Glock in his belt. The look on his face was calm and focused, but it was the sense of quiet urgency that shook her. He quickly left and she locked the door behind him.

Teren walked over to the south window, pulling the curtain aside. It was still light, with the sun hovering near the western horizon. She saw the huge main gate, and it was closed. There were two guards inside the gate and two outside of it. She watched, her heart beating a little more strongly, as Nolan trotted down the slight incline toward the entrance to Kitra. What was going on?

Generally, she never knew about the security that Ayman had surrounding Kitra, nor was she educated about security measures. Had one of the guards seen something? Was someone driving down the highway toward their gates at this hour? Normally at this time of day, there was no traffic in or out of Kitra. They were very far off the beaten path.

She watched as Ayman arrived in his desert camouflage uniform. She was relieved that he was the one guarding Kitra. He and Nolan talked, and a guard came over, pointing east of them, across the flat grasslands. *What had he seen or heard?* Curiosity burned at her, but Teren wasn't going to disobey Nolan's order to remain in her duplex. She saw Ayman hand Nolan a pair of binoculars and he slowly scanned the east. She nibbled on her lower lip, feeling low-level anxiety mounting.

It was almost too much for her to absorb. For seven years she'd lived happily at Kitra and never felt threatened unless she had to drive into Khartoum. Was Uzan in the vicinity? Had he hired mercenary thugs from some gang in the slums of Khartoum, who were now out there scouting around?

Teren knew that Kitra was strategically situated on that slight knoll above the sea-level desert floor. She remembered Ayman once saying that no matter what direction, his soldiers would see man, beast, or vehicle coming from miles away. He emphasized that it was very well placed. Teren remembered teasing him about building a moat around Kitra to make sure it was really safe, like the European castles did during the Middle Ages. They'd gotten a good laugh out of that one. Ayman had studied at the military school and was intimately familiar with the art of war.

Feeling chilled, Teren saw two more soldiers arrive, both with their M4s on their shoulders. Normally they carried the rifles with the barrel pointed down to the earth. Now the barrels were pointing skyward. Teren didn't know what that meant, but it didn't feel good.

Tomorrow morning at nine a.m., all the department heads would be notified in a meeting of Sharan's threat against Kitra and Teren. She knew everyone would be very upset by the news and a pall would come over this happy, carefree place—one that gave so many women and children help and support. Of course, Nolan had assured her that only the department heads would know.

Teren wasn't sure that was wise, but Farida had wanted those in a supervisory capacity at Kitra to know about the situation. She didn't want everyone at Kitra dipped in the terror, and Teren knew such information would stain the entire community. Still, it bothered her. What if one of their employees went into Khartoum not knowing what else was swirling around Kitra?

Teren knew she was a civilian. Now she wished she had more military knowledge and education so she could appreciate Farida's decision-making process. Her husband, Ameer, was a civilian too, but she knew Ayman and Farida worked in close support of one another. After all, Kitra's safety depended upon them. Teren was sure Farida knew a lot more about security, because Ayman would have educated her enough to grasp possibly dangerous situations.

Damn! She normally didn't cuss, but it felt good to think the word under the circumstances. She saw Nolan and Ayman slip through the gates and walk off to one side where she could no longer see them. The other two guards were very alert, looking eastward. What on earth was out there?

★

Nolan knocked lightly on Teren's door an hour later. It was dusk, and above him, he could see the first stars starting to glimmer in the coming night sky. When she threw open the door, he stepped inside.

"What's going on?" she demanded nervously.

Nolan turned, shutting and locking the door. He shed his jacket and pulled the Glock out of his belt. "Let's go the kitchen. I could use a bottle of water if you have one." He was parched. Teren looked worried and upset, her mouth compressed. He joined her and she handed him a cold bottle of water from the refrigerator.

"Thanks," he murmured, opening it. He took her hand in his. "Come on, sit down with me at the table, okay?"

Heartened that her long fingers were curving around his, he saw some of the worry lighten in her grim expression.

Teren sat down. He pulled out another chair, sitting at her elbow. Finishing off the pint of water, he wiped his mouth. "The guards spotted movement east of Kitra," he told her. "At first, they thought it might be a herd of feral camels. Ayman makes sure each guardhouse has a good set of binoculars. The head of the detachment checked it out. There was dust rising in the east, which was unusual for this time of day." He saw Teren tensing. "It wasn't a herd of camels, and it wasn't a caravan coming into Khartoum. The lead sentry saw three *haflas* with men riding on the flatbed, armed."

A breath stole out of her. "Oh no…"

He placed his hand over hers. "That was when the guard called Ayman, alerting him to the situation. And then Ayman called me. We met down at the gate. I looked at the group of *haflas* and they were about two miles away. There are a lot of shadows on the desert this time of day, so all I could make out were three of them with six men on each flatbed with AK-47s. I gave Ayman the binoculars and he confirmed my siting."

"Was it Uzan?" she demanded, strangling on the name.

"We don't know. Ayman was telling me that sometimes the Sudanese Army has warfare games in given areas. This could have been one of them."

"But there are only dirt roads out in that area."

"Those are good for war games," Nolan assured her.

"Was Ayman worried?"

"Concerned was more like it. He's calling a general in Khartoum whom he knows right now to find out."

"What if it wasn't war games, Nolan?"

He had thought the same thing. "The men were dressed in Sudanese Army uniforms. What was out of place is that they were carrying AK-47s. Terrorists are well known to favor that particular weapon. The Sudanese Army has some, but their main rifle is an M4."

"What do you make of this?"

"Nothing yet. I'm just taking in all the information," he told her bluntly, squeezing her icy fingers. "It may be a false alarm, Teren. Nothing more." He could see her worry by the way she was tucking her lower lip between her teeth, brow furrowed. At least he could be here with her, give her a sense of safety.

"Is this what it's going to be like from now on, Nolan?"

Hearing the apprehension in her tone, he grimaced. "I'm afraid so."

"Has Ayman heard from his undercover men in the slums yet?"

Shaking his head, he said, "That's a delicate operation, Teren. It's going to take time. Those men have to be extra careful. If they appear to stand out compared to those who live there, they could be killed."

"Yes, they are paranoid in the slums. They trust no one but their own gangs."

He knew Teren usually went to bed between nine and ten p.m. because she was up at four thirty every morning. "Why don't you get a bath to help you relax?"

"Good idea," she grumped, releasing his hand. Teren gave him a softened look. "I worry about you too, Nolan."

"I know you do, but I'm the one you should worry about least, okay? And don't let that wild imagination of yours take flight. We've got everything handled." He wanted to sound confident for her sake and saw some of the tension ease from her face.

Rolling her eyes, Teren managed a sliver of a sour smile. "Guilty as charged. I'll try not to. That bath sounds like a good idea."

Nolan watched her walk down the hall toward her bedroom. Growling to himself, he wished Ayman would call him. His gut told him it was probably a war games group. Ayman had been neutral about it, but Nolan had a hunch he was actually very concerned. However, until Nolan heard from him, he wasn't going to let his imagination take over. His world was hard facts and logic, backed up with a helluva lot of experience.

TEREN PADDED OUT on her bare feet into her living room, expecting to find Nolan there, but he was gone. She toweled off her damp hair, moving to the opened inner door.

"Nolan? Are you in there?" she called. Teren searched the empty living room and kitchen.

"Yeah, I'm here…"

She saw him come out of the other end of the duplex, having been in the bedroom. He was naked from the waist up, a towel around his hips and one across his shoulders. His hair was wet, and his flesh gleamed from the shower he'd just taken as he padded toward her. Swallowing, she stopped dead still, her heart rate soaring. Nolan was so powerful-looking without clothing. His chest was sprinkled with dark hair, emphasizing the deep muscling, and accentuating the lithe movement of his upper body. He wasn't bulky but taut and hard. And he was simply beautiful to Teren.

Forcing herself to look at his eyes, she asked, "I'm sorry…did Ayman call you yet?"

Nolan came to a stop about six feet away from Teren. He'd seen her eyes widen and he felt her appreciation of his body. "Yes. It was a training exercise, was all." He held on to the ends of the white towel around his shoulders. "You can sleep well tonight, Teren."

"That's such good news!" she whispered, her hand against her throat. There was a dangerous sensation around Nolan and the dark blue of his gaze was locked with hers. She felt so much, unable to sort it all out. Uppermost, he was so sexy that male charisma dripped off him, and she could feel her lower body reacting instantly to her view of him half-clothed. "I'm heading to bed," she said, her voice a little strained. "Is it all right if I go jogging tomorrow at five a.m.? Will you come with me?"

He nodded. "Sure, I'll always be at your side any time you're outside Kitra's gate, Teren. That won't change for the duration of the PSD. Get some sleep. You've had a pretty rough day."

She gave him a warm look. "It was tough on you too, Nolan. Thank you for sharing with me. It means a lot." Teren turned away, knowing that if she didn't, she might step forward and do something bold and crazy: ask Nolan to take her to bed and love her. So turning, she hurried away to prevent herself from issuing, either verbally or with her body, such a life-changing invitation.

Musing, Nolan watched Teren move away from him. She wore a pair of loose lavender cotton pajama bottoms with a sleeveless tee of the same color. With her hair half-dry, the towel over one shoulder, she looked fetching. He hadn't meant to be half-naked, but when she'd called for him, it had sounded urgent. Pushing his fingers through his wet hair, Nolan turned and headed to the bathroom.

THE MORNING AIR was slightly cool. Teren jogged with Nolan along the berm of the asphalt highway. It was quiet except for their running shoes slapping the dry, hard clay soil. She spotted a few rabbits hopping around, seeking out the tough green bushes that thrived in the hot Sudanese desert to hide within. Off in the distance, she heard a pack of hyenas yipping but couldn't see them. There were what she called "knobs of hills" here and there across the otherwise pancake-flat grasslands. They were two hundred or so feet tall, rising like bumps out of the sea-level surface.

Having Nolan moving fluidly at her shoulder, his Glock in a holster at his side, made her feel safer. There was no one around at this time of early morning. Traffic to and from Kitra usually started at ten a.m. and was finished by three p.m. on weekdays. Teren expected to find no traffic on the ribbon of highway and she saw none. She'd slept hard last night, her last thoughts settling on Nolan and how sexy he'd looked in that towel draped around his waist. Her dreams had been torrid: they were finally in bed together doing things she'd never imagined participating in. These dreams were a first for her and left her shaken and yearning for relief.

She couldn't look into his eyes this morning and not remember he'd lost the woman he loved, as well as their unborn baby. She saw him in a whole new light and could feel the last of her walls crumbling around her heart.

"Two point five miles," Nolan told her now, starting to slow down to make the turn back to Kitra.

"Wow, it didn't seem like it," she said, breathing easily as she turned around on the highway.

"You were lost deep in thought," he teased, joining her on the other side of the highway.

Teren laughed a little. "Yeah, I nosedived, didn't I?"

"You're a techie. You're used to putting a hundred percent focus on whatever you're doing."

She slid him a glance as they picked up the pace once more. "You do the same thing."

"Guilty," Nolan admitted with a boyish grin.

There was a new, vibrant energy throbbing invisibly between them. The intimacy was there, just waiting. Nolan had entrusted her with the most horrific event of his life. He had so much courage that, in her eyes and heart, he was a modern-day warrior with morals and values from long ago. Not everyone held themselves to a higher standard, but Nolan did. He also treated her as an equal, if not putting her on a pedestal at times, and that was so refreshing.

"Farida has never had this kind of threat to Kitra…not that I know of," she said to him. "I wonder how she'll take the report from you and Ayman this morning."

"From what Wyatt told me at Artemis before I came out here, Teren, he'd had a number of serious events reported by Farida and Ayman. She probably kept that intel to herself for a lot of good reasons. I don't think this potential intrusion is going to catch her off guard. It's not going to make anyone's day, but Farida strikes me as a very solid leader who's pretty much unflappable."

"I think you're right. I'm glad Artemis is working so closely with us."

"They're just coming online, but their whole focus is on keeping their locations, the people they serve, and the staff, protected."

"And I had to be the poster child they cut their teeth on," she grumped, shaking her head, frowning.

"Two years ago there was an attack on another Delos charity down in La Fortuna, Costa Rica," he told her as he looked at his watch, marking the time. "Two teachers were murdered and their school was burned to the ground. A third woman, Lia Cassidy, the administrator, escaped into the jungle and lived to tell us about it. But then the drug lord, who was pissed at them for hiding his mistress from him, took out a hit on Lia as well. That's when the Culver family kicked into gear. They hired a security contractor like me to protect her. His name is Cav Jordan. And then Dilara and Robert Culver, who own Delos, flew down there to start the rebuilding of the school and hiring new teachers. They fought back by bringing in a security team to allow the construction of the new facility to be completed. The happy ending was that the drug lord was put out of business and the children of that town are thriving with the school nearby."

"I didn't know any of this," she murmured, worried. "What happened?"

"They eventually captured the drug lord who instigated the murders and the burning of their school. Lia, the woman who survived because of her security contractor, now works at Artemis in Alexandria. So does Cav. They're happily married and working in different departments at the security company. They have a little one-year-old girl, Sophia."

"I love happy endings," Teren said, seeing the gates of Kitra in the distance. Looking at her watch, she said, "Cool-down time."

In more ways than one, Nolan thought as he cut his stride and watched her ponytail settle between her shoulders. He enjoyed seeing Teren in skimpy jogging clothes; her blue shorts and white sleeveless tee left little to his imagination. His hand itched to explore every part of her lovely, gleaming body, but he sent his desire packing, reminding himself that patience paid off—for all concerned. He just hoped that a time for loving would come sooner than later…

CHAPTER 14

ENVER UZAN LISTENED closely to Nazir, who had been employed at Kitra before being fired. They sat in a tent in the slums near Bachir's tent. Nazir was a young, restless Sudanese, sweat dripping off his dark temples, his eyes red and bloodshot. Like many child soldiers in western Sudan, he'd become addicted to heroin and cocaine, the drugs of choice given to them before they went in to kill their enemies. That way, the young boys using the AK-47s fired without feeling or social conscience. It also made them bold and risk-taking; they didn't care if they received wounds or were killed themselves. Earlier, he'd seen Nazir's forearms as he pushed up the sleeves of his white robe: a number of nicks and scars, and at least two holes indicating bullet wounds from his past.

Bachir, who was crazy as far as Uzan was concerned, had loudly boasted that he could produce one of his soldiers who had worked at Kitra. But it would cost Uzan many Sudanese pounds. The mercenary was interested in the layout of the charity, and having access to an employee who had worked there and seen it firsthand was worth the price. Besides, his employer, Zakir Sharan, was a billionaire. He could afford to lay out one thousand pounds to speak to Nazir.

Quickly, Nazir drew Kitra with a stick on the red ground between them, then proceeded to show Uzan everything. Because Kitra was so far out in the middle of the grasslands and built strategically on a small hill, it posed a number of problems for Uzan to approach it without being spotted. Studying the layout, he rubbed his neatly groomed black beard. The place was huge—much larger than he'd anticipated.

"What of security?" he demanded of Nazir.

Nazir's eyes widened. "Captain Ayman Taban has soldiers who protect Kitra."

Uzan had heard Taban's name. As a member of the upper ranks of al-Qaeda, he knew the players in all the countries of the Middle East and Africa.

"He retired and works there now?" he demanded.

"Yes, sir, he does."

Scowling, Uzan's mouth tightened. "Are sentries posted in Kitra?"

"Yes, and he has three jeeps going around outside the seven-foot red clay wall too, twenty-four hours a day."

That made things even worse for Uzan. "Are there any nearby villages?"

"Yes, one that is two miles south of Kitra. And then there are several more. Some as far away as twenty-five miles from the charity."

"Do they visit Kitra?"

Nodding, Nazir said, "From the nearest village, which has a very large herd of cattle, the women bring butter to Kitra. They exchange the butter for clothes that are sewn there or for money."

"But it's always women?"

"Yes."

"Are there camel caravans that pass nearby?"

"Sometimes, yes." Nazir brightened and sat up from where he crouched opposite Uzan. "By the time they have crossed the desert from the east, they need water. There are huge water troughs that Kitra keeps filled for all animals, but they are located outside the north wall."

"Are these caravans allowed to use them?"

"Yes. Sometimes, the master of the caravan will go inside Kitra and bargain for other things, such as the fabric and material used by the women who sew for the charity. They trade fresh dates for the material."

"Are these men allowed to walk freely around Kitra when they enter to bargain?"

"No, they are always escorted by at least one armed soldier, usually two. They are not allowed to move freely within Kitra."

Uzan scowled more deeply. "Do the people who run this charity ever go outside its walls?" If he couldn't get in, maybe he could arrange an attack against a group of them outside those big iron gates.

"Yes," Nazir said. "Kitra has its own medical doctor and staff—a doctor and three nurses. They have an optician for people who need glasses and eye examinations. There is also a dentist and two assistants. They often go by *hafla*, visiting surrounding villages, giving medical aid, vaccinations, and dental and eye care for the people. Several times a year, foreign doctors come in and volunteer their services to the villages as well."

Uzan unrolled a map, placing it down on the rug laid over the hard-packed dirt in front of him. He stared in the half-light provided by the open tent flap, studying the area surrounding Kitra. "Do they have a schedule when they do this?"

"Oh, at least once every month, two or three *haflas* bearing volunteer doctors and nurses from around the world are driven out to a faraway village, sahib."

"What about Teren Lambert? Does she ever go with them?"

"Yes, often she accompanies them, because she speaks Arabic and many of the local village dialects. She is the doctors' interpreter and translator. Her job is very important and she is always going on these rounds."

"Who else interprets for these groups?"

"Only she. It is part of her duties as an administrator to get volunteers from around the world to come into Kitra for a week to help Sudanese villagers. She maintains a monthly record of such visits by foreigners."

That looked promising to Uzan. "So, she does this monthly?"

"When I was there, she left many times each month for such duties."

"I need a schedule."

Nazir wiped his sweaty face with his large hand. "Then you need to send a man to the villages south of Kitra to find out when the next medical team is going out for a visit. News is often passed by word of mouth to nearby villages and all the people walk to the location where they'll be cared for by the medical team."

Uzan wished he had a good hacker with him so he could get him to break into Kitra's servers to snoop around. He would call Sharan about the possibility. If not successful, he was going to have to do this the old-fashioned way. "You know these villages, Nazir?"

"Yes, sahib, I do. I would often go along with them to collect medical garbage so it wouldn't be left behind in a village and spread disease."

Grunting, Uzan said, "Then get going. How long will it take you?"

"Do you want the earliest visit by the medical people? Or should I go to all villages and find out their summer schedule?"

"Find one that has the summer schedule and then see me." He'd need time to buy a group of mercenaries who weren't drugged up to their eyeballs. Uzan entertained kidnapping Teren Lambert. It appeared, under the circumstances, the easiest route to creating serious disruption to Kitra and to Delos. He stared over at the soldier. "And take no drugs. I want you clearheaded. I'll give you a satellite phone and teach you how to use it. When you arrive at a village that has Kitra's full visiting schedule, you'll call me. I'll write the information down on this map. Once you get me all the information, then I can form my plan. You'll be paid in full after you get me that intel."

Instantly, Nazir was on his sandaled feet. "Yes, sahib."

TEREN'S STOMACH WAS knotted and rolled as they completed their somber meeting for the supervisors at Kitra. No one was smiling now that Ayman and Nolan had finished giving them their briefing. Teren had sat next to Farida, who would reach over and pat her hand every once in a while, attuned to her being upset because she had been targeted by Sharan. *Who wouldn't be?* Teren wondered. It wasn't every day she was put on a hit list by a major al-Qaeda organization. There had also been a Skype session with Wyatt Lockwood, who had updated everyone from Artemis. They were sending over two drones that would be kept inside Kitra. Plus, two ex–Air Force drone pilots would be arriving with the pilotless aircraft. They would live within the walls of Kitra. That made Teren feel better. Those eyes in the sky could see for many miles, trolling along at twenty-thousand feet, unseen and unheard by those below. They would provide real-time intel for such things as Sudanese Army maneuvers, camel caravans, or anyone driving on the road to Kitra.

Sometimes, during the briefing, she'd felt Nolan's gaze on her and looked up to see him watching her. Each time, she felt that warm cloak of protection surrounding her. Teren had argued with Wyatt that she should leave Kitra to keep it safe and no longer be a target of Sharan. Wyatt had quickly punctured her argument, saying it was the charity at large that was under potential attack. And that the entire American, Turkish, and Greek families who owned Delos were also targets, not just Kitra.

She was only a "secondary target," which didn't make her feel any better.

It was near lunchtime when they broke to go back to their offices. Farida and Hadii surrounded her, hugged her, kissed her cheeks, and told her that they loved her and would protect her. It brought tears to Teren's eyes as she hugged them back. When she'd turned, Nolan was waiting at the door to the conference room. She managed a weak smile as she walked around the table and approached him.

"Why don't we have lunch at the duplex?" he said, cupping her elbow, leading her out onto the busy hall. "I think you need some quiet time."

She fell into step with him. "That obvious, huh?"

"You're pale, Teren." And then he said more gently, "You have every reason to feel the way you do."

"Yeah, I feel like one of those rabbits we see every morning out there when we jog. They're defenseless, too." She felt his fingers tighten a little more around her elbow, and she wanted to be close to him because he fed her courage, chasing some of her fear away.

"Starting tonight, I want to show you some self-defense moves so you can protect yourself if you are attacked."

"Okay, that sounds positive. But do you think that will happen?" She risked a look up at his impassive expression. Throughout the briefing, Nolan had worn his game face. She could tell nothing of what he was feeling. She was glad it came off as soon as they walked together.

"Being prepared is nine-tenths of surviving, Teren."

"You're right," she agreed, frowning.

"You already know how to use a pistol because Ayman taught you, and he's had you get out on that small shooting range outside Kitra every couple of weeks to keep your aim sharp."

"I know," she whispered. "But honestly, Nolan? I could never fire a pistol at anyone with the intent of hurting them. I just don't have it in me. I told Ayman that too, but he insisted I learn."

Nolan pushed open the main door that led out to the shady courtyard. "Don't you think you could pull a trigger if you saw a man coming at you with the intent to kidnap or harm you?"

Her stomach rolled big-time as they walked down the red tile sidewalk. Around her, many of the employees were coming out for lunch, looking forward to eating at the picnic tables beneath the shade of the trees. "I-I don't know, Nolan."

He decided to change the topic. "It's okay," he said, trying to reassure her, leading her toward her duplex. Overhead, a few puffy clouds were gathering. Nolan wished it would thunderstorm in the afternoon, cutting the unbearable heat and cooling off the burning grasslands surrounding Kitra.

Halting at her door, he opened it for her. Teren suddenly stiffened and jerked out of his grasp. He heard her gulp and give him an anxious look, her hand over her mouth as she tore past him, running down the hall toward the bathroom.

For a second, Nolan was stunned. He suddenly realized that it was Teren's sensitive-stomach issue. Cursing, he quickly shut the door, locked it, and cleared the place. Then he hurried down the hall toward where she'd disappeared.

He heard her retching and walked into her large bathroom. He felt sick himself as he saw her kneeling in front of the toilet, gripping it as she dry-heaved.

He knew she'd feel embarrassed by him seeing her like this. Grabbing a glass of water and dampening a nearby cloth, he walked over, crouching down, his arm light around her waist. He saw the abject misery in her features, the darkness in her eyes. Shakily, she took the water, drank a little, and spat into the bowl. She did it three times before returning the glass to him.

Leaning up, he flushed the toilet. And then he handed her the damp cloth.

"Here," he urged. "Wipe your nose and mouth." Helplessness clawed at Nolan. He could see the terror in her eyes as she straightened, wiping the cloth against her face with trembling fingers.

He released her waist and gently smoothed her tee against her hunched shoulders. She was shaking uncontrollably.

"I-I'm sorry," she whispered brokenly.

"Don't be," he said gruffly. He took the cloth and handed her the glass. "Rinse your mouth out one more time." Her fingers were chilled as she wrapped her hands around it, giving him a look of apology. Her face glistened with perspiration. He ached to take away her pain, her fear, stilling his hand on her shoulder, trying to steady her. When Teren was finished, he took the cup, setting it on a nearby counter. "Feel like getting up yet?"

"Just let me kneel here for a moment." She put her face in her hands and hung her head.

"Take your time," Nolan said calmly. He moved his hand across her hair, smoothing it away from her face. "It's going to be all right, Teren," he rasped, sliding his arm around her shoulders, urging her to lean against his body for support. He pressed a kiss to her hair, wanting to will away all the terror he felt around her.

Once more, Teren had pushed all her feelings deep down inside her until they welled up in the form of vomiting. Was this something she'd done as a child, too? Now he felt her lean into him, entrusting herself to him.

"Think you're going to have another round?"

With a shake of her head, she muttered, "No...I get so weak afterward. I-it takes me a few minutes to gather myself. I'm so sorry, Nolan...I didn't want you to see me like this. It's humiliating..."

The strangled emotions in her voice tore his heart open. "Hey," he growled. "No apologies. Remember, when we're scared, the body reacts. It's just what it does, Teren. There's no shame in it, sweetheart. I'm the one who should be apologizing, anyway. I pushed you over the edge." He saw her hands fall away and she barely looked up at him.

"I was already there," she admitted hoarsely. "Help me stand, Nolan, please? I want to get out of here."

He gave her a faint smile. "I'll do better than that. Hold on." In one smooth, unbroken motion, he lifted Teren into his arms, walking her out of the bathroom and taking her down the hall to her bedroom. He nudged the door open with the toe of his boot and then gently placed her on the bed.

Teren had wrapped her arms around his shoulders, wearily resting her forehead against his neck as he carried her down the hall. She trusted him, and his heart soared with that knowledge.

"Why don't you rest for a while?" He sat her down, their hips brushing against one another. He'd brought up a pale pink knitted blanket that she had on the end of her bed. Tucking it in around her to her waist, he watched her skin become less pale. What Teren needed was to be fussed over, and Nolan was more than willing to give that to her.

"Th-thanks," she whispered. She pushed some of her hair away from her face, fingers trembling. "I can't stay here long, Nolan. I have to be back at work in an hour."

He shook his head and said, "I'll let Farida know you need to take the afternoon off, Teren. She'll understand. And I won't tell her why. She knows you're upset about this. Anyone would be, so just rest. Promise?"

Closing her eyes, Teren said hollowly, "Okay…yes, call her? I can do what I need to do this afternoon from my computer here in my home office. There are a lot of things that need to be done by the end of the day, Nolan."

He patted her hip. "I'll call her. Now, go to sleep for a while. I don't think you got a lot of sleep last night, did you?"

Sighing, Teren grimaced. "No…not a lot. This is just weighing on me…"

He forced himself to rise, because what Nolan really wanted to do was curve her beside him, hold her, and allow her to feel the protection she desperately needed, but to do that would be a foolish move on his part. Teren was already vulnerable, and he knew he couldn't resist loving her if she were in his arms.

"Understandable," he agreed gently. "I'll crack the door, but I'll be around. I'm not leaving you alone here. And I'll let Farida know you're working from home this afternoon. If you need me, I'll be out in your living room."

Teren closed her eyes and moved to her side, tucking her face against the pillow, exhausted. Very soon, she spiraled into a deep, healing sleep, knowing Nolan was nearby, protecting her.

EVERY ONCE IN a while, Nolan would quietly check in on Teren. She was sleeping soundly, having pulled the pink blanket over her shoulders. What concerned him was the fact that she'd gone into a fetal position of protection, knees drawn up to her torso. It showed him just how frightened she was. The body never lied. A person could lie, but the body always told the truth. Those nonverbal reactions spoke volumes.

He had called Farida hours earlier. It was three p.m., and Nolan was going to let Teren sleep as long as she wanted. Fear physically drained people—he had seen it dozens of times while on the job. It was shock robbing the body instead of supporting it. And Ayman's unflinching report of what was going on made every supervisor in that room upset as they tried to deal with their own stunned reactions.

He imagined Teren felt like a piece of raw meat thrown out on a sidewalk with no way to protect herself in that meeting.

At four p.m. Nolan peeked into her bedroom and saw her slowly open her eyes, lying on her back, the blanket across her lower body.

"Hey, sleepyhead," he teased, easing into the room. "How are you feeling?"

Yawning, her hand against her mouth, Teren mumbled, "I just woke up…"

Nolan eased his bulk onto the edge of the bed, their hips barely touching. He saw how drowsy her eyes looked. Her hair was mussed and he slid a few strands away from her left eye. "You needed the sleep."

"I had nightmares last night," she admitted thickly, slowly pulling herself up and leaning back against the headboard. "I woke myself up screaming in one of them."

"I didn't hear you." Teren's shoulders were slumped, and she looked more like a child waking up than an adult. Coming out of sleep was when a person had no shields in place. Nolan hungrily absorbed Teren's drowsy state, seeing no fear in her eyes. Reaching out, he caressed her cheek. "You're not pale anymore, either. That's good."

Her skin was soft and firm beneath his fingertips. Her lips parted. She was pure innocence to Nolan in that moment, reacting positively to his touch, a rosy glow coming to her cheeks. It was a sign that she enjoyed it.

Something deep within Teren broke the moment Nolan slid his hand along her cheek. It was from her past. Maybe shame. Guilt? She wasn't sure. Lifting her chin, she looked directly into his eyes, saw the desire for her in their depths, felt it warmly embracing her. Without thinking, she followed her heart for once and leaned toward him, framing his face with her hands and leaning up…up to meet and slide against his mouth. She moved beyond her fear, beyond that age-old shame, because her heart blossomed fiercely beneath Nolan's care and tenderness toward her. All she wanted—and all she needed—was to kiss him, to give back to him a small token for what he'd given unselfishly to her this past week.

Nolan froze for a split second but then swept her hard against him, hungrily taking her mouth like a man starved for sustenance—for her. She drowned in the strength of his lips caressing hers. Eager to feel him closer, just as hungry as he was, she melted into his embrace, pressed against him, their hearts thundering in wild unison. Teren lost herself in his male warmth, that beautiful mouth of his teasing, cajoling, and pleasuring her until a moan rose within her, flames licking down to her nipples, her lower body clenching, which screamed to be satisfied and touched by no one else but him.

Drifting in the heat of his mouth sliding provocatively against hers, nudging open her lips, inviting her to match him, she surrendered herself to Nolan completely, giving herself to him, even her ravaged heart.

Losing herself in his scent—the sweetness of the grasslands, the dried sweat on his skin, and that aphrodisiac that was only Nolan—made her thighs clench as he moved his fingers through her hair, caressing her scalp, wild licks of electricity skittering across it. His breathing grew shallow and she opened up more to him, brushing shyly against his tongue. Teren heard him groan and the vibration rippled through her body, tightening her nipples to an almost painful degree. It had been so long since she'd wanted to be touched. Now there wasn't a place on her body where she didn't want Nolan's exploring hands.

He tore his mouth from hers, his eyes slits, burning with want of her. "Teren—"

"No, I want you," she pleaded huskily, sliding her hand across his rough bearded jaw, holding his gaze. "I need you…" She saw his gaze soften, felt a powerful wave of emotions crashing against her. "You want me. I know you do. Nothing's ever felt so right to me, Nolan…"

Teren had never begged to be loved by a man. She saw the hesitation in his eyes and tasted him on her lips, wanting to kiss him into oblivion, her fingers moving across his nape, seeing the pleasure come to his eyes as he studied her intently.

"I don't have any condoms on me, Teren."

His voice was thick with desire. She shook her head. "It's the right time of month for me, Nolan. I'm clean, sexually speaking. You?"

"Same here, I'm clean." He grazed her hair. "You're sure, Teren?"

"Very sure. I've never been more sure of anything in my life than you." She fought back hot tears. Nolan moved her soul. He didn't know it, but he held her heart in his large, calloused hands. There was so much she'd withheld from him. Teren wanted to change that, now and in the future. She saw so much in Nolan's expression: desire, torrid heat, hesitancy. Reaching up, she allowed her fingers to drift down from his jaw, across his neck to his shoulder. "I won't break," she whispered, trying to lighten the worry she saw in his expression. "It's been two years since I was with a man, so we need to go slow."

His features softened more.

"We will," he promised her thickly. "You just need to tell me if you're uncomfortable or you don't like something I do, Teren. This is about us loving one another. It's not a one-way street. All right?"

"Yes," she whispered, easing away from him, pushing the blanket aside. He wore a black T-shirt and jeans. The fabric stretched across his chest, and she allowed herself to salivate as she got on her knees and opened her hands, spreading them across Nolan's taut body, closing her eyes, absorbing him into her in every possible way. And he wasn't idle, either, pulling up the edge on her tee. In moments, he had removed the material, revealing her white cotton bra.

The instant his large, roughened palms enclosed her breasts, she whimpered, her fingers stilling on his chest. And then his thumbs caressed the tight peaks thrusting outward against the fabric and she uttered a serrated cry, the sharp electric shocks like small earthquakes rolling down through her.

Her mind disappeared. That was the only way to describe it. His hands were now commanding her body, his lips now caressing her neck, trailing a path of different, wild sensations throughout her. Teren had never experienced foreplay like this. The men she had known were always in a hurry, wanting to get into her, satisfy themselves. But Nolan was taking his time, teasing her with small nips, a lick, and then a lingering kiss across her throat, moving on to her prominent collarbones. Soft sounds left her lips, and her breathing changed, becoming more chaotic as he eased the hooks free, pulling off her bra.

CHAPTER 15

Nolan made a growling sound of pleasure as he saw how perfectly formed her breasts were. He could see the faint throb of her heart on the left side of her chest and ravished one of those hardened rosy peaks. Teren's fingers dug into his arms as he leaned down to taste the first nipple. Her cries overcame his caution and hardened him to the point of pain. *You are mine,* Nolan silently promised her as his mind began to disintegrate in the scalding heat of her twisting hips, which were begging for more of what he was giving her. He wanted to love her until he fused her body, heart, and soul to him.

Teren started to protest that she should be a full partner in their lovemaking, but Nolan shook his head, giving her a heated look. "You've had so much taken from you this week, Teren. Let me give you something that's positive in return. Just this once?"

The man had a way with words, she decided. But that didn't mean Teren was going to lie there and be passive—that wasn't in her nature. Nolan must have seen that challenging glint in her eye. "Just this once," she whispered.

"I like the wild woman you hide inside yourself, sweetheart. And I'm more than happy to see her come out and spread her wings with me."

By now, she was naked and so was he, their clothes in a heap on the tile floor near the bed. Nolan's eyes swept her from her head to her delicate toes, with a blend of lust and tenderness. He lightly moved his hand from her shoulder, gliding across her arm, and picked up her fingers and kissed each one of them.

At that point, Teren lost all arguments about sharing this session. She knew she wasn't the most experienced or skilled woman at loving a man, but what she knew she intended to share with Nolan. And as he knelt at her feet, opening her legs just enough to place his knees between them, she closed her eyes in anticipation. His fingers were long, teasing, and gentle as he caressed the outsides of her ankles and calves, moving his index fingers beneath each of her knees. A fiery bolt of pleasure raced up through her and directly into her wet, throbbing channel. Already, Teren could feel the hot juices spilling out of her body, coating the insides of her thighs.

There was magic in Nolan's exploring hands as he moved away from those erotic spots behind each of her knees and slid his fingers upward as if imprinting every inch of her into his mind and heart. He cupped each of her long, curved upper limbs and growled her name. His voice was low and alerted every nerve that he was going to take her. Teren had no idea what her body was doing at this point, lost in wave after wave of delicious heat from his caresses. He slid his hands beneath her upper legs and opened her even more. She was grateful for his slow, steady approach, because she didn't know what to expect next. Or what he expected from her. Resting her hands on his lower arms as he widened her, she saw his eyes become hooded and fiercely intense. She held his gaze, her heart pounding, the throb increasing at her aching gate.

NOLAN EASED HIS hands from beneath her firm, strong thighs and blanketed her with his body. She was so slender and rounded beneath him as he leaned over, taking her lips, cherishing her. Teren responded instantly, her fingers curving around his shoulders, wanting to pull him down upon her. Already, as he worshipped her soft, opening mouth, wet with so much promise, he could smell her sex scent, and it flowed like a hungry, awakening river through him.

Nolan wanted to rush but knew better. She hadn't had sex in two years, which was like being a virgin all over again. More than anything, he wanted Teren so wet that she would dampen the blanket beneath her. He wanted her ripe, needing him as urgently as he needed her.

When he left her lips, Teren's fingers dug into his shoulders, her hips mercilessly rubbing against his thick erection. Nolan gritted his teeth to control himself. Yeah, she was a wild one, all right, so natural and uninhibited with him. That was a gift too, and Nolan recognized it as just another wonderful facet of Teren. He appreciated the restless strength of her body matching, stroking, and teasing his.

Nolan rose up, seeking and finding one of her taut nipples, pulling it strongly into his mouth, suckling her without mercy. She came apart on him, her long legs threading between his, capturing him, holding his hips in place so she could arch against his erection. The move exploded his mind and he thrust slowly into her, feeling just how damned tight she really was. But she was wet. Her juices were warm and thickly coating him the moment he made a few short, rhythmic pulses inside her.

Nolan wasn't prepared for the orgasm that he triggered in her as he lavished that swollen pearl at her entrance with only a few strokes. He'd done so little to tease one out of her, and yet her hoarse shout of surprise, her back arching against him, her fingers tight against his shoulders, told him it was one hell of an orgasm. And he was going to prolong it for her, easing more deeply into her, his strokes longer, more powerful, drowning in the beauty of her sobs and cries. For someone as slender and graceful as she was, Teren was damned strong, clutching him, but he twisted and moved his hips with controlled strength, feeling her juices pour around him, lubricating her so that he could continue to cradle her within the rapture he saw in her features.

Teren lay panting and gasping beneath him as the orgasm finally began to subside. It made Nolan feel good to see that rosy flush blossom across her upper body, flood her features, her eyes dazed with satiation as she lay limp beneath him.

He stilled himself, giving her the time she needed to allow her shattering orgasm to continue giving her ripples of heat that massaged her lower body. The ecstasy shining in her eyes made him smile.

"That good, huh?" he teased, keeping most of his weight off her except where they were joined.

"Oh…" she managed to say. "What on earth happened?"

Taken aback, Nolan grinned. "Really? Tell me you've had orgasms before…"

Rolling her head weakly from side to side, Teren couldn't even lift her hand, she felt so exhausted by the experience. "Is that what it was?" She licked her lips, feeling the currents of electricity continuing to throb and crackle deep within her. She felt awash with excruciating pleasure she'd never felt before.

Nolan moved his hand slowly up Teren's arm, feeling the dampness of her flesh, shocked by her reply but hiding his reaction. He wasn't going to humiliate her by saying something stupid like, "I thought all women knew what an orgasm felt like." That wasn't true. It's just that the women he'd bedded knew the score, wanted to be pleased as much as he did, so it was mutual and satisfying as partners to know what was expected from one another.

He studied her, soft strands stuck to her brow, absorbing this special moment of discovery with her. Pride rose within him; he knew he'd introduced her to a realm of incredible satisfaction. His lips twitched as she closed her eyes, and she made a pleased sound in her throat, a careless smile floating across her well-kissed lips.

At that moment, his heart opened wide to Teren. This was where he could introduce her to a whole new world: erotic pleasure of the finest kind. He'd had a lot of female bed partners as a Delta Force operator before marrying Linda, and they'd taught him a lot. And he was grateful, because now he could teach Teren about this new world she'd just stumbled into with him.

"This is just the best," Teren drawled, her Southern accent more noticeable, barely opening her eyes, looking up at Nolan, thinking how handsome he was. And he was hers. She could feel him thick and hard within her, and never had she felt more satisfied than right now. This man knew how to love her, no question. She weakly lifted her hand, fingers caressing his thick, hard biceps. "You know, Farida and Hadii were always telling me about how wonderful it was to have an orgasm. I pretended to know what they were talking about." She frowned and looked away for a moment. "I was afraid to admit to them I didn't know what one was."

Nolan leaned over, kissing her brow, then her cheek, and rasped, "It's okay that you didn't admit it. That's our little secret." He lifted his head, holding her adoring gaze. He swore he saw something shining in her eyes for him. He didn't want to call it love. Maybe lust? Yet their connection with one another was palpable. Beautiful.

They barely knew one another, and yet, lying here, blanketing her body with his, nothing had ever felt so right to him. He felt as if he'd come home, and the realization skittered through him like sunlight spread across a dark, barren land that he'd inhabited for too long. Teren made him feel again. Fully. Completely.

Nolan drew strands away from her brow, memorizing this moment because it was so special and life-altering. Teren's mouth was so beautifully shaped, and when those soft corners rose a little, he smiled, too, feeling her trust.

He twisted his hips slightly and she whimpered, her smile increasing, lashes sweeping downward.

"That feels so good, Nolan." She slid her hands across his powerful shoulders, raising her hips, moving with him, loving how in sync they were with one another. "Don't…stop…please…"

A sound of agreement rumbled through his chest as he eased as deep as he could go inside her. Teren was limber, athletic, passionate, and unafraid to meet and meld with him. "Let's see if we can coax your body to gift you again," he growled, and he leaned down, capturing her other nipple, sucking it just enough to make her gasp, because he knew the sensation would send her body bursting into another realm of rapture. And it did. Her hips ground against his and her breath quickened, turning into a pant as he thrust long and steadily, reaching that sweet spot so deep within her.

This time he was going to release his steel control. This time, he was going to ride that explosive wave he felt beginning to release within her.

Teren's whole world shimmered before her closed eyes; she felt as if there were fireworks going off deep within her. Nolan was thrusting into her, and each time he stroked that spot, more of her orgasm reacted to his powerful caress within her. She cried out, feeling him suddenly grow rigid, hearing him grunt, an explosive breath leaving his contorted lips. She whirled into the scalding heat of that second violent orgasm. This one threw her into a rapturous state, floating as she felt his damp skin sliding against her own, his hot breath against her face. And then he climaxed, growling her name, framing her face between his large hands, his perspiring brow pressed against her own. She swam in such pleasure that all she could do was moan and cry out. At last, she had felt the power of what Farida and Hadii had called "good loving."

NOLAN SLOWLY ROUSED himself. After that climax, he had been utterly spent and he'd eased out of Teren, drawing her back into his arms and cradling her beside him. He'd haphazardly pulled that blanket over both of them after capturing her long legs within his. Teren had nestled her head against his neck, her arm limp across his torso, plastered sweetly against him, warm, damp, sharing that musky sexual scent. She fell asleep immediately, but he forced himself to remain awake for a while, because he wanted to remember how it felt to lie with a woman who had loved him with such an open heart and untrammeled passion.

Nolan knew without a doubt that he and Teren could fall in love with one another. It didn't matter whether they said the words, admitted it, or even discussed it. He knew it. Just as he'd known when he had met Linda that she was the woman he would marry. Maybe it was part of how he saw his black-and-white world.

Just as when they met, he knew she was the right woman for him, Teren had experienced the same thing. Nolan had never thought he'd find another woman he could envision a life with, but he had. And in one of the remotest places on the planet. *Go figure.*

He inhaled her subtle cinnamon fragrance, sure now that she used it in a spicy oil on her hair. Her sex scent combined with that fragrance on her skin drove him crazy, making him want her once more. Moving his hand, he caressed Teren's shoulder, allowing his fingers to trail down her long, curved spine. She had such a sweet ass, her cheeks full, in part, due to her jogging. Teren was in remarkable shape for someone who sat at a desk five days a week. His mouth curved faintly. He liked caressing her, feeling the satin firmness of her skin beneath his roughened fingertips. He loved how her slow, moist breath fanned across his neck and upper chest.

Closing his eyes, Nolan felt like a desperate thief, wanting to remember every second of his time spent with Teren. His world was one of constant chaos and change. And with the danger swirling around them right now, he couldn't even plan anything with her—for them—although he wanted to. He wanted to take her to meet his charming, sweet-natured mother in Galway Bay. Nolan knew they'd get along well.

He wanted to take her to his farmhouse he'd bought outside Alexandria, Virginia. He was ten miles from the security company, in a home situated on thirty acres of rolling green grass and a stand of woods nearby. The farmhouse was over a hundred years old, and it needed a lot of work. Nolan had bought it thinking that between assignments, he would gut the place, take it back to its original condition, and over time, restore it. The money he made as a security operator was a hundred and fifty thousand dollars a year, enough to easily cover the expenses of reclaiming his new home. And now he dreamed of taking Teren to some of the finest antique stores in the area to hunt for period pieces to decorate the place once the rooms were finished—providing she liked old things. She might have other ideas.

He smiled. It didn't matter to him, because all he wanted to do was make her happy. That farmhouse would reflect both of them, but mostly her, and Nolan was fine with that.

Yet, in another way, that farmhouse reflected him: both were in desperate need of inner repair, a mess right now. Symbolically, Nolan saw Teren as the reason to support his own healing work, to finally release the past, to make peace with it so he could have a present and future once more. She brought new possibilities and new life to him. It surged through him twenty-four hours a day since he'd met her. He could only feel it, absorb it, and then feel her care for him, healing him in some of the darkest corners of himself.

Teren realized none of this, but Nolan would share it with her when the time was right.

And with those last thoughts, Nolan dropped off into a deep, restorative sleep himself, Teren warm, soft, and sweet against him.

TEREN WAS DISORIENTED as she slowly pulled out of the halls of sleep. Her first impression, one that powerfully opened her heart, was that she was in Nolan's arms, sleeping against his long, hard body. She became aware of his slow, deep breathing, his one arm curved around her shoulders, keeping her as close as she could get to him. Forcing her eyes open, she saw it was dark. She had no idea how much time had passed. The blanket covered her and she was warm. Just getting used to seeing Nolan's tight, solid form following the line of her own body made her smile a little. Her lower body was cranky now, but she knew why. Nolan wasn't a normal-sized man and she hadn't had sex in years. What amazed her was the warmth still radiating within her from those earth-shattering orgasms he'd coaxed out of her. Now Teren knew what that achy feeling meant.

She had to ask herself, was she falling in love with Nolan? It was there, hanging silently before her. Teren had always wanted to fall in love but never thought she would. How she felt toward Nolan was so refreshingly different from the feelings she'd had for the few other lovers in her life. It was so rich, intense, and filled with promise.

She slid her hand across his chest, the silky, dark strands moving between her exploring fingers. While Nolan made her feel safe in a whole new way, she felt equally fervent about protecting him. And she found herself worrying about him. She'd never worried about a man before this.

Bottom line, Teren didn't want to lose Nolan now that she had discovered him. She wanted to spend every moment she could with him, sleep at his side each night, make love with him, pleasure him like he'd pleasured her. Those were her new priorities.

A niggling doubt slithered through her, dampening some of her idealism and need for Nolan. She hoped it was something serious and possibly long-lasting taking root between them. Hadii and Farida had told her on many occasions about what love was, what it looked like, how a man acted toward the woman he loved and how it affected a woman's heart, mind, and soul. If they were right, Teren had already seen what she thought might be love in Nolan's eyes when he looked at her. He didn't hide how he felt, and she was grateful. And she had all the signs and symptoms of beginning to fall in love with him, according to her two friends.

Alas, that created another, much larger problem. It stared at her like the monster from her past that it was. Fear grew in Teren as she wondered what Nolan would think of her decision at the age of eighteen. Would he see her differently when she told him the truth? Would he harshly judge her as her family and community had? That niggling fear turned into bona fide terror within Teren.

Her palm lay against Nolan's heart. She could feel the slow, solid thud of it. How badly she wanted to keep him in her life. The way he looked at her made her feel incredibly beautiful, wanton, and unafraid. Nolan seemed to revel in her being fully who she really was. But her past was not perfect. Far from it. And it could make him lose respect for her, become disappointed in her, or worse, be ashamed of her choices and not want anything to do with her ever again.

More than anything, she knew she had to divulge the truth to Nolan. This couldn't wait. Teren had not planned to be in bed with him, to have him love her so well and so thoroughly. It had just happened. There was such a naturalness that vibrated subtly between them, a trusting openness each gave to the other. Would Teren's revelations break the connection she cherished so much with him? Her past could shatter her present. Destroy it. She wanted to cry but forced back the reaction.

As if sensing her confusion, Nolan awakened. She felt him move his hand that rested above the blanket across her waist, tighten momentarily and then lift away. His fingers trailed down her cheek, nudging aside thick strands of hair that had fallen across her face. Hungrily, Teren absorbed his contact, wanting so badly to have Nolan touch her tenderly, just like this, forever.

"You all right?" Nolan muttered drowsily, pushing himself up on one elbow, staring down at Teren. He could feel an edginess to her. Was she sorry she'd gone to bed with him? He searched her dark gray eyes, sensing a lot of turmoil. Sliding his hand against her jaw, trying to soothe her, he saw her eyes fill with tears.

"Talk to me," he coaxed gruffly, feeling a sense of dread. "What's wrong, Teren?" His voice, at first drowsy with sleep, was now fully alert.

"I need to tell you something, Nolan," she whispered, pulling out of his embrace. Lamenting the loss of his holding her, Teren slowly sat up, pulling the blanket around her waist, tucking her leg beneath her and keeping the other half across his lower body. Her heart pounded in her chest as she prepared to tell Nolan about her past.

He looked boyish right now, all the normal hardness she saw in his face during the day gone. His brows dipped and she felt his full and immediate focus.

"Okay," he rasped, pushing upward. "But you're going to tell me with you in my arms. Come here." Nolan leaned back against the headboard and then coaxed Teren into his arms, pulling the blanket up, covering her. He watched her gulp several times, as if trying to stop unknown emotions from surfacing within her.

Nolan situated Teren against him, her leg across his, and he arranged the fabric around her waist, making sure she was kept warm. "Now," he said gruffly, kissing her hair, "tell me what's bothering you."

A part of him was relieved as she sighed and laid her head on his shoulder, her palm coming to rest on the center of his chest. At least she hadn't pushed him away. Then he felt her tense, as if struggling with some invisible energy. He kissed her forehead and eased his fingers across her temple, pushing her dark hair aside so he could fully look into her eyes, now glistening with tears.

Her voice was low and torn-sounding. "Nolan...I've lived in fear of telling you about this . . ."

He felt her tremble and wanted to soothe her worries. "Whatever it is," he promised, "we'll handle it together, Teren. All right?"

Just his reassurance gave Teren the courage she needed. "Okay," she managed to say, her voice strained. She flattened her palm against his chest, desperately grateful for his arms around her. They gave her the strength to speak.

"After I graduated from high school, I'd never been so happy. I left for a nearby community college in a much larger town near Louisville. It was the first time I'd ever been alone in such a large city, Nolan. I was starry-eyed, excited, and so happy to be free of my smothering family. I signed up for a degree in computer science and had my whole life planned. I was going to get a two-year degree. My family didn't have money to send me, so I went out and found two part-time jobs, both waitressing. I lived in a small apartment off campus with two other girls who were doing the same thing I was."

Nolan moved his fingers slowly up and down her arm, feeling Teren begin to relax just a tad. Her words were rushed, tumbling out of her. Sensing something tragic in the offing, he eased his fingers through her clean, silky hair, knowing how much she enjoyed that. "You had a rough road ahead of you, Teren, but you had a dream to fulfill and you went after it. I'm proud of you."

Nolan heard her draw in a jerky breath and then relax just a tiny bit more in his arms, but she was still on guard, as if trying to protect herself from an imminent blow. He squeezed her gently, rasping against her ear, "Tell me. Remember, we're in this together, Teren. We'll handle it, sweetheart."

She shut her eyes, and two tears squeezed from them, running down her pale cheeks. Her fingers tightened against his chest. "I'd just started school, Nolan. I-I was suddenly feeling like I was in the eye of a hurricane. I had so many boys wanting to go out with me and date me. I'd never had a boyfriend before. It threw me off. I loved their attention. I thought it was wonderful, but I felt scared and confused because I didn't know what I should do or say. One guy, Tony, was really complimentary. He would show up after my classes, carry my books for me, ask me out to have a hamburger at the student union. He made me laugh. And I loved that he devoted so much attention to me." She took a deep breath and pressed her face into his neck. "It hurts so much to admit all this…"

"You were innocent, Teren. You came out of a rural environment. And you weren't socialized to the world of boys dating girls. I'm sure you felt uncomfortable, and you were exploring yourself and men. There's nothing wrong with that. It's a natural occurrence."

A tiny trickle of relief shot through Teren. Nolan understood. "You're right. I didn't know what was happening. All I knew was that I felt so special, when I'd never felt that way before."

"Sweetheart, you're a beautiful young woman. I imagine at eighteen you looked so damned fresh and innocent to a lot of those guys who were a lot more experienced and on the prowl for someone just like you. But you didn't know that, so there's no crime in you not realizing it." Again, he squeezed her a little more closely to him, wanting to give Teren emotional support.

Lifting her hand, Teren quickly wiped the tears off her face. "Believe me, I know that now. I didn't know it then, which is what got me in so much trouble, Nolan."

"Go on," he urged her quietly.

Teren hadn't realized how desperate she was to hear Nolan's low, thick voice against her ear. She moved her hand restlessly across his chest, the words strained. "Tony prided himself on knowing about all kinds of wines. I had never had a drink of alcohol in my life, Nolan. He would sit and show me books on types of wine. He was always excited by the different reds and whites. And he taught me about them. One night, he said he'd borrowed a friend's car and we were going to go to a wine tasting. I wasn't sure I wanted to go, but he insisted and I gave in."

"Why did you hesitate?"

She compressed her lips. "I-I don't know. Something didn't feel right, but I didn't want to disappoint him. I was afraid he'd drop me. I finally had a boyfriend for the first time in my life and I didn't want to lose him."

"Well," Nolan said, "that about sums up every eighteen-year-old girl's thoughts." He cut her an amused look. "Right?"

"When I was in high school, girls who were fifteen or older had boyfriends, and I never had one. I guess I was jealous."

"And now that you had one? All of that played into your decision?"

Nodding, she said in a disappointed tone, "Yes."

"Teenagers make more mistakes per square inch than any other age group," Nolan informed her. "Twenty-somethings aren't far behind. That's how we learn, Teren. Maybe our parents told us to not do this or that, but we didn't always listen. We were at an age of what I call 'exploration,' taking risks and finding out what each of our choices taught us."

"I see that now. I wish I'd seen it then."

"Did Tony take you to a wine tasting?"

"He took me to a seedy motel. I asked him why we were there. He said the wine tasting was in a room. We'd go there and taste different wines. I was scared, but I didn't want to make a scene because he was so convincing, smiling, and telling me I'd enjoy it." Teren pushed the tears off her face. "There were three bottles of wine on a dresser in that motel room. I'd never been in a motel before, so I was curious. Tony poured me a little wine and asked me to taste it. He asked me to sit down and I did. I drank some of it and it tasted god-awful."

"A taste for wine is something we develop," Nolan said, seeing her eyes darken.

"I guess. It tasted horribly sour and bad. He urged me to drink the whole glass."

"A whole glass of wine?" Nolan asked, alarmed.

"Yes. Why?" Teren twisted a look up at him.

"At a wine tasting? There's usually half an ounce to an ounce of a particular wine in a glass. He didn't bring you there for that. He'd tricked you."

"Oh." Teren gave him a frustrated look. "See? Even now, I didn't know that."

"What happened then?" Nolan coaxed, drying her damp cheek with his thumb.

"I remember I got up and felt horribly tired, like I wanted to go to sleep immediately. It was the weirdest thing, Nolan. My feet felt like they'd suddenly grown twenty-pound weights on each of them. I found it hard to talk, to think…"

Nolan tried to keep the anger out of his tone. "He drugged you, Teren."

"Yes, only I didn't know that until the next day when I found myself naked, lying on the bed, and Tony was gone." She felt Nolan tense. He slid his arm around her, holding her tightly against him. Never had his embrace felt so welcome, so strong.

"He drugged and raped you, didn't he?"

Teren heard his tightly controlled lethal tone and closed her eyes, nodding. "I didn't know what happened," she whispered, her voice scratchy. "I was cold because there was no heat in the room; all my clothes were in a pile by the side of the bed. I felt sore and my lower body hurt."

Nolan mentally cursed, continuing to move his hand soothingly up and down her back, feeling the tension in her. "You'd been a virgin."

"Yes."

"What did you do then?" he asked, easing his arms open enough so that he could face her, look into her glistening eyes, which reflected so much hurt.

"I don't know what all he did. I found bite marks on my breasts, on my stomach, and on the insides of my thighs. I saw blood on the covers. I was sore and I hurt." She glanced up at Nolan, his face tight, mouth thinned, eyes filled with rage. But he was holding her gently, giving her the strength to go on. "I took a shower, cleaned myself off the best I could. I threw up several times. I was so miserable, and it was almost too much to try to think what to do next."

"Because the drug was still in your bloodstream—that's probably why you threw up." Nolan felt the urge to find this bastard but held on to his emotions, knowing that if he appeared upset, Teren would retreat and possibly stop sharing the incident. He knew her well enough to know he should remain stable and level-headed to keep her calm.

"Yes. I walked three miles back to the apartment. My roommate knew something was wrong and asked me, but I wouldn't tell her anything. I went to my room and slept the rest of the day."

"Did you confront Tony?"

"No. I was afraid to. He disappeared for about two weeks and then he came back, using that same charm, that same smile on me. He said he wanted to take me to another motel."

"The bastard had balls," Nolan growled.

"I told him no. I told him to go away and leave me alone. He got really angry, his hands curled into fists, and he scared me to death with his temper. I got away from him as fast as I could."

"Did he leave you alone, though?"

Teren heard the wariness in Nolan's tone. "He began to stalk me. I was so scared. About three months after he'd raped me, I began throwing up every morning. My roommate knew by this time what Tony had done to me. She said I was probably pregnant." Risking a look over at Nolan, she saw bleakness come to his narrowed eyes. His arms automatically tightened around her.

Teren forced herself to push forward. "The test came back, and it showed I was pregnant. I didn't know what to do, Nolan. I couldn't go home and tell my parents what happened. They'd have been ashamed of me. They'd have shunned me, and I was afraid they'd disown me and kick me out of the house, telling me to never come back to see them again. And my three brothers? My God, if they'd found out, they'd have crucified me with questions until I told them it was Tony. And then they'd have gone after him and probably killed him."

"What did you do?" he asked her quietly, cupping her face, holding her stormy gaze.

"This is the worst part," she warned him. Without thinking she pulled his hand from her cheek, gripping it, holding it in her lap. "I went to Tony and told him he'd gotten me pregnant. He became very quiet. He said we needed to talk, that he'd take care of the situation. He'd help me. I was angry at him then, but he grabbed me by the arm and hauled me out of the college and into his car. He said we were going somewhere. I screamed at him to let me out, but he'd locked the door. When we arrived at that same horrible, seedy motel, I started crying. I thought he was going to rape me again. I fought him, but he was too strong. He got me into a first-floor room and slammed the door, locking it behind him."

She felt Nolan's hand, so warm and comforting, twine with her damp fingers. Teren felt if she didn't grip his large, callused hand, she'd be lost.

"I tried to run past him, tried to rip that door open. The next thing I knew, he'd hit me so hard in the jaw, I felt bones breaking in my face. I remember falling…and that's all…"

Sniffing, Teren didn't have the courage to look at Nolan. Gripping his hand, she closed her eyes, the words tumbling out of her. "I woke up three weeks later in a hospital. My parents were there, standing guard over me. At first, I didn't even remember my name, but over the hours after I became conscious, I started remembering things. My parents just sat there, staring at me. I felt horrible. They left and later, the doctor came in. He checked me out, and then a nurse came in and told me I'd had a miscarriage, that I'd lost my baby. She went through a list of broken bones I'd sustained. I just lay there, not able to really comprehend it all."

"He beat the hell out of you," Nolan ground out, holding her close, wanting to protect her but unable. "He probably counted on knocking you out and then hitting you in the belly to force the miscarriage."

She felt so tired and worn, as if carrying this load by herself for so long had taken an enormous toll on her soul. "Yes, that's what the nurse told me. Only, when he hit me in the face several times, he gave me a serious concussion, and I was in a coma for three weeks. I don't remember much after that. I know I slept a lot. And every time I'd wake up, one of my family or one of the parishioners from our church was with me. It helped me. I felt guilty and ashamed. The women who came and sat and prayed for me from the church didn't look at me like I was a slut. Some were even kind to me, and I needed that so badly…"

It took every kind of control that Nolan had ever had to remain relaxed, allowing Teren a place to hide and tell her story. He'd seen that her nose had been broken previously the first day he'd met her, but he'd had no idea how it had occurred. A killing rage flowed through him. "How were you feeling then about the baby?" Nolan knew how much she loved those Sudanese children, and they loved her equally. They were always tagging along with her, holding her hands, pulling on her pant legs, touching her, wanting to be close to her. Teren was a natural mother. And to lose her child like that?

Gently, he kissed her cheek, feeling the wetness of her tears beneath his mouth. She was crying silently, clinging to him, her head buried beneath his chin, holding him. Holding on.

After weeping, she said, "It took me a couple of years, Nolan, to come to grips with all of it. I was so young, so green. The grief over the loss of my baby was the last to come up and be dealt with. First, I had to deal with the shame and humiliation my family put me through. In their eyes, I'd sinned so badly there was no forgiveness ever coming from them. They shunned me."

Shaking her head, Teren felt so much of her fear dissolving beneath Nolan's quiet, steadying presence. She was amazed he wasn't judging her like everyone else had. It gave her even more courage to say, "I ended up, after getting well, having to go to court and testify against Tony. The jury gave him twenty-five years in prison. That was a relief, because I'd feared he would be set free, and that he'd find and kill me the next time."

Smoothing her hair, Nolan kissed her temple, grazing her shoulders, trying to get her to release the backlog of tension she carried in them. "Yeah, he would have, Teren. What did you do then?"

"I went back to school and finished my degree. I couldn't go home. I was persona non grata to everyone. I put my head down, took on two part-time jobs, paid my way through the two-year course in computer science, and graduated. At one of the job fairs on campus, I met some wonderful people from Delos. They were hiring programmers, but they needed them for fieldwork in third-world countries. When I found out that they had a charity near Khartoum, Sudan, I leaped at the chance, and they hired me on the spot. I spent a year in Darfur and then transferred here to Kitra."

Brushing the dark hair sprinkled across his chest, she added, "I've never been sorry for my decision. Living here at Kitra has been so very healing for me, Nolan. Farida and Hadii adopted me like the lost puppy I was. They always teased me that I was their younger sister whose skin was lighter than theirs, but we carried the same color of blood, the same heart. I liked the way they saw me. I wasn't white and they weren't black. We were women who lived our lives loving what we were doing. That brought us together as a wonderful team that's been so great for the past seven years."

"And your baby? When did that loss hit you?" Nolan knew it had taken him years afterward to come out of the shock of losing Linda. One day, unexpectedly, the grief exploded through him, hurling him into a vat so painful and filled with loss, he thought he'd never make his way through it all. But he had. Barely.

Looking down at Teren, he eased her against his shoulder, studying her in the near-darkness, her cheeks glistening with tears. The small light out in the hall shed just enough illumination into the room so he could see her anguished eyes.

"The third year I was here at Kitra, there was a rash of abused women who had come to Kitra pregnant. It just ripped off that scab inside me." She grimaced and looked away. "I wasn't much good for about three months after that, paralyzed by the grief of losing my own baby. I never told anyone why. Farida and Hadii thought it was my reaction to the losses of the women. They weren't far from the truth…"

"I'm glad they were here to support you," he whispered, shaking his head. "You're so damn strong, Teren. You really are."

"I don't feel strong, Nolan. I feel a hollowness right here." She pressed her hand against her belly. "Even now, I sometimes dream about my lost baby coming to me, and we talk and we laugh with one another. I always wake up with this ache of loss in my heart. Every time that dream happens, it heals another little part of me."

"Yeah," he rumbled. "It sure as hell is a process, isn't it?"

She gave him a sad look of understanding. "You lost your wife and your baby. I just can't imagine what you've gone through, Nolan." She eased away from him, sitting up, facing him, her legs crossed beneath the blanket. "You aren't judging me, are you?"

He gave her a perplexed look. "No. Why would I do that, Teren? You didn't do anything wrong. You were young and innocent, and you trusted. You did the best you could at the time."

She pulled in a ragged breath. "I thought...well...I thought you might not want to be around me anymore after you found out what I did."

Nolan stared at her, the silence thickening. "Let's get this clear, Teren: you did not do this to yourself. It was done *to* you. Tony drugged and raped you. Got you pregnant. And then when he found out, he wanted to get rid of the baby. And I think he really wanted to kill you and probably thought he had." His mouth turned downward, his words grating. "But you lived, Teren. You survived."

"I carry so much guilt over it, Nolan. Even to this day..."

"Because your family sees you as having done something wrong."

"Yes. I'm older now, but it still sneaks up on me sometimes. Most days," Teren shrugged wearily, "I blow it off. But when you came smashing into my life, I was so drawn to you, it scared me."

"Did you think I was another Tony?"

"No...never. You're the exact opposite of him, Nolan. What I did fear was you knowing what had happened to me, that you'd blame me for it, for my poor choices, or see me as something less than you saw me before."

She bit down on her lower lip, watching his expression turn tender. He reached out to her.

"I don't want you away from me right now, Teren. Come here." He held his hand out to her. He could see her need to be silently supported and loved no matter what she thought she'd done. Nolan realized that she was still seeing life through that faulty lens of her parents' misshapen religious beliefs, making her feel judged and hounding her to this day. At least she was aware of it and was fighting not to let it run her life.

When she placed her damp fingers into his hand, he smiled gently, tugging her back into his arms—where she belonged. And if he had anything to say about it, she would be staying with him forever.

CHAPTER 16

TEREN WAS HAPPY—THERE was no getting around it. Where had two weeks gone? She was sitting with the children around the fountain, waiting for Nolan, who was finishing up a meeting with Ayman in his office. The children, boys and girls, all between four and eight years old, squirmed and wanted to get as close as they could to her, like little bookends. Two girls sat in her lap. The boys crowded on either side of her. She drank in their smiles, the happy glow in their brown eyes. Their laughter made her heart expand even more—if that was possible.

It was five thirty p.m., and everyone was lining up at the dining room entrance. The children standing in line with their mothers had spotted her and raced over to where she was sitting. Within moments, Teren was laughing with them, kissing them, ruffling their neatly cut hair, and enclosing her arms around as many as she could fit beside her. The mothers in line smiled and waved in her direction. Often in the past, when Teren had time, she would help out at the childcare center with the Sudanese women who ran that portion of Kitra. She loved playing with the children, enjoying their innate intelligence, burning curiosity, and innocent trust of everyone.

The heat today was at its maximum, nearly a hundred degrees. Breathing was like drawing superheated air into her lungs. Teren would be glad to see September come, when it would be a little less hot. The sky was a pale, cloudless blue. For the moment, she forgot about Enver Uzan and Zakir Sharan's promise to harm Kitra—or her.

The last two weeks had been a dream. Every night she slept with Nolan. And nearly every night, they made love to one another. Her body glowed with the memory of his skills and loving her. Teren wasn't sure if it was love, since neither had said the word. Perhaps it was care? She railed silently over her lack of experience in relationships. Judging from what Hadii and Farida had said about what it felt like being in love, she was falling in love with Nolan. Every day, in so many large and small ways, he showed his care for her, and Teren tried to do the same.

Now Teren smiled at the wriggling, giggling children surrounding her and spoke to them in Arabic and English. All children at Kitra were taught both languages, which would give them a huge advantage as they grew up. Anyone who knew English could get a job over someone who did not, since English was the primary international language.

When she spotted Nolan leaving the building and walking down the courtyard, her heart swelled with fierce emotion for him. Every day, he wore that safari jacket. She knew there was a pistol beneath its folds. He was her guard and never lost his focus. Only when they were alone, in their duplex, would he relax. Even then, Teren could feel his alertness, although it wasn't obvious. It was just a sense around him that she'd picked up. And every day they had become more and more in tune with one another. They were starting to finish sentences for one another, and when it happened, they'd laugh over it.

She felt heat stirring deep within her as she met his narrowing eyes, and felt that incredible, invisible embrace surround her. She hoped she knew what it was: the love he felt for her. That and a sense of protection, which was helping her cope with the present threat that hung silently over their heads.

As Nolan neared, he slowed down, his eyes growing amused, a smile tugging at the corners of his mouth. The children called him "Asad," or "the Lion." In their world, where they were still open and trusted their instincts, they sensed Nolan's power but were unafraid of him. Teren knew that these children—at least many of them—had been abused by their fathers or other male relatives. But with Nolan, they showed that they loved him. It was as if they sensed the same thing around him as she did: that he was a big, strong, devoted guard dog. However, in their world, where the lion ruled, they saw him as the lordly king of the desert—admiring, respectful, but still loving them openly because like her, he gave them affection. In fact, in the past two weeks, Teren had seen the children begin to gravitate to him just as much as they did to her.

Nolan was showing these children that a man could be affectionate, kiss, hug, and laugh with them. Teren looked forward to coming to the fountain with Nolan, because the kids, with their invisible antennae, always knew when they would arrive. They'd come racing around the building to join them. If it was during the heat of the day, and everyone was suffering from the burning sun overhead, Nolan usually engaged the boys in a water fight. And then the little girls got involved, as did Teren. They all ended up wet, dripping, and laughing. Within fifteen minutes afterward, their clothes had dried out. And sometimes the employees, if free for a few minutes, would come and join them. Water always splotched around the fountain afterward, everyone grinning, wet, and feeling cooler in the unrelenting heat.

Several of the boys broke from beneath Teren's arms, rushing down the red tiled walk toward Nolan, calling, "Asad! Asad!" Two more little girls snuggled in coyly beneath her arms, smiling up sweetly at her. Teren smiled down at them, her arms curving around them. Laughter bubbled up in her throat as the two young boys, ages four and six, flew down the walk, arms wide open, flinging themselves at Nolan. She watched as he knelt down on one knee, grinning, calling them by name, his arms open to embrace them. The boys slammed into his hard body, screeching with delight. Nolan easily took their tiny hurtling forms into him, their thin arms wrapping eagerly around his neck. She heard them begging him to lift them up and carry them, one of their favorite games with him. He would offer children horseback rides and make neighing sounds, then go galloping around the fountain with one of them. And then he'd offload that child and take the next one begging for a ride. Teren had seen him do a circuit around the fountain twenty times for twenty excited children. Horseback rides were an American thing, and Teren would sit at the fountain, watching the sheer joy and anticipation mirrored in each child's face and in the faces of their mothers.

Nolan had brought a positive male influence to Kitra—just as the Sudanese men who worked here did. It was good that these abuse survivors had this experience with such men.

Nolan picked up the boys easily in his arms and they shrieked, hugging him with their child's strength. He grinned past them, holding Teren's smile, her eyes clear and light with joy. His heart raced with such intense and powerful feelings of love for this woman. As he deposited his two boys on the concrete lip where Teren sat with the rest of the children, he told the boys in Arabic that no, there wouldn't be any horseback rides right now. Each boy looked disappointed, making sad little sounds, their expressions pleading as they begged Nolan to give them a ride anyway.

He ruffled their hair and told them no. The boys made more sounds and kept holding on to his hand and jacket, giving him pleading looks.

"You've really started something with horseback rides," Teren said, chuckling as she released her children, gently urging them back to their mothers, who were just about ready to enter the dining room.

"Tell me about it," he said, grinning. The flock of children scattered like startled birds, heading back to their mothers. In a few moments Nolan found himself alone with Teren. His smile deepened as he placed his arm around her waist, wanting to kiss her but refraining in public. Nolan was aware of Teren's stature here at Kitra and didn't want to diminish it. Children especially found their affectionate public behavior strange. In the Sudanese culture, women were separated from men, unlike in America. The children found them fascinating and curious, always watching them.

"Ready for dinner? I don't know about you, but I'm starved." Nolan walked with her toward their duplex down at the bottom of the small knoll. He kept his hand around her waist and enjoyed how her slender body touched his as they walked. She looked wanton, her hair caught up on top of her head with that clip, loose strands straight and falling on each side of her face. Her favorite color, he'd discovered, was pink. Today, she was wearing a cap-sleeved pale pink tee, her ivory cargo pants, which hung loosely on her frame, and her leather sandals.

"I'm hungry," she murmured, giving him a wicked look, her arm around his waist.

Tipping his head back, he laughed fully. "Uh-oh, I know that look."

A grin pulled at her lips as they continued their walk to their duplex. "What look?"

Nolan released her, unlocking the door to her apartment. "I think," he said in a low, teasing tone, looking into her glinting eyes, "that you have come to really enjoy those nightly orgasms, Ms. Lambert."

Teren stepped to one side, knowing Nolan would go in and clear both duplexes. "They're wonderful," she murmured. "Farida and Hadii were right as rain about that."

He looked around as he pushed the door open, his focus shifting. Nolan didn't like to expose the pistol out in public. He gazed around the low-lit apartment, a cool rush of air from the air-conditioning evaporating some of the sweat on his face. Pulling the Glock from beneath his jacket, he shifted focus entirely. The threat to Kitra and Teren was still there—it hadn't gone away.

Teren leaned against the stucco of the building until Nolan reappeared minutes later. He'd shed his jacket and pistol.

"All clear," he said. "Come on in."

The moment she closed and locked the door behind her, Nolan swept her into his arms, his mouth bearing down on her lips, brushing them, teasing her. She moaned and slipped her arms around his neck, rubbing her body against his, feeling his erection beneath his jeans. "Mmm, is this called getting dessert before dinner?" she asked, licking his lower lip, nudging her hips suggestively against his.

Hearing his low growl, she felt her lower body readying itself for pleasure, warmth beginning to flood her. Nolan laughed, a rumble in his chest as he ravished her wet lips, kissing each smiling corner of her mouth, luxuriating in the sparkle in her eyes as she held his gaze. Teren slid her fingers through his short, dark hair, his scalp prickling with pleasure.

★

IN TWO WEEKS, Teren had turned into the fastest learner Nolan had ever encountered. She might have started out innocently enough, but she took to his teaching in earnest. Once he loved her in a certain position, she learned from it. And it had tripled the pleasure for both of them as a result. There was so much more he wanted to share with her.

Sure, he was aware that the threat was ongoing, and it kept Nolan up some nights after making love with Teren, trying to figure out what Uzan was up to. Ayman's three men were still undercover in the slums of Khartoum, coming up empty-handed regarding the al-Qaeda officer. No doubt Uzan was a sly fox who knew how to hide in the slums. It left Nolan concerned, and always on guard as a result.

"You're dessert *anytime*," Nolan whispered against her smiling lips, drowning in the pearlescent shine in her eyes. A giddy joy bolted through him, and he realized that in the last two weeks his closed-up heart had flung itself wide open once more. He loved Teren. The connection he had with her was so deep, he couldn't see where it began or ended. Was it the same for her? Nolan knew her experiences with men were different, and he didn't dare project what he felt on her. He was a patient man.

He'd been hesitant to allow that feeling in again, and he would always love Linda. She would be a permanent resident in his mind and heart until the day he died. But Teren brought something new, exciting, and enlivening that he'd never experienced before. She widened him in areas he'd never trod and made him dig deep into his psyche. Her insights were startling revelations, for him and about him.

Nolan had come to cherish their exploratory talks with one another after they'd made love, lying in one another's arms, damp and satiated. She was truly dessert for his soul, whether she realized it or not. Nolan silently promised Teren he would one day share that realization with her because daily, he was seeing her confidence in herself, and in them, grow.

Teren smiled and eased out of his arms. "If we keep kissing I'm going to drag you into the bedroom, Mr. Steele, and I'm not letting you out of there."

He grazed her mussed hair. "Okay, I'll stop for now. My turn to make dinner. What do we have in the fridge?"

"Leftovers," she said, squeezing his hand and then releasing it.

"Want some cold water?"

"Yes, but I want to get changed first, and then I'll help you in the kitchen."

Nolan nodded, heading for his duplex apartment. This was their routine: get out of their sweaty clothes, shower, and then change into some comfortable evening clothes. "Meet you in thirty," he told her.

TEREN NOSHED ON Sudanese tomato salad, goat cheese, and some leftover *kissra*. Nolan had finished off several barbecued goat steaks, gobbled down a huge salad that she'd made for him earlier, and eaten enough for two people. He worked out in the gym every day, without fail, and they jogged their five miles every other day, too. She loved when Nolan wore one of those revealing muscle shirts that embraced the beauty of his hard, rock-solid body. He was truly her own personal eye candy!

"You know that in two days I'll be taking that Belgian group of arriving doctors and nurses to Zalta, that village along the river?"

"Yeah," he said, wiping his mouth on a white linen napkin. "Ayman and I were going over the route this afternoon."

"Hmm, is that why you were late?"

Nodding, Nolan took his fork and speared a tomato from her plate. Teren ate like a bird, although she had been eating more since they'd started living together. "Yes. I've got the list of medical people's names, and we'll have three vans from Khartoum coming to bring them here tomorrow afternoon. Right now, they're at a hotel in the city. Ayman's soldiers will dress as civilians, be their drivers, and bring them out here. Farida has the visitors' duplexes ready for them. Everything seems in order."

"Good thing I speak French, too," she said. "I'll be translating between them and the villagers, who only know Arabic plus their own tribal language."

"We'll be out there for five days straight." He frowned. "I wish you didn't have to be gone that long from Kitra."

Teren shrugged. A week ago, Nolan had argued with Ayman to keep her at Kitra. He didn't disagree with Nolan, but the problem was there was no other translator. Teren understood his concern for her safety, citing the dangers that lurked unknown out there. Did Uzan know about their schedule of medical visits to the various villages? Could he possibly be lying in wait for her to arrive at this village? No one knew the answers. Nolan had been adamant that she stay at Kitra. She had persuaded him, with Ayman's support, that her medical assistance to the regional villages was important. Grudgingly, Nolan had yielded, but she'd seen the raw concern in his eyes as they left Ayman's office that day.

She gave him a tender look, knowing he was on edge about it. "I've been doing this for seven years, Nolan. I love doing it. We get doctors, dentists, and optometrists who donate their help to the villages around Kitra. It's a worthwhile use of my time. This is your first time, so I'm sure it's hectic to plan."

"It is. That's a village of nearly three-hundred people, Teren. I know you know that place like the back of your hand, but I don't. We're taking extra soldiers with us because Ayman wants you protected. Plus, if Uzan decided to attack, he'd have a good opportunity."

"What do you mean?"

"That village sits on the Nile River. It's in an oasis for starters, so there are lots of palm trees, a lot of underbrush and high grass, plus stands of papyrus, on both sides of that river. Ayman showed me the area online with Google satellite photos. While it's a terrific place for the village, with its water, shade, and ability to irrigate crops, it's a hell of a place to try to keep you safe."

"It's the biggest village in the area," she said, becoming somber, nibbling at some greens. She tore a piece of bread from the loaf of *kissra*. "You do know that I'll be running around here and there—are you going to be able to keep up with me?" she teased, trying to allay the worry she saw in his eyes.

"Absolutely. I'm not leaving your side in that kind of environment and circumstance."

"All the camel caravans come through that oasis, too. They do a lot of trading with the villagers while they rest up their camels. Those poor creatures can drink gallons of water from the nearby Nile."

"Do you have a particular hut you sleep in?"

"Yes, normally I sleep with all the female nurses and dental assistants. You know: Sudanese tradition."

"Well, not this time," he warned her. "I talked to Ayman about this and he agrees, you should be with me at night. Those are straw-walled huts, and anyone could pull open a side and slip in."

"That will cause a few raised eyebrows, Nolan. These villagers are very traditional in their customs. Women sleep with women. Men sleep with men. Even married couples don't sleep together."

"Ayman had a fix for it," he told her confidently. "We'll just tell everyone we're married and that in America, a husband sleeps with his wife."

Giving him a wry look, Teren said, "Ayman's wily."

"Yes, and I'm glad. You can't be left unguarded, Teren. It just isn't going to happen. Ayman thinks that this white lie will work and the chief won't cause a fuss about it."

"The chief knows Americans from the medical teams that have visited them over the years. And there have been husband-and-wife doctors or nurses. They've always slept together in a small hut in those cases."

"That's what Ayman was saying. I don't believe the village chief will raise one eyebrow, much less two."

Teren could see the relief in Nolan's eyes. He rarely allowed her to know he was concerned about something, but tonight he was. She chalked it up to his worry about her being outside the safety of Kitra's walls. She covered her hand with his. "It will be all right. The whole village will be in celebration over the medical people arriving. There's lots of dancing, ceremony, and laughter. These are good people and they so appreciate what Kitra does for them. We'll also be bringing our own food for our medical teams. That way, the villagers won't bear the brunt of giving away hard-won food to visitors."

"I like the food we have here," he said. "I'm not keen on bush food unless it's the last resort."

Grimly, Teren said, "I agree, especially in southern Sudan, where Ebola and the Marburg virus are carried by fruit bats. And hammerhead bats, one of the carriers, are a huge meat source for the tribes down there."

"Well," Nolan grumped, "you sure as hell won't find me in a market buying some of those bats as meat. No way in hell."

"We're lucky, we don't have those types of bats up here because we're in the grasslands, not the jungle. People up here eat bats, too, but they aren't carriers of Ebola or Marburg."

"Like I said, bush meat isn't something I want to eat for any reason."

"Have you had to?" she asked, finishing off the tomato salad. If she asked Nolan about his life as an undercover Delta Force agent, he would often give her general details.

"Many times," he said, shaking his head. "We're vaccinated up to our eyeballs for all kinds of diseases you can pick up here in Africa, but there's no vaccine for viruses like Ebola, Crimean fever, Lassa, or Marburg."

"I know. Well, no worries, okay? I talked to Nafeesa this morning and she's got most of the food provisions made and packed. They're all ready to go."

"This is when I'm really glad to have MREs—'meals ready to eat'—around."

She grinned. "We do a lot of packaging of meals when we have to go out like this, which is at least once every three months. Nafeesa is a brilliant chef. She does a lot of goat jerky, and dried fruits and vegetables. Then all we have to do is add water. And we carry clean water and pots and pans, and never drink from any village water source. Too dangerous."

"Tell me about it," he muttered. "Sometimes I had to drink brownish water and was hoping like hell it wasn't full of brain-eating parasites."

"And yet, here you are," she teased, smiling over at him. "Fit, healthy, and very, very sexy."

Giving her a heated glance, Nolan said, "What's for dessert?" He saw Teren give him a coy look, her cheeks suffusing with pink. She was still an innocent, still learning to embrace herself as a sexual woman. Two weeks had shown her the beauty of having a skilled man as her lover. She was blossoming before his eyes in the best of ways. Even more, Nolan appreciated her honest responses to him pleasuring her. Some women pretended to be satisfied when they weren't, but she didn't.

Her expressions, that smoky sound in her voice as he teased her, increased to a peak where she would orgasm. That couldn't be faked.

"Well," she said, looking suggestively down the hall toward her bedroom. "I was thinking that you could be my dessert."

"I like your boldness." It was as if their time together had released Teren in many positive ways. Nolan understood the importance of partners who fed each other praise, support, and love. He'd been lucky enough to be married to Linda and knew what a good marriage consisted of. Linda had taught him a lot, but he'd equally contributed. The same kind of healthy connection had just automatically sprung up between him and Teren.

Every day, Nolan was seeing Teren flourish in exciting and unexpected ways, and he loved her for her eagerness to explore all her potential. The influence of family, right or wrong, played hell on most people. Teren had come from one that might have had good intentions, but her personality, who she could become, had been deeply suppressed. *Until now.*

"My turn today," she told him archly, standing and pushing the chair back. "I've been thinking of how I was going to undress and make love with you tonight."

"Did you get any work done in your office today, I wonder?" he chuckled, rising. Nolan picked up their plates and flatware while Teren gathered up the salt and pepper shakers and the butter dish.

"Very funny," she sniffed, then grinned broadly. "Of course I did."

They stood side by side at the sink, their hips brushing against one another.

"Do you hear that?" Teren said, lifting her head.

Nolan frowned, hearing a tinkle of bells. "What is it?"

Pulling the curtain aside, Teren said, "Look. It's a camel caravan!" She hurried through the dishes. "They come through here off and on. The caravans don't carry cell phones on them, so they can't call ahead and let us know they're arriving."

Nolan dried his hands, studying the line of about twenty-five dromedary camels that were carrying loads. There were at least ten men in long white flowing robes walking beside them. The bells they heard were part of the decorations around each camel's neck. Nolan knew that if a camel ever got loose, its owner could find the camel by the sound of the bells. They were made of brass, hand-painted, and usually came from India. Anywhere between three and ten of those bells were around each camel's long neck.

"Been a while since I saw a caravan," he murmured. "What's the SOP—standard operating procedure—on one coming to Kitra?"

"They have to remain outside the walls of Kitra. The guards on the outer gate will guide them to three, huge wooden water troughs placed alongside the north wall. They can refill them with water from the nearby faucets. Those camels will consume a *lot* of water."

"Do you go out and talk with them?" Nolan asked, seeing the excitement in her eyes. He was concerned that Uzan might try to sneak close to Kitra in disguise as a camel driver. He put nothing past the enemy soldier.

"Yes. I *love* camels! I know some people hate them, but they have such gorgeous, liquid brown eyes and those long, long lashes over them."

He gave her a sour look. "I got bitten by one once. He turned on me so damned fast, he took my hand and arm up to my elbow in a millisecond. Surprised the hell out of me." Nolan pointed to several deep scars along his forearm. "The camel was unhappy with how heavy his load was and took it out on me as I walked past him."

Teren moved her fingertips over the small white scars that dotted his forearm. "Ouch. Their bite is really bad."

"Well," he said drily, "at least he didn't spit in my face."

Wrinkling her nose, Teren said, "Ugh…that's worse than a bite! They regurgitate part of their meal and spit it at someone who has pissed them off. The smell is horrible!"

"Yeah, tell me about it. Been there and had it done to me."

"Don't wanna be a camel jockey, eh?" she teased.

"No. Not even, I'll get my jacket and pistol." When he returned, he became serious, placing his hands on her shoulders. "You're going to have to stay behind. I'm sorry."

Teren became somber, her excitement dissolving. "I forgot all about the threat," she admitted, frowning.

"Uzan could be among them. I just want to be extra watchful," he said, seeing all her childlike enthusiasm wane.

"I understand. I'll wait for you here by the door." Caravans came through about once a month, and she loved going out to talk with the head driver, finding out what stories he had to tell. Usually, they camped outside the walls for one or two days while they and their animals rested up.

Kitra was a well-known camel oasis. Here, water was plentiful, and the fruit-tree orchard lent shade to everyone. Tamping down on her sadness that she couldn't go out this time, Teren understood why.

CHAPTER 17

THE VILLAGE OF Zalta, which was Arabic for "grazing," was pastoral, rural, and peaceful. Enver Uzan melted into the village as someone passing through. He smiled beneath the cloth he wore across his nose and lower face. He'd dressed like the rest of the Sudanese tribe of this farming village, who raised cattle. Like the populace, he wore a long white robe and white turban, so that he blended in.

Nazir had found out from his own network that Kitra was sending out a three-van Belgian medical team to this village. This community was thriving, very busy, and a crossroads to many other areas of Sudan because it was built on the Blue Nile, a major river. They were used to strangers in their village, and it didn't raise any eyebrows. Enver had found out the Kitra medical team was to arrive here this morning.

He stood near one of the stucco, single-story houses and watched the villagers wake up to greet a new day. It was barely light, but he had driven in with his own fleet of vehicles during the night. Sudan's roads were mostly dirt, filled with potholes, and ungraded; there were no asphalt highways in this immediate region. Where he came from, in Pakistan, the major cities had paved streets.

His men were well hidden, away from the main village in a nearby forested area, remaining with the three vehicles, all Land Rovers. This was a vehicle that could take a beating and still keep running. Enver had rented them in Khartoum, paying a hefty price to do so, but the desert-toned vehicles, already badly dented up and rusted from years of abuse on Sudan's dirt roads, suited his plan. Nazir knew this village and had given him a detailed layout.

Only one thing concerned Enver. When Nazir had asked him what he was going to do, he hadn't told him. He'd hired Nazir as one of the drivers of the three Land Rovers. He was getting paid three times the usual amount for a driver, so Nazir nodded and asked nothing more. He worked in the employ of crazy Bachir. The other men, the best that could be found to kidnap Teren Lambert, were up for it, but they weren't formally trained soldiers as he would have preferred. These were not his men, and he wouldn't trust them as he would his own.

But money spoke volumes, and the eight soldiers with him had their weapons hidden in the vehicles. They pretended to blend into the village as he had, and weapons would be used only if necessary. Uzan wasn't interested in a bloody assault. Just the quiet theft of the American woman was his mission, with no blood spilled. Except hers. Later. When they were finished with her.

The sky was turning a pale pink as dawn broke over the large, flat green pastures where the Kenana cattle grazed. This was a very comfortable village in comparison to most, especially with the Nile winding nearby. There were ditches around these large pastures, telling Uzan that the officials employed irrigation to keep the grass growing for their zebu-like, short-horned white cattle. The pastures completely surrounded the village of three-hundred tribespeople.

The rich lived in modern, one-story stucco homes instead of the hundreds of grass huts that sat on the outskirts of the village. He snorted at the evidence of the class system, even out here.

He'd seen a number of empty grass huts on the north, south, and east sides of the village. They were being prepared for the coming medical group from Kitra. Nazir was their point man to find out particulars, fading into the populace to ask questions and find out where each medical group would be working. Uzan had walked from one end of the awakening village to the other. It appeared that medical staff would be in the north, the eye doctors in the east, and the dental team in the south. Already, he was seeing women in brightly colored clothes, their heads covered, doing last-minute tidying up, sweeping around these designated areas. Where would Teren Lambert be? That was all he cared about.

The cattle were lowing back and forth to one another. The cows' udders were heavy with milk, and frisky brownish-red calves frolicked and kicked up their heels. In a smaller pasture were the yearlings, now weaned from their mothers' milk, playing in the cool dawn morning.

The women emerged from their huts, placing blackened kettles on tripods over smoldering fires of dried cow dung. Their children soon appeared, and it was a peaceful scene as morning arrived. However, at some point, Uzan was going to create one hell of an uproar. He preferred executing a swift kidnapping of Teren Lambert, and his mind moved over several plans he'd concocted. He still wasn't sure which one he'd use; it depended upon how things developed.

Uzan would have to see how the Kitra medical teams set up and behaved. Either way, Lambert would be his by the end of this day. He wanted her alive and unharmed. Later, once he got her back into the slums of Khartoum, that would markedly change. He would let his boss, Lord Zakir Sharan, know that he had his targeted hostage. And whatever Sharan wanted, he would get. Uzan was prepared to carry out any order, especially against an American woman. Personally, he hated them. They were the devil's spawn.

NOLAN REMAINED OUT of the way, keeping a few feet from Teren after the medical vans drove into Zalta. It was nearly nine a.m., and the sun rose, spreading heat across the land, the sky a pale blue. The smell of cattle, of green pastures, and the river nearby, filled his nostrils. The village was near the Blue Nile, and he was familiar with this area because of his Delta Force undercover activities over the years.

Zalta was a thriving, large rural village. And it was one of the few places where people weren't on the edge of starvation all the time. The leader, a chief, had gone to the University of Khartoum when he was a young man and had a degree in agriculture, which had certainly helped put this place on solid economic footing.

Wearing his usual safari jacket over a black T-shirt and blue jeans, Nolan wore a level-two Kevlar vest beneath his T-shirt today, the Glock in place beneath the jacket. He'd tried to get Teren to wear a vest, but she refused, saying that everyone who saw the vest on her, would be asking what it was. Then they'd ask her why she was wearing it. There was no way she wanted to scare the populace, telling them she was a target. Not wishing to argue with her, Nolan understood her position. There was little to no protection for her in this type of village; and he certainly didn't want the people of this village to know she might be stalked by their enemy. In the end, he gave into Teren's request against his better judgment.

Nolan remained alert and on guard as women in bright colored robes worked with Teren. She was speaking in their unique tribal language, giving them directions, pointing here and there as the dental team unloaded. Village men eagerly came forward, dressed in their white robes and white caps, to help carry the equipment into the huts that were being used as makeshift clinics.

This was the last van to set up its station in the southern part of the village. The dental team's hut was a highly popular place to gather. Nolan also saw many villagers lining up at the medical doctors' hut area to the north of them. In the east, the ophthalmologists and optometrists had many older residents, all of them complaining of losing their eyesight, mostly due to cataracts, and seeking medical help.

Teren had said that the team of ophthalmologists would be doing surgery today on many of the elders in order to remove those cataracts from their eyes.

Then they would be able to see again. It was a miracle!

Teren wore a red scarf over her hair—which she'd piled up on top of her head—and her normal attire of a dark blue tee covered by a long-sleeved white blouse. She had chosen jeans and boots instead of her usual loose-fitting cargo pants and sandals. The people of this village, she'd told Nolan on the drive here, were used to European and American dress codes. All the European women wore headscarves to honor the Islamic customs of the country; but instead of head-to-toe robes, they all wore green or blue scrub uniforms.

This village had profited greatly by quarterly visits from medical volunteers over the years, and the customs were noticeably relaxed. Nolan thought that was a good idea under the circumstances, as there were few doctors out in these areas at all. The chief of the village was a wise man. He was getting free medical services for his people every three months.

Remaining in the background, Nolan scanned the crowds of people. The chatter was high, laughter was frequent, and there were long lines of adults and children. The kids, as always, were restless and didn't want to stand quietly waiting in line. Soon, Nolan saw a lot of them playing tag, laughing and squealing with delight, running in and around the patient adults. The cattle in the pastures were being tended, too. Nolan saw young boys taking armloads of sorghum, one of the mainstays for the cattle, and dumping them into wooden troughs along one side of the fenced-in pasture.

The scent of cereal cooking in tripod pots had a nutlike aroma to it. The smell of smoke came from the dried cow dung burning beneath the pots. Nothing was wasted out here.

Nolan scanned the crowd again. He saw Ayman in village garb, his pistol hidden in the folds of his white robe as he walked like a quiet wolf, threading silently among the unaware villagers in another area. He had brought six of his soldiers with him. They were all in disguise, also wearing village garb, but each had a pistol on him, hidden out of sight. They were making the rounds, looking for anything that seemed out of place. So far, it was a peaceful village filled with expectant, anxious people seeking medical help.

Nolan was never fooled by such a scene, however. He'd been in too many close calls and scrapes in other Sudanese villages where peace could be ripped away in a millisecond as a rebel group of soldiers drove into it, guns firing, murdering those unable to get out of their way fast enough. No, in his experience, there was no place in Sudan that was honestly peaceful. Except maybe Kitra. Teren had told him that Delos had two other charities in Sudan. One was east, at Port Sudan, and the other was on the western side of Sudan, in a rundown, poverty-stricken area.

★

TEREN CAUGHT SIGHT of Nolan near the round grass hut where the team of dental technicians was sitting down with paper and pens at a makeshift table. They were there to take the names of the patients waiting in line for attention. She gave Nolan a sunny smile, but he didn't respond, his face set, his eyes reminding her of a guardian lion. Her heart warmed, because they'd made love earlier that morning before leaving Kitra. Even now, her body glowed subtly with memories of his skill in pleasing her. Equally, Teren felt much more confidence in being able to please Nolan. It was no longer one-sided, as it had been in the beginning.

She saw the worry banked deep in his eyes and knew he was very unhappy about her being out in the open like this without a protective vest. But the joy, the laughter, the smiles of the people, and the delight in the children's faces made her smile in return. This was a safe village, and she had tried her best to convince Nolan of that.

He didn't buy it. She understood his job was to protect her and was happy that he took it seriously. Still, as she gazed around at the busy village, the air alive with excitement and expectation, she felt joy moving through her. There was so much good that this medical team would do for these people.

She saw a dentist waving a hand to beckon her. Time to translate! Nodding, Teren eased through the lines, excusing herself and making her way over to the dentist seating a young girl in her chair to be worked on. Teren was carrying a radio and knew that she'd be running to each of the areas all day long, providing translation when needed.

Even better, Ayman knew English, and so did two of his other soldiers, who were in disguise. They all had radios on them, including Nolan, and were all on the same channel, so they could easily communicate with each other.

UZAN WATCHED AND waited. It was past noon, past prayers, and the village was a throbbing, crowded place. He saw the difference being made by the volunteer medical teams and watched Teren move from one area to another. She was always smiling, always providing translation. The people clearly knew her: the women came up to hug her effusively, and the children followed her around because she carried candy in her pockets and gave it out freely to them.

What he didn't like was that American male always nearby. Whoever he was, he looked lethal, probably a security contractor with a military background. Uzan knew his own kind, and it was easy to spot this man and separate him from everyone else. He tailed Lambert wherever she went. Not close, but at a distance, close enough to be a shield if she needed one. Yes, he was her bodyguard, no question.

There were other men in the village he watched carefully, too. The Land Rovers had been parked behind a swampy area within the forest, out of sight, hidden by a huge stand of papyrus waving in the inconstant breeze. So far, no one had gone into that area, where his three drivers waited to be summoned. Under no circumstance did he want Nazir to show his face here for fear that the Kitra people would instantly recognize him.

Uzan had a radio on him hidden in the folds of his robe. His other soldiers blended in well with the villagers. He stood out slightly because he was light-skinned, and more than a few villagers took a long, hard look at him because he was different from them. Still, he knew that Egyptians and other Middle Eastern tribes that walked with the camel caravans were his color, too. They probably thought he was one of them, which was fine with him. But he had no camels with him, so that made him suspect.

One thing he had learned long ago was to pick up the pattern on a quarry. It took until late afternoon, just before the clinics would close up for the day, for him to identify all the players, understand the rhythm of Lambert's activity, and call his men into certain areas of the village. Patience was definitely a virtue in this work, and Uzan felt confident that he could now create a diversion and know when to strike. He moved behind a round thatched hut, pulled out his radio, and told the drivers to get ready. They would meet him at a specific spot after he'd kidnapped Lambert. His heart began to pound in anticipation. He was going to enjoy this attack. It would catch all the villagers, including that American security contractor, completely off guard!

TEREN WAS AT the north end of the village with the medical doctors, standing outside one of the huts, translating for a physician who had just finished examining a young mother's baby. She had lost sight of Nolan, but normally she didn't see him around because he was able to blend in with others. Fifteen villagers had crowded around the doctor and mother, all relatives of the baby, listening intently as Teren spoke in their language to the anxious mother.

Suddenly, Teren heard a high-pitched shriek.

"*Abu someet! Abu someet!*" a woman screamed in the center of the village. She was panicked, jerking her finger in the direction of a stucco home, the door open.

Teren turned, frowning. "*Abu someet*" was Arabic for "father of agate." And it was specifically applied to the black-necked spitting cobra. They were common in this area—and deadly. Cobras lived in families, and normally they hunted at night, but not this particular cobra. They hunted in the pastures around the village during the day. Everyone feared cobras; she saw at least fifty people suddenly stampede, running as far away as they could get from the house where the cobra had been sighted.

Suddenly, the mother next to her screamed, leaping away from the doctor, and Teren saw an olive-green cobra with a black upper body and white rings around its neck. Her eyes widened. She was within spitting distance of the snake!

People squealed in terror and ran into one another, trying to get away from the cobra, which now stood, waving slowly back and forth with its strong upper body, right near Teren.

Teren froze. She knew cobras lived in families. What didn't make sense was that they would enter a busy village like this. Normally, cobras lived where it was quiet, so they wouldn't be disturbed by too many humans.

A third scream erupted deeper in the village, and now the whole community became like a huge, moving, panicked wave. Teren pushed the doctor, frozen in fear, away from the cobra. She turned, leaping back, not wanting contact with the cobra's venom, which it could spit six feet. It could land in her eyes or on her skin. Terrified, she ran behind the hut to save herself.

As she did, a hand closed over her mouth, yanking her backward off her feet. Teren screamed, and her hands flew up as a man's hard-muscled arm closed across her throat. She was jerked off her feet and she saw a flash. Too late, she realized it was a needle! It sank deep into her upper arm and she fought, panic rising in her. Her boots struck the ground, and she felt herself being dragged farther away from the hut. She tried to scream, but the man's hand was covering her mouth and nose. And then Teren felt her legs becoming weak. She heard the roar of vehicles suddenly surround her as dust rolled over the area. People were screaming and running. *Nolan! Where was Nolan!*

Suddenly, gunfire split the panicked air and Teren saw two dark-skinned men with hatred in their eyes advancing upon her. In seconds, they'd lifted her up into the back of a Land Rover, dumping her inside. Her head slammed onto the metal floor, stunning her, and she collapsed into a heap, unable to move. Drugged! She'd been drugged! Again! It was the last thing Teren remembered before she lost consciousness.

NOLAN FIRED AS the spitting cobra was lifting its upper body to strike at the nearby doctor. He blew its head off, then, cursing, he swung around, trying to locate Teren. She'd been there a split second before. People were in turmoil, panic filling the air. At least three cobras had suddenly appeared in different parts of the village as pandemonium reigned.

He heard the roar of engines and turned on his heel. There were three

Land Rovers racing toward him, just outside the village. He barked into the radio to Ayman, knowing instinctively that this was a distraction. Teren had been captured!

Where was she?

He jerked to the left; the last place he'd seen her was at the hut. A boy came running up, screaming that Teren had been taken by bad men in a Land Rover.

Gunfire suddenly whined past his head and Nolan shoved the boy to the ground, ordering him to stay down and cover his head. The child instantly obeyed while Nolan hit the earth, rolling and trying to see where the shooter was. He saw one Land Rover, windows down, filled with men with AK-47s firing into his immediate area.

People cried out. Some fell, wounded. More bullets spat around him, temporarily blinding him as he shot back.

Where was Teren?

More rounds, clearly focused on him. He had to move! Nolan rolled twice more as the Land Rover raced toward him. He heard Ayman's shout of orders over the tumult, saw him pushing through the terrified crowd, getting shoved back by people who saw the vehicles, saw the winking of yellow and red as bullets spat from the rifles at them.

The world had suddenly exploded around Nolan. He heard the dreaded *thunk* of a rocket propelled grenade, or RPG, being triggered. *Shit!* He hunkered against the dusty earth, hands over his ears, mouth open. If he didn't keep his mouth open, the pressure that RPG created would turn his lungs to jelly. And then he'd die of suffocation.

The RPG sailed between two other round huts, both exploding into fire, the reeds flying like a thousand needles into the air. The powerful wave pulsated like an invisible fist through the northern part of the village as people were hurled off their feet.

Screams!

Shouts!

The smell of burning huts invaded Nolan's nostrils as he rolled over, gripping his Glock, shoving himself up to his feet. He heard the screech of tires. Heard the wail of engines behind the hut, where he staggered to his feet. His nose was bleeding, the blood running over his lips and chin as he raced around the hut.

He slid to a halt as he saw three Land Rovers hightailing it across the yellowed grassland, heading north on the road leading to Khartoum. There was no way he could fire, because he knew instinctively that Teren was in one of those vehicles. And he couldn't see anything because of the rising, boiling yellow clouds of dust as they made good in their escape.

Sonofabitch!

Wiping his nose with the back of his hand, Nolan gripped the radio, telling Ayman to get to one of the medical vans. Teren had been kidnapped! They had to go after them! Worse, the drone that was being sent to Kitra had not yet arrived. Nolan ran toward the nearest van, dodging people and flames from the two burning huts. He remained on the radio, telling Ayman where to meet him. Within three minutes, Ayman arrived with his six men. Nolan jumped into the driver's seat, and in moments the entire team was in the vehicle. Nolan stomped on the accelerator, the van fishtailing and roaring out of the village, heading in pursuit of the vehicles, which were now at least a mile ahead of them.

Ayman was on the radio again, calling the Sudanese Army for help. He turned to Nolan. "Has that drone arrived yet to Kitra?"

"Hell no!" he snarled, both hands on the wheel, holding the van steady over the uneven dirt road. Everything in the van shook and trembled. The sound of gravel crunching under the tires filled the air.

"Did you see Teren?" Ayman shouted to Nolan.

"No. But a boy came running up to me, telling me she was dragged fighting into a Land Rover."

Ayman yelled over the wind whipping through the van, "Someone threw those cobras into the village to create a diversion."

Mouth flattening, Nolan said, "It damn well worked, too!"

"Did you see any of the enemy?"

"Just some soldiers in white robes in the third van. They were carrying AK-47s. They were disguised as villagers. Just like we were," he added, swallowing hard.

The worst had happened: Teren had been kidnapped! Nolan was sure it had to be someone that Zakir Sharan had sent to do just that—Enver Uzan, most likely. Why hadn't they seen and identified them? He knew part of the answer: distraction.

Teren had been moving constantly from one location to another. She had a pattern of movement, and whoever had observed her saw it and then used it against her. The bastard knew where to create the diversion by releasing those cobras from gunnysacks, letting them loose in the crowds.

His twisting gut nearly made him cry out, but Nolan stuffed it down. His whole focus was on catching up to that fleet of fleeing vehicles. The more he pushed the van, the more dangerous it became for all of them. One wrong move on a gravel road and the van could skid and flip over several times before stopping. They could all be killed. Nolan had to weigh their lives against the speed necessary to catch up to the kidnappers who held Teren. *Was she all right? Had they killed her already? Wounded her? Drugged her?* His mind went to the darkest corners of possibility, and then he shut it all down. He couldn't go there and remain focused. It could kill him and the rest of these men if he didn't stop right now.

"It *has* to be Uzan," Ayman shouted, his face sweaty and dirt encrusted. He gripped the doorframe with his hand, his mouth contorted. "They wanted Teren!"

Nolan's mouth pulled in deeply at the corners. His knuckles were white as he skillfully guided the van over the jarring road. They weren't catching up with them, but they weren't being left behind, either. What he'd have liked to do was call in an air strike, though he knew he couldn't have the jet hit the vehicles because Teren was in one of them. But a well-placed air strike in front of the lead Land Rover could force the vehicle to stop or slow down just enough so they could reach them.

"How many men, do you think?" Ayman demanded.

"I saw six in that last vehicle. There were three vehicles. Eighteen men?"

"Yes." Ayman turned, grim. "And we have eight."

"Good odds," Nolan growled, his eyes slitted, focused on the straight road ahead of them. There was nothing but yellow dust clouds spiraling and billowing above to show them the enemy's location.

Ayman ordered his soldiers to get ready for combat. Luckily, they had put a cardboard box in each van filled with M4 magazines and extra mags for their Glock pistols as well. The soldiers tore off their outerwear, revealing their Sudanese Army uniforms. Another man crawled into the rear of the van, dragging the heavy ammo box forward. The soldiers began to pass the clips around between themselves. Another man handed Ayman magazines for his and Nolan's Glock pistols.

Teren...God, I love you. Hang on, hang on...we'll get you out of this...

It was a litany in Nolan's head, sweat rolling down his temples, dust collecting on him with the windows open. He cursed himself. He hadn't told Teren yet that he loved her. He had wanted to but felt it was too soon. She was still climbing out of that foxhole where she'd lived so long alone, abandoned by her family. They'd only had three weeks with one another. *Three weeks.* And now he didn't know if they'd ever share another moment together.

CHAPTER 18

NOLAN'S MIND WHIRLED, considering his strategies. They couldn't see through the clouds of dust to take a shot, and he wanted to blow the tires to slow down the nearest vehicle. But a stray bullet might wound or kill Teren, and he wouldn't risk it. And yet, as fast as they were going, some sixty miles per hour, twice the speed they should have been driving on this road, they weren't closing the gap on the fleeing enemy vehicles, either.

"I wish," Ayman growled, "that we had that drone Wyatt Lockwood was sending us. It would help so much."

Nolan grimaced. "You got any ideas on how to stop these dudes? I'm not going to be able to drive any faster or I'll wreck the van and probably kill all of us."

Ayman tugged at the black baseball cap he wore. "No. Just follow them. Maybe one of them will run out of gas. Maybe crash. That road leads past Kitra and on to Khartoum. Teren is in one of those vehicles. We don't know which one. We can't take a chance of firing and possibly hitting her." Exasperation was plainly written all over his face. "And even if we could get close enough, we can't ram them to stop them, either."

"I can't get close enough to do anything," Nolan muttered, even more frustrated.

"Something will happen. They can't keep up that speed. They'll wreck themselves," Ayman told him, scowling.

Yes, and what would happen to Teren if she was in the vehicle that crashed? Nolan wanted to ask, but bit it back. He'd had such dreams for them. And damn it, from the moment he'd met Teren, he'd started seeing a future with her. Hope had infused him when he thought he'd lost the capacity to ever feel it again after his family's murder. There was something so bright, so idealistic and innocent inside her that she had breathed new, hopeful life back into him. Now she *was* his life.

Nolan had dared to hope once again…

But now?

As an operator, he knew all the possible playbook strategies in a situation like this—and not one of them held a good outcome for Teren. He felt his heart ripping open, the pain excruciating across his chest. He couldn't go through this again! He just couldn't! And yet, here he was: facing the ruthless reality of possibly losing Teren. Losing her before he'd ever had a chance to dream and build a life with her.

Nolan knew that she loved him. She'd never said the words, but that didn't matter. He'd seen it in her eyes, and in the way those perfectly shaped lips that sent him into such heat and instant need, would tilt. Yes, Teren loved him.

He wasn't a man to pray, because he'd seen too much. He'd survived when others hadn't. Prayers had never helped him or the fellow Delta operators whom he'd befriended over the years. They braved death so many times together. Then, suddenly, one would be ripped out of his life in a split second. *Gone.* He would never hear him laugh or speak again. No, normally Nolan didn't pray because it didn't do any good.

And yet, he was praying that something…someone…some twist of fate would intervene to save Teren's life, keep her from dying. Because if this fleet of enemy vehicles reached Khartoum, Teren would be lost to him forever. They'd hide her in those miserable slums, and even if Ayman asked the Sudanese Army to go tent by tent searching for Teren, they would never find her.

The loss would be unbearable.

Teren, I love you. Hang on…just hang on…I can't lose you…I can't…

MEANWHILE, TEREN WAS jolted heavily, shaking her out of unconsciousness. She was thrown halfway across the back of the Land Rover, bruising her thigh. Dazed, feeling the heavy jolt, the noise outside sounding like she was in a blender with gravel, she slowly blinked. At first, everything was blurred as Teren heard yelling. Men were screaming at one another above the grinding, earsplitting noises. The vehicle she was in was sliding back and forth and bumping violently up and down, then side to side once more.

What on earth? Where was she, and where were they taking her?

Her mind spun in circles, refusing to work. She lay on the dusty corrugated metal floor. Closing her eyes, Teren tried desperately to think, placing her palm between her head and that hard, unforgiving metal deck. Her heart was thudding heavily in her chest. She tasted terror along with the dirt in her mouth. Opening her eyes again, she realized that she was in a Land Rover, and everything suddenly became starkly clear.

Then her vision blurred, and it took another five minutes before Teren put it all together. She had been drugged and kidnapped.

Her captor was Uzan, whom she recognized from the photo Nolan had shown her. His black eyes were filled with hatred. It was the last thing Teren remembered. She had fought hard to get loose from his chokehold, but the syringe he'd punched into her arm had rendered her too weak to resist him.

Oh God. Her greatest nightmare had arrived.

She was in trouble. Where was Nolan? Her mind shorted out, then cleared. Her mouth was dry, her skin sweaty, grit sticking to it. Lifting her other hand, she felt more strength returning. Not much, but more than she had before. The vehicle swerved, jumped, and then fishtailed as she was slapped against a side panel with bruising force.

Opening her eyes, Teren stared out the dust-streaked rear window. She knew the Land Rover opened from the rear. Forcing her mind to work, she recognized it as an older model, probably a 2000. And she saw a huge, knobby-treaded tire attached on the outside of the vehicle. On the other side of the window was a small metal ladder that would take a person to the top of the vehicle. Her eyes focused. There was the handle that opened that door outward right in front of her.

How fast were they driving? It felt like they were going over sixty miles an hour, way too fast for this gravel road. She slowly rolled onto her back and lifted her head slightly toward the seat in front of her. She saw three men, all with rifles, sitting there. She was barely able to see the sides of their dark-skinned, sweaty faces. Terror struck her then and Teren realized their attention was not on her. Rather, their gazes were all riveted forward. That was good.

The door handle stared back at her.

She knew the Land Rover had electronic controls. Had someone locked that handle from the dashboard? If they had, she couldn't escape from this vehicle. She could hear the roar of the engine, the big tire treads biting deep into the road's gravel, spewing it up like a geyser behind them. There was only one way to go on this road, and that was north, from Zalta toward Khartoum. And it was at Kitra that the road changed from gravel to asphalt.

How far away was she from the village? Teren lifted her wrist, squinting to see the time on her watch. A half hour had passed, and her mind was working better with each passing moment. Teren licked her dry lower lip, trying to gauge the speed of the vehicle again. If the door handle was not locked, she could twist it open and roll out.

And at what speed? She could tear herself up if it was as fast as she thought it was. She'd kill herself if she landed on the gravel road, striking her unprotected head. But glancing up at the hard, set faces of the men sitting in that seat scared her even more. She'd been kidnapped. And Teren knew it was by Uzan. How many vehicles were there? Was this the only one? Was there another one nearby? Because if she tried to escape and there was a second enemy car behind her, it would hit and run over her and she'd die.

But what other choice did she have? Teren knew Uzan would kill her, probably behead her on video for the world to see. Closing her eyes, she was suddenly overwhelmed with a fierce love for Nolan. Somehow, she knew he would try to save her. So would Ayman and his soldiers. But where were they? Could they reach her in time? So many questions and no answers!

Teren thought about getting up on her knees and trying to grab one of the AK-47 rifles held by those three hardened soldiers but presently, she wasn't that strong. And she didn't know how to use one. No, it wasn't an option.

The only option she had was to try to escape through that rear door if it was unlocked. That was the only way she'd get out of this vehicle. Slowly leaning forward, she peered through the rear window, which was dusted with yellow grit. Behind them was another Land Rover. She saw men with AK-47s sticking out the windows. Teren tried to see beyond the yellow clouds kicked up behind that Rover but couldn't see through the dust. Were Nolan and Ayman somewhere behind them?

Teren felt desperation eating through her like burning acid. Either way, she'd never see Nolan again. Tears filled Teren's eyes and she collapsed on the floor, getting violently bumped around once more, bruising her sore hip.

Her mind worked behind her closed eyes. A half hour would put them many miles north of the village. She knew the road well. There was a tight curve farther up the road, if her memory was correct. It was a ninety-degree turn, because the Blue Nile swung abruptly into the dry grasslands. The river's yearly flooding had forced them to redirect the road at that point. Had they already driven past it while she was unconscious? Or did they have yet to slow down for that curve? She didn't know.

Teren closed her eyes, one hand beneath her head and the other clasped against her breast. She pretended to be unconscious in case one of the armed men turned around to check on her. That curve where the Blue Nile met the road was roughly a hundred feet from the river. There were huge stands of papyrus thickly lining the bank in that area. The tall, thin reeds grew in huge groups, creating a green wall that could be ten to fifteen feet high and up to a mile long by the riverbank. It was the perfect hiding spot for her.

If she could get the rear door sprung open when the Rover slowed for that curve, she could leap out, make a dash for the papyrus stands, and hide inside them.

Teren knew someone would see her. The men in that vehicle following hers would jam on the brakes and probably start shooting at her. But she didn't have a choice. It was either make a break for freedom or die.

★

AYMAN JABBED HIS finger toward the windshield. "Up here, about a mile farther, is that ninety-degree curve, Nolan. Everyone's going to have to slow down. They won't be able to do anything else. It's near the bank of the river. That's our chance to make up some distance between us and them."

Nolan nodded. His hands ached on the wheel, he was holding it so hard, constantly working to keep the van from skidding or flipping. The dust was thick ahead, and he couldn't see through it. "If we can run up on them, we can see them without dust between us."

"Yes," Ayman shouted. He turned, snapping orders to his soldiers, who got ready to use their weapons. "I propose we speed up to that point, brake to a sudden stop, leap out, and run through the dust clouds, firing at the tires on all three vehicles as we see them. They'll be slow-moving targets, and the vehicles will be crowded together. It's a perfect spot to engage them. And we'll go after any soldiers who are firing at us, as well. We'll be able to see if Teren is in one of those vehicles by that time."

Grimly, Nolan nodded. They were heavily outgunned, but Ayman's men were military trained, and so was he. "Do you think Uzan has military-trained soldiers with him?"

"No, impossible. He's probably hired thugs from the slums. They aren't marksmen like my soldiers at Kitra. Those hired men in the Land Rovers are outgunned. They are just bodies carrying weapons they may or may not know how to use. We have the advantage even though we only have eight soldiers."

Mouth tightening, Nolan nodded. "Then we have a chance. We just need to try to locate Teren."

"Yes." Ayman nodded. He pulled out his Glock, placing a round in the chamber.

Nolan was glad he was wearing a level-two Kevlar vest. Ayman had ordered all of them to wear the vest beneath their clothing. If Uzan's goons weren't military trained, then they stood a small chance of victory. A very small one. Eighteen men against eight weren't good odds. But where was Teren?

THE VEHICLES BEGAN to slow. Teren inched toward the rear, her heart pounding in her ears. She was shaky. The drug was wearing off, but she still wasn't as strong as she wished. Her mind, however, was clear for the moment. Glancing over her shoulder, she felt the vehicle slow even more. She couldn't chance a look out the rear window, because the men in the Land Rover behind them might have radios they could use to call the first vehicle if they saw her moving about, alerting the soldiers that she was conscious. Mouth dry, Teren saw all three soldiers ahead of her were ignoring her. They probably thought she was still unconscious from the drug. *Let them.*

The moment the Land Rover slowed to a crawl, Teren jerked at the handle and gasped. It opened!

Adrenaline shot through her. She pushed the rear door open, and it swung wide. The vehicle behind her was a good thirty feet away. Spotting the papyrus, she leaped out and landed hard on her hands and knees. Pain and burning sensations reared up her hands and into her arms, the gravel biting deeply into her flesh.

Get up! Get up!

Scrambling, terror galvanizing her, she ran and wobbled on unsteady feet, lunging toward the riverbank ahead of her. Her feet slipping on the gravel, Teren weaved and staggered toward the river's bank. She heard a screech of brakes behind her as men started yelling.

Hurry! Hurry!

She was suddenly enclosed in billowing yellow dust clouds as she sprinted like a wounded, winded animal toward the papyrus stands. Suddenly, bullets were being fired. The world shattered around her as she dove into the thick, heavy wall of greenery, bullets singing around her like bees angrily flying and buzzing around her head. Flailing, Teren was pushed by the knowledge that those men would come after her. Her legs were weakening. Her breath tore out of her in ragged gasps. She lunged repeatedly through the stand, boots suddenly in mud, until she was knee-deep in the brackish green water of the slow-moving Nile. She pushed onward, knowing she had to get on the other side of the stand and then work to swim downriver to get away from them.

Bullets whined all around her. They made plunging, gulping sounds as they struck the water far away from where she flailed. The goons didn't know where she was! That sparked a surge of hope, and she dove forward again, landing on her belly, warm water splashing around her. Suddenly, Teren found herself beyond the stand of reeds. The Blue Nile, dark green, moving lazily, was a hundred feet wide and stretched in front of her. Sobbing for breath, soaked, tears streaming down her face, she threw herself into the water, striking out with strong strokes, paralleling the papyrus.

The water had Nile crocodiles in it, and Teren knew the risks only too well. She was splashing, making sounds that would draw any of those aggressive crocs in her direction. But it was either be shot and recaptured by Uzan or risk getting attacked by a thousand-pound crocodile. Both her hands were bleeding, cut open on her dive out the vehicle.

Then she heard other sounds. More vehicles were suddenly screeching to a halt. More gunfire erupted. It sounded like a war was going on behind her.

Focused, Teren swam about a tenth of a mile and then slowly worked her way back into the thick wall of reeds to hide. Her body was weakening, and her arms felt like they weighed fifty pounds. She couldn't swim anymore. Instead, she had to hide and hope her strength would return. If Uzan's men were hunting for her, there would be no footprints to follow, and the water would cover up her route of escape. The only other way she could be found was by the movement of the reeds. They were at least eight to ten feet tall and would wave slightly where she was threading through them. She had to be very careful and go very slowly, so as not to have them give her position away and show Uzan's men where she was hiding.

As she slipped back into the reeds, mouth open, breathing raggedly, Teren's booted feet struck the muddy bottom of the Nile. Pushing forward, she fought to get inside the thick stand and hide. The gunfire behind her was horrific. The air was alive with booming, thundering, angry sounds reverberating throughout the area. It felt as if her heart would tear out of her chest, she was breathing so hard, the drug still in her system, slowing her down, weakening her until she could barely walk.

There were unexpected explosions. Huge ones! She jerked and looked south. Black smoke columns were rising. Terrified and confused, Teren didn't want to wait around and try to figure out what had just happened. She kept moving slowly through the reeds in knee-deep Nile water, completely enclosed by the shielding, thick papyrus. She had to keep slogging southward, back toward the village to get help, because sooner or later, Uzan's men would try to recapture her. That couldn't happen. Papyrus stands could grow for a mile or more along the Nile and then suddenly stop. She'd be in the open and an easy target to spot once the papyrus disappeared. Her weakness terrified her; her knees felt wobbly, and she was barely able to take another step forward at the moment.

Teren realized at that point she'd have to swim across the river and risk being pursued by a nearby crocodile or Uzan's men on this side of the bank. If men didn't spot her and start shooting, then the hungry crocodiles would come after her, seeing her as food. Teren had no way to defend herself. But those were her options. Plus, if this weakness from the drug continued, she'd drown, because she didn't have the physical strength to swim very far. If she could get across the river to the other bank, there were stands of brush and trees nearby. There, she could run and hide within them, working her way back to Zalta, where a wooden bridge across the Nile would take her to the village and she could get help.

More explosions rocked the area. The pressure waves beat down upon her like fists suddenly striking her body. She flinched, holding her hands to her ears, which were aching with pain, crouching as she was pummeled repeatedly by the invisible waves rolling through the immediate area. What was happening? Why was there so much gunfire and so many explosions? Maybe Nolan and Ayman had arrived. They might have followed Uzan...

Her hands were shaky, and she continued to inch ahead, afraid to make splashing noises for fear of alerting a crocodile lurking nearby. Pain drifted up from her knees. Stymied, she glanced down, surprised to see dark stains on her jeans—blood loss, from her knees being torn up after she leaped onto the gravel from the Rover. They were bleeding a lot. *Too much.* Crocs could smell blood in the water a mile away. Teren knew she was in trouble, seeing her red blood slowly moving in and around the reeds, following the current. She kept pushing through the slender, thick reeds, careful how much noise she made. Her breathing wasn't as harsh, but her heart was still thudding heavily, making her gasp for air.

Suddenly, everything grew silent. The gunfire stopped. Halting, Teren looked up toward the area from where she had escaped. She saw several black, roiling columns of smoke but heard no more firing. All there was now was the *lap, lap, lap* of the quietly moving Blue Nile outside the reed beds in which she stood.

She suddenly felt her body give up and gripped some reeds on either side of her, trying to remain upright. The drug was cycling through her again, debilitating her body and her mind. Closing her eyes, Teren bent over, feeling lightheaded, trying to keep from passing out. She had pushed her drugged body about as far as it was going to go. The adrenaline that had fueled her escape was gone. Now she was crashing.

Mouth dry, she tried to swallow but couldn't. There was no way she was going to drink the water; it was infested with all kinds of bacteria, fecal matter from animals, and God knew what else. Her fingers tightened around the reeds and she began to sway. *No! I can't pass out now! I can't!*

Clinging to the reeds, her fingers slipping down their strong stalks, Teren tried to focus on surrounding sounds. Panic struck her. A croc could move with total silence and only the subtle movement of the reeds he swam through would give away his position. Had the heavy bleeding from her knees flowed through the water and now out in the main current? She was sure it had. A croc could have already picked up its scent and now be tracing it back to where she presently stood. Teren was utterly spent, barely able to even feel fear at this point. The massive power of the drug robbed her of strength and she was mentally spiraling downward. Fearful she'd pass out, she turned, weaving unsteadily toward the shore. If she did pass out, a croc could find her, bite her legs, and drag her into deeper water, drowning her.

No! Fight! Fight!

Teren's mouth grew thin, and she willed herself to move her foot out of the sucking mud. *One step at a time.* She loved Nolan. She wasn't going to give up! Even now, she didn't know if Nolan was nearby or not. Or dead. Teren felt woozy, closing her eyes, pushing forward, head bent down. Every step felt as if she had a hundred pounds of extra weight on each foot. Her heart was thudding like a drum that felt like it was going to rip out of her chest. She had to keep moving! Somehow, she had to get into shallower water in case she lost consciousness and fell face-first into it; she could suffocate and drown. Fear of dying sparked through her.

Suddenly, her vision blurring, she spotted the damp bank of the river just ahead, and water was now sloshing around her ankles, the mud deeper, hampering her efforts even more. She was beyond exhaustion. There were the crackling sounds of something on fire, and she wearily glanced upward, seeing three distinct columns of black smoke now rising lazily into the air, carried east by an unseen breeze. Staggering, she blearily focused on the bank that was so close. Teren felt out of her body, floating, her vision spotty and darkening. *The bank. Get to the bank.* The mud was like thick, black hands pulling downward on her boots. It was a battle between life and death.

Teren pitched forward. A small cry tore out of her as her legs collapsed beneath her. She felt herself falling. Her head struck the muddy bank. Her arms were thrown outward, fingers digging into the soft, damp soil of the bank, trying to pull herself a few more inches out of the water. The coolness of the mud against her right temple and cheek felt soothing as she slumped against it, facing the blackness racing toward her. The last thought she had was that at least half her body was up on the shore and the lower half was in very shallow water. Teren hoped the reeds had hidden her well enough from the patrolling crocs that had smelled her blood and were now following the trail that would eventually lead to her.

NOLAN FINISHED TIGHTENING the plastic flex cuffs around the wrists of the survivors of the firefight. Ayman and one of his soldiers had suffered slight, grazing wounds. Around him, he grimly perused ten dead men, all enemies, sprawled over the area, the other eight survivors now captured and with various nonthreatening wounds. But Teren wasn't among them. Where was she?

Ayman came over, his brown eyes thundercloud angry as he gripped the collar of one man. "Nazir!" he yelled into his face, jerking Nazir toward him. "Where is Teren?"

The young Sudanese had sustained an upper-arm wound. He winced as Ayman brought up his fist, threatening to strike him. His arms were behind him, thick wrists cuffed, and he was incapacitated. "Don't hit me!" he cried out. "Don't!"

Breathing like an angry bull, Ayman pressed his face into Nazir's terrified one. "Where is Teren Lambert? Tell me or I'll put a bullet in your head right now!" He pulled out the Glock, pressing the barrel of it hard against the man's sweaty temple.

"S-she escaped!" he cried out. "When we slowed down for the curve, she jumped out the back of the second Land Rover!"

"Where were you?" Ayman snarled. "How did you know this?"

"I-I was driving the Rover behind her. I saw her do it. S-she ran toward the Nile. She disappeared into the reeds! I swear, that's the last I saw of her!"

Nolan listened, his face expressionless as he assessed the frightened man.

"Was she hurt?" Nolan demanded in Arabic.

"Uzan drugged her," he cried. "I had nothing to do with this! I was only hired to drive!"

"Did she injure herself when she escaped from the Rover?" Ayman angrily demanded.

"I-I saw her fall out onto the road. She landed hard on her hands and knees. A-and then, she took off fast, like a gazelle, and raced for the reeds. I-I don't know if she's injured or not."

Nolan traded a grim glance with Ayman. The Sudanese Army soldiers were picking up all the discarded weapons, keeping them in one heap and away from the cuffed enemies.

"Which way did she go? Upstream or downstream?" Ayman growled, holding Nazir's wide, bloodshot eyes.

"I-I don't know! I swear by Allah, I don't know! Don't shoot me, Ayman! Spare me!" he shrieked. "I did Teren no harm! No harm! I swear it!"

Nolan's lips drew away from his teeth. "Where's Uzan? He isn't here. Where did he go?"

Nazir gulped. "I-I don't know! Everything…everything got confused, the gunfire…"

Yeah, Nolan thought, *damn right there was gunfire*. It was like the OK Corral, everyone firing at everyone else at point-blank range. But only he, Ayman, and Ayman's men hit their targets, unlike the thugs, who were rattled and really didn't know how to shoot calmly during a firefight. Nolan said nothing, sending Nazir a hard, threatening look.

Ayman snarled in disgust and slammed Nazir back onto the dusty ground. He landed hard and rolled away.

Straightening, Ayman turned to Nolan. "Uzan escaped. I'll bet he headed into the reeds just like Teren did."

That scared Nolan more than anything else. Uzan could be going in the same direction as Teren. What if they accidentally ran into one another? "Which way would she go, Ayman?"

"She would head upriver toward the village." Ayman pointed south. "Teren's not stupid. She would know there was help there. The people of the village would aid her. She would swim or work her way through the reeds along the river. This bed of reeds goes for a mile south and then ends—if she made it that far. She would probably try to swim across the Nile to the other bank, because she could go hide in the brush and trees you see farther down on that side of the river. That stand of trees goes all the way to the pastures of Zalta. I'm sure she'd go that direction, because she'd be well hidden, out of the water, and out of sight of Uzan's men."

Wiping his mouth, Nolan released a spent mag on his Glock and shoved in another one with the palm of his hand. "My gut tells me Uzan will do the same thing."

"Yes, I fear that," Ayman muttered, worried.

"I'm going to find her."

"We'll search with you," Ayman promised, and ordered three of his soldiers to come with them. The others would guard the prisoners. Earlier, Ayman had called for a Sudanese Army transport truck to be driven from Khartoum to this spot to pick up all the prisoners. It was already under way and would arrive in three hours.

But a lot could happen in three hours…

CHAPTER 19

NOLAN SPENT NEARLY ten minutes trotting slowly down the bank of the Nile, searching for Teren. His heart rate skyrocketed as he glimpsed her unconscious halfway up the muddy bank. He made a sharp, silent gesture to Ayman, who was about ten feet behind him. The soldiers had trailed slowly behind their captain, trying to see if they could locate Uzan. Nolan had barely spotted Teren because the thick reeds were nearly impenetrable. It had been the sun striking her hair, a color that was out of the ordinary if anyone was looking at the wall of green papyrus. His years as an operator had honed his vision to look for what was out of place, and her hair color, brown, stood in stark contrast to the green wall of reeds.

He wanted to run to her but knew Uzan could be waiting for one of them to approach Teren, who lay unmoving. Nolan swallowed hard. Sweat was running down his temples. He held the Glock ready in both hands, crouching and moving sideways, his gaze ruthlessly sweeping around Teren. Was she dead? He didn't think so because her skin, although muddied, was not gray, which would indicate she had passed.

Let her live…let her live…

His heart was pounding so hard that it was blocking his exceptional hearing ability. A great white heron flew overhead. Another bird, a white egret, landed in the top of one of the slowly waving papyri. Nolan knew if there was another human near Teren, the egret wouldn't have landed. The bird landed because Teren might have been strange-looking and out of place, but she wasn't moving and therefore was not a threat. If Uzan was nearby, chances were he would be crouched and waiting, or moving. Either way, the bird would see the man's eyes, see him blinking, and take off, not feeling comfortable enough to perch.

His fingers were sweaty around the Glock, his breath shallow, as he approached Teren. Ayman was coming up silently behind him, intently scanning the papyrus, his Glock drawn and prepared to fire. Having another military-trained partner took a huge load off Nolan's shoulders. He was used to working in a team situation and Ayman would have his back as he swiftly moved forward.

Now, directly on top of the bank in a crouch, Nolan swept the area where Teren lay one more time. Crocs, he knew, were a secondary threat, and he remained on guard, looking for eyes and a partial snout floating in the water approaching her legs.

A soldier ran swiftly by him, rifle at the ready, his eyes riveted on the reeds around Teren. He was acting as a decoy so that Teren could be rescued.

Nolan was grateful for the tactic, which gave him time to jam the Glock into his waistband and leap down the bank to get Teren the hell out of there. *Let her be alive!! Let her be all right.* His eyes missed nothing as he slipped and slid down the sandy ocher embankment, the heels of his boots sinking into the black ooze near the waterline. He saw no blood on her body, just mud on her soaked clothing. Her lips were parted, eyes shut, hands above her head, as if she was trying to claw her way up the bank when she lost consciousness.

Knowing she'd been drugged, Nolan approached her from the rear, keeping a watchful eye on the surrounding area. The reeds were so thick, nothing could be seen except at very close range. He knelt down on one knee, slipping his hand beneath her neck, the ends of her hair and half her face, coated in mud. Wanting to scream, wanting to become impatient, Nolan knew better. He had no idea of the possible extent of her injuries.

Ayman came, standing on the bank. "Clear," he told Nolan, still scanning the river beyond the reed beds.

"I need your help," Nolan said gruffly, directing him to come down in the front of where Teren lay. "Do you see any blood on her? Any wounds?"

Ayman scowled, slipping and sliding down the ten-foot embankment, kneeling in front of Teren. "No. She's been drugged. Probably unconscious due to that alone." He ran his hands over Teren swiftly and knowingly, as Nolan did, checking her hips, legs, and knees, and then he helped drag her lower body out of the water. "She looks fine," Ayman rasped, still warily watching the reeds surrounding them.

"I'm going to pick her up," Nolan growled. "Help me?" Because he was standing on unstable sand and mud, he didn't want to try to pick Teren up and then slip and fall with her in his arms.

"Go," Ayman said, steadying her as Nolan slid his other arm beneath her bent, wet legs.

In a moment, with Ayman's support, Nolan was able to bring Teren into his arms. She was limp, her head lolling back against his shoulder. Ayman brought one of her arms up, placing it against her body, helping Nolan get up the slippery bank.

Ayman growled, "Look," he pointed to her torn pants around her injured knees, blood still leaking down her legs.

Once on top of the bank, Nolan swiftly walked over to a nearby tree and laid Teren down under its shade. The second soldier joined Ayman, hunting for Uzan. Nolan's heart was aching with dread as he tipped Teren's chin upward so that she could breathe more easily.

Ayman pulled out his satellite phone from the harness he wore. "I'm calling for a helicopter from Khartoum," he called to Nolan. "Teren needs medical assistance now."

Nolan nodded his agreement. He was well trained in emergency medicine and moved his two fingers against Teren's carotid artery on the side of her slender neck. Her pulse was slow but strong. A little of the terror he felt dissolved. Her skin was a good color, although her face was muddy and colorless, indicating drug overdose.

He was no stranger to such a thing. He wished for blankets, for an IV to give her life-sustaining fluids, but out here, there was nothing available.

"What about the medical doctors in Zalta?"

"They won't have drug overdose medication to pull her out of this," Ayman said, punching the numbers into his sat phone. "I can get a helo out here in thirty minutes with everything we need to get her out of this drugged state...you just keep her stable."

Yeah, that was as good as it got out in this third-world country, and Nolan knew it. Nodding, he tried to remove some of the wet mud from Teren's slack face. He'd kissed those lips of hers, listened to her breathy, smoky laughter, seen her gray eyes, like soft diamonds, dance with amusement. And now, she lay like a broken doll, limp and unmoving as he knelt beside her. He waved his hand, keeping the pesky flies away from her face and exposed arms. As Ayman made the emergency request from the Sudanese Army in Khartoum, Nolan checked her front and back for any other injuries—to his relief, he found none.

Suddenly, M4 gunfire erupted upriver. Nolan automatically threw himself over Teren, going for his pistol. Ayman had whirled around, sat phone at his ear, his other hand going for his Glock.

Nolan saw his soldiers firing into the reeds upstream. He remained with Teren, protecting her with his body. Unable to see anything, he held the Glock at the ready.

Ayman was craning his neck, not firing either. He finally connected with the Army in Khartoum, quickly speaking in Arabic, ordering a helicopter and medical specialists to their GPS coordinates.

Abruptly, the shooting stopped. *What the hell?* Nolan craned his neck, frustrated that he could only see the soldiers on the reed bed of the bank, rifles pointed into them.

Nolan, tense, remained where he was, watching, waiting. The mud on Teren's body coated his, but all he could think of was, *had they found Uzan? Killed him?* He watched as the soldiers suddenly leaped down the embankment, splashing into the reeds, charging into and out of them, rifles up and prepared to fire once more.

Ayman signed off on the sat phone. "Stay here," he ordered Nolan, sprinting toward his men. Easing away from Teren, Nolan stood and walked around her, crouching nearby, fully alert. His gaze swept up and down the reed stands along the bank. Then he heard shouts.

Nolan froze.

He saw Ayman leap into the reeds, Glock up in his hand. He quickly disappeared into them. Were they chasing Uzan? Nolan would bet on it. If they hadn't wounded or killed the bastard, he was probably trying to swim across the Nile to escape to the other side.

Suddenly, a man's terrifying shriek ripped through the air. Nolan stood, eyes fixed on where the scream had originated.

More screams. Wailing.

Worried, Nolan thought it was one of Ayman's soldiers. He couldn't see anything beyond the papyrus screen. Damn it!

And then, sudden quiet.

Nolan remained at his post and knelt near Teren's shoulder, reaching out, sliding his hand gently across it, trying to give her some sense of safety even though she was unconscious. Nolan knew her life was still in jeopardy. What kind of drug had Uzan given her? Had she been overdosed? It could kill her unless they got her to a hospital in time to neutralize the medicine.

Desperate, Nolan wanted to take Teren into his arms, hold her close, give her his warmth, his strength. As he watched her slack face, his heart lurched in terror of losing her forever.

NOLAN SAT ON the edge of Teren's hospital bed in a private, air-conditioned room at the medical center in Khartoum. Everything was quiet. Night had fallen hours ago and he'd continued to stand watch over her. Two dedicated nurses had gently washed her hair and body, removing all the mud and blood on her hands and knees, placing her in a clean, soft blue nightgown. She lay beneath the covers of the bed, still and pale. There was nothing to do but wait, the doctors told him.

Nolan gazed at her bruised arm. There were two IVs in her: one feeding her necessary fluids, the other an antidrug medication to counter the drug Uzan had given to her. Slowly, he was seeing signs of change come into her face, the waxen look giving way to a bit of color. The nurses had combed her hair and had tended to her as if she were their own beloved child. Nolan was grateful for their care and gentleness with Teren.

The doctor had come in earlier and told him Teren had been given an opiate drug. "Guaranteed to knock a Kenana bull to its knees." It had felled Teren, too. The anti-opiate drug was now helping to neutralize the rest of it in her body. No one was sure when Teren would regain consciousness, but they knew that eventually she would. Nolan felt his knees weakening when the doctor reassured him that she would survive this. At first, he advised Nolan, she'd awaken and be terribly disoriented, her mind muddled, unsure of where she was. Nolan promised to stay with her when she regained consciousness.

Ayman had already dropped by and listened to the doctor's prognosis for Teren. His hardened face softened over the good news. He'd shaken Nolan's hand, clapped him on the shoulder to comfort him, and then left for Kitra, his soldiers guarding the door to Teren's hospital room. Ayman took no risks under the circumstances. There could be other enemies out there who, if they found out she was here, would attack and try to kill Teren. Uzan's remaining goons they'd captured earlier had been turned over to the police and would be properly dealt with, never to see the outside of a prison again. Sudan dealt harshly with kidnappers.

Nolan saw Teren's eyelids quiver. He slid his fingers around her cool hand, watching her intently. Color began to flood her cheeks, and he knew that she would become conscious shortly. His heart lifted, the dread beginning to dissolve. He loved her so much and once she was coherent, Nolan wasn't going to hold back that admission any longer. He'd come too close to losing her.

His fingers tightened around Teren's, silently reassuring her and mentally begging her to return to him and the love that had never been given words.

As her dark-brown lashes lifted, Nolan saw the confusion in her murky-looking gray eyes. And then she uttered a low sound of protest, trying to lick her lower lip but not succeeding.

Nolan realized she was thirsty. Cupping her cheek, he felt the warmth returning to her body. Her lashes lifted marginally as he lightly stroked her cheek.

"Teren? It's Nolan. You're here in the Khartoum hospital with me, and you're safe." He tried to keep the wobble of emotions out of his low voice but didn't succeed. Her brows slowly drew down, and she closed her eyes again. He didn't want her to dive back into that drugged state again but knew that she could. Leaning over, he pressed a kiss to her forehead, inhaling her special scent. The nurses had used a shampoo with a cinnamon fragrance, and he smiled a little as he lifted his mouth away from her forehead.

"You're coming out of a drug haze, sweetheart, but you're going to be all right…" His voice still shook as he gazed at her. She emanated such an ethereal innocence. It had nothing to do with her age, her maturity, or her life experiences. It was simply a part of her, of who she was from the time she'd been born until this minute. He grazed her cheek as she stared uncomprehendingly up at him.

"Teren? Do you understand me?"

Nolan watched her blink owlishly, as if those words had to go through a layer of gauze before they reached her barely functioning mind. He stroked her damp, cool fingers, which lay across her blanketed stomach. Touch was so healing and powerful. Nolan watched as she gradually focused on his hand against her cheek, warm and calloused, giving her something to orient herself by.

Joy surged through him as he saw her huge black pupils begin to enlarge. Before, they had been small and pinpointed, indicating the drug in her system. Now they were opening—a good sign. There was a small lamp on in the room, nothing bright that might blind her or make her squint. As he removed his hand, he saw Teren's eyes change, as if she missed his contact with her.

Hope surged through him as he watched her fighting the drug, trying to reach more awareness. After about fifteen minutes, her gaze finally settled on his face. Teren looked at him, and Nolan's joy tripled. He knew she recognized him this time. Reaching out, he pushed a few strands of hair away from her brow. "Welcome back, sweetheart…"

Tears stung his eyes as he saw just a hint of one corner of her mouth curve upward in response. For the first time, Teren's fingers wrapped weakly around his. Swallowing several times, Nolan felt tears rolling down his cheeks. How he loved Teren with every fiber of his being! She was the woman he wanted to marry. To carry his children. To grow old together with. All future dreams, he knew. But now they would have a chance to work in that direction together. He had such an incredible vision for them and wanted so much to speak about what lay like a dream within him.

"Nolan…you came…" Her voice was husky, cracking with emotion.

"You knew I would," he rasped, tenderly kissing her lips. "You're not leaving my side anymore, Teren," he told her as he eased away, holding her clouded gaze. His heart soared as her tentative smile strengthened. Already, he could feel her fingers getting stronger, too. Finally, that drug was being washed out of her system.

"Uzan…"

"He's gone and won't ever hurt you again," he said. Nolan knew her mind wasn't working well. He couldn't speak at length because her attention was still wandering, thanks to the powerful drug given to her. "I'll tell you more later. Are you thirsty?"

Instantly, her eyes widened.

"Thought so," he murmured, releasing her hand and getting off the edge of the bed. "Let me get you some water, Teren."

It took another hour before Teren was truly coherent. She was desperate for water and drank almost a quart. Nolan had buzzed the nurse's station for help. Later, the doctor, a man in his fifties, kind and bespectacled, came to assess Teren's progress. He spoke fluent English with an Arabic lilt and held her hand, patting it, slowly going over the fact she'd been unconscious due to the drug given to her.

Nolan had stood on the opposite side of her bed, her other hand in his. He wasn't about to let her go. *No way.* Right now, he could see that terror would grip her for a moment, then dissolve, only to return later. He was familiar with drugs and what they did to a person mentally, physically, and emotionally. They were a toxic tide within the body that came and went. And when they washed through a person, the victim would experience all kinds of nightmarish events. Emotions could rip out of their control and make them a puddle of feelings. He could see Teren going through this now. That was why he wasn't going to leave her alone. He'd be here when her emotions became magnified and tore through her. It was a rollercoaster ride coming off a drug like this.

When the doctor finished his explanation, he nodded gravely toward Nolan. "It will take several more hours for Miss Lambert to become fully conscious, Mr. Steele. I'll have one of my nurses bring her in some hearty chicken soup. Perhaps she'll be up to eating it. You can feed her, yes?"

"Yes," Nolan agreed, holding Teren's murky gaze.

"She may drift and suddenly fall asleep on you," the doctor warned. "Do not be alarmed. This is a natural healing cycle for her body. She might sleep an hour or two and then wake up once more. Every time this occurs she will be more aware, stronger mentally, and her brain will work better."

Nolan didn't want to let the doctor know what he knew. As a Delta operator, he'd had his share of times drugging an enemy to capture them and take them to the CIA to be interrogated. "Thanks for letting me know, doctor."

Nodding, the doctor bowed his head and then left.

Shortly after that, Nolan watched Teren slide back into oblivion. It was a waiting game, but one he was more than willing to participate in. Pulling up a chair next to her bed, he sat down, crossing his arms and resting his head against them. Capturing Teren's listless hand, he folded it gently within his own and closed his eyes. It had been one hell of a day and he was exhausted.

D<small>AWN WAS CRAWLING</small> up on the horizon, cleansing Khartoum with a watercolor pink wash as the light increased, highlighting the pencil-thin minarets, the call to prayer echoing across the city. Teren slowly dragged her lids open. She felt almost normal, her strength returning rapidly, her brain coming out of its fog and engaging with her wandering, half-formed thoughts. She became aware of a man's warm, callused hand around her own, and she moved her head to the right.

Her heart warmed as she saw Nolan asleep, head buried in his arms along the side of her bed, his massive hand wrapped protectively around hers.

Joy surged through her and Teren smiled softly, closing her eyes, so grateful that Nolan was here with her. Slowly, she moved her fingers up and down his roughened hand. He was so strong and enduring. She loved him. That thought melted through her like welcoming rain across a dry, thirsty desert, sending tendrils of incredible joy to every part of herself. She had survived. She was alive. And Nolan was here...with her. She slowly recalled what he had told her earlier.

Nolan stirred as she caressed his fingers. It was a special moment when he drowsily lifted his head, his eyes filled with sleep, his hair boyishly mussed. That unshaven beard of his darkened and emphasized the hard planes of his face. Teren watched him shake off the sleep, saw the deep exhaustion in his murky eyes, saw the love shining in them for her alone. She managed a weak smile.

"I'm alive...I thought I was going to die, Nolan. But I'm here. With you..." Her voice cracked, tears spilling hotly from her eyes, dribbling down her cheeks. Teren closed her fingers over his, seeing the anguish, the hope, flaring in his expression. His fingers curved gently around hers, and he stiffly eased upward after remaining in one position for so many hours. Then, perching his hip on the side of her bed, he leaned down and whispered, "You're home."

His words were filled with so much emotion—he was barely keeping control. He leaned down and placed his hands flat against her pillow on either side of her head, their faces inches apart. Her lips parted and he drowned in the sight of her coming back to him, her wide gray eyes framed by those thick lashes.

He placed his mouth against her brow, feeling the natural warmth of her skin beneath his lips. No longer was her flesh chilled and damp due to the drug in her system. He slowly placed light kisses across her hairline, trailing a few more down her temple, caressing her cheek before seeking and finding that sculptured, soft mouth of hers. Nolan groaned as Teren turned toward him, seeking him, hungrily pressing her lips against his.

Her flesh tingled, reminding Teren she really was alive, that she had escaped from the kidnappers. She didn't know how yet, but right now all she wanted...all she needed...was Nolan's strong, skilled mouth curving tenderly against her own, celebrating her life with his own. Drowning in his gently searching lips, feeling her tension melting away as he cupped her cheek, drawing her mouth more surely against his own, Teren made a happy sound in her throat.

Just his male scent, the way his mouth took hers, worshipped her, his hand eliciting more pleasure as he caressed her cheek, trailing his fingers along the side of her slender neck, pulled Teren back into the present. She was here with the man she loved. And never had she been more clear about her love for him, as his mouth tenderly molded against hers, shared his need of her, than in this scalding moment of coming together. Of welcoming one another back into each other's life. Because Teren had thought for sure that she was going to die, thought she'd never see Nolan again.

She made a mewling sound of unhappiness as Nolan reluctantly dragged his mouth from hers, their breathing fast and shallow. Staring up at him, she whispered, "I love you, Nolan…"

His face crumpled with so many withheld emotions, and she saw tears in his eyes—tears he didn't try to hide or wipe away. His love was life to her, and like a sponge, she drew it into her widening heart, the joy rushing through her.

"I love you…you are my life, Teren," Nolan managed to say gruffly, lifting his hand, smoothing it across her mussed hair. "I wasn't sure I would ever be able to tell you that. I was sorry I hadn't shared it with you earlier, but it was too soon…"

"I understand," she said brokenly. "I lay in that Land Rover thinking the same thing. I wanted so badly to let you know I loved you. I was so afraid I was going to die and you'd never know…"

He nodded. "We weren't sure we could get to you in time after you'd been kidnapped. But we did. It was too close, Teren. Too close. I nearly lost you…"

She lay there beneath his burning, intense gaze, absorbing him into every cell of her being. Her heart bounded with joy, with love. Teren saw Nolan's agony from nearly losing her and realized that her kidnapping had torn him apart. Nolan had lost his wife and the baby she'd carried, and had been sure he was going to lose Teren, too.

"I didn't want to die, Nolan." Teren swallowed hard and looked away, struggling to contain her rampant emotions. "I fought to live. I fought to come back to you…"

"You fought and escaped. We found that out later, after we caught up with you. It was Nazir, who drove the third Land Rover, who told us you had bailed out of the rear of the middle Rover, escaped down to the river, and disappeared into the reeds."

She sniffled and nodded. "I didn't know if you knew I'd been kidnapped or not, Nolan. I woke up in the back of the vehicle and looked out the window. There was another Rover behind us, and so many thick, yellow dust clouds that I couldn't see beyond it. I was trying to see if you were behind us…"

"We were within a mile of you but invisible to you in that dust," he muttered, straightening up on the bed, his hip against hers, holding her hand. "Can I get you something? Water? Food?"

"N-no…just you."

"Well," he said wryly, "you've got me, sweetheart. I'm not going anywhere."

She looked around the room, which was now growing lighter as the dawn deepened in the east. "Where are we?"

"Khartoum. The medical center. The doc says you're going to be fine. Your knees are pretty well chewed up from landing on them on that gravel road, but he took care of them for you. Your palms have some cuts and scratches and you're pretty bruised up here and there. Mostly, you're dealing with a drug overdose in your system, and he said you'll come out of it within the next twenty-four hours. Do you feel up to me telling you what happened?"

"Yes," she whispered, pushing more strands from her brow. "I lost sight of you, Nolan, when that spitting cobra came out of nowhere from behind the hut where I was standing with the doctor and a patient."

"Uzan created a distraction by releasing three cobras into the village. He planned it well, because the villagers stampeded in the directions he wanted. He grabbed you by that hut, pulled you behind it, and hit you with a syringe of drugs, knocking you out. I was twenty feet away from you, but I'd been distracted by the cobra. Fortunately, a young boy saw you being kidnapped and ran over to tell me. I then contacted Ayman and his soldiers, and we took off after you."

Teren gave a resigned sigh. "Can you help me sit up?"

Nolan flipped a switch on the bed and it slowly whirred up, moving Teren into a comfortable semi-seated position. He sat down on the bed, facing her, and she curved her fingers into his.

"I recognized Uzan when he grabbed me and dragged me behind that hut. I saw the flash of the needle, and I remember the pain in my upper arm. I fought hard, Nolan, I really did. I was so panicked. But then my body just went limp on me, and the last thing I remember is being tossed into the back of a Land Rover by two of his men."

"Yeah, that's about right from what the boy told me," he agreed, smoothing his fingers over hers. "I had to dodge panicking, screaming people and kill the damned cobra that stood between me and where Uzan had taken you. I raced around the hut to see the three Land Rovers heading north. The kid saw it all happen. He didn't know which vehicle you were in, Teren." His mouth flattened and Nolan gave her a caring look. "I wasn't going to shoot indiscriminately at them, because I was afraid I might hit you instead."

A nurse appeared and smiled. She took Teren's vitals and wrote them down on the chart hanging on the end of the bed, stopping their conversation for a moment. Nolan remained patient. There was more to tell her.

CHAPTER 20

AFTER THE NURSE left, Teren drank some cold water that Nolan had poured for her, her mind clearing even more. "Did Ayman and his soldiers come with you?" Teren asked, her voice still hoarse.

"Yes, we took one of the vans that brought the medical team in. I couldn't drive fast enough to catch up to you. We were going sixty miles an hour, and that was dangerous because one wrong move and I could have flipped our van over and killed all of us. Uzan and his three Land Rovers were going the same speed, but they had a mile's head start on us. We couldn't catch up until we hit that ninety-degree curve where everyone had to slow way down."

"I remember getting bounced around a lot," Teren recalled, her hand over his, feeling his quiet strength feeding her. "I knew my only possible escape was out the rear door, but I didn't know if the handle was locked or not. I peeked out the back to see another Rover behind us, and I knew I had one chance to make a break for it."

"At that ninety-degree corner?"

"Yes." Teren rolled her eyes. "I'm so glad I knew this road so well, Nolan. I was hoping we hadn't passed it yet. My mind was woozy and kept shorting out. They'd left me untied. I don't know why, but they did. They probably figured I was so drugged up, I would never regain consciousness. I couldn't just sit up and look around because that would let everyone in front of me know that I was conscious. I didn't want the soldiers in the seat ahead of me to know I'd awakened."

Grimly, Nolan said, "Uzan probably thought he'd given you enough drugs to make you unconscious until they reached Khartoum."

A cold shiver moved up Teren's back. "I figured he'd disappear with me into the slums, Nolan. You'd never have found me again if that had happened," she whispered, remembering how terrified she'd been at the thought. She felt his fingers tighten around hers, as if to reassure her.

"You were so damned brave, jumping out of that vehicle," Nolan rasped, reaching out to touch her cheek.

"It worked," Teren whispered with relief. "I don't remember much because my mind was all over the place from the drug. I knew if I made it to the reeds and the river, Uzan would send his soldiers after me. If that happened, I wasn't sure I'd survive." Teren shrugged, lifting one shoulder because she felt stiff, bruised, and sore all over. "I had to try, Nolan, because I loved you…I wanted—needed—a chance to have some kind of life with you."

"We're going to discuss that in the coming days," he promised her, moving his hand slowly up and down her forearm. "When you feel better."

"Good," she said, wiping tears from her eyes, the drug still making her overly emotional. "Because there's a lot I need to discuss with you, too."

"And we will," he promised her, caressing the top of her tousled hair. "You managed to get away from Uzan. We raced up to the Land Rovers and slammed on the brakes. They weren't expecting us and Ayman and his soldiers took most of them down. I tried to find Uzan in the firefight but didn't. And I couldn't find you, either. I was afraid he'd captured you and dragged you off into the reeds of the river."

"I never saw him, Nolan. I heard a lot of gunfire at one point, so that was probably when you and Ayman arrived and you attacked them."

"Probably. One of Uzan's men had an RPG. After Ayman deduced you weren't in any of the vehicles, he ordered his soldiers who had hand grenades to throw them at the Land Rovers, destroying all three of them so they couldn't take off again." He smiled a little. "Ayman's one hell of an Army officer. He directed the entire firefight. He's a good man, Teren."

"I've never seen him in action until now," she said, her voice husky with tears. "I felt the blast waves from those grenades, though; they about knocked me over. It was awful and those waves almost punctured my eardrums."

"Yeah, it was a helluva firefight, but it didn't last long. Once we got the goons in flex cuffs, Ayman found Nazir among the survivors."

Eyes widening, Teren gasped. "Nazir? He was there? Oh, no!"

Nolan saw the betrayal in her eyes, the hurt that Nazir would turn on her. "Yeah. He told Ayman that you'd escaped out of the middle Rover and dove into the reed beds of the Nile. He wasn't sure which way you went after you disappeared."

"Oh," Teren choked out in despair. "Nazir was doing so well at Kitra until he tried to break into my duplex."

"He came from Darfur, one of the most torn-up, miserable pieces of real estate on this earth. He was a child soldier, Teren. He couldn't overcome his past." He lowered his voice, leaning forward to wipe the tears off her cheeks. "I'm sorry. I know you liked him, and everyone at Kitra had faith that he could succeed."

"This—this is just so awful to realize, Nolan."

"Well, in his own way he did help us. He gave up the intel on you to Ayman when he asked where you'd been taken."

She pressed her hands to her face. "He had a dark heart, Nolan. No one at Kitra saw it."

"The darkness in him overwhelmed the good in him," he said gently, seeing the regret and grief in her eyes. Teren's love for people was one-hundred percent. She never withheld her heart from anyone, no matter what their pasts consisted of when they came to Kitra for help. And while it was a weakness she paid for in situations like this, Nolan also knew it was one of her greatest strengths. "Everyone at Kitra did the best they could to help Nazir. It was his responsibility to make healthy choices for himself, and he couldn't."

Gulping, she took a tissue that Nolan offered her, blowing her nose and wiping her eyes. Gripping it in her hands, she managed to ask, "But he's alive? He'll live?"

"Yes, just a scratch on his arm. Ayman and his soldiers killed ten out of the eighteen men who were hired by Uzan."

She wiped her eyes with a trembling hand. "You said Uzan was dead?" She saw Nolan's blue eyes glint with feral satisfaction.

"You were unconscious on the bank of the Nile. Uzan had headed north like you had after he escaped the firefight by slipping into the reed beds. It was a good thing you had lost consciousness on the bank, Teren, because he probably passed within ten feet of where you lay and didn't spot you."

Her hand automatically went to her throat. "No…"

"Yeah," Nolan growled. "But the reeds are so thick and because you were lying still, he never caught sight of you halfway up that bank."

"He was using the reeds to hide while he worked his way toward Zalta?"

"Yes, just like you were. Only the drugs wiped you out, and you went unconscious. I don't know if he was hunting you down or not. Probably was, but he also had to escape us, so he changed his priorities to save his own hide."

Teren's mouth thinned and she shivered. "He'd have killed me if he'd found me."

"Yes, I'm sure he would have. Once we spotted you, Ayman and I lifted you off that muddy bank and I carried you to a nearby tree and put you down in the shade. About that time, two of Ayman's soldiers spotted Uzan south of where we'd located you." Pleasure vibrated in his low tone. "Uzan was swimming across the river. He was halfway across it when Ayman's soldiers saw two crocodiles swimming toward him."

"Oh, God…" Teren whispered, her eyes widening. "Don't tell me…"

"Yeah, they let the crocs finish the bastard off," Nolan said in a gritty tone filled with pleasure. "I didn't know any of this until after I heard Uzan's screams. I didn't see it happen, but Ayman's soldiers said the crocs got him, dragged him beneath the waters, and he never resurfaced." He smiled tightly. "A fitting end for a killer like him."

Blanching, Teren leaned against the bed, her hand across her closed eyes, feeling relief soar through her. "But…what a horrible way to die…" She allowed her hand to fall away from her eyes, holding Nolan's flat, dark stare. There was no remorse in his expression. "You never recovered his body?"

"No. Ayman said they might find some of his torn clothing drifting down the Nile toward Zalta's bridge over the river in a few days, but that's all. Crocs aren't picky eaters. They consume a whole carcass."

Her throat closed up and she nodded. "All the while I was using the reeds to hide in, I was so fearful of a croc finding me, Nolan. I didn't know my knees were bleeding until I looked down and saw the blood in the water around them. And then I really panicked, because I know crocs can smell blood a mile away and follow the trail until they find the bleeder." She sighed heavily. "I started getting dizzy and nauseous, so I headed for shore, knowing my blood was tainting the water. I think I passed out before I could get completely out of the water."

"You must have, because the lower half of you was still in the water when I found you, Teren. You got lucky."

"What—what do you think Uzan would have done to me if he'd captured me and made it back to Khartoum with me?"

Grimacing, Nolan said soothingly, "It's not important to conjecture, Teren. It didn't happen." He gave her a pleading look, knowing that this trauma was going to affect her for a long, long time to come. Nolan had no wish to add to the trauma possibilities, giving her even more nightmares. She'd have plenty already based upon yesterday's experiences. "What I want you to do now is just focus on the positives, not on the scary things that didn't happen. Okay?"

"Yes, that's a good idea." Teren looked around the room. It was now flooded with a wash of pink light, the sun about to come up above the horizon. "When can we go home to Kitra? I don't like hospitals."

Nolan smiled a little. "Sometime today. Your doctor will want to check you over one more time and then he'll release you. Ayman has two *haflas* standing by with a driver. He has three soldiers guarding the door here in the hospital and they will follow us home. I'll make a call to him and then we'll leave for Kitra." He saw relief instantly come to Teren's pale features. The drug was still in her, but not as much as before.

"That sounds so good, Nolan. I-I really need Kitra. My friends…the children…the mothers…and you…"

"I know you do," he rasped, taking her hand, holding it, wanting to infuse her with his strength, his calm.

"And I need you more than anything else in my life, Nolan," she admitted, clinging to his gaze. "Just you."

Nolan moved closer, easing Teren into his arms. She sighed brokenly, her head coming to rest on his shoulder, their brows touching. He closed his eyes as she weakly slid her arms around his waist, holding him as hard as she could, realizing that she was still not anywhere near her full strength.

Sliding his fingers through her loose, unbound hair, he whispered, "You've got me, Teren. I'm not ever leaving your side again. Not ever."

NEVER HAD TEREN felt better than when Nolan and Ayman walked her slowly, on unsure legs, into her duplex. They had arrived at Kitra near midnight. The village was sleeping quietly and Ayman had met them at the main gate. She was exhausted but happy to be home. At the door, Ayman swung it open and stepped aside.

"I've already cleared your duplex. Go rest, Teren," he urged her quietly. "You've had a very rough time the past few days."

Teren held his glittering gaze beneath the porch light. "I will, Uncle. Thank you…for everything."

"Farida wants you to come back to work when you feel up to it. Take your time," Ayman counseled. "Your two office assistants are in charge of the online store. They are doing just fine, so don't worry, all right?"

"Okay," she whispered, giving him a look of gratefulness. Reaching out, she squeezed Ayman's long, strong hand. "Thank you, again—for everything…for rescuing me." She saw the man's eyes glint with tears, but then just as quickly, they disappeared. His fingers were comforting and warm around her hand.

"Allah was good to us today, my child. His angels will guard you as you sleep, Teren. Good night." He released her hand, stepping outside the entrance.

Nolan watched Ayman and his soldiers move silently along the walk, heading toward their duplexes on the other side of the admin building. He slipped his arm around Teren and she leaned against him, needing his solid strength. "Come on. Let's get you inside. Does a hot bath sound good to you?"

Did it ever! "Very much," Teren admitted wearily. Someone had thoughtfully brought some of the wildflowers that grew nearby along the edges of their massive gardens and put them in a small blue vase on the coffee table. It was an endearing touch, and again, she found herself close to tears. Teren had never cried so much, off and on, as she had today. Nolan had reassured her it was the drug working its way out of her system, that it made everyone super-emotional and that the crying was good for her.

Teren was tired of crying, but she knew she'd suffered a life-changing trauma, so she wasn't as hard on herself as she might have been.

Closing the door, Nolan locked it. He took Teren directly to the large bathroom and had her sit down on the small stool while he got the water running in the tub. She moved slowly, still somewhat uncoordinated. Nolan understood it was the drug. Kneeling down, he eased her boots off her feet, setting them aside. The darkness in her eyes told him that she was crashing, which wasn't unusual. In minutes, he had her undressed. He tested the warmth of the water with his fingers and satisfied, helped Teren climb into the huge garden tub. He felt relief when she sighed and smiled as she eased into the water.

"Just soak," he advised. "I'll be back in a little bit."

Nolan, out of habit, cleared his apartment, leaving the door standing open between them. Teren was going to sleep with him at her side. He wouldn't leave her alone to deal with what he knew would haunt her sleeping hours. As an operator, after a firefight, the nightmares would torment him for a week or so. It was just a way for him to work out the emotional trauma of the situation. It would be no different for Teren. But he'd be there for her. She wouldn't have to go through this alone like he always had.

Nolan was sure that she wasn't in any way prepared for what could happen to her. PTSD was real, and she'd nearly died. It would raise its ugly head again and again in Teren. A fierce love for her overwhelmed him as he walked into her bedroom and drew down the sheet and the chenille bedspread.

Later, Nolan joined her in bed after taking a long, hot shower that dissolved some of his stiffness. The brutal demands on his body had left their impact on his joints and hot water always eased their soreness. The night light in the hall spilled hazily into her bedroom. Teren had dressed in a pink sleeveless tee with her thin pink cotton pajama bottoms on. It hurt him to see that she lay asleep on her side in the middle of the bed, knees drawn up toward her body. That fetal position told him that even in sleep, she felt threatened.

Naked, his skin damp from the heat of the shower, he slipped in beside Teren, his body wrapped around hers, her back curved against the front of him. Nolan didn't try to force her to stretch out her legs along his. He wanted her to sleep because he knew that would heal her more quickly than anything else. The shock of the event was still with Teren and would remain with her for weeks, maybe months, to come. Every person reacted to trauma differently. In some, it left quickly—while in others, it could take longer.

As Nolan slid his arm beneath her neck, folding his other arm around the front of her, gently bringing Teren fully against him, he heard a little sound of comfort in her throat. She sensed him with her even though she was asleep. Nolan felt grateful as she sagged against him. It was enough.

TEREN HEARD THE roosters crowing outside her duplex window and their noise broke her out of a deep sleep. Frustrated, not wanting to be roused, she fought against surfacing. Ordinarily, she awoke quickly, fully alert, but now her sluggish brain whispered that she was still healing from being kidnapped.

As she stirred, she felt comfortably warm, the sheet across her lower body, her hand beneath her cheek on the pillow. Somewhere, she heard music, a harp. It was an instrument she hadn't heard in a long time. She dragged her lids open, listening to it. The door to her bedroom was partially open and soothing music drifted quietly through the room. It was a beautiful sound and it brought back memories of her childhood, of Christmas at church, of a woman parishioner who was a harpist. Those were happy times for Teren.

Snuggling her face deep into the pillow, a new happiness thrummed through her, chasing away the cloudiness of sleep. *Nolan.* Teren allowed herself to feel her love for him. Before the kidnapping she had tried to downplay it, tried to explain it away, tried to hide from it because she'd fallen so swiftly for the man. People just didn't suddenly fall in love like that, did they? Wasn't a long time needed in order to know for sure? At least that is what her inexperienced mind told her. But her heart had other desires, never listening to her brain—and it desired Nolan now, not later.

Teren once more regretted her lack of worldliness about men and relationships in general. But right now, that didn't matter. Whatever questions she had had about being powerfully attracted to Nolan on every level had been more than answered, and she was at peace with herself and her decision.

She heard a noise at the door and barely lifted her head. "Nolan…" He stood in the doorway, leaning casually against the jamb, a cup of coffee in hand. He was dressed in that revealing dark green T-shirt and those body-sculpting jeans, and she felt her whole body flare to life. The man was sensual, sexy, and hers. All hers. She managed a partial, sleepy smile, slowly pushing up into a sitting position.

"That coffee smells so good."

"It's got cream and sugar in it," he warned. "Want it?" He held it toward her. Nolan couldn't stop the hunger that swept through him as Teren sat up, looking like the disheveled but beautiful young woman that she was. Her hair was tousled and soft around her drowsy features. The tee she wore brought out the slenderness of her body, her proud shoulders, and those small, tempting breasts of hers, the nipples pressing strongly against the cotton fabric. Most of all, as he held her cloudy gaze Nolan saw clarity in her eyes. Teren was fully here in her body, not drifting in and out from that opiate that she'd been given.

Gratitude flooded him as he saw her nod and stretch her hand in his direction for the bright yellow ceramic cup he was holding.

Nolan sat down on the bed facing her, easing the mug between her long, artistic hands. He smiled into her eyes and watched as she brought the steaming coffee to her lips, tentatively sipping it and then blowing across it to cool it. Just watching how her lips moved sent fire through him. Already, he could feel his erection pressing against the zipper of his jeans. Nolan knew that sex wasn't the answer for Teren right now—she needed a safe environment and she needed to be comforted. She had to let him know what felt right to her because he knew coming out of a drugged state, a person's emotions could whiplash around at a moment's notice. Teren would probably be in that unpredictable state for two or three more days.

"Mmm," Teren said, sipping the coffee with relish. "This tastes so good. Thank you."

"It's probably got more sugar in it than you're used to," Nolan said, hooking his one leg up on the bed and pushing it beneath him, his other foot resting on the floor. "Gives you instant energy."

Teren absorbed Nolan's quiet, steady nearness. "I don't normally drink coffee with sugar in it," she admitted. "What time is it, Nolan?" The clock was on the nightstand behind her, and she didn't want to twist around to look at it. Her body felt a lot less stiff and sore than it had been last night before she soaked in that warm tub of water. Leaning against the carved wooden headboard, she drew her legs up near her body, feeling her cranky, bruised knees protest. Nolan had put more antiseptic on both of them after she'd gotten out of the bath. He'd carefully dressed her injured knees before she went to bed to protect her stitched flesh.

Glancing at his watch, he said, "Ten a.m." He saw the surprise flare in her eyes. "You needed it," he stressed darkly. "And you have the day off, so relax."

"Ten," Teren muttered. "I *never* sleep that long!"

"Shock is the culprit," he said, moving his hand lightly down her leg beneath the light blue sheet.

"I'll bet you could write a book about what trauma does to people," she muttered, sipping the coffee and feeling her strength increasing. "You seem to know exactly where I'm at and what I'm feeling, Nolan. To do that, it must have happened to you." And then she thought about the worst shock in his life: losing Linda and his baby. There was no question Nolan had dealt with tragedy—and survived.

Teren wasn't so sure she would have recovered from a blow one-tenth as serious as Nolan's had been. It served to tell her just how strong he was mentally and emotionally. He was such a rock, so steady and solid. Teren felt like a cork bobbing on the ocean in comparison. But she'd always been that way because she lived, for the most part, on her passion and her emotions.

"As an operator, I've had a few shocks," he admitted quietly. "I always like your insight, Teren. The way you think. The way you see yourself and others." He caressed her foot, his fingers making light patterns around her covered ankle.

"It's just who I am," she offered softly, feeling the tenderness of his touch. It made Teren feel valued, important to Nolan, emphasizing how much he really loved her. "And you? You didn't get the psychological depth you have without experience, without a lot of events happening in your life."

He snorted a little and gave her a bemused look. "Age coupled with experience hopefully gives everyone a little maturity and a drop of wisdom, sweetheart. You have a natural ability to read others. It's a gift you were born with. I saw that in you from the moment we met at the airport." His hand tightened around her foot for a moment. "I'm going to spend the next few days detailing just why I love you so much, Teren. I knew all these things about you beforehand. We haven't been together that long, and I was waiting for a better time to share them with you. Then after this kidnapping attempt, I said to hell with it. I was going to let you know exactly how I felt about you and why I love you so much. You're an extraordinary woman, but I don't think you see that in yourself—but I do. And I'm going to show you every day, in large and small ways, who you are, your skills, your wisdom, your compassion, and that very, very large heart of yours that has room for strangers and friends alike."

She finished the coffee, leaning over and placing the cup on the nightstand. Sweeping joy shimmered through her as Nolan's low, gritty voice flowed like sweet falling rain on the parched land surrounding Kitra. She eased her legs slowly down until they were straight beneath the sheet. "I don't see any of that in me, Nolan." Reaching out, she tangled her fingers in his own, holding his intense gaze. The man, she thought, was a mind reader—there was nothing she could hide from him. Not that Teren ever wanted to. She was curious as to how he saw her, because he made her feel so good, so positive about herself.

Compared to her family of origin, who always cut her down, belittled her, made her feel badly about herself, Nolan was like sunshine spilling into the darkness of her soul, illuminating her, showing her that she had beauty and purpose. He saw her as someone to be valued. That was such a freeing realization, and her heart was grateful that he saw her in that light.

"Well, I intend to remedy that, Teren. Ayman, Farida, Nafeesa, and Abit all see what I see in you. They may not give it my words exactly, but they see who you are. Why do you think you're so loved here at Kitra? Everyone here wants your touch, your smile. And you're able to give your love freely to everyone. As wounded as you were by your family, you had the inner strength, faith, or whatever else you want to call it, to work through your own pain, heal yourself, and turn around and give love in return to others. That's remarkable in my book because not a whole lot of people can do that." He squeezed her fingers. "That's just one more reason why I fell in love with you."

"You make me sound like a saint," she protested, giving a shake of her head. "I'm human, Nolan. I make mistakes every day."

"We all do. But not everyone has the capacity you have for loving others, Teren."

She sobered. "Well, what else is there?"

He smiled a little. "Indeed."

"Every human owns a heart, Nolan. Every human has the same capacity that I carry in me."

"I would argue that while that's true, not every human being has the strength or desire to attain the level of caring that you operate at every day, without ever thinking about it. And no, you're not a saint. And yes, you make mistakes. But I love you just the way you are."

And now she had to give back to the man who had changed her life. "I love you so much, Nolan." Her voice trembled. "I tried so hard to push you away from me before because the power of our attraction scared me. I-I'd just never felt what I felt for you. Plus, I was such a neophyte, I didn't have the experience I needed to understand what was happening to me…to us."

"Your heart knew, Teren. Just like mine did." Nolan squeezed her hand. "We were both trying to run away from admitting our love to one another for different reasons. I was afraid to admit how I felt toward you because of losing my family. I fought it every day, but you were like fog and just eased in between all the shields I'd put up to stop me from saying I'd fallen in love with you."

"Because you were afraid if you fell in love with me, you could lose me like you'd lost your family?"

Nolan was stunned by the depth of her understanding of him. "Yes," he admitted, his emotions nearly overwhelming him. "Yes, that was it exactly."

She saw the grief and loss in his eyes, comprehending it on an even deeper level than before. She'd almost lost him. The tragedy he'd endured scored her heart and deepened her understanding of what Nolan had gone through and somehow, had managed to survive.

Curling her hand around his, she saw him close his eyes for a moment, feeling him battling back a lot of emotions. She knew Nolan wasn't the kind of man to cry in front of anyone. Teren hoped that someday he would entrust her fully with himself. Her intuition told her that he would, and she tightened her fingers around his, giving him a tender look as he opened his eyes, staring at her. More than anything, she wanted to help him heal from his horribly tragic past. For the first time in her life she understood the power of love, from one heart to another. And she would surround Nolan with her love, helping him to gently allow the past to remain a part of him but orient himself toward the present—and a future with her.

CHAPTER 21

AFTER BREAKFAST WITH Nolan, Teren wanted to see Farida and check in with her hardworking office staff. Her knees were painful, but the more she walked and moved around, the less stiff they became. It was a small price to pay for her freedom. The morning was warming up, the sky cloudless, the shafts of sunlight flowing strongly across the ruffling grass of the flat land around them. Kitra throbbed with life, everyone had finished breakfast and gone to their respective places of work or schooling.

Teren loved the pulsating energy of this place, but today she appreciated it as never before. Nolan accompanied her to Farida's office in the admin building and stayed in the background. Everyone in the building had heard that Teren had just arrived and soon, the huge office was filled with well-wishers and Teren's friends. Laughter rang in the air, her friends hugged her, and there were a lot of tears of relief that she was alive and safe. Nolan began to understand the family atmosphere of Kitra as never before, because clearly, Teren was part of the fabric of this place. She cried with her friends and Nolan wanted to comfort her, but he realized Teren's friends were her spiritual family, supporting her through this experience, giving their love to her. This morning over breakfast in her duplex, Nolan learned that she was rarely in touch with her real family in Kentucky. She sent them an email every three months or so, somewhat impersonal, just letting them know she was happy where she was.

When Ayman entered the noisy, joyful office, he spotted Nolan and nodded, then crooked a finger, asking Nolan to come with him. Teren was safe here, so Nolan left and met the security officer out in the highly polished hall.

"What's up?" Nolan asked. He saw that Ayman's face was filled with concern.

"I just got off the satellite phone with Tal over at Artemis," he said. "Their security people have been in touch with the CIA. They're picking up cell phone chatter out of Pakistan about Enver Uzan."

Scowling, Nolan leaned against the metal lockers alongside the wall, arms across his chest, studying Ayman. "What kind of chatter?"

Shrugging, Ayman said, "Tal didn't tell me her sources, but I've put it together. Zakir Sharan is monitored by U.S. satellites passing overhead. Every time he uses a cell phone, it's picked up. For whatever reason, he didn't use an encrypted one this time and the CIA picked him up talking to someone in Khartoum. The man he talked to is another officer with al-Qaeda. The CIA is running intel on him to see what they have in their database on him right now."

"What's the bottom line?" Nolan demanded, not liking the situation.

Ayman rubbed his jaw, giving him a worried look. "Sharan has figured out that Uzan is dead or missing in action. It's likely he's sent a second officer to go after Teren. I'm sorry. It's not to be unexpected under the circumstances. Sharan still wants to go after her."

"Sonofabitch!" Nolan allowed his arms to fall to his sides as he glared over at Ayman. "We have to get her out of here, then. He's focused on her as a way to make a statement about Kitra and the other Delos charities in Sudan."

"Right. Tal came to that same conclusion," Ayman murmured. He sighed. "They want Teren back on U.S. soil, Nolan. They're ordering her home. I'm sure when she goes to look at her emails in her office, she'll find that order. Tal is sending a company jet right now to Khartoum's airport. They want her out of this country as soon as possible. They want to remove the threat from Teren, as well as from Kitra."

Clenching his teeth, Nolan knew this news would shatter Teren. This was her home. Her family. "This is going to be hard on her."

"I know," Ayman murmured, reaching out, patting his shoulder. "We'll miss her as much as she'll miss us. But Tal is right: Teren's life is in jeopardy if she continues to remain here. Sharan isn't going to stop trying to get to her. He sees her as a symbol, a soft target, easy to go after. Kitra is too well fortified, and he knows that. He'll never be able to breach our walls or destroy what is here. But he can go after a lone American woman because she's constantly outside Kitra's walls helping medical teams in the nearby villages."

Anger moved through Nolan along with frustration. "All right," he growled. "Let her be with her friends for right now and I'll tell her later."

"Bring Teren to my office after that, please. She is like a daughter to me and my family. I think she will listen to me about the seriousness of this situation, when she might hope to convince someone here at Kitra to allow her to stay. She won't want to hear this news, but I can impress it upon her. Better that it comes from me than from you."

Sadness moved through Nolan. Their love was barely taking hold with one another, and now this. "You're right. I was hoping against hope that with Uzan killed, Sharan might move on. But I figured he'd send another assassin to go after her, too. I didn't want to go there, but here it is…"

Grimly, Ayman said, "He's a man on a mission. He's fixated."

"Does Tal think Sharan will move his focus elsewhere if Teren is gone?"

Nodding, he said, "Yes, but then it becomes a scramble to find who he's going to target next. It's clear from the conversation the CIA taped that he wants an American man or woman working at a Delos charity. He wants to set an example. We have two other charities here in Sudan, and both have an American working with them. They could become his next targets of opportunity."

"My thoughts also," Nolan growled.

"No one is sure yet what target Sharan will choose or who he is going to focus on after Teren is removed from Kitra. It's a constant worry. Wyatt is convening a high-level meeting with the NSA and CIA over at Langley right now. They're putting all the scraps of intel and cell phone calls together, trying to figure out where Sharan might focus his hatred and attack next."

"But the only clear piece of intel," Nolan said, "is that Sharan is going to go after a U.S. citizen who works for Delos. Is that correct?"

"Yes," Ayman said, unhappy. "As you know, Tal and Matt killed both his sons in Afghanistan. So, from what I can see, Sharan is focused on anyone who is a U.S. citizen and works for a Delos charity. It's just a question of where he will strike next."

Shaking his head, Nolan muttered, "That puts Delos in a helluva bind."

"I've worked with Dilara Culver, who runs Delos from their headquarters in Alexandria, Virginia, for many years, Nolan. She's the sweetest, kindest, and most generous person I have ever met. She helped build Kitra into what it's become today. She hired me and my soldiers, putting out a lot of money to ensure that this place would be safe for those who need help and support." Ayman shook his head. "I hate to see that it's come to this. Sharan's sons were evil. They were in no way Muslims. One was an opium warlord, the other dealt in kidnapping women and children and selling them into the global sex-trafficking trade."

"Like father, like sons," Nolan ground out.

"Yes. The planet is better off without their kind. But now, Sharan believes in an eye-for-an-eye revenge, and he's sworn a lifelong vendetta against Delos charities around the world. He won't give up. He's one of the richest men in the world. He's got the money. He can hire anyone, and he's already got a replacement in Khartoum to go after a new target of opportunity. Again."

Aching for Teren, Nolan rasped, "She doesn't need this on top of just surviving that kidnapping, Ayman. It's going to total her. You know that."

Patting Nolan's arm, he said gently, "Yes, and that's why you must bring Teren to my office. This can't wait…and she will have your support. You will help her through this."

TEREN WIPED HER eyes and gave Nolan a tender look as she walked with him down the hall toward Ayman's office. "It's so wonderful to see everyone again. When I was in that Land Rover, I kept thinking I'd never see you to tell you I loved you and that I'd never see anyone here at Kitra again, either."

Nolan squeezed her hand and then released it, his heart heavy with sadness for Teren. She didn't know what was coming, and he knew it would devastate her further. "They love you and you love them, Teren."

"It's so good to be back home…"

He heard the quaver in her voice and winced inwardly. Maybe it *was* better that Ayman tell her how her life was going to change in the next twenty-four hours. Nolan wanted to protect Teren from the new unexpected shock, but there wasn't any way around it. He slowed his stride, pushing open Ayman's partially opened door.

Teren smiled as she entered Ayman's office. "Come here," she said, opening her arms. "I just need to hug you, Uncle."

Nolan quietly closed the door, watching Teren squeeze Ayman breathless. He knew how much of a part this man had played in her new, positive, healthy life. He was like a much-loved uncle she'd never had, but one that she needed. There was affection shining in Ayman's dark eyes as he walked her to one of the two chairs in front of his large, wooden desk.

"Have a seat, child," he said. Ayman gestured to Nolan to come and sit next to her.

"It's just so good to be home," Teren bubbled, crossing her legs, her hands in her lap, smiling at Ayman as he sat down.

"And we're relieved you are back here with us," Ayman told her. He became somber, opening his hands on the desk, looking into Teren's dancing gray eyes. "Teren, we've learned of some new and very disturbing developments, and you need to be aware of them," he began in a deep, gentle tone.

Nolan watched Teren's face lose color, her eyes widening, and he felt the shock emanating from her as Ayman quietly went over the CIA information with her. Her fingers dug into the arms of the chair where she sat, and he saw the fine tension leap through her. She sat forward a little more, her shoulders drawing upward. Damn it, this wasn't fair to her. She was barely over being kidnapped and nearly killed. At one point, she turned and looked at him after Ayman had finished.

"Is this threat real, Nolan?"

His mouth twisted. Reaching out, he placed his hand over her arm. "It's very real, Teren. It's not something that can be ignored."

"B-but," Teren stammered, looking toward Ayman's set expression, "what does this mean? Is Kitra a target again?"

"It will be if you don't leave," Ayman said gently. "No one wants this, but you've seen what Sharan is capable of, Teren. As long as you remain at Kitra, we all remain a target."

"Oh," she whispered in a strained voice, her hands against her mouth. Tears burned in her eyes. She clung to Ayman's unhappy gaze, which was filled with regret. Her heart twisted in her chest. "I won't let Kitra be a target, Uncle. You know that."

"I knew you would understand, my child," Ayman said heavily. "It would be like putting your family at risk if you remained. I know how hard this is for you, Teren. You are as much a part of us as we are of you. Kitra has bloomed because you came here with your ideas, your heart, vision, and passion."

Teren suddenly stood up, unable to remain still. She wrapped her arms around herself, pacing the office in utter turmoil. Nolan's expression mirrored hers. He knew how much the people of Kitra meant to her heart and soul, and now she had to leave them to protect what she loved so much.

Gulping back tears, Teren tried to think through everything. She finally halted, looking at both men.

"What's the plan, then? Tal must have one."

"She does," Ayman said, and he told her.

Nolan watched Teren blanch, darkness, grief, and shock coming to her eyes when Ayman finished telling her about the plan of action. He eased out of the chair, walking over to her. As he opened his arms, she came to him, and he was never more relieved. Nolan knew that this could have torn apart their fragile love that had just taken root. Instead, Teren went to him and let him hold her tightly. He felt the tension in her, felt her trying to do the right thing for the right reasons. Felt her jamming her tears of grief deep inside, trying to put on a brave face. But Teren wasn't an operator who could put on a mask and hide how she felt. No, she lived daily on her emotions, every one of them readable to all.

She buried her face against his shoulder. Threading his fingers through her loose hair, Nolan wanted so badly to remove the pain he felt around Teren—but he couldn't. All he could do was be there for her. After nearly dying, she was now being ripped away from the family she loved. Nolan couldn't think of anything worse than what was happening to her right now. It was a death of another sort—and equally devastating.

Ayman slowly stood up and walked around his desk. He came and placed his hand on Teren's sunken shoulder. "There is much hope here, Teren, even though you haven't seen it yet. Come and sit down. There's more, and it is good news for you."

Nolan didn't know what he was talking about but eased Teren out of his arms, walking her over to the chairs. He saw the anguish in her eyes.

Sitting tensely, Teren asked, "What else, Uncle?"

"Tal wants to offer you a job at Artemis, their security company. The umbrella company is Delos. She wants to offer you a position in their IT department. The website for Kitra's store is something she wants for every Delos charity around the world. She wants you to head up that department. You would work under Alexa, her younger sister, who runs the school program. They took your vision for Kitra, and now they want to maximize it for all the other charities. It's a good thing, Teren. You can do it safely while living in the U.S., and you'd be spreading your vision of the Internet store globally to all the other Delos charities. A store will increase the livelihood of people around the world, wherever a Delos charity is located. They'll have money to buy more food for their families and it will also give the women of each family a way to make a living. It's a win-win for everyone, and I think you know that."

Miserably, Teren nodded. "That's a wonderful position they're offering to me," she admitted, her voice hollow.

"And," Ayman added, giving her a gentle smile, "we will always be in touch with you by Skype, Teren. We have that facility here. We can call you up anytime and see how you are doing—and we will want you to call us, too."

Right now, Teren was too upset to even think about that, but she knew Ayman was trying his best to help her. "I-I'll miss all of you so much, Uncle," she whispered, her voice breaking.

"While you might not be here in body, Teren, in a way, you will always be with us in spirit. Your vision is important. What you've achieved here at Kitra you can now duplicate and spread around the world through all the other Delos charities. Think of how many more women, children, and families you will be helping! If you stayed here, that wouldn't happen. Kitra would continue to thrive, but you're much more than Kitra. I feel in my heart"—he pressed his hand to his chest—"that Tal really does acknowledge your global vision. And she's supporting you. You will have your own department. You will have people working beneath you that you'll train and guide. Good work deserves good support, and Artemis is offering all of that to you."

She searched Ayman's long face, heard the love in his voice for her, saw it in his warm gaze as he held hers. "It's just so much to take in all at once," she managed to say.

"I know. But as you have told me so many times in the past, when one door closes, another immediately opens up. And this is so, Teren, even for you. Kitra will miss you, but Artemis is opening a door to you that will help so many more people improve the quality of their lives around the world. Isn't that a worthy cause to pursue?"

She smiled brokenly, tears running down her cheeks. "You've been like a wonderful, wise, loving uncle to me, Ayman."

Tears glittered in his eyes, his mouth compressed. Placing his hand on her shoulder again, he said gruffly, "I will continue to be, if you'll allow me that honor. You will always be our adopted child, Teren. No matter where in the world you go, you are always in our hearts and minds. We will stay in touch. That, I promise."

THE GULFSTREAM G650, part of Delos's fleet of aircrafts, spanned the Atlantic Ocean, heading for Reagan National Airport near Washington, D.C. The Delos fleet had only red and yellow stripes running from nose to tail, down the center of the fuselage, to hint at its identity. The Delos symbol was nowhere in sight. That had been removed from the fleet over a year ago to prevent their planes from being easily identified or targeted precisely because they were Delos-owned jets. Now that Sharan had made a promise to destroy the global charity, security had to ramp up.

Nolan watched Teren sleeping on a leather couch placed along the opposite bulkhead from where he sat. She was covered in a warm wool blanket, her legs drawn up toward her chest. She had cried after boarding the jet at the Khartoum airport. Ayman, Farida, and all her friends had driven there to see her off. The Sudanese were people of the heart, and there were no dry eyes in the terminal. It took everything Nolan had not to cry with them. The amount of love between them and Teren had made him wonder if she would ever get over being torn away from Kitra.

She had clung to Nolan during these last twenty-four hours, adrift and grief-stricken—and he'd held her, been her anchor. He reassured her that she would make wonderful friendships of equal depth at Artemis. Weekly Skype calls to Sudan would be a gentle lifeline for Teren as she adjusted to her new job and new life. Already, Ayman and Farida had promised that they would fly to the U.S. to visit with her, and that helped Teren greatly. It tore Nolan up that her own family was incapable of supporting her at all, but he was also grateful to the Sudanese who loved her fiercely, and that love would not dim with time or space. There was a heart loyalty between them, and it would exist forever.

He looked out the oval window, the dawn rising with the aircraft at max throttle, just under Mach one, heading for the East Coast of the U.S. He'd been on the communications links that the aircraft provided. It had Wi-Fi, an encrypted satellite phone, and the latest electronic security.

Nolan had asked Wyatt to get someone to his farmhouse, and get it cleaned up and welcoming for him and Teren. It would be her new home, he hoped. Nolan knew her heart wouldn't be focused on the farmhouse he'd bought because there was too much grief and loss for her to work through right now. But he wanted to make a home for her—a place where she could feel safe and thrive as never before. He silently promised her that even though he'd never said the words out loud.

Looking out the window of the jet, he saw the dark green of the Atlantic thirty-five thousand feet below where they flew. He saw the whitecaps, the long rows of waves moving relentlessly to some unseen destination.

Sharan was like that—an evil blot on Delos, relentless in pursuing his revenge against them. And any American working for Delos was a potential target. No one could have guessed this would happen.

The world was in an insanity spiral as far as Nolan was concerned, and darkness and evil were flourishing more and more daily. At Delos, they were going to be confronting it head-on. And thankfully, those who owned Delos were billionaires from their container shipping businesses across the globe, so they could afford to ratchet up the security of Artemus, hire the right people, and watch out for their enemies who were determined to make sure Delos wouldn't survive.

Moving stiffly in the comfortable leather chair, Nolan found peace by gazing at Teren's sleeping features. Her hair was caught up in a long barrette at the back of her head. She was on the wings of sleep, and for that, Nolan was grateful. He'd already talked to Tal and Wyatt about her physical and emotional state, and they understood. When a Delos limousine picked them up at the airport, they would be taken directly to his farmhouse in the country. It was peaceful and quiet—the perfect place to help her adapt to this sudden change in her life.

Nolan knew that eventually Teren would adjust. She would come to realize her life was her own once more and she wouldn't have to keep looking over her shoulder, wondering when she'd be kidnapped again by one of Sharan or Rasari's minions. She would create a new family within Artemis, because they really were a family company, not one of those heartless global corporations that cared nothing for the humans who worked for them.

Teren would have Nolan there, to listen to her, to hold her when she wept, to show her the beauty of this new life they could create together. Nolan believed their love would survive this and was going to fight for both of them to give it a chance. He didn't question Teren's love for him; he knew it was there.

Nolan held on to this hope because Teren reached for him when things got bad. She trusted him above all else.

Teren knew about the Culver family history, but he did, primarily through Matt Culver, who had been an Army Delta Force operator like him. They'd served together in Afghanistan, and sometimes his team would work either directly or indirectly with Matt's team. Nolan had been able to share this with Teren, and he'd seen some hint of interest when he told her much more about them. He emphasized that they were a tight family, just like her family at Kitra. Then he'd seen a glimmer of hope come to Teren's eyes. Heartened, he'd told her about Tal and Alexa, the women of the family. He filled her in on Dilara and Robert Culver, the parents of these children who ran Artemis. And Nolan had seen more hope grow in Teren's desolate expression. More than anything, he'd tried to build the vision that she was moving from one loving family to another. Here, too, she would be a loved, respected family member, embraced and welcomed, just as she had been at Kitra.

She'd already told him on the flight that when she came back to the States, she would not go back to Kentucky to visit her family. It would just reopen that wound from the past that had never healed between them. Nolan agreed with her. They'd only want Teren back if she'd throw away who she was to fit their idea of who she should be. That wouldn't happen.

Teren wasn't even sure she would let them know she'd returned stateside, such was the depth of the wound within her. Nolan acquiesced to whatever she wanted to do about it. In the future, he hoped that some kind of bridge between them might be rebuilt. But he wasn't sure. And neither was Teren. Her family, her real one, was back in Kitra. It was up to him to build her another family of equal love and caring here in Virginia.

And there was nothing Nolan wanted more.

CHAPTER 22

Teren loved Nolan's two-story, mid-nineteenth-century Virginia farmhouse. They stood together on the redbrick walk, which had a herringbone pattern, looking at it with appreciation. The fall afternoon was warm and the smell of decaying leaves permeated her senses. She was jet-lagged but couldn't deny how appealing the white farmhouse with dark brown shutters was—it felt like home to her. Leaning wearily against Nolan, his arm across her shoulders, she whispered, "It's beautiful, Nolan. Did you know? I love antiques and anything from another era?"

"No I didn't, but that's good to hear. This place is old all right, and it needs a lot of TLC. I think after I roll up my sleeves and get to repairing it, it'll be a home you can love even more." He gazed over at Teren, seeing her tender glance toward him.

She knew how much he'd gone through for her, but she didn't know that he'd feared their love might not weather the storm that surrounded her. Looking at her now, Nolan knew it was his fear from the past that was eating at him. Teren loved him. Period. That wasn't going to change.

"I love the wraparound porch," she said, gesturing to it. "And the swing. I love swings."

"You never told me that."

She smiled faintly, drowning in his eyes, absorbing his quiet stability, the effortless way his care embraced her and made her feel as if everything was going to be all right. "We never had time to talk about things like this, did we?"

"Well," he said gruffly, "we will now."

Nodding, Teren's gaze moved across the railing around the porch. At one time, it had been a screened-in porch, but that was now gone. "Are the mosquitoes in Virginia like the ones in Kentucky, always pests during the summer months?"

"Yep," he said. "Which is why I'm going to put up new screens next spring. I'd like us to use that swing on the porch and not be constantly batting at them."

The trees surrounding the farmhouse formed a palette of orange, yellow, and red colors against the backdrop of the green pasture behind the home. There was a red barn, two stories high, with paint peeling off the sides; the roof was rounded and the shingles looked worn.

Still, Teren felt a new surge of hope slowly moving through her. The place was in a cul-de-sac at the end of a narrow asphalt road. The wooden rail fencing needed a lot of TLC, too. "I wonder," she murmured, resting her head against Nolan's shoulder, "if the former owners loved this place as much as you do."

"I'm sure they did. But it's fallen into disrepair over the last twenty-five years."

"Was it abandoned?"

"No. The last surviving family member died two years ago, and there were no heirs, so it was put on the market by the family attorney and it finally found a new owner: me."

"I'm sure that house rang with happiness and laughter, tears and loss, and now holds many memories," she whispered, gazing at it.

He pressed a kiss to her hair. "I'd like to make new memories in it with you, Teren," he said, and saw her love for him reflected in the depths of her eyes. "How do you feel about that?" Inwardly, Nolan held his breath. He knew Teren was jet-lagged and emotionally strung out, but he needed to give her a foundation for her new life. "This will be a place where we can create new memories. Where we can dream together, and you can envision the colors you'd like to have in each of the rooms. The outside of the house can be any color you like. You can put antiques you've chosen in them and make this a real home for us."

"Yes . . . yes, that sounds wonderful, Nolan. I don't want a life without you in it. I know it's too soon, but now we have the time. Here," she moved her chin in the direction of the farmhouse, "we aren't under threat. We're safe here. We can relax, be ourselves, and have a real chance to explore one another."

She slid her fingers across his jaw, which needed to be shaved. "This farmhouse sort of looks like both of us right now: in a state of becoming. I love the symbolism, the overlay of how it looks and how each of us was abandoned in one way or another. But now, here we are, together. We have each other."

Teren watched his eyes grow dark with emotion, narrowing hungrily as he gazed at her. She went on, "Things happen for reasons, I've seen that in my own life. I've had time to think and feel my way through the stages of my life, and so far, I'm a better person now than before. My own family doesn't accept who I am, but Uncle Ayman and the people of Kitra welcomed me with open arms. They loved me just the way I am. They didn't try to change me." She cupped Nolan's cheek, a fierce love tunneling through her. "You welcomed me the same way. I feel like I'm growing, I'm opening up, blooming. I've been moved from one family I love in Sudan to this new family here, with you."

He slid his hands across her shoulders, feeling no tension in them. The way she languidly leaned against him made Nolan's heart soar. "We'll make a family, Teren. That's my promise to you. Whatever you want…I want it for you. I want you happy. I like hearing your laugh. I love holding you in my arms at night, holding you close to me in bed. I like hearing you think out loud, how you see life around you, how it touches and affects you." He leaned down, taking her lips, feeling her instant response, that happy sound vibrating in her slender throat as he deepened the kiss with her.

His world melted and dissolved beneath her mouth, her lips gliding against his; he felt her arms tighten around his shoulders, her fingers sliding through his short hair at the nape of his neck. She smelled so good to him, felt so alive and soft within his tight embrace, and Nolan absorbed the joy surrounding them.

As Teren eased her lips from his, he stared down and saw desire in her stormy gray eyes. "And now I'm going to carry you over the threshold," he growled, and he swept her up into his arms. Teren gave a surprised, happy laugh, her arms around his neck, her brow pressed against his jaw as he walked to the porch and climbed the creaking wooden stairs. Nolan unlocked the door and pushed it open with the toe of his boot. Light poured in through the curtained windows, flooding the foyer. He carried her to the right, into a high-ceilinged, formal living room. It was one of two places he'd already been working on to bring back to its original nineteenth-century charm.

Easing her down but keeping his arm around her waist, Nolan watched Teren take in the warm, bright room. He'd chosen American rococo revival antiques and a rosewood sofa with a small bird pattern of blue silk. There was an armchair, plus two sitting chairs with it. The huge redbrick fireplace went from floor to ceiling. There was a sideboard along one wall from the same period, and the wallpaper matched the period as well—pale cream with small lavender buds of roses and green leaves here and there. The matching cream-colored curtains were filmy, drawn back to allow the afternoon light to flood the room. They, too, were designed with plants and flowers throughout the texture of the fabric.

"This," Teren breathed in amazement, "is gorgeous, Nolan." She looked up at him. "Was it like this when you bought it? Or did you decorate it?"

"No, it was a gutted empty room," he said. "The floor was in bad shape and I replaced it with a light-colored oak that had originally been installed in it. The carpet beneath the sofa and chairs I bought from an antique dealer in

Alexandria, which I think you'll love to explore. This is a hand-woven striped eighteenth-century rug. The rosewood furniture I got at an estate sale in the Shenandoah Valley, west of here."

"So," she said, "you used your weekends to hunt for just the right pieces?"

"Yep," he said, looking at the joy shining in her eyes. "Do you like what I've done so far?"

"I love it! I love the color of the rosewood, the light in here. The striped blue, green, and gray rug just pulls it all together. And that fireplace is awesome."

"So?" Nolan murmured, bringing her into his arms. "You think you might want to stay with me and help me restore this old farmhouse and make it our own?"

Teren reached up, claiming his smiling mouth, drowning in the dark blue of his eyes, which held heat, promise, and love for her alone. She pressed her hips against his, holding him tightly, kissing him with everything she felt for him. She wasn't disappointed as Nolan gave a low groan, hungrily plundering her mouth, sliding his hands down her torso, capturing her hips, holding her tight against his pelvis, letting her know he wanted her in other ways, too.

Her whole lower body flared to life, despite the jet lag. The warmth of the room, the light, and his male fragrance all combined to make Teren deliriously happy. As they broke their kiss, breathing faster, staring at one another, Teren whispered, "I love you, Nolan Steele. That's *never* going to change, no matter where in the world we live."

He tunneled his fingers through her hair at her temple, kissing her brow, her nose, and then her lips. "Good, because I feel the same way about you, sweetheart. Are you ready for a tour of the rest of our home?"

His eager words brought tears to her eyes. *Our home*. How wonderful that sounded. Nolan led her across the foyer and down the hall a little way to the left, where she found a huge L-shaped kitchen. It was badly in need of loving work and care, but she saw the bones of the huge double sink and wooden counter. The rows of windows made the place feel light and airy. An old iron woodstove was in the room, along with a modern refrigerator and gas-fed cook stove. The cupboards made her gasp. Each one had colorful stained glass on its front. The white painted wood only made the ancient stained glass look more colorful. "I love this," she exclaimed, touching the glass in wonderment.

"It's original from when the first owners built this house," Nolan told her. "I've been working with a museum expert on this, and she's helping to clean and refurbish the glass so it will last another hundred and fifty years."

"It's just so beautiful." Teren turned, absorbing the huge area. "This kitchen has so much potential, Nolan."

"Sort of like us?" He grinned and saw her lips curve and a sparkle come to her eyes for the first time. It was as if he could sense life flooding back into her, returning, much like the Nile flooded the land surrounding it, making it fertile and abundant once more.

"Yes," she whispered. "Just like us."

"Well," he teased, "if there's hope for this farmhouse, then there's hope for us!"

She kissed him for a long, long time, languishing against him. "Yes, there's lots and lots of hope for us, Nolan."

AT ARTEMIS HEADQUARTERS, Teren tried to tamp down her nervousness as she was led into one of the large mission planning rooms deep below the ground to a secret, well-protected part of the security company. Nolan had her hand and was leading her into a room where the door had been slid open. They'd had a week together with no demands other than living together in the farmhouse, and Teren hadn't known how desperately she'd needed those fulfilling seven days with Nolan until now.

As lonely as she was for her friends in Kitra, he had filled her days with laughter as they worked on the farmhouse together, sharing stories with her. They'd filled their nights, hungrily seeking each other in bed, their lovemaking reaching new levels of passion. Her body still pulsed with the memory of Nolan loving her earlier this morning, long before this nine a.m. meeting. She was to meet the Culver family and then take a tour of the huge security facility. After the tour, she would talk at length with Alexa Culver and her team, who worked with the Home School portion of Delos. At one time Alexa had headed up another division, but later, had made a lateral move to this one.

Entering the room, Teren saw many people standing and chatting with one another. Matt Culver had driven down to the house to see Nolan, a fellow Delta Force buddy, midweek. Teren recognized him and felt better at least knowing one person in the room. Matt was the first to come forward, a smile of welcome on his face, his hand offered to Teren.

"Hey, welcome aboard our little ship, camouflaged by the surrounding farmhouse. Do you like how we hid Artemis?"

Smiling, Teren took his hand and shook it. "It's incredible. It's absolutely invisible to the outside world. From the road it looks like an old, still-functioning farmhouse."

A woman with shining black hair curled around her shoulders, wearing a gray pantsuit, her green eyes sparkling, came up beside Matt. "Teren? I'm Tal Culver-Lockwood. Welcome! We're really glad to see you."

Teren started to shake her hand, but Tal's smile deepened and she stepped forward, lightly hugging her 'hello' instead. It was unexpected, but the gesture warmed Teren, and she felt already accepted.

As Tal stepped back, releasing her, she became more serious. "Even more important, welcome to our family. You have a new home now, Teren, and we're really eager to have you with us as a part of it."

She couldn't have heard more welcoming words. "Thanks, Tal. You have no idea how much that means to me."

Matt threw his arm around his big sister. "Tal here is the big, broody mother hen of Artemis. You gotta watch her, or she'll start calling you one of her peeps." He gave his sister a great big, warm grin, squeezing her shoulders and then releasing her.

Tal snorted. "I'm broody all right. Especially with you and Alexa."

"Someone call my name?"

Teren saw a shorter woman wearing an emerald-green pantsuit, her red hair gathered back into a single braid, slip between Tal and Matt. Her hazel eyes danced with mischief.

"Teren? I'm Alexa Culver-Hunter. I've been dying to meet you!" She threw her arms around Teren, hugging her enthusiastically.

Laughing a little, Teren hugged Alexa back. "Same here. It's so nice to meet you." And it was, because now Tal, Matt, and Alexa were surrounding her, almost in an embrace. She was struck by their sincerity and warmth, and it was obvious they were family members, given the resemblances and the loving looks they exchanged. Matt mercilessly teased them, and she saw their love for one another dancing in their eyes. Just this one vignette made some of her grief over leaving Kitra melt away. These three people were confident, vulnerable, and friendly, hoping she'd accept them as they'd accepted her.

"Come on," Tal urged, touching Teren's elbow. "Would you like to sit down?" She guided her to the front of the long, oval mahogany table.

"Yes, thank you." Teren was impressed that one half of it was a surface computer, state-of-the-art with two huge viewing screens on two different walls of the room.

Nolan followed, falling into a conversation with Matt. As Teren sat down, Nolan took the seat to her right, Alexa to her left. There was coffee, tea, and doughnuts for everyone. The air was festive, with a lot of laughter and smiles, Teren noted. The door to the planning room remained open, other members coming in shortly.

In no time, she'd met Gage Hunter, Alexa's husband, and Wyatt Lockwood, Tal's other half. Matt said his wife, Dr. Dara McKinley-Culver, was inviting Teren and Nolan over to dinner that night at their condo. There were other individuals in the room as well. Soon, with so many new names and faces, Teren said laughing, that she'd need a few days to remember all their names. That brought collective grins with nods of agreement from everyone.

Tal sat at the other end of the table, her coffee in hand, opposite Teren. As the room quieted, everyone looked to Tal.

"Teren, as you can see, we're kind of a big, warm, sloppy family of sorts." She smiled. "And it's like this around here all the time. We do very, very serious work here at Artemis, but we also play as hard as we work. Matt, especially, is a culprit and plays jokes on all of us from time to time, just to keep us from getting too serious."

"That's just good mental health," Matt piped up, smiling smugly, sipping his coffee.

"You'll have to watch him, Teren, if he comes into your office," Alexa warned with a giggle. "He's well-known for planting tiny cameras around and then showing the video to all of us at a Mission Planning meeting later on the big wall screen."

"Well," Matt drawled, "I am, after all, Delta Force. We're black ops to the bone, sis."

Teren smiled. "Looks like I need to keep Nolan nearby."

"Oh," Tal said, "he's going to be closer to you than you think, Teren."

Teren gave Nolan a questioning look. He shrugged and looked over at Tal. "Ask her," he said to her, a slight smile on his face.

"We're such a black-ops group, Teren. You don't know about my background, but I was an officer in the Marine Corps and the head of a sniper unit at Bagram. Matt was Delta Force. Alexa here flew A-10 Warthogs and risked her life from the air to bomb and strafe the Taliban to keep our men and women safe on the ground in Afghanistan. And here, most of what we do is undercover as well. We've offered Nolan a job at Artemis. We want him to become part of our Africa Consulting Team, so when we pull a mission anywhere on that continent, we have people who are boots on the ground in a particular country. That way we can utilize their knowledge and experiences."

"And," Alexa said to Teren, "I want you on my team, but you need to see our facility first and understand what your job entails with me in the Home School Foundation Department."

Teren looked at Nolan. "Did you know about this?"

He gave her an apologetic look. "Remember when Matt came out last week?"

"Yes."

"He offered me this new job here at HQ, which would take me off being assigned to missions around the world, but I didn't want to say anything or make a decision on it until you came here, Teren. I needed to see if you felt like a fit with Artemis. If you want the job, then I'm taking the job here at the security company and we'll be together."

She colored a little, all eyes on them. It was as if all of them knew that they were already a couple deeply in love with one another. "That's fair," she murmured. Gazing over at Alexa, she said, "I'd love to sit down with you about the job you want to offer me."

"No worries. You and I are going to spend the rest of the morning together as soon as we get out of here," Alexa promised her. "And then Tal, Matt, and I have lunch at a nearby inn."

"And," Matt said, "don't forget, you and Nolan are going to have dinner with Dara and me tonight. She's been cooking all day. It's her day off and she wants to really welcome you home with us."

"That sounds wonderful," Teren said, overwhelmed by the energy, warmth, and cozy atmosphere in the room. "I'd love to meet Dara."

"Yes," Tal intoned, "she's the better half of my jokester brother."

Everyone chuckled, nodding their heads in unison.

"As you can see," Matt said, pretending to be wounded by his big sister's words, "I'm crucified here daily."

"Only because you're nailing all of us in our offices with the Instagram videos you're taking of us when we don't know about it," Wyatt drawled, an easy Texas grin spreading across his face.

Nolan reached over, touching Teren's hand. "Don't worry, Matt won't pick on you."

"Pooh!" Alexa said. "How's that?"

Nolan arched an eyebrow at her. "Matt is my Delta Force brother. Teren's my gal, and he's not gonna pick on her because she's part of our Delta Force family. Okay?"

Wrinkling her nose, Alexa muttered in Teren's direction, "You're getting off easy."

"Well, her office will be an official safe zone," Matt proclaimed to everyone. "Because she belongs to a Delta operator. We do take care of our own."

Nolan gave Teren a pleased look. "See?"

Teren smiled and shook her head. "There are all kinds of families here at Artemis, aren't there?"

Everyone nodded simultaneously, as if they'd trained for this moment.

Alexa reached over and tapped Teren's hand. "We *are* family. We're not some big, heartless corporation. You'll find that out right away. We are people with passion and we love what we do, and we're good at it. But there are also bad days, Teren, when things go sideways. I can't tell you how many times I've come down here to an empty planning room to scream out my fury, or cry, or do both. These rooms are soundproofed and have the latest composite materials in the walls to stop any kind of electronic or other type of snooping into our facility."

Tal lifted her chin, looking at Teren's soft expression. "And just like family, when there's a bad day we circle the wagons. We're there for that person or department. We know that we deal in life-and-death issues every day. And as much as we want a mission to go right and to help, sometimes it doesn't. So, while you may see us as a pretty loosey-goosey kind of organization right now, on a tight mission where lives are in the balance, we get damned serious, damned fast. There's a lot of intensity in Artemis. Not in every department, but Mission Planning is usually a pretty tightly strung area."

"Which is why," Wyatt drawled, leaning his elbows on the table, holding Teren's gaze, "they have me leading this group of sorry-looking characters. I'm very laid-back, and I don't get my knickers in a twist when things go south. It's a SEAL thing. But," he continued, looking up and down the table with a sly grin, "not everyone here is from Texas. Pity, because if they were, they wouldn't get uptight like Tal has noted."

"I'm glad I don't have to work with you," Teren admitted, giving him an apologetic look. "It's nothing personal, Wyatt, but I don't work well in that kind of high-stress environment."

"Most of us don't," Alexa huffed. "You'll find my department just the opposite of Wyatt's. We're a happy group, doing happy things for others. There's a lot of laughter and super-creative people who love education and know the value of our kids all over the world."

"That really sounds lovely," Teren admitted, absorbing Alexa's ebullience. She was like a sun glowing in the room, so alive and caring. Alexa was just the type of person she wanted to work with. Nolan hadn't been wrong in his assessment of the three Culvers; they truly were genuine, sincere, and family-oriented—everything that she needed to thrive.

"Speaking of that," Tal said as the table quieted, "I've been studying what you've created online for Kitra. Matt, Alexa, and I have looked at the numbers and the sales on the clothing that your Sudanese women are making on their treadle machines. They're impressive, Teren. Having that Internet store has allowed you to sell their goods around the world, and not just to African countries."

"Right," Teren murmured. "I wanted to expand the type of goods they sewed. For example, an apron is a European and North American item of clothing that can be added. I did a lot of research on the different types of fabrics that are worn by men and women in a particular continent and country. Over the years, I've expanded their sewing into many different areas and as a result, it makes Kitra more money. We have high sales in Scandinavia for our crocheted and knitted cap and scarf sets."

"I particularly love what you do for the children," Alexa said, gushing with enthusiasm. "You make those silly little sock monkeys that are coming back in fashion here in the U.S. Only you make them for Africa, Europe, and South America, each a little different so the colors appeal to that particular region and group of people. They're your best seller right now."

"It's nothing short of brilliant," Tal complimented Teren. "You're far more than a software designer. You're truly a visionary, and you have a global grasp of what's popular or common on every continent. There aren't many people who have that capacity, Teren. That's why we wanted to hire you. And you will have your own department. You'll be able to hire others who are like you and you'll have the final say on such things. We want you to feel like you're a part of a huge family, with your own little family in your department. Sort of like those Russian dolls where, when you open one up, there's another, slightly smaller doll contained in it. And when you open that one up, there's another."

Teren shrugged a little. "I guess I've never seen myself like that, Tal."

Alexa made a soft sound in her throat. "Teren, let us see your potential, your skills. Trust us to place you in your own department, to do what you do best: help women learn how to sew, learn how to market their clothing online, and then sell those wares to the world."

"Which," Matt said, giving Teren a kind look, "is what you've been doing at Kitra for the last seven years. And look how Kitra has prospered. Look at how many more women and children we're able to take in and help because of the money made from your vision."

Teren sat there, absorbing all their sincere, passionate compliments and their admiration and respect for her. She felt Nolan nearby, felt his pride in her, and briefly glanced over at him. She saw, radiating from him, not only pride but the depth of his love shining in his eyes, there for all to see.

CHAPTER 23

WITH A SOFT sigh, Teren sank against Nolan's hard, sweaty body. She nuzzled beneath his jaw, smiling, eyes closed, feeling the undulations of pleasure flooding through her lower body. He made a sound of satisfaction, kissing her tousled hair, sweeping her against him. The late-November moonlight flowed silently into the large bedroom where they lay, breathing fast and shallow, languishing against one another, fulfilled.

Barely opening her eyes, Teren was content to be held against Nolan, feeling his fierce love for her, his lips resting against her damp temple, inhaling his fragrance, the scent of their shared sex. There was such a sweet vibration rolling through her and she stretched upward to kiss the column of his thick neck, tasting the salt of his perspiration on her lips.

"Every time is better," she whispered.

Nolan eased his embrace, placing Teren on her back, studying her shadowed face caressed by moonlight through the nearby window. He drank in her shimmering, happy gaze, the way those sculpted lips curved upward, telling him how well he'd satisfied her. There was nothing more he wanted to do for this woman than make her smile like that, see the happiness glimmering in her peaceful eyes. "It's you," he rasped, kissing her smooth brow. "You inspire me, Teren."

"Mmm, well, I think we inspire one another, don't you?"

She heard a rumble in his chest, her lips drawing upward. Absorbing the vibration, her heart swelled with love for him.

"Most definitely," he managed to say, sliding his fingers through her loose hair, grazing her cheek. Nolan pushed himself up on one elbow, wanting to memorize Teren right now. Her cheeks were flushed, her eyes warm with love for him, her fingers caressing his damp shoulder, the moonlight accentuating her naked beauty as she lay beside him.

"Love gives us this gift," he told her, his voice roughened with emotion. Glancing at the clock on the nearby nightstand, he added wryly, "And the gift of being sleep-deprived is the price we pay."

Smiling softly, she skimmed her fingers down his tightly-muscled arm, which kept her hip pinned comfortably against him. "Do you think Tal, Matt, and Alexa notice it?"

He laughed. "I think they see us drinking more coffee in the morning. But we put in our eight hours and we get a lot done, so I don't think they're concerned at all."

Sobering, she said, "Then maybe it's time, Nolan?" She saw him cock his head, confusion coming to his eyes.

"For what, sweetheart?"

"Well, we've finished the parlor, the kitchen, and this bedroom," she began quietly, making invisible patterns across his large biceps. Stilling her hand, she wrapped her fingers around his upper arm, holding his concerned, shadowed gaze. "I know we haven't made anything official yet, Nolan, but I want to know what you think about something."

Nolan felt the sudden tentativeness within Teren. He could see worry in her eyes, or maybe it was concern about something new; he wasn't sure. The last two months, she'd not only become a part of the Artemis family, she'd thrived as never before. He wanted to think it was the love blossoming between them, giving them the deep roots required to make their lives something that would last forever. There was no question that Artemis and Teren hummed together as a smoothly working team. In two months, she had accomplished so much, laying out a grand plan for the software she'd already written, so that it could be sent to every Delos charity that wanted it. Nolan had recognized early on her intelligence and her far-seeing capability, but he knew that Tal, Matt, and Alexa were blown away by her visionary abilities. Teren was such a major asset to Artemis—and to him as well, but in a different, far more personal way.

"Tell me what's on your mind." Nolan knew that when Teren had tried to share her ideas with her family, they'd shut her down. To this day, she struggled with speaking her mind. Nolan had made it his personal mission to get her to open up and trust him and talk at length with him. He would not interrupt her. Not like her family always did as a way to control her and shut her up.

Their most important talks seemed to come up after loving one another and tonight was no different. He leaned down, caressing her lips, wanting to erase the worry he saw in her eyes. Nolan would never turn away from her, never not be interested in what she had to say, or how she saw her world—or their world.

"Come on," he teased with a growl. "Fess up." He felt Teren quiver with laughter.

She sighed, cupping his jaw. "I love you, Nolan. I never want anything else in this life except you." She looked away for a moment, as if to gather her thoughts, then tilted her chin, holding his warm, amused gaze, she whispered, "And that's one reason why I want to get pregnant. I want to carry your baby…our child. Are you okay with that?"

Stunned, Nolan responded with his heart. "Oh, sweetheart, I'd like that more than you can ever know. I want as many kids as you think you want, Teren."

Staring up at him, the tears running down her face, she sniffed, "I-I was so worried, Nolan…"

"Why?" he rasped, kissing her gently, her mouth warm and inviting beneath his.

"Because, you lost your wife…your baby…I wasn't sure you'd ever want another child, Nolan—risking it all again. Oh, I know I'm a worrier, but I had to ask you, I had to know."

He took her hand from his cheek, placing a kiss in the center of her palm. "I'm glad you asked, Teren. I've always loved children. I dreamed of being a father before." He gripped her hand, placing it over his heart, holding it there. "I want to be a father to the children we'll have. Okay? I want you pregnant and happy, being a mother, and me learning to be a good parent."

She searched Nolan's glimmering eyes, saw tears in them, and knew he was thinking of his losses from the past. "There are five bedrooms upstairs in this farmhouse," she said, her voice quavering. "When I first saw your house and we toured it, the moment we went up the stairs and I saw those huge rooms, I pictured children in four of them. I know I'm a dreamer, but I honestly saw them, Nolan. I felt like it was a movie playing out in front of my eyes."

He slid his hand down her shoulder and caressed her arm. "You've always been a dreamer, sweetheart. And I like sharing your dreams with you."

"Then four kids doesn't scare you?"

He grinned boyishly. "Should it?"

She smiled and shook her head. "I saw two boys and two girls."

"Then we'll just have to make it happen." There was such a rush of joy that came over her face, Nolan thought he was going to die of happiness. Taking his hand, he moved it gently across her soft abdomen. "And I'm fine with whatever nature decrees for us. I don't care if it's four girls or four boys, or anything in between. I think we can get those rooms finished over the winter."

He stilled his hand on her belly. "You choose the colors, decorate them however you want, Teren. I'll just do the work, the painting or wallpapering for you. All right?"

"Oh, Nolan!" She reached up and threw her arms around his neck, squeezing him so hard he lost his breath. "Thank you! You have no idea how much this means to me!"

He sat up and leaned his back against the carved rosewood headboard, pulling her into his arms and across his lap. Teren enjoyed snuggling like this after they made love, and he craved holding her afterward, listening to her talk in wispy, faraway tones, her head nestled on his shoulder, their gazes locked into one another as they shared the contents of dreams and wishes from their hearts. She folded against him, burrowing her brow against his jaw, never releasing her arm from around his shoulder. "When do you want to start?" he asked, already knowing the answer, trying to keep the amusement out of his low, roughened tone.

"Tonight? Later, I mean…no condom this time?"

"Okay, I can do that," he promised solemnly, smiling into the darkness of their bedroom. "Are you close to ovulation time?"

"Yes…"

"Good." Nolan smoothed her curved back with his hand, feeling the firm warmth of her flesh. There was such a feeling of bubbling joy around Teren, he hungrily scooped it into his heart, his soul. "You were made to be a mother, Teren. You're going to be such a natural at it. I saw how you mothered all those babies and children at Kitra, and how much they responded and loved you in return."

Closing his eyes, Nolan could picture their children, knowing that they would have two very dedicated and loving parents raising them. They wouldn't be latchkey children, raised by a daycare facility or a succession of babysitters. Already at Artemis, Tal had sent out a directive that female employees who became pregnant would not only get a year's maternity leave but if possible, could also work from home the first year. And right now, a nursery was available at Artemis with everything a mother and baby could need. And breastfeeding was more than welcome if a mother wanted to come back to work before that year of leave was up. Tal wanted Artemis to be parent, mother, and baby friendly.

And those women who already had young children would have their own facility in another area of Artemis. Moms and dads would be able to visit their children on breaks and at lunch. That way, Tal felt her employees' children would not feel completely abandoned by their parents. They would be in-house and available, and Tal hoped it would be a healthy environment for the entire family. Nolan remembered how happy Teren when she'd discovered that directive in her welcome packet. He should have suspected then that she was ready for that step into motherhood, but he'd missed the sign.

He smiled to himself, embracing her, inhaling her scent, listening to that sigh that told him she was happy. "You know," he said, kissing her hair, "if you want to stay home full-time, you can. I make more than enough money,

Teren."

"I was thinking about that," she admitted quietly, moving her fingers across his collarbone. "Because of the type of work I do, I could work full-time at home. I'd have the baby in a little bassinet nearby. I'd be there for her or him when I was needed—and I very much want to breastfeed."

"I'm sure Alexa would be more than willing to accommodate anything you suggest. You're far too valuable to them, sweetheart. They'll take you, your vision, and your dreams any way you want to share them with them."

"I love Artemis and I love the people there, Nolan."

"I know you do."

"I think it's fully possible that at times, when Alexa has a department meeting, I can be there for it—or at least via Skype, if necessary."

"Why not? You can do a whole online meeting. I wouldn't worry about that. Alexa loves you and your ideas, and dotes on you just like those kids at Kitra did." He smiled, feeling her sigh, as if he'd helped her take a load she was silently carrying off her shoulders.

Someday, he hoped, by living with him Teren would eventually dissolve her childhood past, replaced by him, by their lives together. Nolan had a hunch that when a baby was born to them, Teren would fully focus on today—not on yesterday or on what she had to suppress from the past.

"You're right," she murmured. "I have so many good options that would allow me to be here in the house."

"Besides, you love to cook and bake."

"I love being at home, Nolan. I truly do."

Nodding, he caressed her hip, holding her against him, giving her that sense of love and safety. "I'll support whatever it is that feels right for you and our baby." He felt Teren nod her head. They shared this invisible connection, he'd discovered. And once they were here in the safety of the U.S., it had strengthened even more between them. Nolan sensed that she might be thinking about becoming pregnant, and smiled.

LATE-NOVEMBER SNOW WAS falling and Teren watched the flakes dancing through the evening sky as she stood at the double sink in the kitchen. All the trees had lost their leaves, gray bare branches poking up, dark and slender, into the gunmetal overcast evening sky. Tal had let everyone leave at noon today because the first snowstorm of the year, shortly after Thanksgiving, was going to blanket the East Coast. She peeled potatoes for an au gratin cheddar cheese casserole.

It had been three weeks since she and Nolan had started making love to one another without a condom and Teren felt subtle differences within herself. It wasn't something she could express in words. It was a quiet feeling within her body. Was she pregnant? Unsure, she wondered where Nolan was. They had left in separate cars from Artemis and he'd kissed her on the lips, saying he had to make a quick run into Alexandria for something and would be home later. That was two hours ago and already the dark shining asphalt ribbon of narrow road leading to their farmhouse was nearly covered with snow.

Teren quickly finished all the prep and slid the potatoes into the stove to bake. The leftover turkey breast and stuffing were warming in some aluminum foil. The Culver family had invited them over for Thanksgiving and Teren had really enjoyed herself because she got to meet the Turkish and Greek sides of their far-flung global relatives. She had helped prepare the food for the huge U-shaped table in the dining room of the Culvers' massive Federal house. Their family had fully absorbed her and Nolan as if they were long-lost cousins, with kisses on the cheeks, hugs, more kisses on the cheeks, and more hugs. Never had she felt so warm inside because the Culvers symbolized the relationship she had always dreamed of having. Now she understood why Tal had created such a cozy atmosphere at Artemis. It was wonderful and she felt so much gratitude for being a part of a greater family who accepted her as she was. She had not expected to be invited to Dilara and Robert Culver's huge home in Alexandria, but it had impressed upon her how starved she'd been for a real family.

Dilara Culver had ample leftover turkey, stuffing, and green bean casserole, and gave them several large containers to take home. Since then, they'd been eating the delicious leftovers—it all tasted so good to Teren. She'd missed the American holidays when she'd lived in Kitra. Now she could celebrate them with Nolan and the people who worked at Artemis.

Kitra had provided her soul food to heal herself from her childhood, and the Sudanese people had accepted her from their hearts. She missed them very much, but being able to Skype them at least once a week helped her so much. It was then that Teren realized she had not lost any of them. Rather, her Sudanese family was now part of her larger global family even though she now lived in America. She'd lost nothing, only gained. That had made her grief and sense of loss dissolve entirely.

Where was Nolan? She craned her neck and peered out of the window, which was now glazed with frost in the corners. Looking down the road, she didn't see any car headlights coming her way. He had a cell phone on him, and surely if he'd been in an accident or gotten stuck in the ice or snow, he'd have called her. What a worrywart she was turning into! Laughing to herself, Teren shook her head. The past week, especially, she had been more emotional than normal. She was easily affected, more tenderhearted than usual, more apt to cry over something she saw on the nightly news or on a documentary TV program.

Nolan provided the tissues, gave her a patient smile, and held her when she felt suddenly weepy.

Teren had just pulled the au gratin potatoes out of the oven when Nolan drove into the garage. The snow was thickening, and she felt relief. Just hearing him come in from the side door and stomp the snow off his boots in the mudroom made all her worry go away. She heard his footsteps coming down the hall toward the kitchen and turned expectantly. He was holding a huge bouquet of red roses tied with green and gold ribbons in his left arm.

"Sorry I'm late. Quite a few fender benders between Alexandria and here. First snowfall of the season and drivers have to get used to it." He held out the roses to her. "For you."

She smiled, inhaling their fragrance. "Mmm, wonderful. There are no roses in Sudan, and I've missed them so much." She leaned over the bouquet, giving Nolan a quick kiss. His dark hair was sparkling here and there with snowflakes that had melted in the short strands. Teren loved the cold, fresh smell, but it was his own unique scent that sent a quiver of yearning to her lower body. "What are these for, Nolan? Are we celebrating something? Thanksgiving has come and gone." She placed them on the drain board and pulled out a large vase from below the sink, filling it with warm water and a teaspoon of sugar.

He shrugged out of his black leather jacket and hung it over the back of a chair. "Well, yes," he said. "There is something to celebrate." He came over, watching her put the two dozen red roses in the vase. Placing his hands on her shoulders, he moved her hair aside, kissing the sensitive nape of her neck.

Giving a little gasp, Teren squealed and dodged his lips, her skin prickling with pleasure. "Nolan! I'll drop these roses if I'm not careful."

Giving her a teasing look, he released her. "Okay, I'll be good. But just for a little while. Can I help you get food on the table?"

Teren always appreciated him helping her. They fell into a routine, placing the hot dishes on metal trivets to protect the tiger-maple table's surface in the dining room. Soon, they were eating their dinner.

"You look a little tired," Nolan said. "Are you feeling okay?"

She smiled. "Now who's being a worrywart? I thought I had that covered." Her heart widened with love as he gave her a boyish look, his eyes dancing with amusement.

"I do kind of like having you around," he teased, finishing everything on his plate. He set it aside, pulling over his cup of coffee.

"I think it's your black-ops ability to see all the teeny, tiny details of a person. I feel just fine. Well…maybe I could use more sleep." She gave him a playful look.

"That's probably true," he admitted. "Because the devil *is* in the details. It could mean my living or dying if I didn't observe closely enough, Teren."

"I'm glad those days are gone, Nolan. I don't think I could ever stand to have you going out on missions like that anymore." She felt full and left a small portion on her plate. Nolan rose and took the plates to the kitchen and came back, holding his hand out to her. "I'm done with my undercover days forever. Come join me in the parlor?"

Surprised, she murmured, "Well…okay…I made a chocolate cake, your favorite. Don't you want a piece of it, Nolan?" She saw the glimmer in his eyes as he took her hand.

"I have dessert of another kind I want to share with you first. We'll have your dessert a little later. Are you ready?"

Rising, she smiled. "Of course I am." She leaned into him, his arm sliding around her shoulders, drawing her gently against him. They walked into the parlor, where a fire blazed in the huge redbrick fireplace. This was Teren's favorite room; the warmth, the snapping and popping of the wood, and the color of the flames were like a meditation to her. She spent most of her free time wrapped up in a pink afghan that Dilara had knitted for her a month ago, lounging on the blue silk sofa, dark blue pillows of the same fabric behind her back, reading a book.

"Come, sit with me," Nolan urged, sitting on one corner of the sofa, gesturing for her to come and snuggle up against him like she loved to do.

Teren noticed a small, red velvet box sitting on the lampstand next to the sofa. "What's that?" she asked. "An early Christmas gift? Is that why you were late tonight?" She sat down beneath his arm, content to lay her head on his shoulder, her brow against his jaw.

"You'd be a good black-ops type," he suggested, leaning over and picking up the box. "You're very observant."

Snorting, Teren said, "I wouldn't last two seconds in the kind of work you did, Nolan."

He chuckled and brought the box over, holding it between his hands so she could look at it. "You're made of strong stuff," he told her in a gritty tone, kissing her brow. "You're a lot stronger than most people I know."

"Nolan, what's in the box?" she asked curiously. "Do I get to open it up now or do I have to wait until Christmas morning?" She was joking, but she saw he'd suddenly become very serious.

"This isn't a Christmas gift, sweetheart. This has been a long time coming, but I felt like it was the right time." He opened the box.

Teren nearly flew out from beneath his arm, her hands pressed to her lips as she gasped, her eyes widening. There on the plush red velvet sat a pink diamond engagement ring. The wedding band was a gleaming gold with intricate designs etched in the metal. "Nolan!"

He chuckled, giving her a wry look. "You just about jumped off the sofa, Teren. It isn't going to bite you." He held it out toward her.

Tears stung her eyes as she slowly reached for the box, barely grazing the large, sparkling engagement ring with a fingertip. "I-I wasn't expecting this, Nolan. We've sort of talked about it from time to time, but we said we felt waiting a bit longer was okay." Teren lifted her chin, holding his warm gaze.

"Just because I wasn't pressing you with the idea didn't mean I wasn't going to do something about it, Teren. Will you marry me? Put up with me? Let me help diaper those babies that will be coming along sooner, not later?" His mouth twitched, love coupled with amusement dancing in his eyes.

She nodded and pulled out the engagement ring. "I will marry you, but only if you'll put it on my finger."

Nolan did, seeing that it was a perfect fit. He'd had Alexa trick Teren about three weeks ago into trying on one of her rings because Nolan thought their fingers were about the same size—and he'd been right. Such was the value of his black-ops mentality.

He smiled fully, seeing the tenderness come to Teren's expression as she slowly moved her hand, watching the stone catch the light from the chandelier above the sofa. He could feel how much she liked the diamond. It reminded him of the color her cheeks would flush after he had pleased her.

"I love this color," she whispered. "It's so mystical, so otherworldly…like a dream come true."

"You are my dream come true," he told her seriously, picking up her hand, admiring the ring on it.

Leaning over, Teren pressed her lips to his, sinking into his waiting arms, surrendering to him, lost in the heat and love Nolan was giving to her in that beautiful moment. Then she lay against him and enjoyed the tenderness of his mouth on hers. This was dessert of the best kind!

Finally, Teren eased up and Nolan moved his hand across her hip and down her thigh. She knew what was coming next and her whole body quivered in anticipation.

"When do you want to get married?" he asked, kissing the curve of her ear. Nolan knew that Teren had not been in contact with her real family since returning home in September. He felt her tense a little as he cradled her in his arms. "I'm all for going in front of a judge in Alexandria and marrying you, Teren. Are you opposed to that?"

"No, I'm not. Could we invite our friends from Artemis?"

"Sure, whoever you want, sweetheart." He saw the tension fade from her expression and happiness replace it. "When?"

"Anytime," she said, giving him a wicked look. Sitting up, she closed the ring box and held it between her hands. "I love you, Nolan. I'd live with you whether I was officially married to you or not."

"I know that. But you're going to carry my children, Teren. I was brought up that way, and while I know it's fashionable for people to live together and never marry, I'm not comfortable with that arrangement."

She nodded. "That's okay. I'm fine with it, Nolan." Giving him a dreamy look, she offered, "Wouldn't it be nice to get married on Christmas Day?"

"Then all I have to do is put a red bow on my head and sit under the Christmas tree next year. I'd be your gift every anniversary."

Laughing, she said, "You're a gift to me every day, Nolan." Teren watched him become sober and his mouth thinned for a moment. She had the feeling he was remembering Linda. Reaching out, she added, "Christmas Day just becomes that much more important to me—to us."

"Okay, we'll let everyone know. I'm sure they'll be happy for us."

Moving back into his arms, Teren wrapped one arm around his waist, closing her eyes, content as never before. She nuzzled against him, kissing his black tee which stretched across his magnificent chest. "I love you, Nolan. Forever."

He whispered her name, holding her tightly in his arms, kissing her temple. "Forever, sweetheart."

THE BEGINNING

Don't miss Lindsay McKenna's next book,
Dangerous
Available from Blue Turtle Publishing!

Turn the page for a sneak peek of *Dangerous*.

Excerpt from
Dangerous

WHAT THE HELL! Dan Malloy groaned in his sleep, his body covered with perspiration, the sheets to his bed twisted and caught between his lower legs. His breath was coming hard and fast. It felt as if his heart was going to rip out of his chest, the pounding of it so loud, fueled with adrenaline, that it sounded like kettle drums pulsing in his ears. He heard the blades of his MH-47 Night Stalker helo he was flying. Heard the calm voice of his co-pilot, Lieutenant Andy Gantry, talking to the Special Forces A team hidden on the slope of a rocky Hindu Kush mountain in the inky darkness. The winds were erratic, trying to toss the bird around. His Nomex green gloves were soaked as he gripped the cyclic and collective, his booted feet playing lightly on the rudders, trying to bring the bird in and not crash it.

His teeth ached, he was clenching them so tightly, his entire focus oriented to the green dials in front of him, trying to land safely to pick up the A team that was comprised of twelve members. The weather was stormy and quixotic, slapping the bird with unseen fists, making it shudder, trying to throw Dan off course. Below, through his NVG's, he saw the green chem lights that had been tossed out by the A team to show him where to land the double bladed helo. Sweat trickled down his temples. His nostrils flared as he smelled the constant odor of kerosene, the fuel used to power the helo. His only focus was landing this damned thing. Lightning flashed, blinding him momentarily.

Shit! Blinking, Dan halted his downward descent, trying to give his eyes time to adjust. They were landing with a thunderstorm racing across the jagged, unforgiving mountains of Afghanistan. The Special Forces team had been out for nearly three weeks hunting HVT's, high value targets. He knew the team was hiding nearby, trying to remain invisible.

Worse, Dan knew that Taliban often encamped for the night in nearby wadis, ravines, that ran vertically up and down the rugged slopes of the Hindu Kush. And there was one within a thousand feet away from where he was to land. Did anyone know if there was encamped enemy within it? Wishing for an Apache escort, an overhead drone, none had been available. If there had been? A drone had infrared capability and would have been able to pick up heat signatures on any humans hiding anywhere nearby. The MH-47 had that same capability, but that instrument went belly up half way to their assigned LZ, landing zone, during this flight. Now, they were blind and it bothered the hell out of Dan.

They didn't know squat about potential nearby tangos. Dan mentally cursed, knowing that due to inclement weather conditions, the drone would have been torn apart with the sixty mile an hour wind gusts that were now pummeling his bird, throwing it off course from landing, again and again. The storm was racing directly down at them. And it was a violent son-of-a-bitch. But Night Stalker pilots, the cream of Army aviation, was expected to fly through any kind of a weather conditions, to pick up a black ops group. These were brave men and women who got the job done, despite the challenges or the potential life-and-death of their assigned mission.

He wanted to wipe the sweat off his face. His eyesight came back and he began to breathe again, nudging his helo forward toward that landing zone once again. In the back of his mind, he knew if Taliban were encamped in that nearby wadi that they could throw an RPG and AK-47 bullets at his bird. They would aim for the rotor assembly to stop the blades from turning. The MH-47 had two rotors and one sat up near the pilot's cabin, the other, near the rear of the helicopter. If either was hit by a bullet? They'd crash. And they'd all die.

Son-of-a-bitch. He'd been on hellacious, challenging missions before, but this one took the cake in his many years of experience. Thunderstorms would pop up at the most unexpected times simply because these mountains made their own weather. No weather forecaster could accurately say whether or not a storm would be created by the shifting, erratic winds created by these dragon-toothed mountains that rose to sixteen-thousand feet high in some places. Right now, he was at nine thousand feet on a steep scree slope. The A team had found the most level spot for them to land, but it was not level at all. They'd done the best they could, being hotly pursued by Taliban. Landing on a slope was perilous. It could be done, but with a thunderstorm looming over them, with unknown possibility of tangos in that nearby wadi close to the LZ, Dan knew they were trapped between a rock and a hard place. His chief gunner had the ramp down and was sitting behind the fifty caliber machine gun, looking for tangos. That was the only defense that his bird had was that weapon.

Andy's calm voice continued to give him directions and elevation. That was his job as copilot, was to give that kind of necessary info so that Dan could devote a hundred percent to his flying skills to this bird and getting it set down, instead of being slapped by a gust of wind and crashing into the side of the mountain. There was so much that could go wrong. His body was so tense, Dan thought he might snap in half. His fingers ached, the perspiration making them slippery and he kept trying to tighten them against the collective and cyclic between them.

Come on…come on….

He saw the chem lights, tiny green dots on the black skin of the mountain slope. The wind gusts were powerful. The bird shuddered violently, shaking as if a dog was shaking off water. The engines would change and deepen. Andy would play with the throttles between their seats, trying to give Dan the power he needed to neutralize the gusts. Any one of them could hurl the bird into the rocky mountainside. Dan was grateful for Andy's years of experience because he needed it now as never before as he inched forward toward those tiny chem lights.

Everything slowed down to movie frames for Dan as he eased his reluctant helo forward. Closer and closer, he inched the thumping, vibrating beast toward that LZ. *Just let me get to it. Let me be able to land without incident.* His ears were keyed to the sound of the engines. His ass was nailed to the seat and he was monitoring vibrations through it because the slightest change could give him a precious life-and-death split second to adjust the cyclic or collective and keep it on course, keep it from crashing. Dan could feel his heart thumping loudly, felt as if his entire chest was vibrating with each hammering pulse of that organ. The adrenaline was racing through his bloodstream, heightening his clarity, making him super aware of all sounds, smells, sensations until his whole world became his senses. It gave him an edge. It allowed him to make the subtle moves of his hands on the instruments, to get the bird on hard ground.

"Over LZ," Andy reported calmly. "Ten feet…..nine feet….eight feet…."

Dan's body felt like it was unyielding steel, caught in the moment. His thighs ached, his booted feet lightly played the rudders as he continued the descent. He couldn't just swiftly plop the bird down. No, it had to go carefully or he'd get into hover-out-of-ground effect, which meant the invisible cushion of air that the helo rode on, was suddenly gone. And if it happened? The bird would drop like a rock out of the sky, crashing. Killing all of them.

"…seven feet…."

God, let me get this bird down safe. Let me get it down safe…

His hands ached, feeling like a raptor's claws frozen around the instruments as he prayed that he'd keep that cushion of air between his bird and that rugged ground that was not level. Sweat stung his eyes and he blinked furiously, trying to clear his vision.

"…..six feet…."

"…..five feet…."

"…three feet…."

The Books of Delos

Title: **Last Chance** (Prologue)
Publish Date: July 15, 2015
Learn more at: delos.lindsaymckenna.com/last-chance

Title: **Nowhere to Hide**
Publish Date: October 13, 2015
Learn more at: delos.lindsaymckenna.com/nowhere-to-hide

Title: **Tangled Pursuit**
Publish Date: November 11, 2015
Learn more at: delos.lindsaymckenna.com/tangled-pursuit

Title: **Forged in Fire**
Publish Date: December 3, 2015
Learn more at: delos.lindsaymckenna.com/forged-in-fire

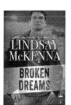
Title: **Broken Dreams**
Publish Date: January 2, 2016
Learn more at: delos.lindsaymckenna.com/broken-dreams

Title: ***Blind Sided***
Publish Date: June 5, 2016
Learn more at: delos.lindsaymckenna.com/blind-sided

Title: ***Secret Dream***
Publish Date: July 25, 2016
Learn more at: delos.lindsaymckenna.com/secret-dream

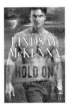

Title: ***Hold On***
Publish Date: August 3, 2016
Learn more at: delos.lindsaymckenna.com/hold-on

Title: ***Hold Me***
Publish Date: August 11, 2016
Learn more at: delos.lindsaymckenna.com/hold-me

Title: ***Unbound Pursuit***
Publish Date: September 29, 2016
Learn more at: delos.lindsaymckenna.com/unbound-pursuit

Title: ***Secrets***
Publish Date: November 21, 2016
Learn more at: delos.lindsaymckenna.com/secrets

Title: **Snowflake's Gift**
Publish Date: February 4, 2017
Learn more at: delos.lindsaymckenna.com/snowflakes-gift

Title: **Never Enough**
Publish Date: March 1, 2017
Learn more at: delos.lindsaymckenna.com/never-enough

Title: **Dream of Me**
Publish Date: May 23, 2017
Learn more at: delos.lindsaymckenna.com/dream-of-me

Title: **Trapped**
Publish Date: July 17, 2017
Learn more at: delos.lindsaymckenna.com/trapped

Title: **Taking A Chance**
Publish Date: August 1, 2017
Learn more at: delos.lindsaymckenna.com/taking-a-chance

Title: **The Hidden Heart**
Publish Date: September 14, 2017
Learn more at: delos.lindsaymckenna.com/the-hidden-heart

Title: ***Boxcar Christmas***
Publish Date: January 1, 2018
Learn more at: delos.lindsaymckenna.com/boxcar-christmas

Everything Delos!

Newsletter

Please visit my newsletter website at newsletter.lindsaymckenna.com. The newsletter will have exclusive information about my books, publishing schedule, giveaways, exclusive cover peeks, and more.

Delos Series Website

Be sure to drop by my website dedicated to the Delos Series at delos.lindsaymckenna.com. There will be new articles on characters, my publishing schedule, and information about each book written by Lindsay.

Made in the USA
Middletown, DE
28 February 2018